# THE SIGN OF THE WEEPING VIRGIN

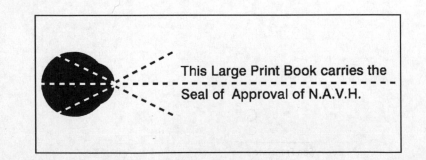

# THE SIGN OF THE WEEPING VIRGIN

## ALANA WHITE

**THORNDIKE PRESS**
*A part of Gale, Cengage Learning*

Detroit • New York • San Francisco • New Haven, Conn • Waterville, Maine • London

GALE
CENGAGE Learning®

**LIBRARY OF CONGRESS CATALOGING-IN-PUBLICATION DATA**

White, Alana.
    The sign of the weeping virgin / by Alana White.
        pages ; cm. — (Thorndike Press large print core)
        ISBN 978-1-4104-5806-3 (hardcover) — ISBN 1-4104-5806-7 (hardcover) 1.
    Italy—Civilization—1268-1559—Fiction. 2. Florence (Italy)—Politics and
    government—1421-1737—Fiction. 3. Renaissance—Italy—Fiction. 4. Art,
    Renaissance—Italy—Fiction. 5. Political fiction. 6. Large type books. I. Title.
    PS3623.H5685S55 2013
    813'.6—dc23                                              2012051209

Published in 2013 by arrangement with Tekno Books and Ed Gorman

Printed in the United States of America
1 2 3 4 5 6 7 17 16 15 14 13

For My Husband,
Who Has Given Me the Gift of Time

# ACKNOWLEDGMENTS

My life has been blessed by libraries, and so I would be remiss if I did not express my heartfelt gratitude for their calm and constant presence therein. In difficult times, they have been my safe place, my haven. In my childhood, they provided me with books — free. Later, they opened up the world of the Italian Renaissance as I began exploring that colorful and complex time in history. Bless Interlibrary Loan, which made it possible for me to place my hands on books written by scholars of the Italian Renaissance, present and past, whose work otherwise would not have been available to me. I want to thank in particular the Nashville Public Library for granting me the private use of one of their lovely, quiet writing rooms: a desk, a lamp, a bookshelf, and me. Heaven.

I want to thank my writing group, the Nashville Writers' Alliance, for many years of solid critiques, particularly Sallie Bissell and Madeena Nolan, who offered invaluable suggestions regarding this work in its early stages. Finally, I want to thank all the group's members for their enduring friendship and support. Family is everything.

# HISTORICAL NOTE

In 1480, Florence was one of five major powers that dominated Italy's patchwork of independent city-states. High on the northern cuff of the sunny, boot-shaped peninsula were Venice and Milan. An oligarchy on the Adriatic Sea with a Doge appointed to rule for life, Venice's lifeblood was maritime trade — spices, slaves, precious metals and luxurious silks — an enterprise threatened by the steady advance of the Ottoman Turks who, by 1460, had, in the name of *jihad,* holy war, made significant inroads in Europe.

West of Venice lay Milan, stronghold of the Sforza dukes. Shifting alliances and family quarrels plagued the ducal succession. Relations between the Duchy of Milan and the Lion of the Adriatic were hostile, with each government aspiring to extend its frontier at the other's expense.

Far to the south, at the ankle of the Italian boot, King Ferrante ruled Naples. The elder of his two sons, Prince Alfonso (also titled Duke of Calabria), was a professional soldier with an eye to using Neapolitan military superiority to make his family's house (the House of Aragon) dominant in Italy.

North of Naples lay the Papal States, presided over in Rome by Pope Sixtus IV. While building and decorating the Sistine Chapel and adding to the Vatican library, Sixtus IV immersed himself in politics. Uncle to a slew of nephews, dedicated to nepotism on a grand scale, he made no fewer than six of them cardinals. For his favorite, Girolamo Riario, Sixtus IV wanted nothing less than a lordship in the Papal States where, in fact, the Pope ruled in name only. While giving lip service to papal authority, local families governed the towns of that sprawling province.

Set in the lush, rolling hills of the Arno Valley, Florence, built on an ancient Roman site, was a Republic whose citizens had clung to the trappings of a democratic form of government since the late thirteenth century. Not for them a king, lord, or duke. To prevent any one man from wielding power, the government changed with breathtaking frequency as members of duly

10

elected committees were replaced by new men who qualified and had their names drawn from a "hat." Ironically, what the fiercely democratic-thinking Florentines had created for themselves was a government that changed so often, Italy's other major powers sought one man or family to deal with, while they considered Florence easy prey.

The Florentine government's wobbly design kept the republic weak at home, too. Over time, within the city walls a select political class had come to rule, dominated by several hundred families. By the mid-1400s, these families in turn were ruled by about five hundred men at whose core the Medici family stood boldly front and center, acting from their palazzo on Via Larga as the *de facto,* or unofficial, leaders of Florence. Why did foreign leaders and Florentine citizens turn to one family for leadership? Because dealing with one family — one man, one faction, one voice — was the only recourse when faced with a government that, for the most part, changed every two months.

Only once over a period of fifty years was the Medici's towering influence truly challenged; this, as described in *The Sign of the Weeping Virgin,* by a rival family in 1478 in

11

a bloody attempt to rid Florence of its leader, the brilliant Renaissance humanist poet and *unelected* statesman, Lorenzo de' Medici, and his supporters — elected and otherwise.

# PROLOGUE

Guid'Antonio entered Florence Cathedral late that Easter Sunday morning, blinking as the front door closed and the sun lost itself to darkness. Inside the sanctuary, he cut through the nave past whooshing torches, jostling men from his path, his aggravation mounting. Already the choir's singular, sweet voice had fallen to a hush, and people were bowing their heads, anticipating the Elevation of the Host. Determined, he pushed through the crowd to Lorenzo de' Medici's dark, muscular figure near the south side of the altar, where they had agreed to meet this morning, but drew back when he glimpsed Lorenzo's brother, Giuliano, strangely isolated with Francesco de' Pazzi and Bernardo Bandini on the far opposite side of the church, near Via Servi. Those three were not friends. Wiry, whey-haired Francesco seemed nervous, snaking his arm around Giuliano's shoulders, casting furtive glances here and there.

Guid'Antonio's eyes flicked toward Lorenzo, and then back again. He did not see Bandini's axe till the blade flashed in the candlelight and sliced down on Giuliano's head. After that, time slowed down, as if luxuriously uncoiling itself in a long dark strand. Giuliano fell to his knees, his hood pouring blood. Francesco jumped on him in wild excitement, ripping his knife into the soft flesh of Giuliano's bare neck. Near them, a boy cried out, "The dome's coming down!" Men, women, and children flailed and fell over one another in a wave of fear and panic.

"No!" Guid'Antonio roared. "Giuliano!" He clawed forward, but repeatedly lost ground, as if ghost hands had hold of his crimson cloak, pulling him back by the hem. "Giuliano!" His good, young friend, stabbed over and over again as if he were a plaything made of scrap cloth, rather than hardened muscle and bone.

Murdered, while Guid'Antonio watched from a distance.

How could he have been so helpless?

He caught the sound of thunder rumbling outside his chateau apartment in Plessis-les-Tours and heard the French wind moan and howl. Restless and sweaty, he threw aside the bedsheet and stared up into the void, bound to memories that sank their talons into him and would not surrender their hold.

Twenty-six April 1478, two years ago. He could still feel the cool air inside Florence Cathedral and smell winter's lingering odor. He could hear the tinkling of the priest's bell. What he saw when he lay awake at night was Giuliano de' Medici on the church pavement with blood pouring from his head.

Pain sliced Guid'Antonio's chest. Why hadn't his gut turned to water when he saw Giuliano with Francesco de' Pazzi and Bernardo Bandini, those two malcontents? Why hadn't a voice inside him shrieked a warning? The Medici and Pazzi families were not friends. Their houses were too old, too well known, and too rich. Rivalries between them were raw. Yet until that April morning, those two mighty Florentine houses had managed the niceties. Swimming the surface of glassy waters, they did not sink.

Lies on top of lies.

Why hadn't he gone to Giuliano when he first noticed him in the church? Why hadn't he stood beside him and prayed? But no. No. Instead of saving Florence's favorite son, he had knelt beside his mutilated body on the cold stone floor and raised his hands to heaven in the raw fullness of disbelief. He had lain across him, protecting him from stampeding sandals, boots, and rough bare feet. He had helped the monks wrap Giuliano's corpse in the young Medici's black velvet cape, deeply grateful Lorenzo had eluded the armed priest who had attacked him, managing only to lightly slice Lorenzo's throat — if what the monks said was true. How could they know? The monks' ink-stained fingers were as shaky as Guid'Antonio's own.

He had accompanied Giuliano home to the Medici Palace through stinking, abandoned alleyways, while other Medici supporters hunted the conspirators down and slaughtered them in the streets like pigs. *What now?* Guid'Antonio had wondered. *What now?* Soon enough, he had received his answer in the shape of this ambassadorship to the French court. His reward for steadfast friendship and loyalty to the Medici, Florence's unofficial first family. But did he deserve it, really? Time and again, he had tried to tell Lorenzo what had happened that bloody Sunday. And each time he had caught the words back in his mouth, consumed with guilt. Since

16

Giuliano's death in the Cathedral, beneath his olive skin, Lorenzo de' Medici's face was watchful and unnaturally pale.

Anyway, didn't all men have secrets?

His chamber was warmer now, the atmosphere lighter by degrees, though outside the windows, the sky over Plessis-les-Tours appeared gloomy and wet. Morning. Nineteen June 1480. In a moment his nephew, Amerigo Vespucci, would enter the richly appointed apartment provided Guid'Antonio by King Louis XI of France, all alight with anticipation and energy, eager to begin their ride across the Apennines and down the Italian peninsula to Tuscany. *"Andiamo,* Uncle Guid'Antonio! Let's go! I can't wait to leave this ball-shriveling French weather!"

And so Ambassador Guid'Antonio Vespucci swung his feet off the feather mattress and reached for his shirt and traveling pants. Rising, he saw himself and Amerigo step out into the pouring rain and sprint toward the stable, where Amerigo had both their horses saddled and waiting. He saw himself shrug into his rain cloak and pull the hood down over his forehead, its oiled edges coiling around his face. Troubled in spirit and uneasy, he saw the ground shifting beneath him as he glanced up at the darkening clouds and rode out into the storm.

# ONE

*Florence, three weeks later. . . .*

He felt like a ghost Guid'Antonio, looming at the courtyard gate in the ethereal hours just before daybreak. Draped in fog, the workshops of the weavers and dyers and loom makers all along Borg'Ognissanti, All Saints Street, were still, the water mills closed down. The sole sound on the air was the faint echo of hooves striking rain-slick stones as a weary but content Amerigo led Flora and Bucephalus around the Vespucci Palace toward the family stables. But no, not so quiet after all, nor completely free of other movement. From where he stood, a hesitant figure alone at the wrought-iron gate, he could see the fountain in the palace garden and hear the soft gurgle of water flowing from the stone lion's jaws. Torches sputtered either side of the gate. In the dim light, he searched his scrip for his key. Amongst the jingle of coins, his fingers found the key, and he inserted it into the lock, only to discover it would not turn over. He jiggled the key, removed it, blew on it and, frowning, tried again without success. "God," he breathed.

"Messer Guid'Antonio," whispered the form detaching itself from the garden shadows. "I'm here. Just a moment, please."

It was not God, but Guid'Antonio's man-servant, Cesare Ridolfi, who unlocked the gate, then swung it open on squeaky hinges. A warm smile lit the young man's face. "Messer Guid'Antonio, welcome home."

"Thank you," Guid'Antonio said, embracing Cesare, patting his back, "but what's this?" He gestured toward the lock, wondering what preternatural force had whispered in Cesare Ridolfi's ear, "Messer Guid'Antonio and Amerigo are arriving home very early today. Moreover, Guid'Antonio will need the lock opened for him at the court-yard gate."

"Changed," Cesare said. "Like so many other things." His arms went out, encompassing the dawn and the stars emerging from behind scattering clouds. "But now, you're home. Will you have a bath to start this interminable day?"

Interminable? Guid'Antonio felt too tired to ask. "No. I'll start it by seeing my wife."

"Ah." Smiling slightly, Cesare slipped back into the shadowy darkness from whence he came.

"Maria?"

Languidly, she turned in the canopied bed, her hair a curtain of black, her cotton nightgown hiked high above shapely thighs. She raised her arms in sleepy welcome.

And then her eyes fluttered open. "Guid'Antonio?"

Yes. Guid'Antonio. For one instant, he paused, standing booted and spurred at their bedchamber door, not liking the direction of his thoughts.

"I don't believe it!" Maria sat up, and, as he crossed the room, she held his gaze with hers. He removed his damp traveling cloak and sat, shivering, on the bed.

"I didn't know when to expect you," she said. "Exactly, I mean." Her eyes searched his, as if he might be an apparition.

"I wanted to surprise you," he said.

"And did!" She laughed with unbridled delight. In the soft light cast by the brass lamps placed here and there around the room, her face shone.

A smile touched Guid'Antonio's lips. His wife was so lovely, her complexion dark olive brown, her skin glowing against the ruby hue of silk bed hangings. In the lamp-light, her hair gleamed like the fine ebony ambitious timber traders transported from afar, black and sweetly smooth to the touch. "You're beautiful," he said, admiring her figure on the bed, the long, graceful legs flowing smoothly from curving hips. He felt shy, now he was here with her after two years.

"What did you expect?" she said. "While you were gone, I'd change into a hag?" Tears welled in her eyes, deep dark pools with glints of gold. "There were times I feared you'd never come home."

"I wanted to." He brushed her hair with his fingers, basking in the pleasure of her touch as she caressed his face, waiting while she traced the line of his jaw and the fine new lines radiating outward from the corners of his eyes.

Her fingers strayed to his temples. Gently, she clasped his face in her hands. What did she see? A man of advancing years drinking in the perfection of his young wife? What did she think? Not only has he been gone two years, he's not as I remembered him?

And then she was down before him, the bare flesh of her knees pressing into the hard marble floor. She removed one of his muddy boots, then the other. She rose up like Aphrodite rising from the sea, her eyes connecting with his, and ran her hands along his thighs. High, her thumbs inside, caressing him. *There.*

A shudder ran through him. He slipped her gown up over her head, and they lay back on the sheets. He kissed her eyelashes, her mouth, and her breasts. "I love your eyes," she said. "Such a tender gray, I can almost see through them."

"*Non parlare, baciami.* Don't talk, kiss me."

She did, her mouth hot and yearning against his. "Do you think you can still satisfy me, Ambassador Guid'Antonio Vespucci?"

"I always have."

"You're mighty sure of yourself."

"Yes," he said.

*Not a whit,* he thought, and then: *When it comes to love, how could I be?*

"The women at King Louis's court must have been half mad in love with you." Gently, she bit his lip.

"More like completely," he said, and she punched him playfully. He felt his passion flare. "Not with me," he amended, "but with Amerigo."

He lied. The French women had flirted relentlessly with him and Amerigo both,

23

particularly when they moved from Paris to King Louis's isolated chateau at Plessis-les-Tours in west-central France. There everyone, including the king, had gathered for cards and music after dinner. And every night, as the ringing laughter and the sound of footsteps dimmed, and the king's entourage bedded down (pillows plumped, covers flipped back, the skirts of satin ball gowns hiked up), he had gone to bed alone.

He yanked his damp shirt up over his head. The roar of blood rushing in his ears almost drowned out the soft scrape of the chamber door, sighing open. Almost. Maria tensed with her fingers pressing into his flesh. Guid'Antonio twisted around. His hand found his belt on the coverlet and drew his knife in one fluid motion.

A small boy stood at the door, his face squeezed into an expression of pure terror. It was their son, Giovanni. "Mama!" he screamed, the candle he was holding shaking violently in his hand. "Why's that man hurting you?"

"Guid'Antonio — let me up!" Maria, fumbling for the sheet, was on her feet and flying across the floor in an instant. Guid'Antonio slipped his dagger beneath the rumpled coverlet, his heart thundering against his ribs.

Maria took the candle. Bending down awkwardly with the taper flaring in one hand, she embraced the child. "Giovanni, where's your nurse? Little one, don't be frightened. That isn't a man — that's your father!"

Her fingers fluttered to her mouth and in the light of the night lamps, the pink flush in her cheeks deepened to a brilliant hue. "I mean he wasn't hurting me, Giovanni, we're just so happy he's come home after so much time in France. Go greet him, my precious pet." She smiled encouragingly at the boy.

Little one? Precious pet? The boy was almost five. Wasn't Giovanni too old to be coddled like a one-year-old? Guid'Antonio extended his hand to his only child, the gift Maria del Vigna had finally given him after half a decade of marriage: a son. Precious and important, so far he was Guid'Antonio's sole heir.

Giovanni brushed the hair from his eyes, dark jewels laced with specks of glinting gold, like his mother's. He watched Guid'Antonio speculatively. "No."

Instinctively, Guid'Antonio sprang up, to do what, he had no idea. Giovanni drew back, his face twisted with fear. Quickly, Guid'Antonio said, "Giovanni, I'm sorry. Maria, the boy and I are strangers."

Maria held Giovanni close in her arms. "He needs time, Guid'Antonio."

"Yes, well, so do I." He strode to the windows, naked. Already the first light of day was seeping through the slats in the wooden window shutters. He unlatched the shutters and propped them up with iron rods. A faint vapor rose from the tiled rooftops stretching like a russet sea across the Santa Maria Novella quarter of Florence. The rain that had pelted him and Amerigo when they rode in through the Prato Gate a short while ago had abated, leaving morning arrayed in a fine gray mist.

"Guid'Antonio?"

He turned, arching one black eyebrow laced with silver.

"Now you're home, we have all the time in the world. Although I believe all I needed was another moment."

All the time in the world. Like Amerigo, Maria was just twenty-six, with complete faith in such words. Guid'Antonio managed a smile, feeling all the weight of his forty-four years. "I hope so, Maria."

"Don't move! I'll fetch Olimpia," she said.

"Olimpia — ?"

"Giovanni's nurse." Maria's brow wrinkled. "I wrote you. Old Silvana died. I'll be back in a moment and show you all

26

you've missed." She hurried off, tugging Giovanni along by the hand, glancing happily over the slender line of her shoulder.

Alone in the bedchamber, Guid'Antonio heard slight laughter, darting, indistinct voices and light footsteps. The palace was coming to life. Eyes closed, he drew a long breath. Then he opened the doors to the tabernacle attached to the chamber wall and, kneeling before the painting of *Our Lady with the Magi Worshipping Christ,* offered up his soul to heaven. After reciting prayers, he bathed using the herbal soap and tepid water that Cesare, as if borne on the morning air, had brought into the apartment the instant Guid'Antonio said, "Amen."

"Cesare, look at you. I failed to notice earlier. You've — grown." Guid'Antonio gestured with both hands.

A pleased expression played around Cesare's beautifully formed lips. "Taller, yes."

A slender young man with a cap of glossy black hair curling at his ears, Cesare stood with perfect posture, gazing back at him. The periwinkle tunic over Cesare's *camicia* was cut from velvet, here in the high heat of summer. But the soft color enhanced the startling violet-blue of Cesare's eyes. *Ah,*

27

*youth,* Guid'Antonio thought. And frowned slightly. Where the devil was Maria?

"You're nineteen now," he said.

"Yes, last month. Do you like the soap?"

"Right now, I'd like any kind of soap. But yes. What kind is it?"

"Lemon thyme. It comforts the heart."

Guid'Antonio laughed dryly. "Then buy a bucket of it from the soap sellers, please."

Cesare handed him a linen towel and in one fluid motion withdrew a cotton shirt from a cypress wood chest and shook it out to remove the folds. "You're off to City Hall, 'less I miss my guess."

"We both know you missing your guess is impossible," Guid'Antonio said.

An odd look, one suspiciously like pity, shone in Cesare's eyes. "What?" Guid'Antonio said.

"Just this: more than your gate latch has changed in Florence these last two years." Scooping laundry into his arms, Cesare strolled to the door and smiled encouragement before vanishing into the hall.

Guid'Antonio stirred uneasily, his face a frown as he removed his cloak from a wooden peg and entered the passageway. The wall torches in the hall smoked, just this moment extinguished. Cesare had

28

vanished the way he had come, in a twinkling.

And in his place Maria stood in the darkness at the top of the stairs. She saw Guid'Antonio's crimson cloak slung over his arm, and her shoulders drooped. "Where are you leaving us for now, Ambassador Vespucci?"

"Only as far as City Hall to surrender my credentials."

"Credentials?" She laughed softly. "You've been absent two years, you arrive home moments ago after a punishing ride, and you can't wait to leave again?"

"Maria —" He made an impatient gesture. "I'll be back by noon, I swear. But for now, Amerigo has dispatched a courier downtown to let the Lord Priors know we're here. I wager he's in the courtyard, pondering my whereabouts."

"Well, we wouldn't want to inconvenience Amerigo, would we?" she said.

Guid'Antonio's jaw tightened, and he licked his lips, parched, wishing he had something to drink. "A while ago, you claimed we have all the time in the world."

"Please don't twist my words against me," she said. "It's insulting. You want to announce yourself, let the Priors know you're back and a force to be reckoned with."

Well, yes. "I only want to tend to final business, Maria."

"What about what I want? But my husband's always gone?"

Jesus, Mary, and Joseph. "Not always, Maria."

"Yes!" Her chin lifted a notch. "This time, France. Before that, four months in Rome, fighting with the Pope."

"Not fighting, Maria. Giuliano had just been slain. In Rome my mission was to prevent a war between us and Pope Sixtus IV, since it was his nephew who masterminded Giuliano's assassination, and Rome is a mighty force to be reckoned with in any circumstance."

"And yet you failed," she said.

His lips felt stiff as he spoke. "I tried, Maria. Our government trusted me with the welfare of the State."

"Lorenzo de' Medici trusted you, you mean. The Florentine government does whatever he says, just like you, even though he has nothing to do with the State."

"Nothing, Maria?"

"You know what I mean."

Yes, he did. Thirty-one-year-old Lorenzo de' Medici was not an *elected* official of the Florentine Republic but, following in his father and grandfather's footsteps, he was

30

the head of the Medici family and its powerful inner circle, both social and political.
Guid'Antonio's circle. Like Lorenzo de'
Medici, whether in office or out, Guid'Antonio had everything to do with the Florentine State, and it with him.

An unpleasant vision of servants and family standing with ears pressed to the palace
walls, listening, flashed before him. "Maria," he said, "our hallway isn't the place for
this."

"Believe me, I know. All I want is for you
to stay with me a while."

All he wanted was to brush by her and
hurry down the narrow stone stairs to the
garden gate. To manage important political
concerns first, then come back home and
— what? Butt heads with her again? No. To
sort out everything. He reminded himself
he was a doctor of law, a highly acclaimed
doctor of law, in point of fact. He couldn't
count the times he had stood before the
magistrates in court, handling a difficult
case. Retreat would have gained him nothing as Florence's special envoy to Rome, to
France, or to any other place. Withdrawal
would gain him nothing here.

Still. "Time and the Lord Priors wait for
no man, Maria. Not even me."

A look of extreme sorrow dawned on her

face. "These last two years there have been times I desperately needed you. Instead, I had to turn to your kinsmen for everything. Even for permission to order new linens for our beds. You were never here. You still aren't. All that's left of you is a shell where once there stood a man."

"What?" he said, staring, drawing back. "What did you say?"

"Nothing."

"Yes, you did. A *shell*? I'm Florence's ambassador to France, for God's sake. I've worked hard for the Vespucci family —"

"For Lorenzo," she said.

Tersely, he said, "They're one and the same. I'm leaving."

"I didn't expect you to stay."

Head held desperately erect, she walked past him into the bedchamber. He heard her footsteps approach the washstand, heard her hair crackle as she attacked it with a brush. He heard the sound of quiet weeping.

He descended the staircase quickly, the heels of his boots ringing solidly against stone, and walked out into the courtyard, where he found Amerigo waiting by the fountain with his worn leather satchel containing his writing pens and ink slung over his shoulder.

"*Andiamo,* Amerigo," he said. "Let's go. It's not wise to keep the Republic of Florence waiting."

# Two

"Praise God, it's good to be home," Amerigo said, excitement rippling in his voice as he and Guid'Antonio quit the Vespucci Palace gate and walked south along Borg'Ognissanti, All Saints Street.

"Yes."

"What's wrong?"

"Nothing."

He felt Amerigo's skeptical glance. The shell of a man? Great God Almighty, what had just transpired between him and his wife? What did she mean? Playing Maria's words over in his mind made his cheeks sting with the fresh heat of anger. Why had he stood in their hallway and allowed her to speak to him thus? Not many men would do. But few men had wives like his beautiful, contentious and hardheaded Maria del Vigna. Hadn't his notary warned him against her when Guid'Antonio approached him ten years ago about arranging the marriage? "She's a virago! A sixteen-year-old girl with a mind of her own! No wonder she's not already betrothed. Messer Vespucci — she reads and writes!"

"So do my sisters. So did my first wife," Guid'Antonio had said back to the little man.

All around him now, Borg'Ognissanti was stretching to life. Yawning merchants unlatched doors and raised squeaky wooden shutters. Awnings dripped, and sunshine warmed the vast piazza between Ognissanti Church and the River Arno. Guid'Antonio drew a deep breath, drawing in the familiar sights and sounds that offered a balm to his soul. "Amerigo —" he said, but broke off as a monk clad in black robes ran from the church garden and crashed headlong into them.

Amerigo slipped in a pile of steaming dung. "Christ!" he yelled, slapping at the glittering green flies buzzing up around his eyes and nose.

"I — oh!" The monk stopped and briefly locked eyes with Guid'Antonio. "Messer Vespucci!" he cried and dashed on down the Borgo.

"What the hell was that?" Amerigo fussed, brushing at his tunic.

"Not 'what' but 'who,' " Guid'Antonio

said. "One of our own, considering his black clothing, and —" Just then two other monks of the Benedictine Order of the Humiliati burst from the church gate and plowed into them. "For God's sake!" Guid'Antonio said, stepping quickly back into the street. "Watch where you're going!"

"A thousand pardons!" said the taller of the two young men. "Ohhh, Messer Vespucci! It's *you*." Alarmed blue eyes shone from the narrow planes of the monk's alert features. His tonsure made a silvery fringe around his face.

Guid'Antonio growled, "Yes." He had no time for this.

"That's *Ambassador* Vespucci to you," Amerigo said. "Now get out of the way so we can go to City Hall and surrender our credentials."

"What?" The tall monk fumbled for words. What did he know of credentials and the Palazzo della Signoria? "I mean to say you don't know me, Messer Vespucci, but I know All Saints is your family church." He gestured toward Ognissanti. "We all know it very well." Gathering his dignity, he drew himself up to his considerable height. "I'm Brother Paolo Dolci, and this is Ferdinando Bongiovi."

Ferdinando poked his head around

Guid'Antonio. "Brother Martino!" he yelled and bolted around them toward the Prato Gate with Brother Paolo giving chase, crying back, "May God have mercy on your souls!"

"*Our* souls? Yours first!" Amerigo said, swearing and wiping his boot with a handful of the straw littering the thoroughfare. "What did he mean by that? If I had my hands on the rascal leading that merry chase, he'd have good reason to run. I just cleaned three weeks' travel off these boots, and now they're covered with shit. Monks!"

Guid'Antonio turned over in his mind the glittering excitement and fear he had witnessed in the faces of the three young men. "Who knows? As for Brother Martino, a heavy burden fueled that high emotion, else, why flee his Benedictine brothers?"

They cut through a byway so narrow and lofty in places, its steep walls never felt the sun. "Ugh," Amerigo said. "Here's an alley ripe with piss and last week's boiled pigeon livers."

Guid'Antonio slowed, his body drawing back. At the far end of the alley, Giuliano de' Medici slumped to his knees, his cloak a black cloud billowing around him. Blood gushed from his head. Guid'Antonio gasped, staring as a scarlet lake spread outward from Giuliano's ruined corpse.

"Uncle! What is it?" Amerigo said.

Guid'Antonio snapped his head toward his nephew. When he looked back down the alley, Giuliano was gone. "Nothing," he said, swallowing hard over the lump lodged deep in his throat. "I thought —" He pushed the image back into its dark hole. "I'm only worn out from the road."

"Me, too," Amerigo said. "Times there were the last three weeks I thought my rear end would wear through the saddle. Do you remember the night I spent talking with the old monk in Piacenza?"

"Absolutely. We were late getting started the next day."

Guid'Antonio started walking again, profoundly shaken by Giuliano's ghostly image. In France, painful memories had gnawed at him, coming out at night like rats. But he had witnessed no visions of Giuliano de' Medici. Now he was home was he to be completely devoured by guilt and grief, when all he wanted was peace in his heart? Thinking of Maria, he choked back a laugh.

"The old fellow kept prattling about the coming of a new heaven and earth. What do you suppose he meant?"

"Annius of Viterbo has been predicting

the defeat of the Turks," Guid'Antonio said. "The building of holy cities and a new Jerusalem."

"Praise God for a miracle! And for sunshine, too," Amerigo said as they entered Piazza Trinita in a golden shaft of light.

"That's the prophet's prediction. The Ottoman Turks embarked on a career of conquest centuries ago in the name of religion. I doubt they'll abandon their mission anytime soon."

"Islam," Amerigo said.

"Yes. Few have managed to hold them back."

"Vlad the Impaler did." Vlad Dracula, the prince of Wallachia, near the kingdom of Hungary.

"How very true," Guid'Antonio said.

A solitary man wearing a full leather apron hurried past them in the direction of Ponte Santa Trinita, off toward their right. Two women, their faces shining with a taut white candescence within their dark hoods, entered Trinita Church on the square. Did they mean to pray before Trinita's miraculous crucifix? Well, Guid'Antonio no longer believed in miracles. Certainly not when it came to the Turks. In 1453, Mehmed II's soldiers had conquered Constantinople and slaughtered King Constantine XI along with

39

his army of Christian defenders. In the aftermath of that massive blow to the Christian world, on the blood-stained floor of Constantinople's Cathedral of Saint Sophia, the young sultan had offered up a prayer of thanksgiving: *There is no god but Allah, and Mohammed is His Prophet!* Mehmed had proclaimed the church a mosque and named the defeated city the capital of the Ottoman Empire, and so it had remained for the last thirty years.

Guid'Antonio's gaze strayed toward the wide side street bearing off to his left. A turn in that direction would lead him to Florence Cathedral. His stomach shrank into a hard ball. He had not stepped inside that holy place since spring 1478. Giuliano's broken body was the stuff of his dreams; how could he face the haunting images within those walls again? He could not. A ghost inhabited that enormous, twilight space. A soul lost and wandering, waiting to be saved. More than one, perhaps.

A red gateway opened off Piazza Trinita onto Via Porta Rossa. He unlatched the gate, let the wooden arm fall back into place with a thud and set a quick pace beneath Palazzo Davizzi's limp crimson banners. "Sometimes, Amerigo, whether or not you believe God has granted a miracle depends on whose side you're on," he said.

"Soap scraps! Used hose!"

"Squirrel pies, pigeon pies, buy my day-old pies!"

"What's this?" Amerigo said as they strode into the market, where vendors in makeshift stalls pitched their wares. "Bargain day in Mercato Nuovo?"

"It appears so." All around the square, rain-soaked silk streamers and ribbons dripped from balcony railings. Banners drooped, mounted on poles. Prominent among the banners was Lorenzo de' Medici's personal standard displaying a golden falcon caught in a net. An odd image for Lorenzo to embrace, or so it had always seemed to Guid'Antonio.

"Thank God our Lorenzo still flies with the Soderini and the Rucellai families and all the others," Amerigo said, his voice grave. "The Pazzi dolphins would be sailing over us now, if Francesco de' Pazzi had his way. Damn his soul to hell for plotting Giuliano's murder."

A muscle jumped in Guid'Antonio's jaw. "Francesco didn't plot it alone, as you well know."

The facts behind Giuliano de' Medici's assassination had been slow in coming — a hard questioning here, sizzling pincers applied to private parts there — and they had led to a startling discovery, since they implicated Florence's powerful neighbors to the south, Rome and Naples. With Francesco de' Pazzi as his pawn, the fall of the house of Medici had been masterminded by Pope Sixtus IV's nephew, Count Girolamo Riario, with the full blessing of the Pope. Fear. Jealousy. Greed. Lorenzo's place as the unofficial ruler of Florence rankled the Pazzi family, particularly Francesco. Francesco's enormously wealthy family of international bankers was equal to the Medicis on Via Larga, or so Francesco believed. Wasn't *he* the head of the Pazzi holdings? Hadn't *he* snaked the all-important Papal account from Lorenzo and put it in his own hands in Rome? *And in retaliation for the loss of that hugely lucrative account — which Lorenzo's family had held for years — had not Lorenzo then tricked the Pazzi family out of a bountiful inheritance it had expected to collect?*

This was personal: an outrage not to be borne. Girolamo Riario understood this. And he understood Francesco, too. Acting from the Vatican, Girolamo had appealed to Francesco's overblown sense of self-importance, his anger, his envy and frustration. Succeed in killing Lorenzo and his only brother, and the Pazzi family would no longer live under the thumb of the Medici brats. Succeed, and Sixtus IV and Girolamo Riario's mercenary troops could creep closer to Florence's frontiers as part of their private scheme to increase their own family's standing in central Italy. In this, they had enlisted the help of the king of Naples, who had his own personal vision of his place in Italy dancing in his head.

"Girolamo Riario was damned two years ago, along with his uncle, the Pope," Guid'Antonio said. "And Francesco is dead." Pulled naked and bleeding from his hiding place at home in the Santa Croce quarter and shoved from a window of City Hall with his hands bound behind his back and a noose around his neck before Giuliano was cold in Via Larga. As news of Giuliano's assassination and the aborted attack on Lorenzo swept through the streets, the Florentine population had not risen up against Lorenzo and welcomed the Pazzi family as its liberators, as pudding-headed Francesco had hoped. No: instead, they had branded Francesco a traitor scheming to hand them over to their enemies and had thrown their support behind Lorenzo, who had stood before them on the balcony of

43

the Medici Palace, his neck wrapped with a bandage whose fabric was stained with blood: the wounded, singular head of his grieving family.

Guid'Antonio smiled to himself. *Unofficial,* indeed.

"Squirrel pies! Crow pies, cheap!"

Amerigo said, "Those pies smell like they've been here forever. I wanted a bite to eat, but now my appetite's flown."

"In writing, please?"

*"Nonna!"* Amerigo called to the old grandmother hawking the tragic little tarts. "You call that dried-up parchment a pie?"

The vendor screwed up her face, her eyes hot beads as Amerigo passed her cart. "Here's a better question, you rich brat: could your soft belly handle it?" She bit into one of the withered pies and hurled it at Amerigo, grinning, showing the black, rotted stubs of her teeth. The crust split, and a burnt crow's leg popped out.

"Christ's ankles!" Amerigo slapped the pie to the ground, where a fawn-colored dog, all paws and bones, snatched the pie up, snarling.

Guid'Antonio glanced at the sun. *"Andiamo,* Amerigo. We're late."

"Jesu! I've never seen such ribs sticking out of a dog! I'd try to get the rope off his

44

neck, but he'd have my hand for something sweet. No fine leather collar for him, now or any other time."

"He's fought bears, then been left to rot."

"For all that, he's managed to survive. And escape."

"He's a Florentine." Along with the sound of his nephew's voice, Guid'Antonio heard the dog's labored breathing and caught the smell of cat urine and moldy bread intermingled as they entered a side street.

"You do know he's following us," Amerigo said. "What manner of cur is that?"

Guid'Antonio glanced back. The dog was *huge.* Black mask across the muzzle, cropped ears, a short, matted dense coat, and curled-down toenails. "A mastiff, a *cane corso Italiano* in a better life."

"Even sadder. An ill fate for a magnificent dog."

"Go on!" Guid'Antonio shooed the animal away. "Give him one bite and we'll have him forever."

"He's already had one bite. The filth posing as a pie, remember? Speaking of filth, I managed a quick bath this morning, given this meeting with the Lord Priors. Still, my body feels whipped as that dog, who's still following us at a safe distance, by the way." Amerigo gave Guid'Antonio a sly glance.

"We haven't seen the last of him."

*"Au contraire,"* Guid'Antonio said.

They stepped into Mercato Vecchio, where daylight was a patch of pale sky overhead, and Amerigo's stomach growled with hunger. "Apparently, despite that burned tart, you've not lost your appetite," Guid'Antonio said.

"Though embarrassed, I will confess it."

City Hall was not far ahead. In a few moments, the Republic's foremost governing council would gather in the Great Hall to hear Guid'Antonio present his report regarding his mission to France. Beside him, Amerigo's stomach roared. "Oh, all right. We'll eat on the way," Guid'Antonio said.

*"Grazie!* I've had my fill of French *cassoulet* and pork with prunes. I want something satisfying. Something Italian."

"So do I," Guid'Antonio said.

He approached a fruit stand, a sagging assembly of rotting wood pegged together in a ramshackle suggestion of shelves. From behind a stack of baskets, an old man appeared, his ferret eyes keen, darting over them.

"What do you want?" the man said, one calloused hand pushing back his hood of coarsely woven cloth.

Guid'Antonio stepped back. The peasant

stank of sheep and sweat. "Two apples and some pecorino." He opened his scrip and tendered a silver penny.

The farmer's gnarled fingers snatched the coin. The apples the man handed him were as brown and withered as the man's face, the sheep's-milk cheese Guid'Antonio bit into, rancid. "Ugh!" He spat the cheese into the dirt.

The mongrel dog launched his body forward and lapped up the found meal. *Two in one day? Unbelievable!* Growling down in his throat, one dull eye rolling up, the mastiff kept close watch on the proceedings.

Repelled by the foul taste of spoiled cheese, Guid'Antonio wiped his lips with his handkerchief, all snowy white linen.

"Scuttle back to your palace kitchen if you don't like my wares," the farmer said. "In the markets, you'll find the pickings slim."

"Slim? Looks to me as if they've given up the ghost," Amerigo said. "What do you expect us to eat?"

The man's stare was as contemptuous as it was hard. "Do you think I care? What do you expect from war?"

Amerigo opened his mouth to speak; gently, Guid'Antonio touched his arm. "Everything will improve, friend, now the

47

war's ended and we have peace again."

The old man barked a laugh. "Where've you been hiding your head? In the well at your country villa?"

Amerigo gasped. "Old man! Have a care!"

"Messer Vespucci!" a friendly voice called out in the piazza. "And Amerigo!" A heavy-set fellow hurried toward them, holding up the hem of his brown *lucco* to keep it tidy as he bustled around the water well in the center of the marketplace. "Welcome home, welcome!"

"It's good to see you, Luca." True, but Christ, here was another delay.

"When did you arrive?"

"Dawn today."

"And already you're out and about in the city. Well, no rest for the weary."

"There doesn't seem to be."

Guid'Antonio knew Luca Landucci better than he did most other men who were not part of the city's ruling elite. In Florence, he often visited Luca's apothecary shop, the Sign of the Stars, to purchase medicaments for the family and sometimes to enlist the druggist's assistance with one or another of Guid'Antonio's private cases of an investigative nature.

"Ser Landucci," Amerigo said, "how's Gostanzo's performance in the *palio* this summer? Exciting as always?"

Guid'Antonio listened with half an ear, aware of the farmer's disdain, the miserable dog retching into the dirt, and the shadows lengthening around them in the market as Luca spoke glowingly of his younger brother, Gostanzo Landucci, of Gostanzo's horse from Barbary, *Il Draghetto,* the Little Dragon, and of the horse races held throughout the year in Tuscany. Prato, Montepulciano, Santa Liperata, and Cortona: those tight little piazzas. Thundering hooves slid on loose pebbles. Horses crashed over stones and into shop walls, leaving the animals and their riders in a tangle of bones, blood, and sweat. The goal? A coveted spot in the championship race in August. *"Palio!"*

"Neither my brother Gostanzo nor any other man takes the banner when Lorenzo de' Medici puts a horse in the mix," Luca grumbled. "No doubt he'll claim the grand prize again next month." Luca muttered something about judges. "Ah, well, Messer Vespucci. How long will you bless Florence with your presence this time around?"

"I won't be leaving again."

Amerigo clasped his chest. "Christ's bones! Does our Lorenzo know?"

"Right now, Luca, we're bound for the Lord Priors," Guid'Antonio said.

The forgotten old farmer spat a gob of phlegm at Guid'Antonio's feet. "Priors? Bastards, is more the like! When you see those nine fools tell them to come into the street so we can whip their Medici asses!"

Amerigo stared, aghast. "Do you *want* to spend the rest of your days in the Stinche?"

Guid'Antonio looked into the farmer's glowing stare. "Why are you so angry?"

"You're a *palleschi!*" the farmer said in reference to the Medici family's emblem, a varying number of *palle,* or balls, in red on a gold field. "A Medici man born and bred."

"Yes," Guid'Antonio said with the confidence born of his family's alliance with the Medici family for the last half century.

"Because of Lorenzo, we went to war with God!"

"Not with God," Guid'Antonio said. "With Pope Sixtus IV."

"The Pope and God are one and the same!" the farmer said, trembling.

"No." Guid'Antonio shook his head. "Sixtus IV, *not* God, declared war on us when his nephew's scheme to cripple our government failed. We have a treaty with the Pope now." Surely the old fellow knew this?

At the first sign of discord, a crowd had started to gather, not unusual in these streets. "What we have," a man shouted

50

from the throng, "is Turks at our gates!" The mastiff eased up onto his haunches, his dim gaze roaming the assembly.

Amerigo's hand flew to his cheek. "Turks? No."

"There are no Turks in Italy," said Guid'Antonio.

A black-gowned woman, as stout as one of the market's empty grain barrels, stabbed her finger in his direction. "You're wrong, Messer Whoever-You-Are in your fine red cloak! They mean to capture us and sell us as slaves, just as they've done to sweet Camilla Rossi da Vinci!" Shouts of alarm underscored the woman's shrill cry.

Guid'Antonio and Amerigo exchanged wary glances. Fear and half-truths ruled this gathering. Guid'Antonio turned to Luca. "What's this about?"

The mastiff, shifting his rheumy gaze from Guid'Antonio to the druggist and back again, slid onto his bony ribcage, prepared to listen and wait.

Luca squared his shoulders. "A little over a week ago, a young woman was traveling out from here when Turks chanced upon her."

No way in hell. With Constantinople as his base, Mehmed II had continued his career of conquest with an eye to converting souls to Islam, yes. As part of his holy war, the Ottoman leader had extended his empire in Europe to the Danube and the Aegean and tightened his control over the Black Sea and had also begun a sixteen-year war with the Venetian Republic, the strongest naval power in the Mediterranean, a war that had ended just two months ago. The northern end of the peninsula was as far as the Turks had ever penetrated, however, and they had not ventured into Italy again. If they had, Guid'Antonio would know about it.

Surely.

"By whose word?" he said.

"That of the Lady Camilla's nurse and her attendant. Praise God, the old woman and the boy escaped the Infidels and lived to tell the tale."

" 'Boy'? Camilla's son, you mean?" All around the piazza, people pushed forward to hear Guid'Antonio and Luca's conversation, their expressions grim.

"No, no, she's sixteen and married but has no children. I mean the boy from the country of the *teste nere.*"

"A black boy? Come all the way from Ethiopia, then." Amerigo's eyes shone with wonder. "There's a fair distance. Across the dark green sea to the slave market at Lisbon, probably. Does he speak Italian?"

"Amerigo." Guid'Antonio put up a finger, a gentle request for quiet. To Luca, he said, "So the boy's the lady's slave."

"Yes."

"How old?"

Luca shrugged. "Twelve or so. The three left Florence and stopped before nightfall in San Gimignano. They were on the road to Bagno a Morba the following day when the Turks attacked."

The Baths of Morba in the Apennine foothills. A thought flickered across Guid'Antonio's mind, but he could not contain it. "Why Turks?" he said.

"They announced themselves with swords flashing and threats in the name of Islam."

Preposterous. But not, Guid'Antonio knew, to the people hanging on their every word here in Mercato Vecchio.

"And her name was Camilla?" Amerigo said.

"Yes. Camilla Rossi da Vinci. Married to the wine merchant Castruccio Senso of the Green Dragon district." Across the river in the Santo Spirito quarter of Florence and from the hilltop town of Vinci, Luca meant.

"They never killed her but made her their slave and whore!" shouted a man in the crowd, a butcher by the look of his blood-

53

spattered apron.

Guid'Antonio grunted. He thought Camilla Rossi was more likely run away with a persuasive young lover than murdered or enslaved by anyone. "Has there been an investigation?"

Luca nodded. "Palla Palmieri conducted one but uncovered nothing."

Guid'Antonio considered this briefly. If his sometimes ally, if not quite friend, Palla Palmieri, Florence's chief of police, had not turned anything up about the missing girl, chances were good this case was closed and forgotten by the authorities, if not by the *popolo minuto,* the people in the street.

A grizzled old monk stepped forward. "Messer Vespucci, the Turkish invasion is a sign from God."

So it was an invasion now. "Of what?" Guid'Antonio said, sharply aware of time slipping through his fingers.

"Of His profound displeasure with Lorenzo de' Medici for taking us to war with Holy Mother Church," the monk intoned, his holier-than-thou voice and the pious expression on his face maddening.

"We are *not* at war with the Church. We never were," Guid'Antonio said. "Only with the Pope. And Lorenzo did not take us there. It was the other way around."

54

"Blasphemy!" the monk cried, shaking his fist. "Because of Lorenzo we've been cast into hell!" Tightly packed, people closed in, their eyes glittering with a fear that verged on madness. The mastiff, struggling to his feet, stood his ground, teeth bared, growling menacingly.

Guid'Antonio felt the breath of the malcontents hot against his face and was beginning to step back when a man hidden in the throng shouted, "What right does Lorenzo have to play the lord over us? He's no duke or king! Would he had died with his brother!"

For one moment, Guid'Antonio stared, speechless.

"Who spoke?" he said, his voice shaking with anger. *More than your gate latch has changed in this town,"* Cesare had said this morning. "Come forward!"

In the eyes of the people, there was a restless shifting.

"Cowards!" He strode into the gathering.

Amerigo glanced at Luca. "Here we go."

Wide-eyed and fearful, people cringed back. "You would disparage Lorenzo, casting him down?" Guid'Antonio said, his words echoing in the square, bouncing and whirling against stone. "You would mock and crush everything the Medici family has done for you in the last half century? For our city, pouring thousands of florins into convents and monasteries? Yes, as far away as Jerusalem! How *dare* you imply Giuliano deserved his fate! He was an innocent!" Guid'Antonio's head pounded, about to explode.

Somewhere a solitary bell began ringing, as though in complete concert with his words. "Not dukes or kings, you say? Yet who does Europe consider the voice of the Florentine Republic — France, Spain, even the king of England, Edward IV? Not to mention the Sforza dukes in Milan, King Ferrante of Naples, the Pope, and the Doge who governs Venice? Lorenzo! And you, wherever you're hiding, you would challenge this? Rue the day a duke or king rules this city! Or a Pope! As it is, we have the brightest voice and the steadiest hand between us and them."

Nearby, Amerigo stood solemn-faced and solid as an oak, the tips of his fingers touching the hilt of his dagger. Guid'Antonio's glance raked the crowd, his pulse hammering in his fists. Eyes round and bright stared back at him. Surely, the devil owned Guid'Antonio Vespucci, just as he owned his accomplice, Lorenzo.

A young bravo, who until now had been content to waste the morning lazing in the shade of the marketplace, drew close. "Ignore them, Messer Vespucci!" To the crowd the youth shouted, "Lorenzo had naught to do with the war but to defend his life and his house! Do you blame him for defending it still?"

A questioning ripple ran over Guid'Antonio. Defending it *still*? How so?

The old farmer, who had remained stiffly by his fruit cart throughout, spoke up. "Say what you will in Lorenzo the Magnificent's favor. You two are apples from the same tree. You think mine are rotten? Here in the starving belly of Florence, we know why the Virgin weeps."

From the youth there came a lusty reply: "And I know it doesn't take much!"

A howl of "Sacrilege!" erupted from the gathering.

"Virgin?" Amerigo said. "Where?"

The appearance of Palla Palmieri riding into the piazza at the head of five armed men had the desired effect. A girl shrieked, *"Ufficiale!"* People shied back. "Disband! Now!" Palla's lithe figure twisted in the saddle. His dark gaze drank in the gathering, memorizing faces.

A tense moment followed. Then muttered

words, and a nervous shifting about. People shook their heads and drifted off, although their faces remained set in anger. Palla caught Guid'Antonio's eye, gave him the familiar knowing grin, and vanished as quickly as he had come. After a moment, the cocky young man who had harangued the gathering settled down at the water well with his *ragazzi*.

Luca blew out a long breath. "Thank God for our police chief. And, Messer Vespucci, for you, as well." Worry creased the druggist's wide brow, and he seemed about to say more. Instead, he gave an eloquent shrug. "Peace be with you."

"And also with you," Guid'Antonio and Amerigo said. "Thank you for standing with us, Luca," Guid'Antonio said. "You're a good man."

Luca smiled uneasily. "A Medici man, like you. I mean — not quite like you. At any rate, Godspeed. And good luck in the coming days."

"Jesus! That old sheep-bugger," Amerigo said once they were away from the market and striding down a muddy side street. "What a wreckage of opinions and misinformation! Verbal arrows fired at us from every direction! 'Down with the Medici'? How

58

dare that fool speak against us? All of them, really, in the open, risking their necks, and for what?" Amerigo frowned. "After all that, I remain confused."

"I've been confused since we first set out this morning and were knocked off our feet by three running monks," Guid'Antonio said. And thought: *Before that, too.*

He glanced back down the passage to be sure a gang of hotheads armed with short knives wasn't tailing them and was relieved to see nothing moving behind them but the drooling *cane corso Italiano* weaving along at their heels.

He made a mental note to have Cesare kill the animal in some humane fashion if — when — it followed them home. Better that than let the dog starve and his corpse rot in the street. "During the war, it was the peasants who lived on bread made from the bark of oaks," he said. Weary and disheartened, he shrugged his incomprehension. "As for the shopkeepers and all the others, I'm as baffled as you."

They quit the alleyway and strode diagonally across Piazza della Signoria toward the flag-bedecked building situated on the piazza's far eastern corner. For pedestrians only, the paved square was free of horses or any other beasts of burden.

A light breeze ruffled the hem of Guid'Antonio's crimson cloak and soothed the flushed hollows of his cheeks. He inhaled deeply, calming his clattering nerves with the sight of the elegant watchtower soaring up from Palazzo della Signoria, or City Hall, into the sunny blue vault of sky. In this city of towers, Arnolfo di Cambio's bell tower loomed over the rest. It and the fortress-like Signoria had commanded this spot in downtown Florence for more than a century. The two structures would stand forever, surely.

"A weeping virgin and a missing married lady," Amerigo was saying. "There's odd talk for a public gathering. And Turks? *Please.* What in Zeus' name could all this mean?"

Guid'Antonio nodded to an acquaintance passing them in the square. *"Buon giorno. Bene, grazie, Augustino."* To Amerigo he said: "Lower your voice, please."

"And as you bespoke, what's this to do with our Lorenzo?"

"Amerigo, *please.*"

In silence, they walked past Donatello's *Marzocco,* the stone lion that was the symbol of Florentine liberty, Guid'Antonio wondering how many others had noticed the animal's fangs were bared in a silent roar.

60

"With our Lorenzo," Amerigo persisted as they entered the dimness of the Palazzo della Signoria's cool, colonnaded courtyard, where a guard with a knife at his belt stood at the bottom of the steps ascending to the Great Hall.

"Amerigo, I haven't the slightest idea," Guid'Antonio said, vaguely aware that behind them in the square the crippled mastiff's curling toenails had come to a clacking halt.

# THREE

Sandro Botticelli, hurrying across the corner of Piazza della Signoria onto a shadowed side street, took a step back into the sun. Eyes narrowed, he watched the two men striding away from him toward City Hall. One wore a lightweight summer cloak of crimson, *the* color of luxury in Florence, given the high cost of the dye, produced as it was from a powder imported from the East, where it was obtained from the ground bodies of the kermes shield louse. His companion wore an expensive purple *giubbia,* one of the new, scandalously short tunics, over thigh-hugging brown hose along with brown leather ankle boots.

Sandro inclined his head. He would recognize Amerigo Vespucci and his celebrated lawyer-uncle, Guid'Antonio, anywhere. Hadn't his family and the Vespuccis lived as neighbors in the Unicorn district of the Santa Maria Novella quarter since before

Sandro was born? Amerigo appeared to have gained some self-assurance, whiling away the hours up north. His booted gait matched his uncle's stride-for-stride, and he wore a new air of easy self-confidence.

Sandro observed Guid'Antonio's broad shoulders. The Vespucci family boss was a remarkably handsome man, with a kind of cool, reserved elegance about him; a long, pleasing neck, silvery-black hair shorn a bit too close around his face — conservative, that — high cheekbones, eyes a pale gray shade. To Sandro, the estimable and sometimes feared Guid'Antonio Vespucci made an altogether agreeable package.

Add to that the man was rich, rich, rich.

Sandro chewed his lip, wondering if he might have acted too hastily just now in Ognissanti Church. He had been seated on creaky wooden scaffolding, his knees touching stone, considering how time was flying up his tunic like Zephyr when he heard the devil scream.

"Lust! Murder! I've defiled this holy place!"

Sandro had snapped around on the plank, squinting along his shoulder, past his almost-finished fresco of *Saint Augustine* lit by torches flaring in iron sconces along the wall. There! A dark figure hurtling from the

63

side chapels toward the altar, robes flapping about him like huge black wings.

The dark dervish howled.

Sandro had watched, horrified, as the creature came to a lurching halt before the altar and beat his breast, his head thrown back in wild abandon. Candles smoked and flared, treacherously close to the miraculous painting of the *Virgin Mary of Santa Maria Impruneta* propped on the altar table. "Mary!" the dark one screamed, falling to his knees. "I brought God down on our heads! I'm not worthy to look on your face. Forgive me! Please!"

Sandro blinked. Since when did Satan repent? Never! Moreover, this agitated figure was tonsured, the top of his head smooth as a baby's bare ass, his fringe a shining black crown. Here was no evil spirit bent on destroying the *Virgin Mary of Santa Maria Impruneta,* but one of the black-robed Benedictine brothers of this church.

"Oh!" the fellow cried. "My Virgin Lady, how often have you wept for me?"

As often as she was so moved, was Sandro's opinion. Who was mortal man to question her timing? He dipped his brush and heard a riot of sound, coming near. "Ferdinando!" cried a high-pitched voice. "This way! Brother Martino's at the altar!

Where else could he be?"

"Yes! Catch him, Brother Paolo! *Run!*"

The dark monk scrambled up and faced the swell of rising voices. "I am Satan's brother! I must leave this holy place!" Whirling from the altar, he ran out the cloister door and into the loggia garden, where he paused, his form awash in streaming sunlight. Midnight's pounding thunderstorm had left the grassy courtyard sparkling, a radiant canvas of glistening silver green. The cloister door wheezed shut, and the church was enclosed in gloomy darkness once more.

Sandro glanced back toward the altar, where Paolo and Ferdinando skittered to a halt. "He's not here! Ferdinando, can you see? My eyes are young but weak — is the Virgin weeping?"

Sandro's pulse slowed. The Mary in the altar painting had first appeared to weep last Wednesday — or, anyway, last Wednesday was when a boy pointed the tears out to his mother. After that, rich merchants and poor farmers alike had poured in from Piazza Ognissanti, heat and hope rising off them in waves, while the ancient almoner of this church rolled his eyes heavenward, his withered ears tuned to the rhythm of the coins jingling in his collection box. "She weeps!" Little by little, though, the Virgin

65

Mary's tears had slowed to a trickle. By Saturday, they had dried up and had not been witnessed again so far as was known.

The little fellow called Ferdinando stared at the painting, his body canted slightly forward. "It's difficult to see in this lack of light. But no, Brother Paolo, Christ's mother is not weeping today."

"Ah, Ferdinando! Thank you." Hastily, Brother Paolo crossed himself, his glance sweeping the nave, sliding over Sandro. Sandro Botticelli was part of the wall, merely one of several craftsmen who had been working here the last few months. Botticelli, Domenico Ghirlandaio: they came and went according to their trade. "Brother Martino!" Paolo called. "There's no cause to leave this place! Father Abbot says God forgives even the most depraved sin!"

*Sin! Sin! Sin!* The word sang up into the abyss and melted in the shadows.

The frown darkening Sandro's brow deepened. "Lust! Murder!" Brother Martino had said. Panic-stricken and agitated, yes. But a murderer? No. Sandro found a fresh brush and applied a tracery of gold along his saint's voluminous hem, his eyes traveling now and again toward the two monks chattering like jackdaws at the altar.

"Reveal yourself, Brother Martin, or

Father Abbot will have my head! Please!" Brother Paolo begged, glancing frantically around.

That probably was not all the abbot would have if he could manage it. It was no secret here in the Santa Maria Novella quarter of Florence that Abbot Roberto Ughi enjoyed riding the lance.

Little Ferdinando snapped his fingers. "Brother Martino's gone! Pouf, in a cloud of smoke!"

"Honestly!"

"Well, he is!"

Brother Paolo huffed, "The question is, gone *where*?"

Ferdinando pointed toward the cloister door. "Through the garden and toward the Prato Gate!" Skirts lifted, the two raced outside into the shining green heat.

Brother Martino had vanished so quickly, he might have ascended into heaven.

Sandro smiled, cocking his ears and listening: silence, at last. In his thirty-five years, he had witnessed some mighty odd behavior, both within church and without. The monks of Ognissanti would deal with their own kind. His mind strayed back to the painted Virgin set upon the altar. Paintings wept, plaster statues oozed tears and blood, and crucifixes were seen to sweat. The

Lord's outrage made manifest in the world was not unusual. In Volterra town a few years ago, people said a boy was born with the head of a bull and a lion's claws and feet. Sandro shivered, envisioning that terrible image.

In his fresco of *Saint Augustine,* he had painted a shelf, and on the shelf, he had drawn a geometry book propped up with the pages open. On impulse — thinking who would ever notice a little joke recorded in the details of a fresco painted in Florence in an old church on Borg'Ognissanti in the spring and summer of 1480? "Here's another painting by Sandro Botticelli. Ho-hum." — he had dipped his brush in black pigment and in Latin, high up in one margin, he had inscribed four lines of poetry. . . .

Now, though, watching straitlaced Guid'Antonio Vespucci and his nephew enter Palazzo della Signoria, where they disappeared up the stairs, Sandro wondered if he had made a grievous error. How angry might the Vespucci family be if any of its members noticed the little joke he had painted into his — their! — fresco of Saint Augustine on the south wall of their family church? After all, one of Amerigo's other uncles, Giorgio

Vespucci, had commissioned the painting. Hurrying into the alleyway, muttering to himself, Sandro crossed himself and prayed for the best.

*Is Brother Martino anywhere about?*
*Brother Martino just slipped out.*
*Slipped out where?*
*Through the Prato Gate for a breath of fresh air.*

# FOUR

Chancellor Bartolomeo Scala whirled from the credenza, parchment paper and a quill pen aloft in his hands. His simple gown, cut from the finest brilliant red cloth, lifted, revealing matching red hose. Fifty years old and a proud but accommodating man, Bartolomeo greeted the Vespuccis warmly. The three men kissed one another's cheeks and Guid'Antonio handed his cloak to Amerigo, who hung it in a pine wardrobe set against the wall.

"You appear well, despite the rigors of three weeks' travel," Bartolomeo said.

"Despite our hot reception in the street, too," Guid'Antonio said.

Bartolomeo's face fell. "What happened?"

Amerigo grimaced. "We had to hear about the disappearance of a local girl and listen to some crazy talk about Infidels having a hand in it."

"They slandered Lorenzo to us,"

70

Guid'Antonio said.

Bartolomeo placed one hand on the grand meeting table, fingers splayed, as if suddenly he felt woozy. "We're as fragile as glass. What are people saying?"

" 'Down with the Medici.' "

Bartolomeo gasped. "Are they mad?"

Amerigo touched his breast. "That's what I wondered, too."

"Are they?" Guid'Antonio said.

Bartolomeo fanned himself. "I'm not one of the nine Lord Priors, but only the Chancellor of the Republic, whose place it is not to discuss private government business with friends, no matter how dear and trustworthy." He stepped to the sideboard and retrieved a straw-covered flask. "Discretion dictates I say no more."

Guid'Antonio wanted to slap him across the face. "Why aren't the Priors here?"

"You're late. They'll be back, when is anyone's guess. How does this wine sit with that of the French? They have quite a good reputation."

Dipping into a deep well of patience, Guid'Antonio said, "Chianti means home. Beside it, French wine pales."

"Amerigo, now you know why your uncle is our most valued diplomat," Bartolomeo said, smiling blandly around.

"I knew already," Amerigo said.

"Ha, Guid'Antonio! Your nephew has a quick tongue."

"He's a Florentine and a Vespucci," Guid'Antonio said.

Bartolomeo studied the vaulted ceiling, as if seeking a safe topic of conversation there in the pattern of rosettes surrounded by *fleurs-de-lis*. "How is our lovely lady, Maria?"

Guid'Antonio recalled the heat of his wife's skin against his as they lay with their bodies touching in the predawn hours of morning. He recalled her anger, and his. "The same. And Maddalena?"

"With child," Bartolomeo said, lowering his gaze, pleased.

A sixth addition to Bartolomeo Scala's already full house. Guid'Antonio nodded. "Praise Mary."

A frown darkened the Chancellor's countenance. "Pray it's a son."

"Pray it survives," Guid'Antonio said. "Along with Maddalena."

"Of course, yes." Bartolomeo flushed crimson, obviously recalling Guid'Antonio's first wife, Taddea, lost in the birthing chamber soon after Guid'Antonio's marriage to her a dozen years ago. Taddea and his newborn son, gone. "Forgive me," Bartolomeo said. "Are you hungry? Have a bite to eat."

"I've no appetite."

Amerigo chose a red apple from the fruit bowl on the meeting table and bit a large, juicy chunk out of it. *"Grazie."*

Footsteps sounded in the outer chamber.

"Sooner than I thought," Bartolomeo said.

The door swung open and a gaunt, white-haired man in a crimson robe with an ermine collar and cuffs loomed before them on the threshold, his ankle-length coat distinguished from the coats of the eight other men by a pattern of stars embroidered in gold thread. He was Tommaso Soderini, the ninth Lord Prior and, therefore, the Gonfaloniere of Justice. The highest-ranking elected official in the Florentine State, Tommaso Soderini was also Lorenzo de' Medici's uncle by marriage.

"Guid'Antonio," Tommaso said with a darkly patient smile. "At last, we hear from you."

Guid'Antonio's mandate as he traveled from Italy to France in October 1478 had been to muster support for the Florentine government in the war the Pope had embarked upon when he realized his nephew's plot to rid the world of Lorenzo and Giuliano de' Medici had missed half its mark — the most important half, twenty-nine-year-old private citizen Lorenzo de' Medici. How dare Florence behead the commanding general of the Pope's army and hang not only his banker, Francesco de' Pazzi, but also the archbishop of Pisa? No matter that general, banker, and cleric were guilty of abetting — and in Francesco's case, committing — murder in a town noted more for its gifted artisans and scholars than for its affairs of state. Florentine politics were more confusing than they were a threat to anyone other than Florence itself, anyway. A democracy, a republic with elected officials, yet actually ruled by one family, the Medici, for half a century? Everywhere except in Italy, people scratched their heads, equally amused and baffled how *Firenze* — the City of Flowers, for goodness' sake — could actually stand as one of the Italian peninsula's five major powers.

From the safety of the Vatican, like an enraged wizard armed with a blazing sword, Sixtus had whirled toward Florence and excommunicated the city. No one within its walls, or even its outlying territories, could marry in church. The dead must be buried in fields and ditches. Churches were closed.

Surely fear for their immortal souls would turn people against that thorn in God's side, Lorenzo. To avoid war with Rome, all Florence had to do was hand Lorenzo over to Sixtus for punishment.

"For what?" Lorenzo wrote in a letter to his ally, King Louis XI of France. "Refusing to die in church along with my brother?"

*"No,"* Florence's Lord Priors said. They considered the attempt to assassinate the Medici family bosses an act of war. But excommunication was a grave matter. How could they thumb their noses at Rome, when it meant condemning their souls to the eternal fires of hell? They couldn't. Consulting texts so old the parchment crumbled to dust in their hands, the Florentine clergy determined the Pope had exceeded his authority. They issued a paper excommunicating *him* and performed Christian rites as usual.

In Bologna, Milan, and Lyons, discussing the situation to the point of exhaustion in his role as government *oratore,* Guid'Antonio had argued for the assembly of a General Council to depose Sixtus IV and reform the Church.

This, while in the territory around Florence, the Pope's hired soldiers stole horses, set fire to mills, burned towns, and slaughtered men, women, and children. Refugees from Brolio, Radda, and Castellina in Chianti poured into the city. With the second winter of the war approaching, Florence had faced certain defeat at the hands of Roman and Neapolitan armies, the latter equipped by King Ferrante, the king of Naples, who had thrown his hand in with the Pope as a possible means of expanding his own private power.

Within Florence, another deadly enemy roamed the streets.

Someone found a man dead of the plague on a bench inside the church of Santa Maria Novella. When a sick boy was discovered in the adjoining piazza, people abandoned him there, loath to touch the child and take him to the hospital. Death carts piled with bodies rattled through the putrid city.

What had begun as a private quarrel between Pope Sixtus IV and Lorenzo de' Medici was driving the Florentine Republic to ruin: no fresh fruit or meat, precious little bread, rats running rampant along the marshy banks of the Arno. When the Italian situation seemed impossibly bleak and Paris lay shrouded in the deep snows of January 1480, Guid'Antonio, still in France, had received astonishing news from Bartolomeo Scala: one month earlier, Lorenzo had sailed to Naples to present King Ferrante with his personal plan for peace.

Lorenzo's move was daring. If it worked, it would strip Sixtus IV of his most powerful ally. But the young, informal leader of Florence in the hands of the Neapolitan king? That thought made Guid'Antonio sweat with fear for his friend and for the future of their city. Lorenzo and King Ferrante had enjoyed friendly relations in the past, but tales of the king's cruelty ran rampant in Italy. People said Ferrante embalmed his enemies and displayed their corpses in the cellars of Castel Dell'Ovo on the Bay of Naples. In France, Guid'Antonio crossed himself and prayed for Lorenzo's safety. Lose Lorenzo, and Florence's legs would be open to the Pope and the nephew many people thought was the Pope's own bastard, the rapacious, insatiable Girolamo Riario.

And then one afternoon in early April 1480 a courier had found Guid'Antonio in Paris walking with Ameliane Vely, one of the young women of the French court, in Louis XI's gardens along the bank of the River Seine, she having chanced upon Guid'Antonio, as was so often the case, whether here among the winding pathways or in the halls of the royal household. Hardly daring to breathe, Guid'Antonio had read Bartolomeo Scala's latest missive from Italy. Two weeks earlier, in mid-March, Lorenzo had arrived home from Naples bearing a peace treaty fixed with King Ferrante's royal seal.

The Parisian sky over Guid'Antonio's head had turned bluer, the sun brighter, the clouds impossibly puffy and white. He broke into an elated smile, hugged Ameliane, and kissed her on the mouth.

Ameliane blushed. "Good news?"

"*Oui!* The war's over."

"Praise God and all the saints."

"Praise God and Lorenzo," Guid'Antonio said, smiling.

Her sparkling gaze flicked toward the rose bushes along the garden path, ripe with tight buds, about to bloom. "And now, Ambassador Guid'Antonio Vespucci, you're no longer obliged to abide here in France?"

"Not much longer. No." Having lost his main ally to Lorenzo, the Pope would now have no choice but to call off his troops. Rome was a mighty power, but even Rome could not fight alone. Still smiling, Guid'Antonio kissed Ameliene's fingertips. "I must tell Amerigo. *Excuze-moi, s'il vous plaît.*"

"*Naturellement.*" She ducked her head. When she looked up, the Italian ambassador was fading down the path, a ghost Guid'Antonio in animated conversation with the courier whose unexpected good news had brought the lovely rare smile to the ambassador's luscious mouth.

"But then," Guid'Antonio said, sitting back in his chair at one end of the meeting table, his gaze fixed on Chairman Tommaso Soderini. "You know most of this already." He passed Chancellor Bartolomeo Scala his credentials written on parchment, in Latin, along with a statement of his expenses on a *per diem* basis.

Tommaso agreed with a slight inclination of the head. Snowy-haired, with bones as frail as a thrush, Tommaso's pale skin made a stark contrast against his robe's vivid crimson hue. "*Grazie,* Guid'Antonio. Your service will be duly noted in our official records." A tiny smile tweaked Tommaso's lips. "Perhaps your sojourn in France will prove your continuing loyalty to Florence."

The other Priors, heretofore glancing impatiently around the chamber, snapped to attention. Beside Guid'Antonio, Amerigo stiffened. Seated at a podium beneath the windows overlooking Piazza della Signoria — those same windows where Francesco de' Pazzi had been hanged — Bartolomeo Scala's assistant, Alessandro Braccesi, sighed deeply.

Continuing loyalty? Guid'Antonio could remind Tommaso Soderini a thing or two about allegiance. He told himself to tread carefully. Tommaso had honey in his mouth and a knife at his belt. Guid'Antonio said, "And I, like you, appreciate Lorenzo's continued trust in both our houses. Despite the traitors who have on occasion lived therein."

Lord Prior Antonio Capponi laughed, reaching for the wine jug near to hand. "There's a sharp parry, Guido! Here's to you, my friend." Capponi's red Prior's coat was unbuttoned over his shoulders, revealing his black quilted *farsetto* and gray cotton shirt: the Capponi family colors.

Across from Capponi, Prior Pierfilippo Pandolfini's eyes radiated impatience. Three gold-enameled fish set in a blue stone decorated the ring on Pierfilippo's hand: the sign of the Pandolfinis. "Guid'Antonio," Pierfilippo said. "You're fresh from the saddle. You can't have heard the latest from Rome."

Rome, Rome, Rome. "Of course not. No."

"Florence is still excommunicated."

Guid'Antonio sat back hard in his chair. "Impossible. Both King Ferrante *and* Sixtus signed Lorenzo's treaty."

"There are always complications," Tommaso Soderini said, smiling thinly.

Guid'Antonio's mind whirled. If Sixtus hadn't lifted the interdict, all the rites of the Church were still forbidden the Florentine people. No wonder the people in the marketplace had been so afraid and angry. No weddings, no baptisms, no burials in holy ground. "Why?" he said. "It makes no sense."

"Because we haven't met the Pope's last demand," Tommaso said.

"Which is?"

Shriveled and purpled with age, Tommaso's lips lifted in a grin. "That we send Lorenzo to him in Rome."

Guid'Antonio jumped up and hit the table with his fist. "The war *began* because we wouldn't give him Lorenzo! Do the last two years mean nothing to that crazy man in the Vatican?" He drew a sharp breath. "What about Lorenzo? What has he said?"

"What he has always said," Antonio Capponi answered. " 'No.' Oh, he'll do whatever's necessary to preserve the Florentine Republic. Just not today. Naples was one edge of the sword, Rome's quite another. He might actually die there."

"Tommaso," Guid'Antonio said, sitting

back down. "What have you advised him to do?"

The older man grunted. "To saddle his horse and ride like the devil to Saint Peter's."

"What? This is news!" Pierfilippo Pandolfini said. "At what cost? To be murdered the instant he enters the Eternal City? It's eternal, all right!"

Lord Prior Piero di Nasi, by nature a quiet man, shifted in his chair. "Come now. That isn't likely to happen."

"Nor was it likely Giuliano would be murdered in the Cathedral," Guid'Antonio said, his temper roaring as he fought memories so sharp, they threatened to cut him to the bone.

Tommaso's fingers caressed his hand-warmer, a round, pewter container polished to resemble silver, then filled with heated coals, here in the high heat of summer. "Lorenzo's treaty is unpopular," he said.

"*Unpopular?* So what? Why?" Guid'Antonio said.

"Because it allows the prince of Naples to remain camped on our southern border, for one thing," Tommaso said.

"In Siena?"

Tommaso shrugged. "Of course."

Guid'Antonio was too stunned to speak.

Prince Alfonso of Naples was the elder of King Ferrante's two sons. A skillful soldier, Alfonso had captained Roman and Neapolitan troops against Florence during the war. And Lorenzo was allowing the warrior prince to remain thirty miles from the Great Hall in Palazzo della Signoria, where the majority of Florence's government leaders now sat? Surely, Alfonso wouldn't mount a surprise attack against them.

Tommaso slathered fresh cream cheese on a thick slice of bread. "King Ferrante wants his son within pissing distance of us. Should opportunity knock, I suppose. Lorenzo agreed to it to bring home the treaty."

"You know our ways," Bartolomeo Scala said, frowning. "Lorenzo gave us peace. Now we gripe about terms. Reason has little to do with it."

Antonio Capponi blew a stray blond hair from his cheek. "The point is, when you add Prince Alfonso's continuing presence to the Turks beating at our door and the Pope's constant interdict, you have a city on the verge of exploding like the cart in Piazza del Duomo on Easter Sunday. But, of course, that's meant to be festive."

He clapped his hands: "Bang!"

Beside Guid'Antonio, Amerigo jumped.

"There are no Turks in Italy," Guid'Antonio said.

"Not for a long time," Piero di Nasi agreed. "But their ships have been sighted off the coast of Rhodes in the Mediterranean Sea."

Amerigo made a squeak of distress. "That's the last home of the Christian crusaders! Against Mehmed the Conqueror's legions, they wouldn't stand the chance of a flea in Hell —" The nine men of the Signoria, along with Chancellor Bartolomeo Scala and his assistant, Alessandro Braccesi, stared at Guid'Antonio's nephew, who had one role to perform in this official government meeting: that of *giovane,* secretary to his uncle.

"We know the island fortress is there," Piero di Nasi said gently. "It has been more than a century."

"People are always seeing Turks," Guid'Antonio said.

"That's because they know Mehmed II still has his eye on the West," Tommaso Soderini said.

"Perhaps, but the Turks in Tuscany are not real."

"Rather like the tears of your weeping painting," Antonio Capponi said, grinning. "They're false — or so we hope," he added, crossing himself.

"My what?" Guid'Antonio said.

"He means the painted image called the *Virgin Mary of Santa Maria Impruneta* brought down from her village and placed on the altar of Ognissanti Church for the spring celebrations," Piero di Nasi said. "Last Wednesday, tears coursed down the Virgin's face."

Stunned, Guid'Antonio said, "Are you sure?"

"There's a question with at least a thousand answers," Tommaso said.

*In my church,* Guid'Antonio thought. *Ognissanti.* "Amerigo," he said, "remind me — how cold and rainy was France?" This garnered a few wry smiles; one man laughed, shrill and nervy.

Beyond the chamber windows, the sun blazed on course across the sky. One raven, then another, cawed. Guid'Antonio sat very still. The Vespuccis had moved from the village of Peretola to the Unicorn district in the Santa Maria Novella quarter of Florence almost one hundred years ago. Since then, they and the Benedictine monks of the Lombard Order of the Humiliati had dominated the neighborhood. In the late 1380s, Guid'Antonio's distant kinsman, silk merchant Simone Vespucci, had built the

85

local hospital, Spedale dei Vespucci, a few steps from the Vespucci Palace. All these years, Vespucci money had decorated the church. Four generations of Vespuccis lay sleeping in its dim stone chapels, Guid'Antonio's mother, his father, his precious first wife, and their baby.

And now a painting of the Virgin was weeping there.

He looked around at the men gathered at the table. "And so — ?"

"And so, Guid'Antonio," Tommaso Soderini said, stone-faced, "these tears in your church have people believing Mary is weeping for their lost souls. They believe God is in a high hot temper because of our defiance of the Pope. Whether by the hand of Mehmed the Conqueror, the prince of Naples, Count Girolamo Riario, or all three, they believe God means to see Florence destroyed and her people roasting in hell like pigs on a spit. And who do they blame?"

Guid'Antonio half-expected the Lord Priors to sing the name out in a loud chorus. Instead, it whispered, unspoken, around the room: *Lorenzo, Lorenzo, Lorenzo.*

Bartolomeo Scala said, "You're a Medici man, Guid'Antonio. So are we all. And you saw how it went against you in the street. It grows worse by the hour."

With a linen cloth, Tommaso wiped crumbs from his mouth. "The time has come for us to satisfy heaven."

"Satisfy Sixtus IV and his nephew, you mean," Guid'Antonio said, his voice grim. "How? By serving them Lorenzo's head on a platter."

Tommaso laughed sourly. "If anyone's head is served on a platter, I doubt it will be my nephew's. He's far too cunn—" Tommaso smiled deliberately. "Far too sharp-witted for that. Whereas if something isn't done to prevent a civil war in our streets, our own heads will land there."

In Tommaso's flat gaze, Guid'Antonio saw fifty years of relentless service to the Florentine Republic and the bitter frustration that must come with Tommaso's role as Lorenzo de' Medici's second. With more legitimate authority than his thirty-one-year-old nephew, certainly. Christ, but for Bartolomeo's secretary, Alessandro Braccesi, and Amerigo, every man in this room wielded more official power than Lorenzo, for all the good it did them. Lorenzo might be uncrowned, but he was the prince of the city, the green grass springing up beneath the feet of everyone who supported the Medici family. Hadn't they — largely, the men in this room — placed the mantle of leadership on Lorenzo's shoulders almost a dozen years ago, when his father died of crippling gout? In December 1469, Lorenzo had been twenty, a strapping youth more interested in poetry and horses than politics. Now they must reckon with the fact power fit him like a second skin.

"Alternatively," Tommaso droned on, "we may find ourselves in exile, with new men as our replacements."

"Exile?" Amerigo went deathly pale. The Vespuccis, the Soderinis, the Medicis and Pandolfinis, stripped of wealth and power and run from the city?

This time, the others ignored Amerigo's intrusion into the conversation. "You might as well tie blocks of stone to our necks and drown us in the Arno," Pierfilippo Pandolfini said.

"Or heave us from yon windows into Piazza della Signoria," Antonio Capponi cut in. "Exactly as we did Francesco and the archbishop of Pisa two years ago."

The *vacca,* the great bell of Arnolfo di Cambio's bell tower, mooed the noonday hour, marking with exact precision the chill quiet pervading the Great Hall. *Exile.* Who could imagine any worse fate? No: even death paled by comparison.

With an impressive air of grace, Tommaso

88

gathered his coat lightly about his shoulders, and rose. "No wonder to me the Virgin was seen weeping. Even I am weary of my nephew's conflict with Pope Sixtus IV."

The old man's brown eyes sought Guid'Antonio. "I must say, former Ambassador Vespucci, I do enjoy your reports. For all the rest of it, if my nephew doesn't want to go to Rome, we can't force him to do it." For an instant, he paused, eyebrows raised. "Or can we?"

Guid'Antonio was donning his cloak when Pierfilippo Pandolfini hurried over. The younger man embraced him, smiling, though his eyes were dark and troubled. "Guid'Antonio, I'm glad to have you home." In an undertone, Pierfilippo said, "Admire my jewelry, quickly!"

"There's a beautifully crafted ring. Who's the maker? Andrea, by the look," Guid'Antonio said.

"Yes, or one of the boys in his shop, though I paid Verrocchio's own price." Pierfilippo lowered his voice. "It's true the current turns against us with all swiftness. But appease Sixtus, my ass! Lorenzo's four months in Naples gave his uncle freedom of action he otherwise never could have managed. A cunning man may accomplish everything in less time. What better opportunity to begin taking the upper hand, which everyone knows Tommaso has always wanted? Missing ladies, miraculous paintings, and civil unrest in our streets. Miraculous *timing,* don't you think?"

Raising his voice, Pierfilippo finished, smiling broadly, "God be with you, friend. We'll get together, have some wine." With that, he took hasty leave.

Guid'Antonio's eyes traveled to the messenger who had entered the chamber and stood speaking with Bartolomeo Scala. He frowned to himself, mulling over Pierfilippo's words while Amerigo slid his writing instruments into his satchel and secured the straps. Could Tommaso Soderini be stirring up trouble on the Pope's coattails in hopes of ruining Lorenzo? If so, who were Tommaso's accomplices? Were the other families who supported Lorenzo in danger? Guid'Antonio rubbed his neck to ease the muscle ache holding him in its grip. With Amerigo at his side, he approached the door.

"Guid'Antonio," Bartolomeo said, beaming, "here's a message from Via Larga."

All eyes shifted their way. Tommaso turned and locked Guid'Antonio in his silver gaze. "And?" Guid'Antonio said.

Bartolomeo smiled his confusion. "From Lorenzo. He needs you there."

"When?"

Bartolomeo hesitated, glancing at the courier, who bowed, murmuring, "*Il Magnifico* didn't say."

"No. *Il Magnifico* wouldn't need to, would he?" Guid'Antonio said.

And so he and Amerigo went back out into Piazza della Signoria, each with his own private thoughts, Amerigo pondering the whys and wherefores of Turks and virgins, holy or otherwise, while Guid'Antonio considered the complex nature of power, desire, and truth. A brief farewell, and Amerigo struck out toward home, whistling tunelessly to himself, and Guid'Antonio strode north toward the Medici Palace in the Golden Lion district of the San Giovanni quarter of the walled city, acutely aware of the battered animal keeping a safe distance behind the heels of his fine leather boots.

# FIVE

Lorenzo, standing at the windows of his ground floor palazzo apartment, looked around with relief and a smile of recognition when Guid'Antonio walked into the room. "So," he said, his brown eyes dark and shining. "Shall I take myself to Rome?"

*"No,"* Guid'Antonio said. They clasped one another, and embraced another moment, Lorenzo every bit as solid and strong as Guid'Antonio remembered him to be. Roused by Guid'Antonio's entrance, the sleek greyhound snoozing before the cold, man-size hearth raised his head before breathing a deep, shuddering sigh and lowering his nose back onto outstretched paws. *I remember you.*

"Guid'Antonio, thank you for coming," Lorenzo said. "So quickly, too. How are you, my friend?"

"Stunned."

"Yes!" Lorenzo said. "The *Virgin Mary of*

*Santa Maria Impruneta* is weeping in Ognis-santi — your family church — and there's a hue and cry in the streets, while I'm blamed for *everything*. Or am, at least, made the solution."

He pulled his thick, dark chestnut hair from his face, holding it aloft before letting it brush back onto his shoulders. Never handsome, but in no respect ill-looking, Lorenzo de' Medici's hair framed dark, irregular features. He wore short boots, ash gray leggings, and a loosely belted tunic of white linen whose plain round collar stopped short at the jagged scar visible at his neck. Well above middle height and light of foot, at the first swipe of the knife-brandishing priest who meant to kill him that bloody April Sunday morning in the Cathedral, he had drawn his sword, fought off his attackers, vaulted the altar railing, and found safety in the sacristy, where he and three friends had bolted the door against the men scampering after them.

"But I've jumped straight into the fray," he said. "Are you hungry?" He grinned. "I doubt you ate much locked in Palazzo della Signoria with our nine Lord Priors."

"Not a bite," Guid'Antonio said, glancing toward the walnut sideboard against one wall, noting the refreshments on silver trays, pottery bowls of mixed olives, fresh oil, bright green melon slices, *prosciutto, salame,* bread seasoned with herbs in the Medici Palace kitchen, and cheese ripe from Lorenzo's dairy farm at Poggio a Caiano. All ready and waiting for Lorenzo's friend and right-hand man, Guid'Antonio Vespucci.

*"Grazie."* He poured water over his fingers and dried them with a linen towel. *Delicious,* he thought, biting into a thick slice of rosemary bread slathered with creamy pale pecorino. And a far cry from the rancid cheese the farmer had palmed off on him in the marketplace today. A farther cry from the old woman's burned crow tart.

"Poggio's up and running?" he said. Lorenzo had begun acquiring property in the countryside between Florence and Pistoia several years ago, only to have the death of his brother and the resulting war bring the farm's progress to a grinding halt.

"By some miracle, it is. Or nearly."

The brindle greyhound eyed Guid'Antonio's bread and stretched up onto his hindquarters. "Mind your manners, Leporarius," Lorenzo said. "You'll have your turn." Lids closed to slits, the hound eased down onto the cool hearthstone. *Hare hunter.* Incredibly swift and spare. "Good dog. Thank you." Lorenzo turned to

Guid'Antonio, grimacing. "I haven't seen Poggio in six months, four spent in wretched Naples courting the king. But God's eyes, Guid'Antonio, what right have I to complain? You've been in France a year."

"Almost two," Guid'Antonio said.

A look of embarrassment suffused Lorenzo's face. "Of course. Forgive me."

A light-fisted knock, the apartment door opened, and Bartolomeo Scala's assistant, Alessandro Braccesi, poked in his head. "From the Chancellor." Alessandro handed Lorenzo the official government notes he had taken during the Lord Priors' meeting. "Messer Vespucci," he said, acknowledging Guid'Antonio, who nodded a greeting, thinking, *Put wings on his heels and call him Mercury. Our own special messenger to the god here in Via Larga.*

"Alessandro, have some of the Brolio. It's excellent," Lorenzo said, his eyes already scanning the papers in his hands.

"*Grazie.* By the way, some boys were tormenting a half-dead mutt at the main gate. I put it out of its misery."

Around Guid'Antonio, the light in the apartment wavered. "Did you?" he said. Lorenzo glanced up, considering him a moment before lowering his gaze back down again.

95

"All it took was a blow to the head," Alessandro said. "With a sharp piece of sandstone. Probably the stone tumbled from some mason's cart. Here —" He leaned toward Lorenzo to decipher a passage splotched with ink.

Guid'Antonio knew he should be grateful. The secretary had saved him — or Cesare — the trouble of dispatching the dog. That empty sack of fur and bones had no benefactor. Never would the mastiff have survived the streets. He massaged his forehead in a futile attempt to ease the tightness gathering there, his gaze drifting to the row of windows set with heavy iron gratings along Via dei Gori on the San Lorenzo side of the Medici palazzo. From beyond the barred windows, there came the sound of voices, wheezy old men trading tales on the stone bench built the length of the wall facing San Lorenzo marketplace and church.

His gaze fell on Lorenzo's writing desk. An oil lamp hung from a brass arm above the rotating reading stand, lighting the poems of Catullus, an ancient work lost for centuries till someone discovered the old parchment stoppering a wine barrel in Rome. Beside the poems, Guid'Antonio saw a letter whose crimson seal remained unbroken. A. POLIZIANO. Lorenzo and Angelo

Poliziano were intimates, yet Lorenzo had cast Angelo's letter aside, unread. Why? And, too, scattered across the marble floor were several pages of writing in Lorenzo's small, precise hand.

Guid'Antonio turned to find Alessandro Braccesi gone and Lorenzo staring at him with frank interest. The heat of embarrassment stung Guid'Antonio's cheeks.

Lorenzo watched him gravely. "These days even the simplest verse is hard won. I've been grappling with that poem for over a year now."

"What do you expect when you hold yourself up to Dante?"

"A decent effort." Anger blazed in Lorenzo's expressive eyes. "There was a time I thought words as valuable as swords. Now, I'm not so sure. Slay Giuliano? How could they do such a terrible thing? Jesus! The Pope! Upon my soul, my honor balks at the prospect of prostrating myself at the feet of that miscreant in Rome, but I will do it, if it means he will lift his ban of excommunication against us."

*Giuliano would already be there,* Guid'Antonio thought. He put down his wine. "What exactly does Sixtus want?"

"Me on my knees before him, he says: his wayward servant humbled before the world.

97

That crazy man takes me for a fool. What he really wants is to whack off my head. Meanwhile, some rival here in our own city is wreaking havoc against me."

Beyond the grated windows, the bells of San Lorenzo tolled, accompanied by church bells all across the city and in the neighboring hills. Closer by, Guid'Antonio caught the sweet peal of Ognissanti. Home. Maria. He strode to the windows and latched the shutters, muting the bells, and whirled back around, his boots firmly set in the heart of the Golden Lion district of his city.

"Who profits most from the discord in our streets? To the point they would risk their necks to set people against you? Surely, whoever it is has a hand in the weeping painting. God's wrath, damning miracles —"

"Against *us,* you mean," Lorenzo said. "Our families, our circle. My spies tell me the Pope's nephew has been whispering in his ear again."

*Girolamo Riario.* If evil walked among men, Girolamo was the devil personified.

For ten years now, Girolamo Riario had fanned the flames of the Pope's hatred for Lorenzo. Girolamo, dead set on using the papacy to acquire land and titles and create a principality for himself in Italy. So far, he

98

had done well.

"Do you know Girolamo's whereabouts?" Guid'Antonio said.

"*Sì, Roma.*" At the hearth, Lorenzo knelt and handed Leporarius a bit of *salame.* "In Rome, Girolamo can keep his tongue stuck in the Pope's ear. Though by now, who knows? The bastard may have gone to Imola for a turn at terrorizing that unfortunate town."

"God Almighty," Guid'Antonio said. "Our troubles with those two began with Imola seven years ago. Seven," he repeated, shaking his head.

"Yes, and they've made the place a viper's nest." They regarded one another, one face mirroring the other's exasperation, and then what could they do but share a sour laugh?

A gruff, toothless man from a poor fishing village in Liguria, on his election as Pope Sixtus IV, Francesco della Rovere had begun advancing his half dozen or so nephews with a bent for nepotism theretofore unequaled, even in Rome. For his pet, Girolamo Riario, Sixtus had set his sights on a lordship in the Papal State, a sprawling province in northern Italy whose cities and towns were part of the Church State but had over time come to be governed by dukes and lords who gave the Church lip service, while ignoring its demands for money and military support.

A toehold there would give Girolamo Riario a base to build up estates and tighten his family's control over the province's rebellious households. His first chance had come when Imola, a small town on the thoroughfare between Florence and the Adriatic Sea on Italy's eastern coast, had come up for sale by its Milanese lord, Galeazzo Maria Sforza. Sixtus, fifty-seven in 1471 and the newly elected Pope, had decided he would buy the town and present it to Girolamo. Lorenzo, twenty-two and ascendant in Florence, had made up his mind Sixtus would do no such thing. From Rome, the Papal State curled around Florence and her environs like a claw. Control this area and you had a good chance of controlling Florence.

In the end, despite wickedly clever maneuverings by Lorenzo, Imola had fallen to the Pope, who had immediately appointed Girolamo its lord and master. All this had come to a head in 1473, and today Lorenzo still battled Sixtus, who spied Lorenzo's dark, shifting shape behind his every failed attempt to make his relatives dominant in Italy. Seven years ago, Lorenzo had unmasked Sixtus IV and Girolamo Riario as major political players in the Italian peninsula. He had challenged the Pope's right to take control of the Papal State and insulted the Pope's family. Worse, Lorenzo had performed these acts in public with the entire peninsula watching the Pope and his nephew made foolish on stage.

For this, Giuliano had died.

For this, there had been war.

For this, Florence still battled Rome.

*Give me that Florentine upstart.*

Guid'Antonio remembered Girolamo Riario well from the contest over Imola, having traveled to that unfortunate little town as Florence's legal representative at the height of that affair, on what amounted to his first "mission" for the youthful Lorenzo. Girolamo was a slender prick of a young man with bobbed hair and moist, prissy lips.

He tapped his mouth with his fingertip, mentally sifting, considering this and that and drawing back. "My bet is on someone local rather than Rome as the source of our troubles here. Currently, I mean."

"What?" A brittle laugh escaped Lorenzo's lips. "Why now?"

"Power? Fortune? First place in the city?"

Lorenzo regarded him with a mild brown stare. "Neither the Pope nor Girolamo

101

Riario, but other men who regard me with suspicion and envy? That would include my Uncle Soderini." Tommaso Soderini, the *official* head spokesman of the Florentine government.

*Dangerous, dangerous waters.* "Surely the monks in Ognissanti are thriving, given the weeping Virgin," Guid'Antonio said. "Would this be the first time a church made a hoax to fill the collection box? No."

The raven-haired monk dashed through Guid'Antonio's mind, along with the two black-robed young men of the Humiliati who had pursued their brother toward the Prato Gate early this morning. Brother Martino, Brother Paolo, and the little novice, Ferdinando Bongiovi. What might that trio have to do with the painting weeping in Ognissanti? Something? Nothing? What of the missing girl — at the hands of Turks, or so some hare brains believed — and the escalating demand for Lorenzo to pack his bags for Rome? Guid'Antonio's imagination, experience, and hours spent handling all manner of complex court cases and tricky investigations warned him not to dismiss any scheme.

"Florence is rich with monks and miracles," Lorenzo said. "And no monk is more devious than the abbot of your church."

True. Guid'Antonio knew this all too well from past experience with Roberto Ughi, the arrogant abbot of Ognissanti. "Have you seen the tears?" he said.

"Haven't I, yes. Last Wednesday the *Virgin Mary of Santa Maria Impruneta* wept as copiously as if for the devil himself." Lorenzo's face clouded. "Yet in my heart I can't believe she wept for me."

"She will if you go to Rome."

Lorenzo waved his hand. "Surely His Holiness isn't truly capable of murder in the Vatican."

"You know as well as I do that madman is capable of anything. As is his nephew." Guid'Antonio left the rest unsaid. *After all, with Francesco de' Pazzi as their pawn, they murdered Giuliano.*

"What choice do I have but to go? All I hear from Bartolomeo Scala, our nail-biting Chancellor, is how an alarmed sense of fatality has overcome our city. Because of the war, the wool and silk trade has declined sharply. The backbone of Florentine industry, as you well know. Business travel and employment have suffered. On and on it goes until I'm sick of hearing it. Predictions of uprisings and exile march daily from the good Chancellor's pen and lips."

103

*"We are as fragile as glass,"* Bartolomeo Scala had said this morning.

"Mercy Jesus, if I could have one hour of quiet, I swear I never would complain!" The frustration in Lorenzo's voice cracked the silence like a hammer cracking marble. By the hearth, Leporarius blinked, staring from one to the other of the two men.

"Nor would I," Guid'Antonio said mildly.

"All I want is peace! How has this happened?" Lorenzo's voice caught, filled with unrestrained emotion. "When was the last time we had peace? Fourteen fifty-four! And then thanks to the Turks."

In 1454, one year after the fall of Constantinople to Mehmed the Conqueror, Italy had united in fear and formed a defensive league to present a united front against foreign aggression. Florence, Venice, Milan, Naples and Rome: eventually, all five major Italian powers had joined the treaty. This only after the Infidels had killed King Constantine, peeled the skin off his face, filled it with straw, displayed it in triumph through the city, and slaughtered the Christian men, women, and children huddled in the Church of Saint Sophia.

"That was a bloody settlement," Guid'Antonio said.

"Aren't they all? Which brings to mind

another matter you may not know about."

"Oh, God," Guid'Antonio said, leaning back against the writing desk with Lorenzo, his arms folded across his chest.

"Did the Priors mention Forli?"

"No." Guid'Antonio's senses heightened as he anticipated more troubling news. Like Imola, Forli town fell within the Papal State on Via Emilia, between Florence and the Adriatic Sea.

Lorenzo filled Guid'Antonio in:

"My agent in Forli sent word last week Sinibaldo Ordelaffi is dangerously ill. Last February, Sinibaldo's father died, leaving Sinibaldo the new lord of Forli, and him a sickly boy. I've written Sinibaldo's mother a letter of caution. If Sinibaldo dies of this fever, Girolamo and his uncle will make a grab for the town. Take it, and Girolamo will have both feet firmly planted on our northern border —" He paused as a rush of footsteps approached the apartment's closed doors.

Guid'Antonio's gaze fastened on the unbolted latch. "Lorenzo," he said, "are you expecting anyone?"

"No!"

They sprang up, hands flying to their daggers, eyes locked on the sole entrance to the chamber. Leporarius stood, growling, his fur spiked along the thin ridge of his back.

*Let Satan himself burst in upon us,* Guid'Antonio silently swore as the doors blew open, *and this time I will plunge my blade hilt-deep into his throat and watch his blood stain the floor.*

# Six

A boy burst into the apartment, all ruddy cheeks and blow-about hair. "Lorenzo!" With that gusty cry, Giovanni de' Medici darted, laughing, toward his startled father. Guid'Antonio blew out a shivery sigh; smoothly, he and Lorenzo sheathed their daggers, glancing ruefully at one another.

Short and thickset, Giovanni de' Medici moved ploddingly. Lorenzo lifted the snub-nosed, roundly built five-year-old and swung him in a circle before putting him down and administering a loving pat on the rump. Guid'Antonio's glance slid toward the hooded hearth and the two jewel encrusted jasper and gold vases jiggling on the mantelpiece; Leporarius dipped his tail and slipped out into the hall.

"Giovanni," Lorenzo said, smiling. "Say *'Buon giorno'* to Guid'Antonio Vespucci."

The boy gazed at Guid'Antonio with squinting eyes. "Are you my father's most trusted friend?"

"I believe I am. Yes."

"My father says so, too. *Buon giorno, Ser Vespucci.*" Giovanni trotted to the sideboard and, reaching up a chubby hand, grabbed a thick slice of herbed rosemary bread.

"Giovanni," Lorenzo began, his voice exasperated. "Mind your manners, please. In Guid'Antonio's instance, the correct address is 'Messer,' as he is a lawyer. Only if he were a notary or ordinary tradesman would you address him as 'Ser.' "

*"Mi dispiace, Messer Vespucci,"* Giovanni managed contritely around a mouthful of bread. Crumbs littered the front of his linen shirt.

Giovanni's tall, well-muscled father looked towards Guid'Antonio and glanced at the ceiling, as if seeking guidance from heaven. The smile on Guid'Antonio's lips faded a bit. Where was *his* Giovanni at this moment? Napping? Playing with — what would his son play with? He had no idea.

Following as it did in Giovanni's boisterous wake, Bianca de' Medici's footstep on the threshold sounded barely audible. Guid'Antonio checked when he saw Lorenzo's sister and saw the sudden heat burn high in her face. No wonder! Bianca de'

108

Medici suffered the spectacularly grievous misfortune of having married Guglielmo de' Pazzi, whose mad brother, Francesco, had butchered Giuliano. For his sister's husband, in the aftermath of the Pazzi Conspiracy, Lorenzo had chosen uncertainty over execution. Now Guglielmo de' Pazzi ate the bitter bread of exile outside the city walls, sentenced to a distance of no closer than five and no farther than twenty miles from Florence. This was a tender mercy Guid'Antonio did not approve. Guglielmo de' Pazzi, with no inkling of his brother's black alliance with the Pope and his nephew?

Guid'Antonio's doubts lingered, and he would not let it go.

Bianca acknowledged him with a slight inclination of the head. "Messer Vespucci, welcome home." With quiet dignity, she turned to Lorenzo. "*Allora?* Now?"

"Yes."

She left momentarily. From beyond the doors, Guid'Antonio heard voices, low and hushed. When Lorenzo's sister returned, she brought with her on her hip a boy of about two years.

"Messer Vespucci." Bianca's voice rang proud yet sweet. "Meet Giuliano's son. Giulio di Giuliano de' Medici."

The boy fixed clear brown eyes on Guid'Antonio and stared unwaveringly at him.

A rush of blood scorched Guid'Antonio's hands and face, and his heart slowed. *Giuliano de' Medici had no children.* But little Giulio's complexion appeared smooth and dark, his eyes darker, his cheeks tinged with pink. Watching Guid'Antonio, the boy ducked his head, a bashful smile lighting his angel face.

Guid'Antonio moved his lips, but no words came. No, never the slightest doubt: this shining boy was Giuliano the Beautiful's by-blow. "How?" he managed, baffled.

Lorenzo's light laugh could not disguise his deep emotion. "In the usual way, I expect."

"But where did you find him?"

"Not on the doorstep. A few months after Giuliano died, the boy's grandmother brought Giulio to us. That was the first we knew of him. After all, everything was not lost," Lorenzo said quietly.

*This is Florence's miracle; this secret child found,* Guid'Antonio thought, his mind racing, one part of him too experienced and too afraid to believe. "Come to me?" he said, and held out his hands to the boy, for Bianca to give him over.

Giulio's inquiring glance sought his aunt; gently, she put him down. "He can walk, Messer Vespucci. If he has good cause."

Walk Giulio did, with his arms extended to Guid'Antonio, all smiles and trust. Guid'Antonio picked the child up and buried his face in the shining black tangle of curls. Hugging the boy, into the sweet, shell pink ear he said softly, "No harm shall ever come to you, my boy. On my life's blood, I swear."

The afternoon had worn almost entirely away when Bianca departed with the two boys, Giovanni de' Medici singing and skipping along beside her while baby Giulio, safe in Bianca's arms, peered over his shoulder at Guid'Antonio, his large eyes dark and glowing. "Bye," came the soft echo of Giulio's voice as he floated from the apartment with his aunt. "Bye, bye."

Guid'Antonio felt keenly the silence engulfing him, now he was alone with Lorenzo, who slid the bolt home and said, "What the people have put up, they may as easily destroy."

"They have no reason to fear you and yours."

"No just reason, true. Nor was there any reason for anyone to kill my brother, except

111

for pride and envy. And yet today, once again, according to City Hall, everything is at stake. Our lives, our homes, our families, our city. They say the weeping Virgin is testament to that. Time and again, people seek proof, signs and symbols to believe in."

"Then it's proof we shall give them," Guid'Antonio said. "Not of our guilt, but of our innocence. It's not we who battle the Church, but the Church that battles us."

Lorenzo's dark features were a somber mask. "All I ask is the truth."

"Good. Because the truth is all we need. I'll find out who's causing the painting to weep; all else unravels there."

In silence, the two men walked across the courtyard garden beneath the late afternoon sky, past Donatello's bronze statue of Judith Slaying Holofernes. With one hand Judith gripped her sword, with the other, she grasped Holofernes' head back by the hair, exposing his naked throat in all its vulnerability. A shiver passed over Guid'Antonio, exactly, he supposed, as Donatello had intended when he sculpted the statue for Lorenzo's grandfather, Cosimo de' Medici.

A gate, high and made of iron, opened onto Via Dei Gori and San Lorenzo marketplace. Lorenzo lifted the inner bolt and moved aside, allowing Guid'Antonio to step into the street. The market was closed, the long stone bench built along the Medici Palace wall empty and shadowed, the gossips having gone home to a porridge made of millet and beans, if they were men of good fortune. Guid'Antonio saw no sign of the dead mastiff. But then Alessandro Braccesi would have entered the palace off Via Larga, through the main gate, just as Guid'Antonio had done earlier today. No doubt the *cane corso Italiano* still lay there with his skull crushed, his carcass trampled by horses' hooves and battered by sandals and hard-heeled boots.

As if on impulse, Guid'Antonio turned back to Lorenzo, frowning a bit, reflective and curious. "What do you think about the young woman captured by Turks?" He shrugged and spread his hands. "As crazy as that may be."

Lorenzo blinked. And blinked again. He moved back into the shadows a pace, his heavy eyebrows drawn together and down. "Camilla Rossi da Vinci, you mean."

"You knew her?"

"As Castruccio Senso's wife, yes. He's a wine merchant, Guid'Antonio. Olives, oil. We employ him to buy and sell wine for us occasionally, but only when necessity dictates. He brought Camilla here three years ago at Christmas. We had a banquet for our business associates." Lorenzo shrugged his broad shoulders. "The man's an idiot."

Guid'Antonio raised his brow in question.

Lorenzo flashed the one-thousand-candle smile. "He's just a fool, Guid'Antonio. Or perhaps not." The smile widened to an unabashed grin. "He didn't stay long that night. He found the attention lavished on his beautiful young wife disconcerting, I believe. One moment they were here, the next, they had vanished like ghosts."

*An interesting analogy,* Guid'Antonio thought. "She's pretty?" he said.

Lorenzo shook his hair back from his face. "As a poppy. Hair black and shiny as silk, and her cheeks? When she blushed, their natural bloom turned full crimson. And she blushed often, always with a shy smile. Particularly when Giuliano caught her eye. Fetching. Ah, well."

Guid'Antonio, heretofore watching a solitary young man untie his horse from an iron ring set in the palace wall, glanced swiftly back to Lorenzo. "Do you suspect a lover?" In Lorenzo's face, he read discomfort. It intrigued him.

"I suspect nothing, Guid'Antonio. But what else explains the lady's disappearance?

114

In her behalf, I will say cuckolding her husband seems contrary to her nature. The night she came here she appeared exceedingly innocent. Still, a girl doesn't have to have lain with a man to see him as a means of escape."

"How 'innocent'?" Guid'Antonio said.

"It was a Christmas gathering," Lorenzo said, beginning to evidence an air of impatience. "We, most of us, anyway, drank and danced and sang."

"Your carnival songs?"

Lorenzo grinned. "Of course. And from Camilla, they drew a rich blush."

"So I would think." *We have some bean pods, long and tender, quite firm and big, first take the tail in hand, then rub it gently up and down . . .*

"At any rate," Lorenzo was saying, "one might even describe Camilla as virginal, but for her married state." His brown eyes twinkled with mischief. "Or because of it, given her husband Castruccio's bandy legs and sour breath."

"And she a young woman of favorable means," Guid'Antonio mused, "traveling with only an old nurse and a slave boy? What route did they take?"

Lorenzo folded his arms over his chest. "From what Palla told me after his inquiry,

115

Camilla's party left Florence and rode as far as San Gimi. There they passed the night. At daybreak, they left for Morba. Not a long distance, Guid'Antonio."

Morba: a small resort town known for its healing spring waters. Guid'Antonio considered Lorenzo's words. And, yes, they matched Luca Landucci's statement in the market this morning. Now, as then, a question flickered briefly in his mind; again, like a vapor of smoke, it evaporated.

"Distance enough for mischief," he said.

Lorenzo shrugged vaguely. "Palla investigated the place where Camilla is said to have disappeared and discovered nothing mysterious. Signs of travelers, yes — it's a well-traveled road. But nothing indicating a struggle with someone bent on committing a crime. Certainly not Turks. Just a rough reed cross put there by locals to ward off devils. And before you ask, yes, Palla questioned the nurse and the boy. Camilla's father, too, at great length. Jacopo Rossi da Vinci."

Guid'Antonio had not had any intention of asking about the investigation conducted by Florence's chief of police: Luca had told him about the investigation earlier today. But Luca had not mentioned Camilla's father, Jacopo. Hmmm. He chewed his lip,

116

his mind stubborn and willful. Like it or not, the girl's disappearance was another charge against Lorenzo, given so many Florentines believed God had unleashed the Turks against them as punishment for Lorenzo's war with the Church. "She disappeared a week ago?" Guid'Antonio said.

"A little over. Yes."

He had just missed it. Damn. "What of the husband, Castruccio Senso?" he said.

"What of him?"

"How has he taken his wife's disappearance?"

Lorenzo snorted. "How would you expect, given she's a beautiful girl of sixteen? Distraught, on the face of it. I've seen him on the street since. And Palla corroborated it."

"You question the merchant's sincerity?"

"I question everything. As do you, according to your nature. The one thing I *know* is this: no corpse, no proof of foul play, no crime, and yet people will lay Camilla Rossi da Vinci at my door, just as they do the weeping painting."

"They already have," Guid'Antonio said and, once again, he turned away.

# SEVEN

A short while after leaving Lorenzo, Guid'Antonio crossed the Vespucci Palace garden, his tired glance seeking the *scrittoio* where he, Amerigo, and Amerigo's brother, Antonio Vespucci, tended the family book-keeping. Antonio had carried the weight of it these last two years: wine, silk, wool, banking, commercial ventures in Bruges, Antwerp, and Ghent. All that and more in a far-flung commercial tapestry whose constant and meticulous care covered the family with vast financial rewards. At the moment, the *scrittoio*'s solid wooden door stood closed and secured with a padlock and iron bolt.

He ascended the stone stairwell, the wall cool beneath the touch of his fingers. He had told Maria he would be home no later than midday. *Jesu.* He imagined her in their bedchamber, poised to strike at him again. Well. He would coax her from her ill humor, kiss her mouth, and play his fingers through her silky hair, willing to let bygones be bygones. He would strike a spark, then hold the blown flame to the wick. Afterward, they would acknowledge how wrong they each had been earlier today. God knew he desired a peaceful marriage with Maria del Vigna.

At the top of the stairs, a shimmer of light appeared.

Quickening his step, he entered the dark corridor and collided with a young girl. In one hand, she held a candle. In the other, she grasped the hand of a small boy. His son, Giovanni.

The girl jumped back, her features startled in the flaring candlelight. "Christ on the Cross!" she yelped. "I took you for an apparition! Who are you?" Scowling, she noted Guid'Antonio's solid form. "What right have you here?"

The question startled him. *"Mi scusi, Signorina. Io sono Guid'Antonio Vespucci."*

In the hallway shadows, the girl's eyes grew round as florins. *"You?* No!" Boldly, cheeks glowing, she examined him up and down. "Here's a pleasant surprise now."

He smiled, gently amused. "And you are?" But of course he knew this must be the indiscriminate young nurse Maria had sought early this morning. Olimpia some-

119

thing or other, the girl who had replaced Giovanni's former caretaker.

"Olimpia Pasquale," she said.

Giovanni appeared fresh from the bath. The boy's cotton nightgown hung in loose folds from his thin shoulders to his bare feet. Soft tendrils of dark damp hair curled around Olimpia's freshly scrubbed face. Her mouth, slightly open, revealed teeth like pearls. She reminded Guid'Antonio of the ethereal beauties Sandro Botticelli was so wont to paint. About her and Giovanni both, he caught the faint scent of apples.

*"Buena sera, Giovanni."* Guid'Antonio bent slightly from the waist with his hands on the tops of his thighs. "How would you like to visit a dairy farm next week where a good friend of ours raises cows?"

Giovanni's frowning expression fell neatly between boredom and disgust. "I've seen cows in the marketplace," he said, his eyes dark and petulant.

Olimpia grinned. "Stallions, too. With mares. Making an impressive display."

Guid'Antonio uttered a sharp laugh. "That I don't doubt. Giovanni, we'll accompany two other boys, one your age, who has the same name, too."

"I know a basketful of Giovannis." The child pursed his lips, and his scowl deep-

120

ened. In Guid'Antonio, his expression found its match.

"This particular boy," he informed his son coldly, "is Giovanni di Lorenzo de' Medici. Believe me, there is none other like him in your basket, no matter how deep or large." He turned toward the girl. *"Buena sera, Signorina."* He made as if to move past them down the corridor.

"Messer Vespucci?"

"Yes."

"You're seeking your wife, I think."

He paused, a warning uncoiling like a snake in his breast. "Yes."

"She's flown."

He stared stupidly at the girl. Flown? At this gray hour, there were few places in the city a respectable woman might go. At any hour, in fact, other than church. "Flown where?" he said.

"To her mother's house. Mona Alessandra del Vigna is ill."

"Ill?" he repeated after the girl, wanting to shake her, feeling like one of the mimics who pantomimed your words in the piazzas on festival days till you wanted to slap them silly. "What do you mean 'ill'?"

"A messenger came to the gate. Mona Maria pulled into her cloak and flew off down the street with him, leaving me with

Giovanni." Olimpia regarded the boy, her expression one of genuine warmth.

Guid'Antonio rubbed the back of his neck, thinking. "Have you seen Amerigo?"

"Ummm-hmmm, he's in the *saletta* with your other kinsmen."

"Send word to me there the instant the lady returns, if you will, *Signorina.*"

Olimpia made a pretty pout. "Not this night, Messer Vespucci. Or tomorrow, either, most like."

He would not falter before this girl. "Why in God's name not?"

"My grandmother has an ache in the gut," Giovanni piped up.

*Don't we both,* Guid'Antonio thought.

"Giovanni," Olimpia protested, but mildly. "Let it suffice to say your *nonna* lies gravely ill."

Guid'Antonio stared at the servant-girl. "How is it Maria didn't mention her mother's condition to me earlier today?"

"Suddenly," Olimpia said. "Perhaps your lady hadn't time enough this morning." Her expression appeared fresh and innocent.

Surely, God danced. Gravely ill, Olimpia had said. Guid'Antonio felt compassion for Mona Alessandra, yes. Who knew better than he how sickness and death waited for no one, including him and his family? But

122

he felt disappointment, too.

"Pray Mary looks over our family tonight," he said, and crossed himself.

Olimpia's brazen glance slid down his chest and legs to his boots and slowly back up again. "You wanted your wife," she said.

"Yes."

"I'll come to your bed tonight."

A jolt shot through his loins. He glanced at Giovanni, who looked back at him without blinking, measuring and distant. Guid'Antonio did not answer at once, sharply aware of the plump curve of Olimpia's breasts beneath the light linen shift: no mere apples there. "Ah, thank you — no." After a moment, he added awkwardly, "Sleep well, Olimpia Pasquale."

"Better than you," she said, the corners of her full mouth tipping up in a smile.

"No doubt." Silently turning away, his face burning with high heat, he descended into the garden, his fingers retracing the walls of the stone stairwell.

*Arista alla fiorentina:* pork loin seasoned with rosemary, garlic, and cloves and then slowly, lovingly, roasted until, crispy on the outside and juicy, with just a sweet trace of pink within, the meat was so tender, you could cut it with one of the forks recently introduced to Florence, thence into the Vespucci household.

Guid'Antonio breathed deeply, inhaling the tantalizing fragrance, making his way back past the courtyard fountain toward the *saletta,* the informal dining room he and his kinsmen shared when they weren't entertaining guests in the *sala* or in one of their private apartments. Familiar voices floated to him, rising and falling in warm camaraderie.

At the sound of his step on the threshold, the four men seated around the trestle table broke into a welcoming chorus. His nephew, Antonio Vespucci, rose and kissed him on both cheeks, his face alight with gladness. "Uncle, you *did* return from France with my little brother! I was beginning to doubt him."

"When have you not?" Amerigo said, and drew the intended laughter.

It had been a difficult day, disappointing, shocking, exhilarating, and tiring by turn. *Thank God for family and home, especially tonight,* Guid'Antonio thought, shrugging off his crimson cloak and tossing it onto one of several pegs near the door. Tapers set in iron sconces suffused the *saletta* with light, making it cozy and intimate. The cooking fire in the hearth illuminated the marbled ochre walls and the red and gold hues in the intricately patterned tile floor.

"Brother Giorgio, Nastagio," he said, greeting Amerigo and Antonio's uncle and father in turn. Both men smiled; neither stood.

Antonio patted the wooden stool between him and Amerigo, and Guid'Antonio sank onto it, safely anchored at last, fanning his loose linen shirt: the kitchen was warm, his underarms wet.

"Look at you, Guid'Antonio," Brother Giorgio Vespucci said. "Is that a halo you're wearing? Or, no, only a trace more silver threaded through your black hair."

"Brother, I wouldn't talk if I were you," Guid'Antonio shot back. "The brown fringe that once ringed your head appears to have gone white as a dove since last I saw you." Beneath his clerical robes, Brother Giorgio's torso appeared round and stout as ever.

Not so, that of Nastagio Vespucci! Rising shakily from the table, Amerigo and Antonio's fifty-four-year-old father offered Guid'Antonio a weak embrace. *Appalling,* Guid'Antonio thought, sinking back down onto his stool. Was this his friend, the merry Nastagio Vespucci, a man whose reputation spoke of his fondness for food, company and drink? In the last two years, Nastagio Vespucci, who was not only Guid'Antonio's kinsman but also one of his closest friends, had turned desperately pale and thin. Antonio's letters to France had said nothing of this. Or so Guid'Antonio supposed; come to think of it, who knew what Antonio Vespucci might have written in private to his brother, Amerigo?

"Try this new wine," Amerigo suggested. "Cesare and Gaspare are bringing our salads."

"I'm floating in wine already," Guid'Antonio said.

Amerigo grinned, shrugging. "Italy was baptized in it."

Guid'Antonio accepted the dark ruby liquid. "Ummm. Nutty and velvety, with a slight sting on the tongue." A *Chianti tipico,* or Chianti-type wine. "From our grapes?"

"Of course," Antonio said. "It suits?"

"Absolutely." Guid'Antonio observed Antonio with a fond smile. People often mistook Antonio for Amerigo, and vice versa. Three years apart in age, both young men were slender and pleasant-faced, with glossy chestnut hair falling past their shoulders. As the Vespucci family's eldest son, Antonio it was who had been sent to Pisa for a university education, rather than Amerigo. Today, like his father and grandfather before him, Antonio was a notary. Thus, in addition to assisting with the family business, in itself a ball-breaking task with both Guid'Antonio and Amerigo absent from home these last two years, Antonio spent grueling hours in City Hall certifying the authenticity of signatures and documents, work as hard on the brain and the back as it was eye-opening.

Was that why behind his naturally cheerful manner, Antonio had acquired a new look of watchfulness?

As for Amerigo, Guid'Antonio doubted employment as his secretary and traveling companion would satisfy Amerigo much longer. Then what?

A small, robust woman blew in from the kitchen with Cesare, Guid'Antonio's willowy manservant, in her wake. Cheeks rosy with heat, Domenica Ridolfi hurried to Guid'Antonio with a pottery mug in one hand and a meat cleaver in the other. "It's about time you showed your handsome face in my kitchen!"

Delighted to see her, Guid'Antonio scooted back his stool and hastily stood with arms outstretched. "Domenica, at last."

Under the cover of his mother's pleased laughter, Cesare said, "Messer Guid'Antonio, you survived City Hall?"

Guid'Antonio's mind slid back to Palazzo della Signoria and Palazzo Medici and forward to the Virgin weeping in Ognissanti. "So far, Cesare. That and more."

Cesare's eyebrows quivered with pride. "Bravo." With a flourish, he set the table, placing dishes on the linen cloth just so, turning knife blades precisely toward majolica plates, lest anyone feel threatened by his neighbor.

Guid'Antonio kissed Domenica's warm cheeks. The woman who had cooked for the Vespucci family since Guid'Antonio was a boy smelled of garlic, olives, and plum wine, the latter sloshing dangerously near the rim of her cup. She hugged him with a strength that would have surprised him had he not been accustomed to it. "Domenica, I beg you, watch the cleaver."

"The only man I'd set this against is the one who would harm you," Domenica said. For all her fifty-six years, the plain headscarf tied loosely at the back of her neck revealed curls more richly black than silver.

"Domenica, pork loin, my favorite dish. You're a saint."

"What did you expect, with you just home from" — she waved her hand — "up Lombardy way." Turning to the sideboard, she

128

sliced a chunk of meat from the roast and offered it to him on the tip of the cleaver. "Is it true the French eat squashed lark?"

"Domenica," Amerigo broke in, laughing. " 'Squashed lark'? And actually, France is farther north of us."

Domenica skewered him with her eyes. "All that matters is the general direction."

"Not," Amerigo said, "when you're traveling."

Guid'Antonio inhaled the fragrance of the tender pork loin. "Not squashed, Domenica. It's called *pâté. Buena sera,* Gaspare," he added, acknowledging the cook's brother, the lightweight old fellow who had just come in from the kitchen, and who seemed in danger of toppling to the tile floor if anyone sneezed in his direction. Gaspare Ridolfi was older than Domenica by a decade and showing all the bone-bent wear of it. He coughed, recovered, and carefully placed a portion of salad greens on each plate.

"Now you've graced us with your presence, I can fry the ravioli. Gaspare! Cesare!" Domenica waved Guid'Antonio back toward the trestle table, where his kinsmen sat watching him, grinning, then sailed into the kitchen with her feather-footed son and her stooped, elderly brother in her wake.

"Are all servants as bold as ours?" Nastagio complained.

Antonio said lightly, "Without a doubt," but his quick glance at his father showed he had heard the truculent note in his father's voice.

Guid'Antonio drizzled olive oil and vinegar onto the wild salad greens gracing his plate and thought back to Olimpia Pasquale. There was bold personified. He poured himself more wine. "How's this one selling?"

Nastagio stirred restlessly. "Well enough to the few who can still afford it."

"Apparently, that's true of everything." Entering the garden off Borg'Ognissanti just now, glancing at the wine-window open to the street, Guid'Antonio had noted the lack of customers who usually appeared at dusk to fill their jugs for a nominal fee.

Cesare, gliding back in from the kitchen, passed the meat on a platter while his mother served the fried ravioli, and Gaspare puttered along behind her, sprinkling the pasta with grated cheese from Parma.

"God," Guid'Antonio groaned, savoring the fine aroma. "I've died and gone to heaven."

"No," Antonio said. "You've come home to Italy."

130

Brother Giorgio's mouth formed a smile as round and red as a ripe cherry. "It takes more to usher a man into heaven than Domenica's *arista* and fried ravioli, Guid'Antonio."

"That's your opinion," Cesare inserted neatly.

Guid'Antonio smiled, blowing on the steaming ravioli on the end of his fork to cool it. The cutlery was new. Silver, with ornate finials in the form of *le vespe,* or wasps, according to the Vespucci family name. "Brother Giorgio, at this particular moment, I'm all content on earth."

Amerigo sopped his bread in olive oil, his face glowing with wine and pleasure. "Me, too. But you saw Lorenzo this afternoon. What did he have to say?"

At the sideboard, the meat platter slipped in Cesare's fingers. He sat the platter down with care and cut his eyes toward Amerigo with marked disapproval.

Nastagio slapped the table. "Amerigo! What does it matter what Lorenzo the Magnificent *says*? More importantly, what does he *do*? Or not do, according to his own selfish nature?"

There was an awkward silence. Amerigo stared at his father. In the quiet, Gaspare crept forward to refill Guid'Antonio's

131

goblet. *"No, grazie."* Guid'Antonio placed his hand lightly over the rim, his gaze fixed on Nastagio, who, it seemed, was as ill-humored as he was unwell. Nastagio Vespucci, a brave supporter of the Medici family, speaking of Lorenzo with such . . . disrespect? What spurred the man? A lingering illness? A raging fever?

Antonio shifted on his stool. "Uncle Guid'Antonio, Amerigo said Alessandra del Vigna is ill."

"Yes. Maria's with her at her house."

"Christ be with the lady," Brother Giorgio intoned, and crossed himself.

Guid'Antonio glanced around and settled on the tried-and-true Amerigo. "Did you get a lot done this afternoon?"

"I did. Uncle Giorgio and I rode to Careggi to visit Marsilio, who welcomed us with open arms and a host of new manuscripts." Marsilio Ficino, the diminutive doctor-philosopher who — having produced the first translations of Plato's dialogues from the original Greek into Latin for Lorenzo's grandfather, amongst many other writings — now kept an oil lamp burning before a marble bust of Plato in his villa foyer and dabbled in magic.

Guid'Antonio frowned. "I meant what did you accomplish here at *home,* Amerigo.

132

Perhaps tomorrow I should tie you down in the *scrittoio,* where surely there's a mountain of paperwork waiting, else you'll be sitting with your uncle Giorgio at Toscanelli's feet, charmed by that old man's ramblings on geography and the limits of the seas."

Spots of pink color bloomed on Amerigo's cheeks. He glanced at Brother Giorgio before speaking. "Scholars come from all over Europe to the University of Florence to attend Marsilio Ficino's lectures. For us, it's just a short ride to his villa. And, yes, as you've surmised, we're meeting at Paolo Toscanelli's tomorrow. Paolo may be in his eighties and his theories bold but, as you well know, his belief we may reach the Orient by sailing west across the sea has people wondering if it may be so. Moreover, having been gone for almost two years, I naturally assumed a few hours in the presence of others would be amenable to us both."

Guid'Antonio was feeling ill-tempered, and he knew it. "I'm sorry," he said. "Today's been a bear. When you come home tomorrow, you, Antonio, and I will review our ledgers."

"I'll be here," Antonio said, sighing deeply.

"That reminds me," Brother Giorgio said, brushing crumbs from the lap of his robe as Cesare whisked around the trestle table, collecting dinner plates, "have we paid Sandro's commission for Ognissanti? Antonio?"

"Haven't we! You'd think he was Masaccio and had painted the glorious frescoes in the Brancacci Chapel, given his price. Higher than a cat's ass, and since he lives just around the corner, I couldn't put him off. He was here at noon today, having just this morning given our new Saint Augustine his final brushstroke."

Put Sandro off? Guid'Antonio frowned. Why would Antonio wish to do that?

"Sandro Botticelli's the best painter in town," Brother Giorgio said. "In all Italy, perhaps."

"Particularly since Masaccio's long dead and buried," Cesare said, adding the last plate to the stack on the sideboard. As the others laughed, with a quick hand he plucked a chunk of meat from the pork roast and slid it into the leather pouch at his waist, a maneuver Guid'Antonio watched with interest. Cesare had no need to purloin food. For whatever reason Cesare desired the leftover meat, why not just take it from the cupboard later this evening? Because Domenica might see Cesare and ask what he was about. What mischief now? Cesare held his spine straight as he made a smooth retreat into the kitchen.

Guid'Antonio reined in his scattered thoughts. "What about the Pollaiuolo brothers? Or Leonardo? When it comes to talented craftsmen."

"Da Vinci? Hands down not dependable." Brother Giorgio brushed another good measure of breadcrumbs from the front of his capacious monk's robe. "It was I who suggested Saint Augustine as Sandro's subject for our fresco. Ghirlandaio completed the Saint Jerome on the near wall. It became quite the competition. I imagine you've yet to see either painting."

"No," Guid'Antonio said. "Nor have I seen our weeping Virgin Mary."

Nastagio barked a sharp, shrill laugh. "Ha! Rest easy on that score, Guid'Antonio! With Lorenzo balking at his chance to save the Republic, in the coming days you'll have plenty of opportunity to see the Virgin's tears and witness more trouble to boot!"

"Father," Amerigo said, frowning, "Lorenzo already saved us once. He did it risking his neck in Naples to secure a peace treaty with the king. Still —" Amerigo glanced at Guid'Antonio. "In City Hall everyone's question is the same. Will Lorenzo now travel to Rome to appease the Pope?"

"No. Florence shouldn't be seen as sub-

135

missive to Sixtus IV."

Brother Giorgio regarded Guid'Antonio with shrewd brown eyes. "However much her people wish to be submissive to the Church?"

"Umph!" Nastagio grunted. "Lorenzo was happy to go to Naples and content to linger there indefinitely. Who knows? He might find a whore's legs open to him in Rome, too."

The color in Antonio's cheeks deepened to dark plum. "Careful, Father, I beg you."

Guid'Antonio's concern for Nastagio mounted. What in God's name was his old friend saying? "Nastagio," he said, "Lorenzo went to Naples to end the war and bring peace to Italy. And did." He felt as if he were addressing a child.

"Peace?" Nastagio hooted. "He went to Naples to salvage his reputation in Florence."

"A not unreasonable motive, Father," Antonio said, measuring out each word, "since Lorenzo and Florence are one and the same. You would do well to remember that."

Nastagio swung his arm out with such vehemence he knocked the wine pitcher from the table's edge, spilling its deep red contents across the floor. "My quibble is our imposter prince stole money from the State treasury to do it!"

"Father!" Antonio said. "Go gently lest you wish us all to hang!"

Guid'Antonio shifted his eyes around the table, silently watching and waiting to see how this would play out.

Exasperated, Amerigo said, "Of *course* Lorenzo used State money to fund the war. It was a State matter done to end our conflict with Sixtus and the king."

"*Our* conflict?" Nastagio's eyes darkened dangerously. "Lucifer's, you mean!"

Amerigo banged both fists on the table. Yes, Nastagio was his father. Yes, he was a respectful son. But he was also twenty-six and Italian. "Lorenzo mortgaged his land in the Mugello Valley to finance his mission to Naples. We were beaten in the field! Our so-called commanders were fighting amongst themselves. Chancellor Scala wrote us saying if what we needed was sluggards to win, we would have been victorious everywhere." He sat back, his chest heaving.

Nastagio did not cuff his youngest son; instead, he stared at him, confusion clouding his face.

*You're the ambassador,* Guid'Antonio thought. *A peacemaker, it is believed.* "Nastagio," he said. "Given the history of the

137

place, Lorenzo could have been murdered in Naples. If it weren't for King Ferrante's admiration —"

"Admiration?" Nastagio laughed shrilly. "If it weren't for the king's daughter-in-law, you mean!" Nastagio lewdly jiggled one forefinger in and out of a circle he made with his other hand.

Brother Giorgio drew back, appalled, one hand clasping the front of his robe.

Guid'Antonio snapped his attention to Antonio. "What is your father saying?"

"Ah —" Antonio cleared his throat, his face bright scarlet. "There were — are — rumors that while Lorenzo was in Naples, he courted Prince Alfonso's wife. Since Alfonso was away in Siena, conducting the war against us here in Tuscany."

A torrent of heat flashed up Guid'Antonio's spine. Ippolita Sforza and Lorenzo de' Medici had met in 1465 when Lorenzo rode north to the Milanese court as Florence's representative at Ippolita's marriage to Prince Alfonso of Naples. Ippolita was twenty that May, Lorenzo a youth of sixteen being groomed to take his father's place as head of the Medici family.

Calmly, he said, "Lorenzo and Ippolita have been devoted friends for fifteen years."

*"Sì,"* agreed Nastagio, and smacked his lips.

A lighter tone, perhaps. "Nastagio," Guid'Antonio said, "do you mean to say that in this enlightened age a man and woman can't be friends?" Guid'Antonio had a female friend himself. *Friend.* And wasn't that a laugh and an enormous falsehood, too? Her name was Francesca Vernacci, and she was the *"medica di casa,"* the doctor of the house, at Spedale dei Vespucci, a short walk from where he now sat. No one other than police chief Palla Palmieri and Lorenzo knew much about Guid'Antonio and Maestra Francesca's past love affair. Theirs was a tortured history that had begun a good twelve years ago, when, after Taddea's untimely death, he had fallen deeply in love with Francesca and had shown her just how deeply time and time again, night after night, and some days, too, worshipping her in her bed. Those days were long gone, buried in the past, but not forgotten, by him, at least. Now, since marrying Maria, he saw Francesca only when she assisted him with his private investigations, say, to establish the time of death in an instance of suspected murder or to identify a particular poison, like Death Cap. *Friend?* He still craved Francesca, loved her deep within his soul, despite the rational explanation she had given him why they could not marry. She was married to the hospital (*his* hospital, he had wanted to shout, but choked back the words), Guid'Antonio must have an heir, and, as she pointed out, she was already in her mid-twenties. He was a Medici man, his was a world of power and politics, hers one of bandages and late hours, of sickness and foul-smelling medicines. "I'm only sorry I couldn't save Taddea and the baby for you," she had said, for Francesca it was who had ministered to Taddea in the end.

Over time, his longing for Francesca Vernacci had become a thirst he could slake by just standing near her, breathing in her scent when they met in her rooms to speak of a case, but it was one he could not entirely quench.

"Enlightened age?" Nastagio said now. "Here's the devil's method, and you would do well to heed it. Who's seen Niccolò Ardinghelli lately? No one has in these streets. Swat the annoying husband away like a fly! Or like a wasp," he said, his voice coy as he wagged his finger at Guid'Antonio. "An ambassadorship can be a sentence of exile, as well as an honor. The trick is knowing which is which."

Guid'Antonio's face burned with increasing heat. Niccolò Ardinghelli was married to Lucrezia Donati. Lucrezia, so the gossips said, was Lorenzo's lover and had been since the green days of their youth. People tittered and pointed behind Ambassador Niccolò Ardinghelli's back; Guid'Antonio had heard them and seen them do it. Poor, cuckolded Niccolò, who spent more time outside Florence tending State affairs than he did at home, tending his own marriage. The eternal devoted ambassador. A Medici man through and through.

Antonio and Amerigo traded glances. Brother Giorgio reached out a restraining hand. "Nastagio, my brother, you're ill, for God's sake. Let me take you to bed."

"For *whose* sake?" Nastagio raved. "God's? Or that of the Antichrist, Lorenzo?"

"Saint Luke, help us," Antonio murmured, covering his face with his hands.

With the sheer force of his will, Guid'Antonio kept his fingers from the hilt of his dagger. He rose steadily, his gaze fixed on his lifelong friend. "Nastagio." The word was a stone in his mouth. "Kinsman or no, from this time forward you will curb your tongue in my presence, lest I cut it out. I will not wink at treason. Nor will I tolerate slander of any kind, certainly not when a lady is involved, no matter who she is, whether Ippolita Sforza, Lucrezia Donati Ardinghelli, or however obliquely, my own spouse."

He shot a withering glance around the table. "Brother Giorgio, lest *you* forget, we're in conflict with Holy Mother Church because Pope Sixtus IV has declared himself the enemy of Lorenzo, and so, of the Florentine State. Moreover, Sixtus refuses to lift his censures against us *not* because he's the Vicar of Christ, but because he's the vicar of his bastard nephew."

Before they had further opportunity to speak, Guid'Antonio was out of the suffocating chamber and striding forth across the city to the Ox district in the Santa Croce quarter of Florence to find Maria.

# EIGHT

She was seated a short distance from the hearth fire when he entered her mother's chamber in the Del Vigna residence. Bathed in the thick odors of incense and candle wax, the air in the modestly furnished room felt oppressively hot against his skin. In the raised bed, Alessandra del Vigna moaned beneath a woolen blanket, while her physician poked his finger in a pewter bowl's lumpy contents. Maria's eyes were closed, her hands limp in the lap of her gown and damask overdress. Surely, she would swelter in this heat meant to sweat the illness from the pores of her mother's skin. Still, the light from the hearth lent Maria's profile a lovely glow.

Guid'Antonio's heart reached out to her. He would help her in the coming days, although for the most part, this duty Maria would perform alone. Her father, her brother, and her two sisters — all were dead from the plague that had ravaged the city in the months after Florence set its course for war. Guid'Antonio had watched her closely back then, while in her grief she drifted about the Vespucci Palace like a specter, her complexion deathly pale. She had eaten very little, becoming so airy and light, he had thought she might vanish before him. Eventually, her wounded soul had learned to live with its terrible loss; slowly, she had come back around. She had her mother to consider, after all. She had Giovanni, then just a boy of three. She had *him*. For a few months at least, until he and Amerigo packed their trunks and turned Flora and Bucephalus toward Paris.

He removed his cloak and placed it on a chest. "Maria?"

She started and turned a glance on him and almost at once, a smile eased her troubled features. She rose and hurried to the threshold to meet him. "Guid'Antonio."

He enfolded her in his arms, holding her so close, he could feel her heartbeat fluttering in her breast. Her body was solid and hot in his embrace, her clothing suffused with the heat of the hearth fire. "How is she?" he said.

Maria's trembling sigh as she took a step back told him everything. She lifted her hair, letting it fan, black and shiny as onyx, around her shoulders. "God knows, Guid'Antonio. Two days ago, when Giovanni and I came visiting, she seemed herself. Now, the pains in her stomach are fearsome; you see how she braces against them. She's so cold, her teeth chatter, yet here it is July and a fire blazing in the hearth. Dottore Camerlini bled her. If only she could sleep."

As if determined not to give herself over to death, Mona Alessandra del Vigna thrashed beneath the cross on the wall behind her bed. *Sleep she will, and the sooner the better, for her own sake,* Guid'Antonio thought.

He buried his face in the smoky fragrance of Maria's hair, brushing his lips against her neck. The contact of his mouth on her flesh hit him hard, like a fist blow to the heart. He wanted to pull her dress down around her shoulders and kiss her nipples till they were rosy and tight. He wanted to fall down on his knees, bunch up her skirt and run his hands up her parted thighs. Quickly, he released her. Such thoughts, at this time and place.

"Guid'Antonio." A note of worry suffused Maria's voice. "Forgive me for this morning. The devil's own disappointment put those harsh words in my mouth. I have no right — what must you have thought when you returned from the Signoria to find me gone?"

His heartbeat slowed. Honor told him to take a step back and confess the truth: he had left her waiting, or so he had thought. Self-preservation reminded him fools rush in where angels fear to tread. Fresh starts, new beginnings. "Hush," he said, cupping her face in his hands, "there's nothing to forgive. If there were, it would be you who should forgive me."

A series of coughs racked Mona Alessandra's body. Maria glanced toward the bed. "Bless you, Guid'Antonio, and God help her. I can't leave her tonight." She gazed at him, her eyes dark pools of sorrow, all her energy spent.

"No. Of course not." He ran his hands down the long sleeves of her gown: beneath the silk fabric, her arms felt warm to the touch. He suppressed a groan. God, he wanted her in bed. Or here, against the hot wall.

Beside the bed, Dottore Camerlini dumped the contents of the sick bowl into Alessandra del Vigna's chamber pot and turned to consult a well-thumbed manuscript. To what end? Maria's mother would die from this sickness that announced itself with sharp twinges in the belly before erupting into fever, chills, and stabbing pain. Guid'Antonio knew it. Maria knew it. Mona Alessandra del Vigna's physician, Dottore Camerlini, knew it. "I'll sit with you tonight," Guid'Antonio said.

But Maria shook her head. "Go home and rest. Soon enough, I'll need all your strength."

"Come outside with me?" he said.

In the shadows of the Del Vigna garden, he inhaled deeply, pulling fresh air into his chest, standing with his wife in the shelter of the loggia in his crimson cloak. Night was upon them now in earnest, the only sound that of their soft breathing. Over the Santa Croce quarter, the moon raced in and out of purple clouds so thick with rain, they appeared about to burst. The fire in the torches burning around the little courtyard danced restlessly, illuminating stone walls caked with grime and soot. The Del Vigna garden showed other signs of neglect, a terracotta vase cracked open by the snow and ice of the past two winters, the bowl in the fountain dry and peeling.

Maria touched his arm. "I haven't had time to do much here, with tending to

Giovanni and other matters at home, and I don't like calling on Antonio. His hands are full as it is."

"I'll send our gardeners here tomorrow," he said.

Large raindrops splattered the ground and the dusty fountain. She said, "Do you expect good weather then? It looks as if a storm might unleash itself on us any moment now."

He drew his finger along her cheek. "I expect nothing, Maria. I only hope," he said, and once more he strode, a solitary figure, out into the night.

Few sensible men traveled the streets of Florence alone after nightfall. But when had Guid'Antonio Vespucci ever been sensible? He unlatched the garden gate and stepped out into Piazza Santa Croce. The sound of the grating iron bolt echoed around the shuttered wooden houses and shops hugging the deserted square. Droplets of rain pelted his face and hair.

Eastward across the piazza, at the end of the great rectangle, Santa Croce Church rose up in the night. Behind that unadorned brick facade, friars devoted to Saint Francis moved through shadows past private family chapels rich with frescoes painted by Gaddi,

Giotto, and Aretino. Guid'Antonio pulled his cloak close around his face and peered through the darkness. A small brick dome rose up past the wall on the eastern side of the monastery's first cloister: the Pazzi family chapel.

The Pazzis hadn't used the chapel in the last couple of years, had they, though God knew they had needed it. All, all had been trapped in the punishing violence unleashed in the city the instant Giuliano de' Medici's knees hit the Cathedral floor. All butchered, beheaded, castrated, hanged, their corpses tossed in the Arno in bloody pieces. All but a few, one of them Bianca de' Medici's husband, Guglielmo de' Pazzi, because he was Giuliano and Lorenzo's friend, had partied and traveled and gone hunting with them on numerous occasions. Amazing.

The wind picked up. Straw and litter whirled outside the darkened shops as the misting rain gathered strength and threatened to come down in sheets. Guid'Antonio hurried into the piazza and drew up short, startled by the sharp burst of white light illuminating the atmosphere. He stopped, startled, watching as glistening crystals of pure white snow cascaded from the sky above his head. Out into the wintry light rode Giuliano in body armor shining like silver. Beneath him, his horse pranced, anticipating the joust. In the stands, bundled in a fur-lined cloak, sat Giuliano's tournament Queen of Beauty, Guid'Antonio's kinswoman, sixteen-year-old Simonetta Vespucci, her cheeks pink and as soft as roses. On Giuliano's banner, Sandro Botticelli had painted Simonetta's image, her cascading blonde hair braided with jewels and pearls, her sheer white gown caressing her voluptuous body.

Guid'Antonio's heart pounded dully as Giuliano's tournament slowly faded from his vision. January 1475. Oh, how he yearned to hold on to that glorious winter morning! Perhaps he should see Dottore Camerlini. A mirthless laugh escaped his lips.

Head bowed, hands shaking, he strode out into the rain. How could they all have been so mad as not to realize they were living in a dream, a bubble whose shape and colors constantly changed, one so fragile, neither prayers nor magic could keep it from bursting? Not long after the tournament, Guid'Antonio had walked with Giuliano behind Simonetta Vespucci's casket as tears flowed unashamedly down Giuliano's cheeks. Death — life! — spared no one, not even the young and impossibly beautiful, not when it came to a sickness in the chest or an assassin's blade.

As was their duty and privilege, Simonetta's husband and her father-in-law, Marco and Piero Vespucci, had also walked in the funeral procession that day. Directly behind them, Guid'Antonio had forced himself to plant one foot solidly in front of the other and keep an even pace. All Florence knew Simonetta and Giuliano had been lovers, though Giuliano de' Medici and Marco Vespucci were lifelong friends.

Black thoughts. Haunting memories.

He moved along the western edge of Piazza Santa Croce and bore left into a crooked lane. Torches in doorways bloomed hesitantly as he passed. A cat slipped into the darkness ahead of him and vanished. Good! Thank God the bony feline hadn't whirled and come bounding back past him, made skittish by some waiting presence. He slowed his step, listening before quitting the tight byway, and heard nothing but the patter of rain.

Out in the open again, he stayed close by the walls of the Stinche. Briefly, he paused and craned his head. The city prison was a massive structure with barred windows cut up so high that from the street they were invisible. Gloomy and stark, the Stinche housed traitors, murderers, and thieves. The list of traitors included Simonetta Vespucci's father-in-law, Piero Vespucci.

A ghost walked across Guid'Antonio's grave. Somewhere in the Stinche, Piero Vespucci sat cuffed and chained. Guid'Antonio quickened his pace, his cheeks smarting with fury and shame. On the day after Giuliano's funeral Mass, Lorenzo and Palla Palmieri had questioned Guid'Antonio, informally, just outside the doors of San Lorenzo Church, where he had gone to pray. The two men had come striding toward him from the courtyard of the Medici garden, exuding an air of grave purpose, daggers in full view. "We found you," Lorenzo had said with the new, dangerous edge he had acquired in the five days since his brother's murder. "Palla has made another arrest." That Lorenzo meant an arrest having to do with the Pazzi Conspiracy was plain.

"Good. Who?" Guid'Antonio said, keenly aware of Palla's mix of bravado and uneasiness, how he bit his lip and glanced toward the marketplace. Palla, who always met even the direst situations directly, if not exactly without guile, in his role as Florence's police chief.

"Piero Vespucci," Lorenzo said. "Your kinsman."

"Piero? Why?" Guid'Antonio's surprise was complete. No deception, no subterfuge.

"For sheltering a man suspected in the plot against the Medici family," Palla said. "Piero gave the fool refuge."

Suspected. It was enough to ruin the family. "Which fool? I thought we hanged most everyone."

"Napoleone Francesi."

"Who escaped justice, thanks to your Piero." Lorenzo's voice was dangerously quiet, revealing no emotion.

"I don't know this Napoleone Francesi," Guid'Antonio said, holding out both hands.

"No?" Lorenzo's eyes shone.

"No. And Piero's not mine. I barely know him."

Lorenzo touched the bandage protecting the flesh wound at his neck, as if reassuring himself the dressing was still there. "I told Palla so."

"You had no inkling Piero Vespucci might be connected to a plot to kill Lorenzo and Giuliano?" Palla said, relief creeping into his voice.

"No."

"Nor Marco?"

"Marco? Did he shelter a suspect, too?"

153

Guid'Antonio said.

A smile twitched Palla's lips. "Not so far as we know. However . . ." He shrugged. *Like father, like son.*

"What will you do with them?" Guid'Antonio said. No need to inquire about motive. Simonetta Vespucci's image stood between them in Piazza San Lorenzo as surely as if she still drew breath in this earthly realm.

"We'll see what we can learn and proceed accordingly." Palla smiled wickedly. "Or vice versa."

"Where are Piero and Marco now?"

"Police headquarters. Piero's there, that is. My men have gone to fetch Marco from home."

"Pray you find him there," Guid'Antonio said.

"I'll find him wherever he goes."

The three men strolled across the marketplace together then, their backs to the church where Giuliano's corpse lay lost in darkness within a marble sarcophagus whose gleaming surface was lit by a burning sea of candles. It was six months later, in October, when Guid'Antonio and Amerigo set out for France, riding beneath the banner of Lorenzo's trust, while Marco Vespucci lived in exile, and Piero moldered

154

behind the walls of the Stinche, his world a stinking river of black.

He stepped over a rushing stream of rainwater and sewage, veering toward Via dei Cartolai, where the booksellers, stationers, and illustrators dwelled. Thunder crashed overhead. Lightning turned the rain to silver needles, and the wind picked up, blowing Guid'Antonio's cloak back from his shoulders. Christ's blood. Was he forever to be pursued by tempestuous weather?

He cut through a black alley, shouldering wet walls, ignoring rats scattering at his feet. It was then a muffled footstep sounded at his back. He spun around, the hairs stiff on the nape of his neck. He strained his ears and heard the rain streaming in rivulets down the walls enclosing him all around.

Alarmed, at Piazza della Signoria, he walked straight out into the rain. The rain was a forceful downpour now, beating against his face. He touched the dagger inside his sodden cloak, sliding his fingers through the narrow slit, and glanced around. City Hall rose up on his left; across from it loomed the Loggia dei Priori, the covered area where Florence's nine Lord Priors received visiting ambassadors and other foreign dignitaries. In the shadows,

155

with rain dripping down their legs, arms, and torsos, the loggia's collection of ancient statues looked oddly menacing.

He could dash past the loggia, sprint toward the river, and bear sharply right, toward Borg'Ognissanti. No! At night the area around the Arno housed ruffians who might be tempted to cut his throat and steal his purse, desperate for a few coins. Better to cut diagonally across Piazza della Signoria and test Fortune in the alleyways. The darkness that hid one man could as well hide another.

He had walked only a few paces out onto the open when the sound of movement pricked his ears again. He spun around and saw — nothing! He walked on, his heart galloping, keeping to the relative safety of the broad, open piazza, his mind preternaturally alert. Lightning cracked and flashed overhead; for one instant night turned into day. Grim and fearful, he maintained his pace. Before him on the lip of the piazza there lay a yawning black corridor.

He walked inside and turned to look back across the piazza. If someone was out there, he was clinging to the shadows. Perhaps his companion had given up the chase on this rain-soaked night. Somewhere in the sleeping neighborhood a baby cried, unsettling his nerves again.

He passed through one short byway after another, retracing the route he and Amerigo had followed on their way to City Hall earlier today, until finally he passed beneath the sopping-wet scarlet flags adorning Palazzo Davizzi. He unlatched the red gate, dropped the wooden arm into place, and stepped into Piazza Trinita.

God's mercy, the rain had all but stopped, the storm reeling off into the countryside. Trinita Church was a welcome sight, though dark and lonely as the grave. On his left, Ponte Trinita spanned the river to the opposite bank. Both piazza and bridge were deserted. At his back, he heard the sound of the latch lifted from the gate. Jesus Christ and Mary! Alarmed, he spun on his heel. "Show your face! Come out!"

Silence.

He sensed eyes boring into him. What the hell did this bastard want? He ducked into the passageway alongside the church and pressed against the raw, wet stones. There he waited, dagger raised. He heard a flurry of motion as someone hurried after him into the black maw. All right, then: one of them would die.

The sound of singing pricked Guid'Antonio's ears. He must be raving mad! No —

157

the singing came from the direction of the bridge, drunken and off-key, accompanied by a lute. It was a gang of young men returning home from some tavern or house of prostitution across the river. From the bridge, they stumbled into the piazza, laughing. "Whoo-hoo, Piccarda! Can you come out to play?"

Trapped between his prey and the youths soaked in rain and wine — armed to the teeth and spoiling for a fight, undoubtedly — Guid'Antonio's pursuer shrank into his cloak. "Whoever you are, come on," Guid'Antonio whispered. He motioned with his free hand. "Do it. *Please.*"

The scrape of the gate opening on the opposite side of the piazza and the drunks falling through it told them both that in a moment they would again face one another alone. "Come on!"

The hooded figure gave a smothered cry. "No!"

He turned and fled, Guid'Antonio's last sight of him the hem of his soaked robe.

"What the hell?" Guid'Antonio leaned against the wall, shaking. In his hand, his dagger felt slippery, drenched with rainwater and sweat. He pulled himself together, quit the alley, and emerged into Piazza Goldoni. Why had the man tailed him? To relieve him of his crimson cloak for resale to the used-clothes dealers? Possibly. To kill him? Why? Christ's nails, he'd only been home one day!

In the coming hours, he would watch his back and warn Amerigo to guard his own safety, too.

Ognissanti Church sat ahead on his right, just beyond Via Porcellana, the street where Sandro Botticelli lived with his family and kept his workshop, Botticelli and Company. Guid'Antonio slipped past the narrow black passage. Beneath his fingers, the church door pushed slowly in. Cool air stung his nostrils. Incense, damp, stone: the smell of loneliness. In the darkness, a few candles flickered here and there.

By Florentine standards, Ognissanti was not a large church. Still, Guid'Antonio's presence disturbed the quiet when he traversed the nave in his cloak, now completely wet and as dark as blood. At this hour the side chapels were deserted, their only inhabitants the bodies of the dead in the lower vaults. His family. On his right, barely visible in the lack of light, were the two frescoes Domenico Ghirlandaio had painted on the Vespucci Chapel's outer wall, the *Madonna of Mercy* and, directly below this, the *Lamentation over the Dead Christ,* with

Ghirlandaio's renderings of Amerigo and his black-garbed uncle Giorgio Vespucci, staring back at Guid'Antonio. Next on the south wall came — oh, yes, Sandro's *Saint Augustine,* the old man garbed in luminous robes of white and orange-gold. Guid'Antonio would know Sandro's hand anywhere, even if Brother Giorgio hadn't mentioned the fresco earlier this evening. He passed the wall painting without a second look, boots squishing as he walked beneath Ognissanti's slender arches toward the painting propped on the altar.

At the altar, he stopped, his gaze fastened on the *Virgin Mary of Santa Maria Impruneta.*

Encircled in a ring of low burning light, the Virgin stared blankly into space. He strode onto the altar, removed a burning candle from a saucer, and held the flame toward her painted eyes, orbs as dry as dust in a vapid face. Glancing up into the lifting vault, he saw only darkness. No ropes and pulleys, no leak in the ceiling. Which reminded him: what had the weather been last Wednesday, when the painting first wept? Had it been raining then? And what about the days from Wednesday to Saturday, when the tears slowed and ceased completely?

He circled the panel: no tiny holes pierced in the wood, no water bucket. Had he truly expected such an easy resolution? He shook his head to clear it. He would begin fresh in the morning. Question people in a quiet way.

He dropped a coin into the collection box, lit a candle, and placed it on a nearby table beside a host of others. Kneeling at the rail, he murmured a prayer for Maria's mother, while from the sacristy on his right there came the soft susurration of voices, the Benedictine brothers of the Humiliati going about some nocturnal business, most like.

And then he heard a brief, whirring sound, and some violent thing dropped down on him from overhead. "Lucifer!" He leapt up, slipped, and knocked against the wooden table. Flaming candles tilted toward the floor. He scanned the altar for his attacker, clasping his knife in one hand, and steadied the table with the other — God! A fire in the church? Appalling! A flurry of sound beat around his shoulders. He slapped at it and ducked. A bird! Trapped in the church and panicky, wings thrumming about its body with the same sense of terror pounding through it as through him. As quickly as it had appeared, the tiny bird flew up and was lost in the void. Guid'Antonio slumped at the altar rail.

"Guid'Antonio," the painting said.

He spun around. The candles at the Virgin Mary's feet guttered and fell still. Her painted eyes watched him blankly. Good Christ. He drew an aching breath, then another, and another, until his breathing slowed. Was it just this morning a distraught young monk had fled this church, giving him and Amerigo such a knock in the street? Brother Martino: a solitary Benedictine, dark eyes all aglow, the hem of his black robe flying behind him as he sprinted toward the Prato Gate with two others of the Humiliati order fast on his heels. Craziness. An apt beginning to a day that slowly and steadily had descended straight to hell.

Near the church front, still shaky, Guid'Antonio stood before Sandro Botticelli's fresco of Saint Augustine.

Botticelli's luminous white, gold, and scarlet brushstrokes brightened the gloomy wall. No surprise there. Guid'Antonio's eye followed the direction of the saint's upward gaze. Toward what? Heaven and the promise of salvation?

But there was something else, too. He squinted, but seeing was difficult in this shadowy atmosphere. At the top of the painting, Sandro had drawn a vermillion shield with a band of blue, and on the blue, a few golden wasps. Brother Giorgio Vespucci had commissioned the wall painting, and so, of course, Sandro had decorated it with the Vespucci family seal. Guid'Antonio made out a fringed tablecloth and a couple of books, one leather bound, the other open to a page scribbled with a few odd markings and, hidden as it was in the shadows, a bit of text he could not make out.

Like Guid'Antonio's spirit, all the rest of Sandro's masterful work was lost in a world of dark, and so he turned away.

# NINE

"Here, Tesoro!" Camilla Rossi da Vinci calls plaintively, and wakes. Hidden in the woods deep in the rustling night, she sits bolt upright on her pallet, the sturdy arms and kind voice of her nurse soothing her within the moment, as she takes Camilla to her breast and holds her close, gently rocking back and forth.

"My girl, sweet girl, it's all right," Margherita coos, "sweet, motherless girl, you're all right, just here now, try to sleep."

"Sleep? How, when I'm held captive? Where's Tesoro? Where?" Camilla glances around, bewildered. "He's taken away my beautiful black treasure, too?" Her thin body shudders, she is chilled despite the tower's oppressive heat, chilled as she remembers her captor's fierce eyes flaring and catching fire when she tore the scarf from his wounded, wild face. She had screamed, she remembers clearly, or is that the sound of her present cries scorching her ears?

"My face! You've seen my face! I ought to kill you for that!" he had railed, grasping her violently, throwing her over his steed like a feather merchant's sack of down. "I ought — !"

"Taken away, yes," Margherita is saying now. "But Tesoro is all right. I'm sure the little horse is fine."

"You're sure? But how?"

Margherita clamps her mouth shut.

At the barred window, Camilla stands alone, a prisoner in a room carved from stone, the hem of her shift touching her bare toes. Behind her, Margherita sits on a stool near the wooden door fixed on the outside with three iron bolts. The nurse is released from the cell from time to time, allowed to come and go every few days to bring food and wine and empty the chamber pot. And always, always Margherita's master accompanies her.

In the darkness Camilla's lustrous hair shines, thick and curling like Tesoro's blue-black mane, brushed with silver in the pearly wash of moonlight. If Camilla thrust her slender hand past the bars, she would feel her fingers lashed by stinging wind and rain. The rain's harsh tears separate her from Florence, where she has lived with her husband, Castruccio Senso, these past few years. But there is no need to reach out for tears; she has her own, glistening wet pools filling her blue eyes. Surrendering to sorrow, she weeps.

In Ognissanti Church, the sanctuary door wheezes shut behind Guid'Antonio, and the candles at the altar flame up, gathering strength, casting the *Virgin Mary of Santa Maria Impruneta* in a veil of glowing yellow light. Silver, shining tears dampen the Virgin Mary's painted cheeks, and a sigh rises in the empty church. Listen and hear its soft, singing hush: *Praise Her, Ever Virgin. Praise Her, the blessed one who weeps.*

# TEN

She troubled Guid'Antonio's dreams, smiling tenderly at him, always just out of reach. Again and again, he beckoned her. He could see her in the mist, her tousled hair caressing her naked breasts. . . .

He sat up in bed, fatigued rather than refreshed after a fitful night of sleep. The chamber felt deadly still, the sheets on the other side of the mattress lukewarm beneath the palm of his reaching hand. Gray fingers of light poked at the window shutters.

He propped the shutters open, bathed under his arms, and dressed in the white tunic embroidered with creamy-colored wasps Cesare had put out for him sometime during the night, slipping in and out on hosed feet. Or had Cesare found some magical method of moving about without sound, like a dryad traveling undetected through the forest and the trees?

He was halfway down the stairs when he

heard a child's loud cries and a solid thumping sound. He walked into the sunshine, frowning. Last night's storm had left the atmosphere clear and the sky a lusty shade of pink. He shivered, remembering the hooded figure hunting him in the rain the previous evening, and how the Virgin had said his name in the shadows of Ognissanti.

Two rug beaters, ruddy-faced, muscular men, had tied a rope across the garden and were flogging a tapestry with straw brooms. Dust flew into their faces, making them sneeze. A clothesline had been stretched across the grass just opposite these men. Cesare, in the act of pinning Guid'Antonio's cloak up to dry, glanced over with a grim expression, then nodded toward little Giovanni, who was weeping beside the fountain.

Guid'Antonio narrowed his gaze. Amerigo's mother, Elisabetta Vespucci, hovered over the boy, fussing, whilst his nurse, Olimpia, down on her knees, rump poking the air, searched the ground at the older woman's tightly shod feet.

Beneath the sole of Guid'Antonio's boots, the grass was whispery and wet. Elisabetta spun around. Only a few years older than Guid'Antonio, Elisabetta Vespucci ruled the household and all therein, exactly as she did her husband, Nastagio, and her sons. Or so she liked to believe.

Her face tightened. "So, Guid'Antonio Vespucci. How good of you to join us before the bells toll midday."

"Why is my son crying?" he said.

Her fists flew to her ample waist. "He weeps like a girl! Over *nothing*! He should save his tears for true sorrow and grief."

Giovanni snuffled, "It's something to me."

"Giovanni, see? I told you I would find it." Olimpia jumped up, rosy-cheeked and smiling, straightening her shift. She handed the boy the small object she had plucked from the ground. "Don't cry, my little lamb."

Elisabetta snorted. "He bleats all the time."

Guid'Antonio's silent gaze passed over Amerigo's mother like a cool breeze. "Son, what had you lost?"

The rug beaters, cursing as they wrestled the leaden-weight wall-hanging from the sagging rope, maneuvered it into a fat sausage on the ground, heaving and kicking their brooms from under their bare feet. Silently Giovanni regarded his toes.

"Messer Vespucci, it's a seashell." Olimpia brushed grass from her bodice and sneezed. Her breasts jiggled. The rug beaters stared. One called out a rude remark. Cesare,

169

marching over, slapped both men on the face, grabbed them by the backs of their shirts, shoved them to the gate, and pitched the brooms after them out onto Borg'Ognissanti.

A smile touched Guid'Antonio's lips.

"Cesare!" Elisabetta huffed. "In God's name, what do you think you're doing?"

"I, *Signora*?" Cesare anchored one hand on his hip. "In a moment, I'm off to find two rug beaters who should know better than to insult our house. Particularly the —" He scanned Olimpia up and down and touched his heart. "Particularly the fair ladies who live herein."

Olimpia blushed, cutting her eyes up at him.

"*Our* house? Cesare Ridolfi, you presume too much!" Elisabetta said. "Before you go anywhere, I mean to ask you about a certain woolen blanket missing from Ognissanti's winter donation box. The blanket is plain brown with narrow blue and yellow stripes at each end. I paid to have the moth holes patched and this morning the blanket's gone." Her voice dropped menacingly. "Stolen from the poor in these hard times."

Cesare's countenance paled. "I know nothing of any stolen woolen blanket."

"Don't lie to me!" Elisabetta said loud

enough for the entire Unicorn district to hear. "You know *everything*!"

Guid'Antonio had had enough of Elisabetta Vespucci's bullying. "Elisabetta," he said in a voice as dangerous as it was composed. "You've insulted my child, and now Cesare, who made this girl a noble gesture, and who has no need ever to steal a blanket, new, old, or otherwise." But then, last night had not Cesare filched leftover pork from the loin his mother had cooked for the evening meal?

Guid'Antonio turned to Olimpia. "Now, for God's sake, Giovanni had lost a shell?"

"Show him, Giovanni," Olimpia said, tossing a speculative glance toward Cesare, who was already halfway out the gate, chasing the rug men.

"Only because you asked me," Giovanni said.

"There!" Elisabetta Vespucci said. "You see what a rotten egg he is? I'll box your ears later, Cesare!" she called toward the borgo. "Something nasty is going on in this house, and I'll not rest till you confess it to me!"

"Elisabetta," Guid'Antonio said evenly, "there's a contest of wills many people would pay several gold florins to see." She glared into his eyes, her heart all but con-

171

sumed by anger, or so to him it seemed.

Giovanni glanced from Guid'Antonio to his red-faced aunt and back again. "It has the sea in it," he said. Ivory-colored with a curve of delicate pink, the small shell fit Giovanni's outstretched hand to perfection.

"Does it?" Guid'Antonio leaned down toward the boy. "That's lovely. May I listen?"

"No!" Giovanni yanked back his hand, gripping the shell so tightly, Guid'Antonio feared it might cut his flesh and cause it to bleed. "Just Mama, Olimpia, and me!"

"Giovanni," Guid'Antonio said, but Elisabetta shook Giovanni vigorously.

"Terrible, terrible boy! Where are your manners, you uncivilized beast?"

"Where are *yours*?" Guid'Antonio roared. "Release him. Now!"

Giovanni kicked her. Olimpia sucked in her breath, her brown eyes round and startled. "God's wounds!" Elisabetta screamed. "The wicked boy attacked me!"

Guid'Antonio grasped his son by the arm. "Giovanni! Look at me. I said *look*!"

Giovanni did as bidden; still, Guid'Antonio felt every fiber in his son's thin body straining to escape his grip. "Giovanni," he said. "Never, *ever* strike an adult. Do so again, and you'll see grave trouble, indeed."

172

Giovanni stuck out his lower lip. "Cesare struck an adult. Two of them, those rug beaters. I saw him. And then he threw them out the gate and pursued them."

Still clutching the shell, Giovanni glared back at Guid'Antonio, his dark eyes sparking with an intensity of emotion that seemed to Guid'Antonio to border on hate. "When's my mother coming home?" the boy said.

"I don't know." Guid'Antonio released him. "Cesare Ridolfi is an adult. You'd do well to remember that, Giovanni. Olimpia, take my son to the nursery."

The two went upstairs, Giovanni pressing the prized seashell to his ear with one hand and holding tight to Olimpia's shift with the other.

Guid'Antonio's white-hot gaze swept toward Elisabetta Vespucci. "Elisabetta, if ever I hear you address my son in like manner again, you will be much the worse for it, I swear."

The woman went rigid. "How dare you, you arrogant pretender? You are not the head of this household. My husband, Nastagio, is! And Brother Giorgio, daring to drag him off at dawn today like — like —"

"Nastagio's gone? Where?" Guid'Antonio said.

"San Felice! As if you didn't know." Her

voice broke. "Like some common criminal or dog you wish to destroy. And why? Why? To keep him from speaking the truth about Lorenzo de' Medici and ruining all your dreams of glory. You're Lorenzo's puppet dancing to the devil's strings! Why *wouldn't* the Virgin Mary weep?"

In a flurry of dark skirts, Elisabetta Vespucci swept up the stone staircase after Olimpia and Giovanni, tossing a terrible glance over her shoulder. "Tell Cesare if he continues to thwart me, I'll have his ears sliced off!"

"Welcome home," Guid'Antonio muttered, crossing the garden to the kitchen. "God help me."

"It's true, 'Tonio —"

Amerigo was leaning against the kitchen door frame with his back to the courtyard, talking to his brother and popping glossy red cherries into his mouth as quickly as Domenica Ridolfi washed the fruit and put it into the pottery bowl on the trestle table beside a basket of mushrooms.

"Beneath their French silks and laces, the *mesdemoiselles* were full ripe. Dark pink and luscious, exactly like these cherries. Of course it was up to me to pluck their stems."

Guid'Antonio touched Amerigo's shoulder. *"Buena mattina."*

Amerigo jumped. "Uncle! *Buena mattina.*" A flush of red crept into Amerigo's cheeks.

"Domenica, Antonio," Guid'Antonio said, smiling despite his inner turmoil. The verbal scuffle with Amerigo and Antonio's mother had been unsettling, at best. Domenica, glancing up from the bucket of water in the kitchen sink, smiled back at him, as different from Elisabetta Vespucci as noonday was from midnight.

The wide red sleeve of Antonio's workday gown fell back along his arm in soft folds as he motioned Guid'Antonio to join him at the table. "Good morning, Uncle."

Guid'Antonio pulled out a stool. "Busy day ahead?"

"As always, yes, merchant papers to review. Spaniards. And a few of the Pazzi documents still want authorizing." In the aftermath of the Pazzi Conspiracy, the Republic had appointed Antonio Vespucci trustee of the Pazzi family's property. That seal of approval had established Antonio as a young man on the rise in the Florentine government. Another important Vespucci milestone and proof Lorenzo de' Medici remained convinced of their fealty.

Antonio grinned. "My baby brother has been telling me how hard he worked in

France."

"Long and hard," Amerigo said, smirking.

Domenica snorted. "Here's more the truth, Amerigo: you're having your hands smacked if you snatch any more of *my* cherries. They're fresh from the street, and who would believe any are available, given the poor circumstances in the market?"

Guid'Antonio poured wine into his cup, added a bit of water, and drank, glancing at his nephews. "Your mother tells me Brother Giorgio has taken Nastagio for a visit to the country."

At once the atmosphere turned grim. Antonio said, "At dawn today, yes. After you left the *saletta* last night, we decided a stay at San Felice would benefit my father in the coming days." San Felice, the site of the Vespucci family villa, was near the town of Peretola, beyond the Prato Gate.

"For his health?" Guid'Antonio said.

"For the health of us all. Pray the clearer air of San Felice helps Nastagio regain his senses. Or at least some sense of perspective."

"Perspective?" Amerigo said, his voice challenging. "What could be worse than this forced departure from his home, for it is an exile of sorts."

Guid'Antonio said, "Exile for him is exile

176

for us all. But better a light sentence now than a more severe one farther down the road."

"At what cost?" Amerigo said. "The loss of all our family pride and honor? For surely people will know —"

Antonio cut across him, "Honor, Amerigo? Unless you've forgotten, I'm first in line for an appointment as a full notary in City Hall, at long last, I might add, though my name could be struck from the list at any moment, should we lose our footing by even one inch. You dare speak of pride and honor? You, who only yesterday returned from a two-year adventure in France, thanks to the good men our father would malign." He glanced at Guid'Antonio. "You and Lorenzo the Magnificent, I mean."

Visibly stung by his brother's anger, Amerigo muttered, "It's worrying, all the same."

Antonio snapped, "You're telling me."

So: more bickering and division within the family. Guid'Antonio drew his hand over his mouth, leaning back on the stool, giving Domenica room to place a loaf of bread on the table along with cheese, apples, and pears. He took more wine and passed the jug around. "Antonio. Last night, you said Lorenzo mortgaged some land to fund the trip to Naples. His finances are unstable as that?"

"Unstable?" Antonio laughed dryly. "Uncle, Lorenzo de' Medici's bankrupt."

*"Never,"* Guid'Antonio said.

Amerigo smacked his forehead. "No! If Lorenzo de' Medici's bankrupt, show me the debtor's prison. 'Tonio, you know he's the richest man in Europe."

Domenica placed a pot of honey on the table, fresh from the Vespucci bees at Peretola. "*Was* the richest," she said. " 'Tonio, you hear it in Palazzo della Signoria, our magnificent City Hall, I hear it in the market from fishmongers and salt dealers. *Il Magnifico*'s scraping the bottom of the barrel." She crossed herself. "So say people in the street."

"This wouldn't be the first time they were wrong," Amerigo said.

Antonio's gaze swept toward the kitchen door and the courtyard beyond it. But for Domenica going about her pots and pans, they were alone. He said: "You know, two years ago the Pope seized the assets of the Medici Bank in Rome and all the Medici property he could lay his hands on."

Guid'Antonio nodded. That had been part of the Pope's war strategy and, yes, it had been a personal financial blow to Lorenzo.

With the closing in Rome, other branches of the Medici banking network, most likely the largest in the world, had collapsed. Milan, and even Avignon in France.

"Given we've been at odds with Naples, the office there is on its last legs," Antonio said. "Rumors are flying about Venice. And —"

"Mama," Amerigo said, smacking his forehead again.

"— the money Lorenzo loaned the English king, Edward IV, for his war against his brother, Richard, is a disaster," Antonio said, "since Edward can't pay Lorenzo back. And isn't that a sad commentary, brother against brother? The London branch closed, anyway. The loan to Edward doesn't seem a very smart decision on Lorenzo's part."

Guid'Antonio glanced toward the garden, where the fountain gurgled softly. "You have the gift of hindsight."

Domenica pulled up a stool and with the hem of her apron wiped beads of perspiration from her forehead. "It's those precious gems and manuscripts he collects. I hear he's no businessman, either. Give him the choice of a ledger or hunting bow, and he'll flash a smile and pick up his quiver every time."

"Domenica," Guid'Antonio protested,

remembering Lorenzo's elaborate plans for the farm at Poggio a Caiano. "Antonio. How are *our* accounts? We said we'd take a look at the ledgers sometime today."

His nephew spread his hands. "Do you have time now?"

*No.* He wanted to press forward with the weeping painting. "Of course," he said.

Halfway across the courtyard, Antonio cast him an unhappy glance. "Banks closed are one thing. This next is strictly private."

Amerigo groaned down in his throat. "What?" Guid'Antonio said.

"Lorenzo has been dipping into his cousins' inheritance."

Beside the spraying water fountain, Amerigo came to an abrupt halt. "He's stealing from 'Zino and 'Vanni's estate?"

"Amerigo, go softly," Guid'Antonio said.

And so they walked in silence beneath the warming sun, Amerigo muttering to himself, Guid'Antonio's thoughts in a tumble. He hadn't expected to hear anything like this. Lorenzo, bankrupt. So strapped for cash, he was "dipping," as Antonio so delicately put it, into the fortune due his two young cousins when they came of age. Lorenzino and Giovanni de' Medici were Lorenzo's legal wards, Lorenzo having been appointed their guardian when their father died four years ago. Lorenzino, the elder of the two brothers, must be . . . how old now? Seventeen? Despite the ten-year difference in their ages, Lorenzino de' Medici and Amerigo Vespucci had a close friendship rooted in Brother Giorgio's teachings. Dante, Petrarch, Heraclitus, Ptolemy, science, mathematics.

"You're certain?" Guid'Antonio said.

"As certain as one may be of news received from a trusted friend. It amounts to about one thousand florins to help finance the war with Rome," Antonio said.

"The war, the war, the war," Amerigo muttered to himself.

"Little brother, the money had to come from somewhere, with our government coffers dry as a bone in the desert," Antonio flared.

"Oh? Well, I can't wait to ask 'Zino how he feels about this," Amerigo said.

"You will ask Lorenzino de' Medici *nothing,*" Guid'Antonio snapped, "unless it's how he feels about peace. Antonio, where does this wealth of financial misery leave us?"

"You'll see," Antonio said.

The walls of the *scrittoio* were close and

dim, the sole light provided by a solitary high window and the single door standing open to the courtyard garden. Together they reviewed the parade of accounts Antonio marched before them, Guid'Antonio with a deepening sense of foreboding. In his absence, mercenary soldiers had raided Vespucci farmland. Vespucci cows, pigs, and poultry had been slaughtered or stolen. The families who lived in small stone houses and worked the farms had been left hungry, scared, and sick till Antonio tended their needs. Who had tended the needs of other families? Guid'Antonio wondered. In some cases no one, given the poverty he had witnessed in Florence since arriving home yesterday morning.

"All our domestic accounts balance as they should," Antonio said, his profile dark under the fall of his chestnut hair. "Food, clothing, repairs, servants. We're not yet in financial trouble, but we must spend wisely here on out, should there be any future emergency."

Say, for example, if they were run out of the city by what seemed to be a growing legion of malcontents. "I see," Guid'Antonio said, noting the dark smudges beneath his nephew's eyes. The war — bearing its weight all alone — had taken a hard toll on

Antonio di Nastagio Vespucci. It had taken a hard toll on everyone. That was why they all should be grateful that, thanks to Lorenzo, the fighting had at last come to an end.

Guid'Antonio strode to the doorway, sweat trickling down his ribs. In the garden, the sun pounded the grass and Domenica's herbs, basil, parsley, rosemary. Spraying water sparkled in the fountain.

Antonio fanned his robe. "The good news is that England and France wanted our wool and wine even during the war."

Guid'Antonio thought how his law practice had suffered during his absence. Too, there were his ambassadorial expenses. Travel, gifts. Who knew when the Republic could afford to reimburse him for those items, let alone pay his *per diem*? Lorenzo dipping into his nephews' money. He said, "I agree we must keep a sharp eye on our expenditures. It seems even we don't have bottomless purses."

Antonio and Amerigo closed the ledgers and locked them in the appropriate chests. "Numbers make me hungry," Amerigo said. "Shall we —"

"No," Antonio said. "Uncle, I assume you have agreed to help Lorenzo with our current crisis." The *Virgin Mary of Santa Maria*

183

*Impruneta* weeping in their church, a missing girl, Turks.

"I have."

"Then you must ride into battle fully armed." Antonio pulled the office door shut, casting them in almost total darkness.

This was not going to be good. Guid'Antonio waited in silence. Amerigo said, "Oh, no."

"How much do you know about Piero?" Their jailed kinsman, Piero Vespucci, Antonio meant.

Anger quickened Guid'Antonio's voice when he said, "He has dragged the family with him into the Stinche." He did not mention his walk past the prison last night, nor the person who had dogged him, either.

Antonio moistened his lips. "Piero and his daughter Genevra have been writing Lorenzo and his mother begging letters."

Amerigo's mouth dropped open. *"Mon Dieu."*

For the first instant, Guid'Antonio thought surely he had misheard. "Begging for what?" he said.

"For Piero's release from the Stinche."

"Why not just throw us from the windows of Palazzo della Signoria now and have it done with?" Amerigo said.

"How do you know?" Guid'Antonio said.

184

"Chancellor Scala showed me the letters. Lorenzo and his mother turned them over to City Hall. Given the Republic's acceptance of Lorenzo as first citizen of the city, the letters are considered State property."

A wave of shame engulfed Guid'Antonio. Yesterday at Palazzo della Signoria, everyone had known about this but him. Forget paintings — *he* wanted to weep. Chancellor Bartolomeo Scala, Chairman Tommaso Soderini, Lord Prior Pierfilippo Pandolfini . . . not to mention Lorenzo, when they spoke in Via Larga.

He masked his agitation, aware of Amerigo and Antonio's sharp scrutiny. Determined to just place one foot in front of the other, moment by moment. "What do the letters say?"

"Our Genevra writes to Lorenzo of her father's failing health and of the cruel irons on his feet, while Piero addresses himself directly to Lucrezia Tornabuoni de' Medici."

"Lorenzo's mother," Amerigo said. "Jesus. What a coward Piero is. What a fool!"

"Claiming neither he nor his son Marco would ever have harmed a hair on Giuliano de'Medici's head. Nor would they have given asylum to Napoleone Francesi, or anyone else who did."

"There are a damned lot of innocents about who wished Giuliano no harm," Amerigo said.

Antonio flashed his brother a quelling glance. "Piero has assured Lorenzo's mother he and Marco always bore Giuliano the greatest affection."

Amerigo chuckled. "With Giuliano screwing Marco's wife and everyone in Florence privy to it? I doubt Marco's generosity went that far. Maybe we should have Piero poisoned."

"Amerigo, that's enough!" Guid'Antonio said. "There's danger all around. Antonio, how stands the matter now?" Probing and already thinking ahead.

"In the Stinche our kinsman is, and in the Stinche he shall remain. Until, as Chancellor Scala believes, Lorenzo decides to have him released."

*Until,* Guid'Antonio thought, *Lorenzo is again fully convinced of the Vespucci family's loyalty to his house.*

Outside in the garden, they stood together in the sun's dazzling presence, shading their eyes and blinking. "I don't think we deserve this aggravation," Amerigo said. "What's next? A plague of locusts to cast a deeper shadow over our family?"

Guid'Antonio regarded his other nephew. " 'Tonio, Maria's house is in poor repair. Tell Cesare to have our gardeners go there and see to the herbs, at least. But first some workmen to clean up the place. I meant to speak with Cesare myself, but I've other business at hand."

"I'll see it's done," Antonio said, hurrying to the gate. "Uncle Guid'Antonio, I have complete faith our fortunes will improve in every direction, now you're here. Not just for us, but for all Florence."

Cesare, now 'Tonio. Guid'Antonio sighed, slightly smiling. "Tell me — have we dealings with a fellow named Castruccio Senso? The wine merchant who's the husband of —"

"The missing girl, Camilla Rossi da Vinci. Yes. Or we did," Antonio said. "We broke with him over padded invoices late last year. Short, tubby, a sparse thatch of mousy brown hair."

And he was married to a girl Lorenzo considered pretty as a poppy. "One thing more. Last Wednesday when the painting first wept — was it raining?"

"No, we had fair weather till you arrived home yesterday evening. Then it poured buckets."

"Ha! No surprise there," Guid'Antonio said.

Amerigo watched his brother hurry down the street. "After all this, shall we go by *Il Leone Rosso* and fortify ourselves with some wine and sausage?"

"No. Time to cut the coat according to the cloth. Past time, in fact. I want to speak with Sandro Botticelli."

# ELEVEN

Guid'Antonio's nose prickled: pine and poplar wood, linseed oil, flour paste and glue made from the clippings of goats' muzzles, feet, sinews, and skin. Wooden shutters attached to a window looking upon the alley stood propped open. In the small bit of gray light thus provided, there loomed the faceless figure of a man attired in a loose white robe. Amerigo jumped back. "Uncle! What is *that*?"

"A wooden mannequin. For Sandro's apprentices to work by."

"It startled me."

"Obviously."

Two boys sat before the white-clad figure. One boy leaned forward, his hair a thick shadow across his cheek as he watched the other lad practice the drawing of clothing with all its difficult tricks. Both youths glanced up, smiling. The two men standing before them were potential customers,

189

wealthy, most like, given their elegant bearing and fine clothing, come to commission something from the master. Good!

A boy of about ten sat apart, gilding a picture frame with paint the same bright color as his own golden tangle of curls. *"Giorno,"* Guid'Antonio said. "Is your master home?"

*"Sì."* Turning halfway round on his stool, the boy gestured toward the rear of the shop, where a man in a loose cotton shirt sat bent over a pen-and-ink sketch with his hosed feet locked around the legs of his stool. Sandro Botticelli's hair, a rich, ginger-gold color, brushed his nape. On the floor beside his scuffed ankle boots lay a wide leather belt, cast off for comfort.

The artisan at work.

Sandro looked up, scowling. Recognition came quickly: Guid'Antonio and Amerigo Vespucci. He drew back a bit. Slowly, the color drained from his face. Brushing at his tunic, he moved toward them with what Guid'Antonio could only call trepidation.

"You've seen your new Saint Augustine," Sandro said in a flat tone.

"No. Or at least not clearly." Guid'Antonio cocked his head. "Why do you mention it?"

Sandro hesitated. "I thought perhaps you had noticed my —" He smiled, waving his fingers lightly in the air. "It's nothing, believe me. But now you're here."

Questions chased through Guid'Antonio's mind. Nothing? Why was Sandro Botticelli so nervous about their presence in his workshop? They had been close neighbors and acquaintances for years. "How are you, Alessandro?" he said, beginning again.

"Fine, today. Tomorrow's another set of sleeves." Sandro poured wine into three cups. "The Unicorn district's alive with news of your arrival. As is all Florence, I expect. After such a lengthy absence."

Amerigo grunted. "Have people mentioned the devil's on our tail?"

"When's Florence ever quiet?"

"Never in my time," Guid'Antonio said. "Is your family well?"

"Everyone except Mariano. My father's ill."

"Mine, too," Amerigo said. "So much so, he's gone to take the air in San Felice." A bitter smile touched Amerigo's lips. "So as not to infect the entire family."

"May God preserve him," Sandro said, crossing himself.

But the shrewd look in Sandro's amber-colored eyes told Guid'Antonio the painter knew all about Nastagio Vespucci's forced exodus to the countryside early this morn-

191

ing. No doubt the entire Santa Maria Novella quarter — all Florence — knew and knew why, too, just as they knew why Piero Vespucci was chained in the bowels of the Stinche.

Guid'Antonio said, "Sandro, you've been in Ognissanti these last few months. Have you noticed any unusual activity there?"

Sandro fixed him with a wide golden stare. "For a time the *Virgin Mary of Santa Maria Impruneta* was weeping. I'm pleased to say she's not one of mine."

Amerigo started to laugh, but sobered, coughing into his fist, when he caught Guid'Antonio's disapproving glance. "When did the tears begin?" Guid'Antonio said.

"A week ago tomorrow in the late afternoon."

Today was Tuesday. "So last Wednesday, then." This seemed to be the truth of it, since several people had given him the same information.

"Yes."

"You remember well."

"Who wouldn't?"

"Who saw them first?" Guid'Antonio said.

"A young boy — it's always children, isn't it? The truly innocent — spied them. In the next instant, people filled the church, praying and beating their breasts." Sandro's eyes flickered, but he stopped there.

"Did you see them?"

"Of course. When I heard the commotion, I flew to Ognissanti."

"You weren't already there working?"

Sandro shook his head. "I had an embroidery design for an altar cloth promised, and —"

"Straight around the corner to the church," Guid'Antonio said.

"Yes."

"What did they look like?"

Sandro gave a quick shrug and a frown. "I've little to add to the official statement I gave Palla Palmieri when he came around asking these same questions."

Guid'Antonio's eyes narrowed. Palla had been to Botticelli and Company? Florence's chief law officer, investigating a religious matter? But then, Guid'Antonio supposed there was good reason for this, given the tears had been turned against Lorenzo. "Palla quizzed you," he said.

"He did." Sandro glanced impatiently toward the drawings on his pine worktable. "He said, 'Yes, no, yes, no,' then was gone like a brisk breeze down the alley in that catlike way of his."

"What did you tell him they looked like?" Guid'Antonio said.

193

Sandro drew a long breath, apparently in lieu of gritting his teeth. "Like tears, Messer Guid'Antonio. Wet and glistening in the glow of countless votives. Amid the uproar, joy and grace reigned in Ognissanti that day."

"Or mass confusion," Amerigo said.

"When did Camilla Rossi da Vinci disappear?" Guid'Antonio said.

"The girl? Eleven days ago, on the first day of the month," Sandro said.

"That's precise."

"Yes."

"*Before* the painting wept," Guid'Antonio said.

"By several days. So what?" Sandro said.

"How did Camilla's disappearance come to be at the hands of Turks?" Beside Guid'Antonio, Amerigo stirred restlessly. This was plowed ground.

"Her old nurse witnessed the attack," Sandro said.

The old woman again. This matched Luca Landucci's version of events surrounding the missing girl and Lorenzo's version, as well. "And people believe the nurse because?"

Sandro threw up his hands. "What reason has she to lie?"

"Money," Amerigo said. "A bribe to mask

194

whatever truly happened."

"That's what I'd like to know," Guid'Antonio said.

"Why do you dismiss the Turks so lightly?" Sandro said. "You know their history."

"I don't dismiss them, except when people bring them to our door. Thank you for the wine, Alessandro."

"Anytime," Sandro said instead of: "What in hell are you really doing here?"

Guid'Antonio smiled. He had interrogated Sandro about the tears, and Sandro had answered as best he could.

"You seem weary," Sandro said, following them to the door.

"So do you," Guid'Antonio said. Outside, he glanced up and down the street. Toward his right, a monk hurried toward Piazza Santa Maria Novella past walls so close, the folds of the man's brown robe brushed the stones on either side.

*"Uno momento, per favore, Messer Guid'Antonio."*

Guid'Antonio whirled. "Yes?"

"Necessity drags me places my pride would rather not go. I would sell my soul to work in the Pope's new chapel in Rome. You were there before going to France. Do you know whether the Holy Father plans to move forward and decorate the walls without us while the interdict is ongoing?"

*Us.* Florence's most celebrated painters: Sandro Botticelli, Domenico Ghirlandaio, the brothers Piero and Antonio Pollaiuolo, Cosimo Rosselli, and the up-and-coming Leonardo da Vinci.

Guid'Antonio regarded Sandro thoughtfully. Sixtus IV had begun building the chapel beside the Vatican seven years ago, in 1473. Now, although the cavernous building was finished, its long inner walls remained blank, because how could the painted decorations go forward without Florence's master craftsmen there to give them places, people, faces? Unthinkable. Although not impossible, given Sixtus's monumental impatience and his determination to make a point with the interdict no matter how his new chapel suffered.

"I have no idea what Sixtus means to do," Guid'Antonio said. "You're right, though, I was in Rome two years ago. And saw the chapel before leaving."

"Christ's wounds." Sandro's hand touched his breast. "You saw the blank walls?"

"I did." In May 1478, mere weeks after Giuliano's assassination, Guid'Antonio had rushed to Rome along with ambassadors from France, Venice, and Milan, anxious to dissuade Sixtus from waging war with Florence and Lorenzo. While Guid'Antonio was there, Bartolomeo Sacchi, the Pope's Vatican librarian, had led the Pope's foreign visitors on a chapel tour, past a temporary curtain and on inside the building. There the men had skirted scaffolding and wheelbarrows, tools, and all manner of debris as Sacchi showed them the dizzyingly high vaulted ceiling — almost seventy feet up — the windows, and the soldiers' quarters above the vault: plainly, Pope Sixtus IV meant the chapel for defense as well as for housing cardinals during conclaves to elect his successors. The building had teemed with laborers, carpenters and brick masons, hammers banging, trowels slapping while rude jokes flew and the builder shouted orders and shook plaster dust from his flyaway, wild black hair.

Guid'Antonio told Sandro this, but not how uncomfortably enclosed the chapel made him feel. As if he were in a tomb. Trapped, like the little sparrow desperately flapping its wings in Ognissanti yesterday evening. His mission to Rome had been short-lived: plainly, Sixtus IV and Girolamo Riario were bent on continuing their pursuit of Lorenzo.

And so after four months, Guid'Antonio had departed the Eternal City, turning his back on the crumbling old Coliseum and the broken Greek and Roman statues and urns jutting up from the surrounding fields. Eventually, the scaffolding had been removed from the chapel some people were calling the Sistine, after Sixtus, who had commissioned it, but the inner walls remained as blank today as they had been the afternoon the laborers packed up their tools and walked to the nearest tavern for wine and bowls of stewed oxtail soup.

"Only the devil Girolamo Riario is privy to the Holy Father's thoughts on the chapel or any other score," Guid'Antonio said, standing in Sandro's workshop doorway.

The artist gestured with his hand, hit the top of the stone door frame, and swore. The raven scavenging for crumbs in the alley cawed, flying up between the sides of the buildings, toward freedom and the full light of day. "I may as well forget going to Rome and throw myself in the Arno! Who knows how long Girolamo Riario will set his uncle against us?"

Guid'Antonio grunted. He wanted the Florentines at work in the Pope's chapel as much as any other man. After all, the place was for the ages. "Don't jump yet, Sandro. Sixtus has spent far too much time, effort, and money to settle for anything less than the best."

"And if he's spent all his patience, too? He'll have the walls done soon, yet we still have this . . . this other wall standing like a mountain between us and the Vatican."

Guid'Antonio gazed steadily at Sandro's frowning face. "A lot of people have suffered."

"Don't tell me. I know!" Sandro jerked his thumb back toward the shop. "Lest something changes soon, we'll all be eating stone soup."

Lorenzo and the war. Lorenzo and the Pope. Pope Sixtus IV held a treasure trove of high cards, even the chapel in Rome. No Tuscan craftsmen would be called there while the Pope battled Florence. Not before Lorenzo rode south and apologized for his — what? Insolence? More for his very presence on God's soil. And the only way *that* was going to happen was over Guid'Antonio's dead body, stone soup, or no.

Sandro drew air into his chest. "In the meanwhile, thank God for the new contract I've signed with Brother Giorgio."

Guid'Antonio glanced at Amerigo, whose eyes immediately locked on the alley's swath of narrow damp ground. "What new contract?" he said.

Amerigo scratched his cheek as if he had

never experienced such an itch. "Likely, he means the portrait Uncle Giorgio recently commissioned."

"Of whom?" Guid'Antonio said.

"Me." Amerigo rocked back on the heels of his boots, grimacing. "It wasn't my idea."

"That and a Saint George for Ognissanti," Sandro intervened. "The latter to honor Brother Giorgio himself."

Guid'Antonio arched a black, silver-laced eyebrow. "I see." Perhaps he should show Brother Giorgio the family account books and teach him the mathematical Rule of Three.

Sandro glanced back and forth between uncle and nephew. His gaze landed solidly on Guid'Antonio, his jaw set in a hard line, his eyes puckered at the corners. "You don't mean to cancel, surely."

"Certainly not. We need another portrait of Amerigo." What was promised was done. But in the back of his mind, Guid'Antonio wondered how much commission Giorgio Vespucci had agreed to pay Sandro Botticelli. Inwardly, he sighed. Whatever Sandro's price, the frame for the portrait would cost more.

"*Bene!* Good!" Sandro said.

"Why did you think we might cancel?" Guid'Antonio said.

Sandro laughed sourly. "War? Pestilence? Triple taxes? Even the greatest families are feeling the squeeze. My light purse aside, I'm more fortunate than many other craftsmen. Even during the war young Lorenzino de' Medici commissioned a large panel painting from me."

*Friend,* Guid'Antonio thought, *I hope Lorenzino has paid you for it.* He kept his eyes off Amerigo, knowing well he wasn't the only one thinking about Lorenzo's raid on his wards' accounts.

Sandro smiled grandly. "Lorenzo, Marsilio Ficino, Angelo Poliziano — everyone had a say in the painting. It's a meadow in spring, a pretty piece, if I say so myself. This was before Angelo fled to Mantua."

"Angelo fled?" Angelo Poliziano was a member of the Medici household and had been for many years. He was a well-known writer, teacher to the Medici children, and Lorenzo's close personal friend. And yet Guid'Antonio remembered Angelo's letter to Lorenzo abandoned on Lorenzo's desk, unread, the wax seal intact. Interesting, this bit.

"Oh, yes," Sandro said, all radiance and good humor now the issue of Amerigo's portrait was tucked away. "He had a terrible fight with Lorenzo. Lorenzo striding

201

off from him in that cool, easy manner, Angelo running after him along the street."

Sandro leaned out into the alley and lowered his voice, although the ruddy-cheeked little girl who had come out from a nearby doorway to bounce a ball in the dirt alley was their only company. "All this, mind you, after Lorenzo had called him a coward in front of the Duomo."

Amerigo stared. "Good God, why?"

"Because Angelo wouldn't go with him to Naples."

"And Angelo didn't draw his blade?"

"Against Lorenzo?" A sharp burst of laughter escaped Sandro's lips. "No, Amerigo, he did not. And, anyway, Lorenzo was right. Angelo Poliziano is a coward."

Irritated, Amerigo said, "Angelo Poliziano is a renowned poet and teacher."

Guid'Antonio gave the painter a hard look. "And angry enough, perhaps, to eventually strike back?"

Sandro relaxed against the door frame, beneath the blue and white workshop sign inscribed *Botticelli & Co.* On the sign was Sandro's painting of Saint Luke, the patron saint of butchers, surgeons, and artists. "Angry and humiliated, too. Their performance made as lively a spectacle as any penned by Lorenzo, if you can imagine it. It was actually quite terrible." Sandro sighed deeply. "I don't doubt Angelo regrets his actions. He loves *Il Magnifico* as both his friend and his livelihood. In spite of everything, we all do."

Guid'Antonio considered this new information. Love made foolish in a public place. Tender feelings bruised — no, *crushed* beneath Lorenzo de' Medici's boots. "What caused the trouble between them?" he asked. "Initially."

"As I say, it began when Lorenzo asked Angelo to accompany him to Naples. In perhaps the first foolish move of his career, our illustrious but hungry poet dared hesitate. After that, Lorenzo wouldn't have him at any price."

"Not smart," Amerigo said. "Had Angelo gone, he could have seen Mount Vesuvius. He could have climbed to the rim and looked out over the Bay of Naples. He could have sailed out from the city and looked west toward Portugal and Spain. He —"

"Sandro," Guid'Antonio said. "One more thing."

Sandro had been about to turn back to the shop. "Yes?"

"Did you ever see the painting begin to weep? The Virgin's painted eyes were dry as sand, and as you stood watching, tears coursed down her cheeks?"

Sandro shook his head. "No. That's not to say I didn't approach the altar from time to time, hoping — well, who knows? When the sanctuary was otherwise empty. Ah, well. Benedetto!" He turned to the golden-haired boy bent over the gilded picture frame. "Leave that. The sun's high overhead. Every crumb in the market will have been sold or stolen by now. Take a few —" He gave Guid'Antonio a meaningful look. "A *very* few coins from my purse and buy bread and cheese for later."

Benedetto's brows shot up. "Yes, Master!"

"And be quick about it. No stopping to gossip."

But Benedetto the Chosen was already past the other two apprentices and laughing as he flew clear of his teacher and the Vespuccis and on down the alley with wings on his feet. Sandro offered his visitors an exaggerated sigh. "Might as well say to a Florentine, 'Don't breathe.' "

"He's hiding something," Amerigo said as they walked down the alley toward Piazza Santa Maria Novella.

"Obviously, Nephew."

"Have you any notion what it is?"

"Not the slightest," Guid'Antonio said.

# Twelve

"Lorenzo de' Medici, a 'mountain'? What in God's name was Sandro thinking? He might as well have called Lorenzo a hindrance to the Republic, then marched to the Bargello and slammed his head on the block for the executioner's axe."

"For God's sake, keep quiet," Guid'Antonio snapped.

Voices bounced and echoed sharply along Florence's high old walls, where ears were plentiful and ready to listen. "Sandro threw caution to the wind. That doesn't mean you should do the same, lest like your father you wind up in San Felice or, like Piero, in the Stinche staring at rats."

Amerigo glanced away, smarting and tight-lipped. Not often was he so rebuffed.

Guid'Antonio touched his arm. "I only want the best for you. For us all." No reply. "Actually, I'm glad Sandro spoke up regarding Lorenzo. Now I know we're on a slippery slope, indeed."

Amerigo slid a glance toward him. "Did you ever doubt it?"

"Sandro sees the opportunity of a lifetime impeded," Guid'Antonio said by way of answer. "And he's worried about keeping food on his table." How much worse for Florence's *popolo minuto,* the Florentine poor engaged in menial trades outside the guilds: shearers and menders dependent on the cloth trade, peddlers, messengers, prostitutes, and pimps who lived hand to mouth and whose stomachs suffered most in times of plague, famine, and war.

"Sandro wants a miracle," Amerigo said.

"Who doesn't?" It bothered Guid'Antonio that everyone he encountered bore Lorenzo a grudge — some with good reason, too.

The strong sun beating down on Piazza Santa Maria Novella started them blinking. On their left, Santa Maria Novella Church rose up imposingly, its inlaid green and white marble face resplendent in the white-hot light pounding down on its walls. Clean, elegant, uncomplicated. How very unlike Guid'Antonio's own life.

In the church square, a gang of boys played *calcio,* yelling and kicking up dust and bits of stone with their bare brown feet as they scrambled for the football. Around their tanned faces, their damp hair flew; sweat streamed in rivulets down their burning cheeks. Guid'Antonio and Amerigo shaded their eyes just in time to see the ball hurtle toward them.

"Watch out!" Amerigo shouted. Gracefully, he lifted his arms and hit the ball back with such swift force it shot beneath the rumpled skirts of the Dominican friar holding forth before a smattering of dazzled students at the church door.

The friar jumped back, his mouth a tiny round "o" as his gaze traveled threateningly around the busy square.

"Oops." Amerigo ducked behind Guid'Antonio.

"Come on." Guid'Antonio cut into the nearest street. In an instant, ochre walls pressed in on them, and the atmosphere dimmed.

"These religious are everywhere," Amerigo observed over the sound of their boots striking the cobblestones. "God's nails, Uncle, do you have any notion where we are?"

Guid'Antonio smiled. "Only vaguely."

Turned around in the city of his birth — how deflating was that? He felt immeasurably fatigued, although the day was not much past its infancy. It was still quite young, in fact, almost intolerably hot, and in this narrow lane, horribly smelly. He dodged a bony canine gnawing a bone mottled with spoiled scraps of flesh, thought fleetingly of the mastiff Alessandro Braccesi had brained with a stray rock, and combed his hands back through his hair.

Overcrowded and blazingly hot, the market and stone loggia alongside the church of Saint Michael in the Garden, Orsanmichele, teemed with livestock and humanity.

"Uncle," Amerigo said, his tone subdued. He indicated the corpse hanging from a scaffold at one edge of the market, a man, judging from the remnants of his clothing, his eyes plucked out by scavenging crows.

"Christ." Guid'Antonio covered his mouth. Add rotting human flesh to the catalogue of foul odors. A hanging? Say what you would about crime and punishment in Florence, the death sentence was rare, except when applied to repeat criminals, immigrants, usually, men who came from the countryside into town to rob the poor of their meager income. Usually, too, hangings occurred at the gallows near the Gate of Justice, just outside Florence's eastern walls, not in one of the city's market-places.

He swerved past two men crouched on their knees, casting dice in the dirt, despising the nearness of all this flesh pressed close together in one place, so he could barely breathe.

"Wretched bastard!" Amerigo whipped around, cursing the old man who stepped down hard on his heel. A vagrant, judging from the sack of holes he carried over his back. "Get away from me! Next time, I'll throttle you!"

"To hell with you, you Medici bootlicker!" the man shouted back. In an instant he vanished, swallowed up by the swarming crowd.

"Amerigo, go easy." Guid'Antonio saw fear and hatred in the eyes surrounding them. He jostled past the roughly clothed peddlers and farmers haggling with cooks who pinched their noses before peeking cautiously into ratty rush baskets. Ahead of him and Amerigo lay a sea of mangy horses, donkey carts, and wagons with sagging wheels. Behind them stood the wealthy shops of silk makers, furniture makers, and silversmiths, where no common wool carder or shearer had ever set foot.

At the arched loggia buzzing with money

changers, tables topped with the bright green cloths of the changers' trade clogged the columned arcade and spilled out into the piazza. Guid'Antonio and Amerigo pressed in beneath the vaulted roof, Amerigo fanning his face and puffing out his cheeks as they joined the line at the nearest table. "At least in here it's shady."

The fellow standing behind them chuckled. "Doubly so, if you include the thieves manning the tables."

Guid'Antonio turned slightly toward him. The fellow wore his hair brushed back from his long, narrow face, and he was freshly shaved, judging from the nicks and cuts along his jaws and chin. He was decently clothed and appeared to be in his middle thirties. Guid'Antonio acknowledged him with a slight nod, smiled down at the boy holding his hand, and left it at that.

The line crawled. Guid'Antonio, shifting restlessly from foot to foot, glanced toward the church of Orsanmichele, his mind traveling inside the multistoried walls to Michelozzo's tabernacle covered in cherubs and encrusted with colored marble, lapis lazuli, gold, and stained glass. All this to house Bernardo Daddi's altar painting of the miraculous Virgin Mary who showed worshippers the path to salvation through personal intercession. Yes. Just ask them — they could offer proof.

Florence was married to miracles, and yet Guid'Antonio meant to expose the latest one as a trick played on the people by mortal men to cast a shadow over Lorenzo de' Medici and his supporters. Within himself, Guid'Antonio groaned. He had bungled investigations before, but this time he must not lose. The stakes were too high. On his shoulders he carried the future of his family, his friends, and the Florentine Republic.

Reining in his impatience — why was he always in the slow line? — he glanced at the gabled niches carved along Orsanmichele's near wall. In each niche (and there were more than a dozen around the church) there stood a marble statue of the patron saint of one of the city's major guilds, touchable, solid, and strong: Nanni di Banco's *Saint Eligius* for the smiths and farriers, Donatello's *Saint Mark* for the linen drapers and used-clothes dealers, Lorenzo Ghiberti's *Saint John the Baptist* for the cloth importers, along with his *Saint Matthew* for the bankers.

*Bankers.* Guid'Antonio turned to the rates posted above the money tables. The grain prices listed on the boards were as disgraceful as the exchange rates. Beside him, Amerigo whispered, "These rates are *pazzo,* crazy! Peas, five lire a bushel and corn, fiftynine soldi? How can people afford to eat?"

"We keep hearing they cannot," Guid'Antonio said, stepping up a pace.

"It's because of the famine," the man behind him said.

"Excuse me?" Guid'Antonio turned back to him.

"The high prices," the man said. "The situation won't change as long as goods are being imported. Naturally, City Hall has been providing grain to those most severely affected by the war. Anything to keep the rabble satiated."

An ancient beggar, flesh and clothing draping off his bones, shifted silently past them, his shoulder brushing Amerigo's. "What, again?" Amerigo cried. The beggar held up his hands in self-defense. Shoulders hunched, he crossed himself and scuttled away.

"I've had enough of this," Amerigo said, starting after him.

"Let it go," Guid'Antonio said.

"You'd best check your purse," their companion said. "These vermin have nimble fingers."

"Not nimble enough to manufacture coins

212

that aren't there," Amerigo fussed, brushing imagined lice from his breast. "I don't like being tried."

"If not your coins, then your undergarments," the man said.

"Father —" The black-eyed boy gripping the man's hand gazed intently up at him. "Maybe the beggar was hungry."

*"Maybe what?"* the boy's father said, his tone so forceful many people in the loggia turned to stare. The child, his arm yanked sharply enough to lift him up off his feet, gasped. His thin face twisted in pain.

"Haven't I warned you to keep quiet until you are addressed?"

Guid'Antonio considered telling the fellow he might well apply the same standard to his own behavior. Instead: "Have I had the pleasure?" he asked.

If the man had been wearing a cap, he would have doffed it. With a grand air, bowing with a flourish, he introduced himself as Ser Lodovico Buonarroti Simoni. The boy, just about five years old, like Guid'Antonio's son, Giovanni, was Buonarroti's second oldest boy. The child's name? Michelangelo Buonarroti. And, yes, Ser Buonarroti knew Messer Guid'Antonio Vespucci, but only by appearance and reputation, much to his sorrow. The Buonarroti family lived in the

213

Santa Croce quarter of Florence, near Guid'Antonio's mother-in-law, Alessandra del Vigna. In Florence — in all Tuscany, surely! — everyone recognized the famous ambassador-jurist Guid'Antonio Vespucci and his faithful nephew, Amerigo.

"Faithful nephew?" Amerigo growled deep in his throat. As for Ser Buonarroti, he was a Medici man by preference and a notary by profession, as well as the former governor of Caprese and Chiusi, two towns east of Florence.

"And an insufferable bastard, too," Guid'Antonio said *sotto voce* to Amerigo, who looked away, grinning.

Buonarroti's attention had returned to his son. " 'Maybe the beggar was hungry,' " he mimicked in a high, child's voice. "As if that concerns men like us!" Buonarroti rolled his eyes. "My son was nursed in the country by common stock, Messer Vespucci, in the fat shape of a stonemason's wife, so I reap what I have sown. Still, what do you do when a babe's mother is frail and her milk dries up? For all that, the boy's sharp enough. At age seven, his brother Lionardo seems good for the Church. This one I'll see made into a successful money changer in the tradition of his great-grandfather. Or into a notary, like me."

Michelangelo's dark eyes stared up at his father, drinking him in. With each piercing word shooting from the man's mouth, the boy's expression turned ever more inward, although for a moment, Guid'Antonio thought he might pipe up again. Instead, the child set his shoulders resolutely and turned his gaze into the distance, as if he saw a larger battle looming, and he was fully armed.

"Uncle Guid'Antonio." Amerigo motioned with his head. "Do you know the bearded ruffian barreling toward us? His gaze is hard upon you."

Brown-skinned, with the sour smell of grapes about his loose clothing, the crab-like fellow pushed through the market, watching Guid'Antonio sideways. His black eyes glittered, the contempt in them a hateful, burning flame.

"I've never seen him before." Guid'Antonio held the man's stare until a jolt flashed between them with such hard force, Guid'Antonio's body stiffened, and he stumbled back.

"Uncle Guid'Antonio?"

"No, no. I'm all right."

Grinning wickedly, the other man glanced away, his stride sure and unbroken. At the purple-and-white canopied wine tent just

215

beyond the loggia, he stopped and leaned menacingly toward the merchant sitting on a stool behind the hinged counter.

A feeling of alarm stole over Guid'Antonio. What had just happened between him and that odd fellow? In those small black eyes, he had glimpsed a hateful challenge.

"Not many thieves are stupid as yon cockroach hanged here last week," Lodovico Buonarroti said.

Guid'Antonio dragged his attention from the wine tent. "Do you know the hanged man's offence?"

"He robbed a coin from one of the banking tables. The fool."

"And was hanged for it? Usually branding or whipping's the strongest penalty for a petty crime."

"Not these days. The Signoria has shown more muscle as of late, all to the good, I say. No man should be allowed to rob another and escape with a tap on the wrist."

Ser Buonarroti chuckled with satisfaction, and Guid'Antonio gave silent thanks he and Amerigo were next up in the line. But Buonarroti had not finished. Leaning around them, he taunted the cashier, "Just like you're about to rob us."

"If you don't like it," the cashier said, thumbing over his shoulder toward the hard-muscled guards armed with axes posted around the loggia, "I suggest you take it up with them."

Buonarroti shrank back into his place. Guid'Antonio loosened the leather strings of his scrip. Whatever the exchange rate today, the traveler's vouchers in his purse had gone a long way in keeping him and his nephew safe from thieves as they rode home the past three weeks. Hmmm. Here was something else he wanted to know: had Camilla Rossi da Vinci been carrying coins or checks, and were any jewels missing from her goods?

*"Robber! Thief!"*

Guid'Antonio spun around. At the wine tent, the stranger who had bedeviled him shouted, *"Bastardo!* You know my grapes are worth twice that amount!"

In the loggia, the buzz of conversation halted.

"If you don't like our projected prices, Jacopo, come back in October during the harvest," the wine merchant suggested civilly. "At the moment, there's nothing —"

Jacopo spat a wad of phlegm that hit its mark straight in the vendor's ruddy face.

The crowd gasped. One of the guardsmen took a step forward, grinning and fondling his axe. At the wine tent, Jacopo shouted,

"Keep your blood money, you thieving Turk!" Turning quickly around, he shoved a path through the gathering. "I'll sell my grapes to Satan before I sell them to you!"

"To Lorenzo, you mean!" someone yelled. "He won't pay you fairly, either!"

*So, the man's a winegrower,* Guid'Antonio thought, watching the malcontent shove back through the crowd. He placed his signature on a check. "Ser Buonarroti," he said as he counted the coins the banker pushed back across the table, "who was that hothead? You know, surely."

"Doesn't everyone? Oh!" Light dawned for Buonarroti. "You've been gone. That was Jacopo Rossi da Vinci, a naturally ill-tempered man, and then his daughter's been kidnapped and ravished by Turks, may the weeping Virgin take pity on her soul," Buonarroti said.

Guid'Antonio shouted, "Amerigo!"

Amerigo shot from the loggia and pushed through the throng. "Here you, halt!"

A farmer led his donkey cart directly into Amerigo's path. Casting a smirk back at Guid'Antonio, Jacopo Rossi da Vinci melted into the milling crowd. Amerigo gave chase for another few moments before returning to the table, crimson-faced. He bent down with his hands on his knees, gasping. "Lost him."

"By now he's halfway to the Prato Gate and on his way home to Vinci. Damn!" Guid'Antonio swore. According to Lorenzo, Palla Palmieri had questioned Camilla's father; but hearing firsthand the winegrower's version of events surrounding Camilla's disappearance appealed to him. To the list of people to be questioned add Jacopo Rossi da Vinci.

He glanced down at little Michelangelo, who was standing quietly beside his father. Quietly, but God, those defiant eyes! Guid'Antonio held the child's dark liquid gaze and smiled. In return he received the whisper of a grin hinting at kinship and recognition.

"Come, Amerigo." Guid'Antonio strode from the loggia, thinking he would give a small fortune to know that child's mind. Deep in those shadowed eyes, he had seen his own son's measuring gaze, and he had felt a ray of hope.

# THIRTEEN

*"Que bella!"* Amerigo kissed his fingertips. "Have you ever seen anything quite so lovely?"

Guid'Antonio cast a glance around the close piazzetta pungent with the smell of dung and overripe fruit, expecting to glimpse the ankle of some pretty maiden. "Where?"

Amerigo pointed to the bakery cart parked near a shady building. "Big fresh buns." He clapped Guid'Antonio soundly on the arm. "Topped with sugar, maybe."

"Sugar?" Guid'Antonio peered at the cart, whose owner beckoned them with both hands, eyes squinting with shifty hope, daring any dogs, beggars, or ragged children to try and steal a crumb of the bread from his cart, sugared or otherwise.

"Best pray, Amerigo. Surely such a precious commodity as sugar is in short supply."

"Do you want anything?" Amerigo said, already halfway across the piazza, light on his feet.

Guid'Antonio drew a shivery breath. "Nothing that baker's selling."

Amerigo returned bearing what Guid'Antonio assumed was first prize on the baker's rack: a bun sprinkled with cinnamon and oozing pure golden honey. "Amazing," Guid'Antonio said.

Amerigo thanked heaven with an airy gesture. He had purchased two buns, in fact. "No sugar, but sweet and good." They started walking again.

"Cinnamon's expensive, Amerigo, coming as it does from the East. Surely there were less —" Guid'Antonio floundered, mentally calculating the number of pennies the buns must have stolen from Amerigo's scrip. "— less costly treats to be had."

Amerigo straightened alertly. "Marco Polo said the best cinnamon comes from Sumatra."

"And if Marco says it's so, it's so," Guid'Antonio said.

"Uncle, get back!" Amerigo jumped sideways, thrusting Guid'Antonio off the street. A rider on horseback pounded past in the opposite direction, so close, his mount's long tail brushed Guid'Antonio's cheek. A courier bearing news, his occupation made clear by his white armband and the white feather in his cap.

"Fathead!" Amerigo yelled after the horseman, who ignored him, grinning over his shoulder in the direction of the pretty miss who had commanded his attention. Before riding into a wide byway, he blew the girl a kiss.

"*Stupido!*" Amerigo said. "Uncle, are you all right?" A second courier galloped past, shouting for pedestrians to clear a path.

Guid'Antonio brushed dust from his tunic. "I've survived worse." Holiness! Was he under siege? He said, "I only wonder what's so important."

"I only wish the first fellow had fallen from the saddle." Amerigo's gaze sought the object of the horseman's attention. "She is remarkably fetching."

About thirteen and still unmarried, for she was uncloaked, the girl wore a gown whose white fabric was so sheer, it appeared spun from butterfly wings. Budding breasts pushed against a row of narrow lace. Pale fingers clutched a prayer book encrusted with glittering gemstones. The girl's maid glowered at Amerigo and hurried her charge along a side street toward Via Porta Rossa.

"Very pretty," Guid'Antonio agreed.

"Now, come along."

"I'll wager she's attending Mass at Trinita," Amerigo said, sucking honey from his thumb and fingers.

"Yet another service unattended by you," Guid'Antonio said.

"Today's one thing, tomorrow's another. If I sweet-talk the girl's maid, the possibilities are limitless."

Guid'Antonio gave him a sharp look. "She's from a good house, Nephew. Her relatives won't have her tampered with. Try secret meetings, and you'll wind up with your cock in a sling." It was no secret to him how candlelit chapels and dark, deserted church naves provided couples with hidden meeting places. God knew Florence was a hive of churches. No telling how many hot professions of love their sacred walls had heard, breathy sighs rising up amongst the brushstrokes of Fra Angelico, Fra Filippo Lippi, Giotto, Masaccio, Verrocchio, Sandro and, oh, so many others, or what those walls had seen.

He had a momentary picture of painted saints staring down on panting, half-clothed youths and maidens, naked boys, frustrated priests. He felt himself harden and paused his step on this feverishly hot July day, clearing his throat, one independent part of him wondering if he was completely mad. No, just horny, like some fourteen-year-old. He cut a look at his nephew. Like Amerigo and every other man still breathing.

The jingling of the doorbell announced their presence in Luca Landucci's apothecary shop at Canto de' Tornaquinci, the tight corner where Via della Spada and Via della Vigna Nuova came together near Palazzo Rucellai. Within the Sign of the Stars, baskets of dried herbs lined one wall and hung from the wooden rafters. Shelves displayed lead-glazed earthenware jars, sapphire blue, golden yellow, and sea green, each labeled in the druggist's neat hand. The shop was small and close with only one window, but the space was fairly lit by the glow of a pair of oil lamps, one at each end of the counter, and by candles burning here and there.

Guid'Antonio was about to ring the service bell when Luca hurried from the curtained back room, carrying a leather-bound journal in one hand. His eyes flickered with surprise when he saw the Vespuccis, and he slid the journal onto a shelf beneath the counter.

*Why?* Guid'Antonio wondered. And: *That diary might make interesting reading. To know*

*Luca Landucci's most private thoughts about the last two years. Come to think of it, conduct a raid on the house of every illustrious Florentine family, and you would have an interesting account of Florentine history, since every man who could scribble words with a pen kept a private chronicle during his lifetime.*

"Surely, neither of you has taken ill since I saw you yesterday morning in Mercato Nuovo?" Luca said.

"No. Maria's mother is ailing."

"I'm sorry. Her symptoms?" Luca said, crossing himself.

"Stomach pains, fever, chills. Dottore Camerlini is dosing her with crushed pearls."

A grumble rose up in Luca's throat. "Dottore Camerlini! Those crackpot remedies are expensive, that's what doctors are about today! Has he administered an enema?"

"Oh, God," Amerigo breathed.

"I don't know," Guid'Antonio said. He had thought to ask Francesca Vernacci to look in on Alessandra del Vigna in Santa Croce. And then, he had thought not. Selfish? Yes. But he could not suffer being together with the good doctor and Maria in the same room. Not again.

Luca held up his hands: No matter. "I'm sure he examined the lady's urine." He glanced at the scales on the counter and at

225

the small statue of Hygeia positioned there. Luca Landucci was *thinking.* On the shelves behind Luca, Guid'Antonio noted the druggist's well-worn copy of the *Antidotario,* the apothecary's textbook.

Luca did not refer to it. Instead, from beneath the counter, he removed a small chest bound with bands of tinned iron. He unlocked the chest with the key from his leather purse, and from the purse removed a second key. Behind the counter in a neat row stood metal vessels with secured lids. Luca unlocked one of these and carefully measured a small portion of seeds into a waxed packet.

Amerigo, his gaze roving the pharmacy, pointed to the remnants of a snake on the ledge at his left shoulder. Head, tail, skin, the latter whispery thin.

"Yes," Luca said, looking up from his scale, "that slippery fellow's innards made a fine tonic, once I removed the poisonous sac. But for your mother-in-law, Messer Vespucci, we have roasted cannabis seeds. Inhaling the fumes will help her relax and induce sleep."

"May I have some?" Amerigo inserted neatly.

Luca handed Guid'Antonio the seed-filled packet. "I'll send round a betony conserve later today. 'Tis good for all disorders. And you should have — the woman who's head of your kitchen? Domenica Ridolfi — have her mix some sweet basil leaves in wine as a tonic to soothe the lady."

Guid'Antonio nodded agreement. "Thank you."

But Luca was not finished. "Here's a small portion of wolfsbane mixed with oils. Your wife or the lady's nurse should rub the patient's aching joints with it, and —" From another vessel, Luca measured a small amount of fragrant oil into a glass vial into which he inserted a stopper. "From Damascus," he said, his tone reverent. "Attar of roses. Tell your wife to bathe her mother's skin twice daily with it. That, along with all the others, should bring the unfortunate lady rest. And with rest comes peace."

*Is that what I need?* Guid'Antonio wondered. *Fragrant attar of roses?* He drew a faint breath and smiled weakly.

"Has she been ill long?" Luca asked.

"From what I understand, no." Guid'Antonio raised his shoulders. "But the outcome's certain."

"Faith," Luca said, and the three men crossed themselves. " 'Tis a pity to succumb to sickness now, after surviving the trials and tribulations of the last few years."

"Which trials?" Guid'Antonio said. "There seem to be so many."

Luca held his hands out in a gesture of dismay. "Christmastime this past year was a disaster! You know Messer Bongiovanni's houses?"

Guid'Antonio nodded yes. Bongiovanni Gianfiggliazzi's houses sat near Ponte Trinita, this side the river. "The Arno overflowed its banks opposite there," Luca said.

Amerigo's eyebrows arrowed up. "Again?"

"It was a disaster," Luca said. "Water flooded the meadowland all along Borg'Ognissanti. People lost their possessions, their homes even. A good number had to flee. The stench afterward was terrible."

Guid'Antonio frowned. "Amerigo, did you know about this?"

Amerigo shook his head. "Apparently, we weren't affected. Directly, I mean."

Ognissanti, flooded, and no one in the family had mentioned it to either of them. But what good would have it have done for anyone to bring the flood to Guid'Antonio's attention? Last Christmas he was in Paris, pacing and staring into the hearth fire, praying Lorenzo would survive Naples. What use notifying him about his beleaguered neighborhood? About his house, his church, his hospital?

"As if excommunication and the terror of war weren't already enough, God unleashed the rains on us," Luca was saying. "Since then, has our lot improved? No."

"Yet you're still a Florentine, rather than Neapolitan or Roman, as you would be if King Ferrante and Pope Sixtus IV had had their way," Guid'Antonio said, staring at him.

A faint blush came up on the other man's skin. "Yes, praise God and Lorenzo."

Guid'Antonio handed Luca payment for the medicines in his scrip. "Luca, how would you go about making a painting weep?"

The druggist gasped. "I never would do such a thing!"

Guid'Antonio raised both hands lightly. "I only wonder how it might be done."

"Our Lord simply has to wish it."

"But if a mortal being were involved," Guid'Antonio pressed. "What then? Someone employing trickery. Water, probably, on the painting's surface."

"That wouldn't be very good for it, would it?" Amerigo said. "A centuries' old panel —"

Guid'Antonio raised his eyebrows, and Amerigo fell silent.

Luca's eyes flicked anxiously to the wasps embroidered in white on Guid'Antonio's plain collar and in the gold trim of Amerigo's pale blue tunic. Straightening to his full height, he said, "I would never *think* about such a sinful act."

Guid'Antonio felt a pound of impatience tempered with a teaspoon of regret. He had no wish to intimidate the druggist, who was a good, kind man. He did not want to play lion to Luca Landucci's mouse. The truth was he needed Luca's help, and one way or another, he meant to have it.

"Forgive me," he said. "Curiosity led me there, nothing more." And wasn't that a whopping lie? "You're aware of the unusual circumstances in Ognissanti. The Virgin's tears are a great concern to Lorenzo, and so as well to me. To all Florentines. To Tuscany. No one wants a civil war in our streets except our enemies."

"Yes," Luca conceded. "I mean — no."

Guid'Antonio started toward the door, smiling good-bye in an off-handed way, as if he regretted mentioning the making of miracles, and was, therefore, dropping the subject. He was not. "Luca," he said, turning. "Yesterday, we spoke of the *palio.* I'm curious about your brother's mount."

"Since when?" Amerigo said.

230

"Since *now.*" Guid'Antonio smiled at Luca. "Does Gostanzo always ride *Draghetto*?"

"Yes." Luca's countenance brightened considerably. "Such a mighty specimen of horseflesh!" Just as suddenly, the druggist's brown eyes narrowed. "Everyone knows my brother, Gostanzo, and they know *Draghetto,* too. The animal's stout heart and how Gostanzo makes him move. Then there's Lorenzo, with a dozen magnificent horses. More! Who knows which mount he'll have his man ride in any race, or how Lorenzo plans to win, whether or not he deserves the prize?"

The druggist caught himself up, shaking with indignation. "This summer everyone in Tuscany has been gambling against the Landuccis."

"They're not complete dunces," Amerigo said.

Luca looked pained. Gloomily, he said, "The final running isn't till next month, and already the banner's lost to *Il Magnifico.*"

Guid'Antonio disagreed. "Gostanzo's competitive and *Draghetto*'s a frontrunner. If your brother had the name of Lorenzo's horse before the final race, he could plan a winning strategy."

"Of course," Luca agreed. "But no one in

231

Christendom knows which horse Lorenzo de' Medici will run on any given day, let alone on the day of the championship race."

"I do," Guid'Antonio said. "Or I will." He smiled guilelessly.

Luca blinked in surprise. "You?"

"Me."

A mix of conflicting emotions battled across Luca's face. "Strategy is everything."

"Yes," Guid'Antonio said, and turned back toward the shop door.

He and Amerigo were on the threshold and the skin on the back of Guid'Antonio's neck was prickling when from behind them in a quiet voice Luca said, "One moment, please."

Guid'Antonio whirled around. "Yes?"

"If I by chance discover anything that might possibly explain the workings of certain mysteries in Ognissanti, where should I send word?"

"To me at home," Guid'Antonio quickly said. "If I'm absent, instruct your messenger to tell Amerigo or Cesare you wish to see me at once. I'll come to you."

"I'll be in touch," Luca said, smiling wickedly. "You can bet your last florin on it. And I will, too."

"How in the name of Zeus will you get

Lorenzo to give you the name of his horse before the race so you can pass it along to our new accomplice?" Amerigo said when they were back out in the street. "Should Luca actually discover how the painting's being made to weep."

"I'll ask him," Guid'Antonio said.

# FOURTEEN

In the gray hours just before daybreak, Tesoro clatters, lost and without a rider, through the Prato Gate and along the deserted thoroughfare where stone dwellings soar to the sky, hemming in the stars of summer high overhead. Close, these buildings, unlike the rolling hills of home, though a memory does stir, this smell of stone rather than lush grass and rich brown earth. The mare has seen this place before.

Close, too, harsh cries and footsteps pounding nearer down the street. "Stop! Stop, you!"

Dead ahead, fire rings a broad piazza. More cries ring out, bouncing against stone. Tesoro rears, neighing shrilly, hooves pawing the air. To one side there is a blind black passageway, to the other, the smell of warm river water. Tired. Exhausted. Heaving. The mare rolls her eyes in terror. Where is *she*?

# Where?
# Where?

# FIFTEEN

Guid'Antonio stared heavy-lidded at his journal. He had brought the leather bound book from the bedchamber into the small space of his *studiolo,* leaving the connecting door ajar, but then had left the cover latched. He had spent the last two days staring idiotically at things and questioning a few people and was not much the wiser for it. Now, after sitting through a hastily called meeting of the Medici faction's insiders deep into the night, he felt like a man hurtling down a snowy mountain slope, while an avalanche pounded after him with such force, it seemed bound to crush him beneath its awesome weight.

In the suffocating early hours after midnight, he had left Palazzo Medici and found his way home to Ognissanti with every bone in his body pleading for rest as he followed winding paths through a web of alleyways and stinking streets. In bed, his eyes wide, as if propped open with sticks, he had stared up at the red velvet canopy whose gathers and pleats in the guttering candlelight were not bright scarlet but deep bruised red.

Now, isolated amongst vaguely lit papers and books, he dipped his pen.

*Riding through the Prato Gate with Amerigo two mornings ago, I never thought to be greeted by such discord in my lady city. Contrary to all expectations, Pope Sixtus IV has not lifted the ecclesiastical penalties he imposed on us at the outset of our fight with him, his nephew, and their fearsome accomplice, King Ferrante of Naples. Instead, the Pontiff continues to demand Lorenzo's presence in Rome. As if that were not cruel enough, Prince Alfonso has not departed Siena on our southern border as we expected him to do once we signed a treaty with his father's kingdom. Instead, the Neapolitan prince acts as lord there in the guise of Florence's military protector while our tax money pays his commission. Ludicrous: this is how Florentines do things.*

*Closer to home, a young woman has been kidnapped or killed at the hands of Turks, or so some fools believe. Since news of Camilla Rossi da Vinci's disappearance reached Florence a little over a week ago, the* Virgin Mary of Santa Maria Impruneta *has been seen —*

*once — weeping in my family church, terror-*
*izing those who interpret the tears as a sign*
*of God's anger with Florence for warring with*
*the Pope, and for Lorenzo's refusal to go to*
*Rome and kneel before him. You would think*
*the sky was raining blood down on our heads.*
*I'm told that at the outset of this holy mad-*
*ness, people rushed the altar in my church,*
*lighting candles and weeping floods of their*
*own, even the desperately poor, offering the*
*monks coins, rather than feeding their own*
*children. On Saturday last the painting's tears*
*ceased, praise Jesus and His mother. Still,*
*the* popolo minuto *grumble and blame us for*
*everything.*

Guid'Antonio experienced an unflattering vision of himself striding into Ognissanti and breaking the centuries-old panel painting over his knee with both fists and shook his head to clear it.

*Now, fresh torments delivered to City Hall*
*by two couriers late yesterday afternoon as*
*Amerigo and I were on our way to speak with*
*Luca Landucci at the Sign of the Stars to enlist*
*his help in Ognissanti. We had just finished*
*our conversation with him and stepped back*
*out onto Canto Tornaquinci when Cesare*
*found us there. "Lorenzo wants you in Via*
*Larga." And so of course, good Medici man*
*that I am, I immediately turned toward the*

*Medici Palace.*

*Although we gathered in Lorenzo de' Medici's house, Lorenzo's uncle, Tommaso Soderini, spoke first, informing us the Pope has now joined hands with Venice. I glanced at Lorenzo, surprised. Yes, said his dark eyes, gazing back at me: the Pope is on the move.*

*Together, Sixtus IV and the Venetians have contributed eight hundred infantrymen toward the security of Forli town on Via Emilia. Forli's fate is of paramount importance to us, since it separates us from the Adriatic Sea. The Pope's nephew and assassin Girolamo Riario will fight to add Forli to his holdings the instant the town's sickly young lord, Sinibaldo Ordelaffi, passes from this world. With Papal and Venetian troops at his command, Girolamo stands close to creating an independent state for himself in Italy, while isolating us in the presence of our enemies.*

*All this as his uncle, the Pope, pats Girolamo's ass and urges him forward.*

*When Tommaso finished speaking, rather than seem completely helpless when it comes to Girolamo's creeping advances, Lorenzo addressed the immediate needs of our city, asking for more grain to be imported as soon as possible and made available for a reasonable price to the people in the marketplace. He did not say how he thought Tommaso and the other Lord Priors might accomplish this. Since Lorenzo's war with Rome, the State treasury is appallingly low. Mercenary soldiers, armor and weapons, compensation for horses wounded, killed, or captured in battle, and so on.*

*"Whatever it takes, we must keep people satiated, so we may keep our place in our town. I will donate a good portion to the hospitals for bread, along with wine and oil," Lorenzo said.*

*Around the table, everyone present murmured how gladly we would follow his lead. As for how to curb Girolamo's constant advances, Lorenzo vowed he will think of something. We cannot muster forces against Rome and Venice. Florence is limping as it is. I watched Lorenzo carefully. I know that resolute tone, and I heard the iron in his voice. People do not call him Lorenzo the Magnificent for nothing. I suspect he already has a plan for the future, not only of Florence, but for all Italy, or has the beginning of something taking shape in his head.*

*12 July In the Year of Our Lord 1480*
*Guid'Antonio Vespucci, Florence*

Guid'Antonio massaged his hands, blinking, blurry-eyed in the wavering yellow light of the airless *studiolo.* The renegade treaty between Rome and Venice worried him. Everything worried him and left him unprepared for daybreak. How could matters get any worse? He was sliding his pen into its case when he heard the rush of footsteps, and they were very near. Leaping up, he pulled his dagger and darted into the bedchamber just as the door flew open.

# Sixteen

Amerigo bounded in. "Wake up, Uncle! Oh!" The sight of Guid'Antonio waiting with knife drawn slowed Amerigo only momentarily. "Uncle Guid'Antonio," he said, stepping back, quivering with excitement. "The girl's dead! Murdered!"

"Girl?" Guid'Antonio sheathed his blade and locked his journal away for safekeeping. "Camilla, you mean? Where was she found, quickly." Impossible! Never would he have thought matters would come to this.

"Ummm —" Amerigo faltered. "Not exactly found, Uncle. Yet."

Guid'Antonio stared. "Murder is an exact word, is it not?"

Droplets of rain dripped off Amerigo's cloak and puddled on the floor. "Of course, yes," he said, "but her horse galloped through the Prato Gate a short while ago. With no rider, its saddle and harness bloody."

"Fresh or dried?" Guid'Antonio said.

"What?"

*"The blood."*

The fragrant water Guid'Antonio splashed on his cheeks did nothing to calm the heat beneath his skin. Swiftly, he glanced around. Where the devil was Cesare when he needed him?

Amerigo handed him a towel. "Who knows? Whether the blood was fresh or dried, I mean."

Guid'Antonio located his boots beside the bed. "And now once again, the Virgin is weeping in Ognissanti. That's smart *and* quick."

"Yes." A wrinkle furrowed Amerigo's brow. "How did you know the Virgin's weeping again?"

"Complete faith in my fellow man. When it comes to knowing, how did you happen by this information?"

Amerigo blew a lock of damp hair off his cheek, grinning. "I was up late."

"And not because you were sleepless and writing in your *journal.*"

"Decidedly not." Amerigo's quick smile faded. "Walking home, I witnessed such commotion as I've never seen in these streets. Swear, I mashed myself against the walls to keep from being trampled by ass

243

dealers and flask makers wailing about the bloodied horse, Turks, and the Virgin, weeping again. Then here comes Palla Palmieri thundering in on horseback, shouting orders."

Guid'Antonio flung his crimson cloak over his shoulder. His white cotton tunic was none too fresh; for now, it must do. "Palla and his *ufficiale*?"

"Decidedly. He warned people to keep away from the lady's horse. Unnecessarily, as everyone on two legs is rushing to Ognissanti to worship the painting."

Guid'Antonio secured his scrip to his belt. "And to throw coins into the monks' hands. You say blood. How, when from the looks of you, it's raining."

"Only in the last short while and lightly as I came home." Amerigo paused, his expression deeply thoughtful. "The Virgin's tears on the heels of the lady's horse do imply someone near had a hand in crafting them. Surely the monks wouldn't hatch such an evil scheme for a few extra coins in the box. Do away with the lady, invent tears in Ognissanti —"

"Men have done worse for less," Guid'Antonio said. "Palla believes the horse in fact does belong to Camilla Rossi da Vinci?"

"Yes. In the hubbub, he told me the gatekeeper who caught up with it knows it as the lady's and took it to the public stable where it's always kept."

"Which one?" Guid'Antonio snuffed the candles and turned down the lamp.

"The Hoof and Hay just inside the gate."

"And Ognissanti?"

"Packed like a crock of sardines."

In the hall, Olimpia Pasquale stood on tiptoe, lighting the morning torches. *"Mattina,"* she said, dimpling as she turned to greet them, her expression as she gazed at Guid'Antonio, glowing.

*"Mattina,"* he answered, caught off guard by the answering warmth her smile ignited in him. "You're not with Giovanni this morning?"

"No." Olimpia reached up to light another torch, her breasts pressing fetchingly against the light fabric of her apron. "Giovanni's with your lady Maria and her mother, as the next few hours may be his grandmother's last. Your lady believed it best."

"Maria sent for him?"

"Um-hm. I walked him there myself. She instructed me to return today with their things and abide there with them until — well. In the meanwhile, I'm lighting morning torches."

Guid'Antonio glanced around the hall. "Have you seen Cesare?"

For one moment, Olimpia hesitated. " 'Tis just now dawn, *Signore.*"

"I did. On my way home," Amerigo slipped in. "He scooted down an alleyway and was lost in the fog."

Olimpia, chewing her lip, stared at the floor.

"Olimpia, tell him —" Guid'Antonio made an airy gesture. "Oh, never mind."

With that, Guid'Antonio and Amerigo hurried downstairs, across the garden and out into Borg'Ognissanti.

Fog, misty and gray, lay like a damp veil over the city, shrouding the rooftops and the Arno, where fishermen in boats cast their nets. Up and down the thoroughfare, people pushed past one another for entrance to Ognissanti, their figures ghostly apparitions in the pale gray atmosphere. Guid'Antonio turned on his heel and walked opposite them toward the Prato Gate.

"God's wounds!" Amerigo exclaimed. "We're not going to see the weeping painting?"

Guid'Antonio shook his head. "Camilla Rossi's horse amongst us here in Florence, rather than kept by her abductors or sold?

246

There's the miracle, I think. We're off to the Hoof and Hay."

"Stand back!" Eyes squinting with brute intent, the burly sergeant posted at the door to the public stable took a threatening step forward.

"Stefano! Stand down." Palla Palmieri moved from the stable into the light, chewing a piece of straw, resting his brown eyes lightly on Guid'Antonio. "You're late." Palla's dagger, cased in leather, rode in full view at his slender waist.

"Right on time for chasing ghosts."

"The horse is real at least." Palla directed them past the police guard and on inside the wooden structure that smelled of oats, sweat, and hay. A chestnut horse poked its nose over the top rail of the first stall and whinnied. From another stall there came the sound of a shovel scraping stone. "The stable keep," Palla said.

"You've seen Camilla's horse? It *is* here?"

"Yes. A dandy little mare." Palla nodded toward the end of the building, past the lengthy row of narrow cubicles. All was quiet there.

A solidly built man whose wild black hair framed muddy eyes set in a ruddy face emerged from the near stall, armed with a manure-caked shovel. He shot Palla a sour look: You're still here? His eyes narrowed further when he saw Palla's companions, one wearing a crimson cloak and wrinkled tunic embroidered with creamy white wasps, the other impressive in tall boots and a purple tunic slit at the neck to show the brocade *farsetto* and rich cotton *camicia* beneath it.

"What's this, then?" the man said. "How many horses do you want? Two?"

"You are the stable keep?" Guid'Antonio said.

"No. I'm King Ferrante of Naples. Can't you tell?"

Guid'Antonio nailed him with a stare. "We've no need of horses for ourselves. Just to inquire about the one found running loose today in the street."

The man's full red lips parted, revealing a mouthful of rotten teeth. "Lady Camilla's mount!" He wagged his head. "The Turks and their dirty work. Enough to sicken my gut. The girl's blood spilled on the saddle, the girl's blood spilled on the bridle, her bl—"

"Show us," Amerigo said.

"Show you what?"

"Her blood!" Oaf!

Palla looked away, mouth turned up at

248

the corners, arms folded neatly across the chest of his plain brown tunic.

The stable keep thumbed toward the police chief, sputtering, "I've been through this with Palmieri! I have work to do."

"All the more reason for you to answer quickly," Amerigo said.

"By whose request?"

"Mine," Guid'Antonio and Palla said.

"First Palmieri, now you, our very own neighborhood snoop, sniffing at doors," the man said. "The all important Vespuccis! Yes, I know who you are. Who doesn't?"

Guid'Antonio studied him mildly. "Watch your tongue or you may need me one day and find I'm nowhere around."

"For all that, the answer's the same: just as I couldn't show our good police chief the lady's blood, neither can I show you."

"Can't? Or won't?" Amerigo said.

The man offered them a sickly brown smile. "Can't. I cleaned the animal's gear."

Guid'Antonio's temper blazed. "It was *evidence.*" He glanced at Palla who, having followed this same, slow curving road a short while earlier, listened with his finely chiseled lips set in a cold smile.

"By her husband's request," the stable keep said.

"Castruccio Senso has already been here?"

Guid'Antonio said.

"Yes, and I do as I'm told," the stable keep said.

Why waste breath asking this dimly lit fellow anything so complex as who, what, when, and where? Instead, sticking to why? Guid'Antonio squelched his anger and inquired how Castruccio Senso knew the horse in question had been found and brought to this particular holding, when there were countless public stables around town.

"Uncle Guid'Antonio," Amerigo cut in, "I told you the gatekeeper recognized the mare and brought her here."

Guid'Antonio held up his palm: Not now.

A light dawned in the eyes of the stable keep. "Because it's *Castruccio*'s horse," he exclaimed. "Tesoro. Or rather, 'tis his lady's. She calls the mare her treasure. When the gateman brought Tesoro here, I sent for Castruccio at his house."

"You recognized the mare because Castruccio Senso typically boards her here," Guid'Antonio said.

"Yes." How could they be so harebrained? And they, the supposed leaders of Florence. No wonder the Republic was in such a mess.

"She's a beauty," the stable keep declared. "Tesoro, I mean. Though the same may be said of the lady, Camilla Rossi da Vinci. A true Madonna herself, and now —" He trembled. "Next, the Turks will fly over our gates with burning wings and devour us with their fangs like the werewolves who prowl our streets at night. Our souls will spend eternity in hell, thanks to the Antichrist who means to destroy our city."

Guid'Antonio ground his teeth. No need to ask which Antichrist the fellow meant. "The blood: was it fresh?"

"How do you mean?"

"Rather than dried," Guid'Antonio said softly.

"Yes."

"How did Castruccio Senso seem when he saw Tesoro today?"

"Seem?" the man said.

"Was he upset, for Christ's sake!" cried Amerigo. "After all, his wife is missing, and this is her horse!"

Palla laughed outright. The stable keep drew back, offended. "What do you think? Castruccio Senso's in a terrible way. He wanted done with the blood, and quickly, too. Though he'll remember the sight well enough, when some hunter stumbles over his wife's corpse, or what the Turks have left of it." The stable keep crossed himself.

"It seems 'quickly' is the operative word

here," Guid'Antonio said, glancing at Palla. "Tesoro's in the back stall?"

"She is. To keep her from harm. And further tampering." Palla turned to Amerigo. "Fetch the animal, please?"

Within the moment, Amerigo was leading Tesoro toward them. "Look at this beauty," he breathed.

Guid'Antonio looked and stared. A splendid black mare, Camilla Rossi da Vinci's horse possessed a proud curving neck and a long mane that was thick and curling. The animal's tail, an abundant fall of shining ebony curls, brushed the stable floor. For all the mare's magnificent appearance, her eyes flickered, showing fear.

"I believe she's an Andalusian," Palla said.

"Absolutely, a Spanish breed." Excitement quavered in Amerigo's voice. "I've heard of them." With gentle hands, he quieted the mare's restive movements, running his fingers over her back and withers, then down each leg, inspecting the hooves, and then the teeth. He rubbed the animal's shoulder gently. "Excellent condition. Well fed, and there are few tangles in this extraordinary mass of curling tail and mane."

Guid'Antonio said, "And yet she's been missing and presumably wandering for almost two weeks."

Palla's dark gaze went to the stable keep. "Do please tell them your explanation for this."

The fellow lifted his hands up in a gesture of helpless wonder. "We are awash in miracles."

Palla cut a smiling glance toward Guid'Antonio. "Remarkable, isn't it, how suddenly He is so prompt with them?"

They stepped into the street. The sun had burned off most of the early morning moisture; the day promised clear blue skies and searing summer heat. "This latest poses more questions than answers," Guid'Antonio said, striding three abreast with Amerigo and Palla along Borg'Ognissanti.

Palla agreed. "One thing's certain. Turks never would have released such a fine animal. Few people would. Be that as it may, *someone* has been tending Tesoro until very early this morning."

"How do you explain the blood?"

Palla laughed sourly. "I, like you, know that's the main question, along with Castruccio Senso's role in this. The harness and saddle are in my custody, should you wish to examine them. Sadly, all evidence of blood is gone."

"How accommodating of you."

253

Palla shrugged. "We both work for the same man."

"I thought Camilla's case was closed. Officially," Guid'Antonio said.

"It is. I count on you to inform me of any progress you make in your private investigation for Lorenzo. Immediately," Palla said.

"You know I will. Palla, was Camilla carrying any coins or wearing any jewelry when she disappeared? There's motive enough for some men to waylay her."

Palla shook his head. "No. Only traveler's checks, according to her cautious husband, none of which have yet come to light."

Amerigo touched Guid'Antonio's sleeve. "Look there."

Ahead of them, Piazza Ognissanti was a mass of men, women, and children elbowing their way through the doors of Ognissanti. Palla said, "There's a dangerous situation. Fear, hot tempers, and a whiff of salvation."

"There's an apt description of the Pope and Lorenzo," Amerigo said.

"Palla," Guid'Antonio said. "You're certain Tesoro was with Camilla when Camilla started out from Florence?"

"Yes. According to her nurse and slave, and a host of eyewitnesses."

"And are we certain there was blood on

Tesoro's gear when the horse bolted through the gate today?"

"The gatekeeper who chased her down confirmed it."

"And the stable keep said the blood was fresh?"

"Yes. I have a shadow on Castruccio," Palla said. "As well as sergeants posted all around here." His gesture included Ognissanti, Trinita, and the byways leading to Santa Maria Novella. "And on Via Larga, too," he said, "should people take their passion outside your church and into the Medici Palace."

Guid'Antonio considered telling Palla about his own shadowed walk through the city two nights ago, on Monday evening. Instead, he said, "Do you know Castruccio Senso's whereabouts last night? Perhaps the horse is meant to lead us away from him."

"He was inside his house. The night watchman confirmed it."

Palla's slight, brown-clad figure cut a wide path through the crowd as he strolled toward the Bargello, the public jail, while Guid'Antonio's mind whirred with questions, foremost among them this: why would a man have evidence, whether fresh or dried (the stable keep said "fresh," but how could they believe that hare brain?) erased that

255

might shed light on his wife's disappearance and possible murder, unless he was guilty of having her killed, or of killing her himself? Tesoro let loose only to be discovered inside the city walls while Castruccio Senso remained within his house suggested additional forces at work.

If the blood truly were Camilla's . . . that meant the girl had been harmed — he recoiled from the word *murdered* — this very day.

This new twist in Camilla Rossi da Vinci's disappearance troubled him.

And what, besides, it had to do with the tears in Ognissanti.

# SEVENTEEN

At the entrance to Ognissanti, Guid'Antonio and Amerigo encountered Brother Battista Bellincioni, the fat almoner of the Benedictine Order of the Humiliati. Tailors, silk merchants, silversmiths, jewelers, and surgeons jostled one another through the narrow portal and on into the nave, along with menders, shearers, and poor kitchen maids smelling of cooking grease. Prostitutes wearing green cowls with bells on their heads, menders, and fishermen: all opened their fists to release precious coins into Bellincioni's wooden collection box.

"Father Abbot wondered how long it would take you to come poking around." The monk sniffed, rising up a bit taller in his sandals, his voice narrow and haughty.

"*Buena mattina* to you as well," Guid'Antonio said. "I came poking around the night before last, too. But of course, you know that. I hear the Virgin Mary's weeping."

Bellincioni's face puckered into a frown. "With good reason, too."

Guid'Antonio nudged Amerigo, who squeezed into the throng of humanity pushing into the church. "What good reason is that?" Guid'Antonio said.

Bellincioni's flabby chin lifted a notch. "Are you here as a worshipper or as a spy for Lorenzo the Magnificent?"

"As one who spends thousands of florins each year decorating this church." Guid'Antonio indicated the wall on the right a short distance behind Bellincioni's squat frame. "Commissioning, for example, the fresco of Saint Augustine Sandro Botticelli just completed. Ah. I love the smell of fresh paint. Don't you?"

Bellincioni scrunched his face and poked the collection box toward Guid'Antonio. "Do you think I know everything?"

"Good God, no, but enough to answer me." From his scrip, Guid'Antonio withdrew a coin and dropped it in the box, where it landed with a metallic *chink.*

"Look around you," the monk hissed, his black eyes radiant and sharp. "Our Blessed Mother is weeping in sorrow for her forgotten children. Not for you or any of your ilk. It's you and men like you who tricked us into taking Communion when Holy Mother

258

Church forbade it. And forbids it still, though no one told us that before or since. It's men like *you* who pull the wool over our eyes time and time again, who gull us into contravening God's will, and who mean for our souls to spend eternity in hell!"

"Not God's will, but the Pope's," Guid'Antonio said.

Bellincioni shook with such indignation, the coins in the collection box clattered, as if they, too, were outraged. "God will punish you! He will punish all of us!" he cried, bouncing up and down on his toes. "He already has, with curses in the streets and empty bellies! Next, He'll send the Infidels to destroy us, just as they destroyed the innocent lady. If ever a mortal woman may innocent be. Cross versus Crescent, here in our own city. The defeat of Christianity, thanks to the devil burrowed in the heart of the Golden Lion district!"

"Shame on you, Bellincioni," Guid'Antonio said, his voice harsh as he spoke. "It's you and men like you who keep this misery flaming. And what would you know of empty bellies? It appears you haven't missed many meals."

"Satan's mouth!" Brother Bellincioni whirled and hastened into the church, seeking the black comfort of his Benedictine brothers.

Dangerous, these religious with their shaven heads and holier-than-thou attitudes. Dangerous, their grip on the scared and needy.

Guid'Antonio slipped into the sanctuary. A man stumbled into him, tugging a little girl along by the hand. A young man pushed against him, elbowing past. Slowly, Guid'Antonio's eyes adjusted to the half-light. In the gloom he smelled sweat and musk mingled with — what? An odor he couldn't identify, something rotten hovering beneath the usual church smell of incense, candle wax, and stone.

He shouldered forward, enveloped in prayers wafting their way toward the vaulted ceiling. "Mary, Mother of God, in coming to know you better, we come to a closer union with God and His Son. Beloved Mary, intercede on our behalf, for we have committed terrible sins. Madonna, save us from eternal damnation and the angels of hell. *Nostra Signora dell'Impruneta, prega per noi!*"

Guid'Antonio sighed, glancing toward the rafters, where he caught no sign of a small brown swallow or any other winged creature poised to swoop down on his head. Where were the singing angels? The white doves bearing the olive branch of peace? Be wary should you see them. He passed the Vespucci Chapel and Sandro's elderly saint, a snowy-haired old man who, if he could talk, would no doubt say he had seen everything. Guid'Antonio glanced away. Farther down the nave, he spied Amerigo at the altar rail and saw him sink onto his knees and bend his head to pray.

On Guid'Antonio's left stood the wooden door leading to the church garden. The door was closed. Toward his right, on the south side of the sanctuary, the monks' full black skirts flapped about their ankles as they sought direction, first one way, then the other, past the chapels built by families like Guid'Antonio's own. His thoughts traveled to another time in another church when hesitation and disbelief held him back until it was too late to save Giuliano de' Medici.

His stomach churned, as if with acid.

Too late.

Too dead.

Stop it!

At the altar, his heart stuttered and stalled. There in a circle of light stood the panel painting: the *Virgin Mary of Santa Maria Impruneta,* just as when he had visited the church two nights past. But now tears trickled from the Virgin's eyes onto her pale

261

cheeks. Tears dampened her painted pearls and the gilded halo encircling the head of the Christ Child seated in her lap. Silvery wet tears, where before he had witnessed only fading red and green paint. At the rail he squeezed in beside Amerigo. Together, they remained on their knees for a long while before the miraculous painting.

After the leaden dimness of the sanctuary, the light of the piazza stung Guid'Antonio's eyes. He inhaled deeply, blinking, filling his chest with air and relishing the intensity of the sun warming his face. Across the square, the waters of the Arno glinted, golden and bold.

"It's almost midday," Amerigo said, lifting his face to the light, as if he, too, felt the need of the sun's healing hand on his lids and cheeks.

Guid'Antonio glanced over his shoulder, watching Brother Bellincioni's monkish replacement thrust the collection box toward the sea of hands paying the entrance fee into Ognissanti — for what else could you call the coins people dropped in the box? "These monks are like weeds," he said. "Where one has been, another pops up."

Amerigo chuckled. "Soon our good Benedictines will be richer than King Midas."

And where there was money, there was power. Guid'Antonio had started to say as much when a woman in rags, clutching a baby on her hip, stumbled blindly into him. Her eyes, filled with dread, locked with his. He stepped aside, and in an instant she vanished, her bony figure swallowed in the church shadows.

"Poor woman. What in God's name is happening to our town? To our church?" Amerigo reached out and gently touched Guid'Antonio's shoulder. "To Tuscany? Who's responsible for this wretched lunacy?"

For the first moment, Guid'Antonio did not answer. His gaze swept across the Arno, up toward San Miniato Church sitting high on a hill overlooking Florence. From where he stood on Borg'Ognissanti, the church appeared plain and small, whereas actually its facade was a graceful design of lustrous Prato green and Carrara white marble. Along with the monastery and Bishop's Palace, the grounds supported by the White Benedictine monks from Monte Oliveto yielded plentiful olive trees, an excellent wine, and thick golden honey.

He let out a long loose sigh, thinking of the ragged woman who had staggered past him just now. Her hair, which once might

263

have been as thick and shiny as Maria's, hung in mousey-brown strands around her shoulders. Her face was pinched, and her coloring so pale, she appeared drained of blood. The sharp scent he had smelled inside Ognissanti was the stench of poverty and fear.

"I don't know who is responsible," he said. "But I swear on my mother's grave, I will find out."

Once more on the move, they turned into a passageway lined with vendors hawking cheap wooden crosses and *Virgin Mary of Santa Maria Impruneta* miniatures. Waving the hucksters away, they crossed a small square, where a blind woman pleaded for money. Amerigo's purse was empty. Guid'Antonio dropped a silver coin into the beggar's gnarled hand and kept walking toward the Golden Lion district and the prince of the city.

"The little horse appears and the Virgin weeps. Who has the wit to devise this hellish scheme? All to bedevil *me.*" Within Palazzo Medici, Lorenzo roamed the confines of his candlelit *studiolo,* his brown eyes dark as oak and glowing with frustration and anger.

"That is the question," Guid'Antonio said.

Moments earlier, alerted by a servant,

Lorenzo had walked toward them from the inner garden courtyard, his smile as bright as the sunshine pouring down on his head. Boot heels clattering on pavement, he had crossed the arcaded loggia with both hands extended in greeting. "*Benvenuti in questa casa!* Thank you for stopping."

He had embraced them both, his manner casual, even breezy, as gawking pedestrians hurried along Via Larga past the palace's main gate. "How was France, Amerigo? Did you meet Catto there?" Angelo Catto, astrologer to King Louis XI.

"In Paris, yes." Amerigo matched Lorenzo's lively tone as he and Guid'Antonio hurried behind him up the curving stone staircase to the Medici family's private quarters. "We spent time with Catto at Monsieur Phillip's apartment. When we weren't at court," Amerigo added hastily.

"Phillip de Commines, now there's a good man. Did Catto read your stars? Did he predict your fate?"

"Yes."

"And?"

"I'm going far in the world," Amerigo said.

"You already have," Lorenzo said, smiling as they walked along a hallway with apartments on either side. "I've never been to France."

Amerigo threw Guid'Antonio a questioning glance. Nor had Amerigo ever been upstairs in the Medici Palace. Guid'Antonio shrugged, assuming they were going to the Medici Chapel, where they could talk without fear of being overheard. God knew he had been there with Lorenzo often enough. But Lorenzo strode past the chapel, turned, and beckoned them into a spacious apartment. A massive bed with hangings embroidered in a pattern of falcons and dormice flashed by. They were in Lorenzo's bedchamber, and their host showed no sign of slowing down.

This was deeper into Lorenzo's private quarters than Guid'Antonio had ever been before, though they were intimate friends. Intriguing. Flattering, even, since in Florence a man's standing was gauged by how far into another man's home he was allowed to penetrate. The word "trustworthy" popped into Guid'Antonio's mind.

Lorenzo lit lamps and candles, and flames danced around them, bathing in golden light the room they had just entered. Looking around, Guid'Antonio felt as if he had stepped into a treasure chest. Above their heads, twelve glazed blue and white Della Robbia tiles jumped to life. On the walls were many shelves of books, some of them

266

newly printed, others ancient illuminated manuscripts. Antique cameos, bronzes, coins, and gems. Gleaming Roman, Byzantine, Persian, and Venetian vases. Add to this a fine walnut desk with a highly polished brass lamp suspended over it for ease of reading.

This was Lorenzo's haven, his most private place, his lair in the heart of the Golden Lion district.

Gingerly, Amerigo touched a book placed shoulder high to him on a near shelf. "I'm almost paralyzed with wonder. So many books. And the illumination so lovely."

Distractedly, Lorenzo said, "Thank you, yes. You're welcome to borrow them whenever you wish."

Guid'Antonio narrowed his eyes. Lorenzo de' Medici's thoughts were not on his prized possessions, but on a weeping painting, a missing girl, and a lost horse, found.

He stirred in the stiff leather chair by Lorenzo's desk as Lorenzo paced the little *studiolo.* "How much do you know?" Guid'Antonio said.

"Not enough. Only hearsay from a servant early this morning. The horse, the Virgin Mary, and still no sign of Camilla Rossi da Vinci. Jesus, Mary, and Joseph." Comb his fingers through his hair as often he might, Lorenzo could not prevent it from falling in dark wings around his face.

"Palla hasn't been here?"

"No."

"He meant to put his sergeants on Via Larga."

Lorenzo whipped around. "At my gate? What message would that send? That I'm a coward? No!"

Guid'Antonio swallowed a protest. Lorenzo's constant public exposure troubled him. In the streets. In Florence Cathedral, when Lorenzo had a will. Guid'Antonio whisked his thoughts away from that vast place. If Lorenzo de' Medici refused police protection, there was little he could do about it. Rather than pursue the issue, he explained in detail how the terrified mare had galloped inside the Prato Gate and how Camilla's husband, Castruccio Senso, had immediately ordered the stable keep to groom the horse and scrub her bloodied tack clean.

"And he did?"

"Naturally."

"Imbecile!" Lorenzo swiped his hand through the air. "That was Castruccio Senso's reaction? To erase all evidence?"

"He wanted no visible reminders of his

268

wife's disappearance or her possible death. *Supposedly,*" Amerigo said, dragging his attention from a copy of Pliny the Elder's *Natural History.*

"*Ignare!* Fool! This grows stranger by the hour." Lorenzo's shadow loomed large on the wall as he paced. "I've been writing letters all morning. Kings, priests. Nothing new there." He massaged his hands as if they ached and wanted comforting. "I had thought Camilla content somewhere. Like you, Guid'Antonio. But given the bloody saddle, how content may she be? Although the blood could have come from any forest creature, rabbit, fox, squirrel. What I *know* is she wouldn't part gently from that fine treasure."

Guid'Antonio feigned calm, as if his heartbeat had not picked up a pace. "You know the horse by name?"

"Tesoro? Naturally. There's no other like that one in this town. Nor like the girl, either." Lorenzo shot him a smiling glance.

Guid'Antonio weighed Lorenzo's words and tucked them away. "So," he said, "whether or not the blood was hers, the lady may have been parted forcibly from her steed."

"Dashing the notion of a scheme betwixt her and a lover," Amerigo said. "No man

269

would be so foolish as that. Part a lady from her pet bird or kitten and draw back a nub. Who, though?" He plucked the *Natural History* from the shelf.

Lorenzo chuckled. "If we knew the answer to that, we'd have an end to this tale."

"The husband?" Guid'Antonio wished Lorenzo would sit down. "Spurred by jealousy? A cuckold. And him, one of your employees."

Lorenzo looked at him, hard. "We've been over this. Yes. Castruccio Senso's a wine dealer. From time to time, he handles our oil and wine, as he does yours, too, no doubt. And *no*. Never Castruccio Senso for any reason. He hasn't the balls."

Guid'Antonio remembered Lorenzo's coat of arms: six *palle,* or balls, five of scarlet and one of sapphire blue emblazoned with three golden *fleurs-de-lis* on a gold field whose design graced everything from the covers of Lorenzo's illuminated manuscripts to his horses' gilded tournament trappings, exactly as his father and grandfather's arms marked the walls of the Medici Palace and countless other buildings they had constructed or rescued and renovated in Florence. Balls, indeed.

He felt as if they were talking in circles and had done so all along. "Who, then?"

"The monks," Amerigo said. "They have balls aplenty."

Lorenzo laughed. "But do they have the brains? And anyway, so elaborate a plot for so few coins? In that case, I'll match them ducat for ducat, if they'll cease this madness."

"If they're our culprits, it's not only for coins, but also for their loyalty to the Pope," Guid'Antonio said.

Lorenzo gazed at him, eyes and mouth stern. "Hang the Pope. And the monks in Ognissanti."

Guid'Antonio closed his eyes a moment, praying for direction. "After things calm down, I mean to return to the church and speak to Abbot Ughi."

"Why not just inspect the painting? See what — who — is causing the Virgin's tears, now they're flowing again."

Guid'Antonio laughed. "And be exposed by the monks, who surely would pounce on me and ridicule me in the street? I don't think so." Besides, he had already inspected the painting and learned nothing, or so it seemed to him.

Lorenzo paced. "Do you really believe Abbot Ughi, that old lecher, will share anything with you other than how pretty his boys are?"

Guid'Antonio's stubborn nature flared. "Perhaps inadvertently." There was not one puzzle here, but two, at least. "Who besides the husband knew Camilla was traveling from the city the week she disappeared?" Sweet Jesus, he was beginning to feel as if he knew this girl. Perhaps he should have inspected Tesoro's mane and tail for some identifying bit of brush or herb when he had occasion to do so at the Hoof and Hay. For some sneaky little leaf growing far out in the *contado.* But he was no gardener or monkish herbalist. And anyway, too late. The dutiful, damned stable keep had groomed the horse.

"Who didn't?" Lorenzo included the world in one flip of his hand. "When Palla interrogated Castruccio Senso after Camilla's disappearance, Castruccio admitted telling anyone who would listen that his wife was off to the baths. Fool."

Guid'Antonio gaped at Lorenzo's broad back moving away from him. "Baths? Which baths do you mean?"

Lorenzo turned, staring. "Ours at Morba."

Here was the detail niggling Guid'Antonio these past three days. The lady was from Vinci, yet people had said she was traveling to Morba. Both Luca Landucci and Lorenzo had told him as much on Monday, but

272

neither had mentioned Morba's baths and its healing waters. He had assumed Camilla was on a family visit, and he had not remarked her destination overmuch. Why Morba? Why to any bathing place?

And who owned the resort at Bagno a Morba, but Lucrezia Tornabuoni de' Medici, that gentle and enterprising lady who, three years ago, had leased the baths, doubled the water supply, added a hotel and rented the sparkling new accommodations to visitors, and her no less a personage than Giuliano and Lorenzo de' Medici's *mother.* Admired, like her son and his castoff friend, Angelo Poliziano, as one of Italy's foremost poets. *Circles,* Guid'Antonio thought. *Chains.*

"Was Camilla ill?" he asked, a man surfacing from a warm, murky lake.

"Not that I know of. But then I wouldn't, would I?" Lorenzo's manner was completely natural.

A young woman off to the Morba Baths, off anywhere, without her husband? Strange. "How odd she traveled alone," Guid'Antonio said.

"Not alone," Amerigo said. "With her nurse and the Moorish slave boy."

"Just so." Guid'Antonio thought about all this and wondered. "Lorenzo, have you had

273

any dealings with Camilla's father, Jacopo? Since he's a winegrower?"

"Pray God, no!" Amerigo cut in. "There's an ill-tempered madman. *Il Magnifico,* yesterday afternoon in Orsanmichele, Jacopo caused such a commotion —"

"No need to digress," Guid'Antonio said, lightly slapping Amerigo on the side of his leg with the back of his hand.

"Jacopo Rossi da Vinci?" Lorenzo said. "You saw him here in Florence? What did he say regarding his daughter?"

"He left Orsanmichele before we could catch up with him," Guid'Antonio said.

" *'Left'?"* Amerigo stared at Guid'Antonio. "He practically —"

"Never *mind,*" Guid'Antonio said.

Lorenzo's eyes traveled from Guid'Antonio to Amerigo and back again. "I don't know Jacopo. My business associates handle these matters. Our silk shops along with the olives and wine, and everything else we own. You do know Palla questioned him. In Vinci town, where Jacopo lives."

"Yes. And?" Guid'Antonio said.

Lorenzo shrugged. "Apparently, Jacopo Rossi da Vinci was quiet as a clam."

Lorenzo's reply was unsatisfying at best, since from what Guid'Antonio had witnessed in the marketplace, Jacopo, with his

274

razor stare, was not a man he would ever call quiet. If, on the other hand, Palla Palmieri had ridden all the way to Vinci a week or so ago and declared Jacopo a dead end, he supposed that should satisfy him. It did not.

"You just came from Ognissanti," Lorenzo said.

"You know we did."

"And?"

"Emotions are high, people scared and angry, the seeds sown for terrible violence."

"Mary!" Lorenzo swore beneath his breath. "I knew as much. We've got to calm Florence down."

"We will. Find the culprit —"

"Yes!" Lorenzo said. "But here's the thing: we've got to gain lost ground in the city and within our circle, as well."

Amerigo lifted his brow and looked at Guid'Antonio, who shook his head. *I don't know where this is going, Amerigo. Stay quiet.*

Lorenzo turned the chair opposite Guid'Antonio around and straddled it, facing him across the desk. "I'll speak bluntly," he said.

"You almost always do."

A little color spread over the high bones in Lorenzo's cheeks. "Who knows how far some of our *friends* will go while we're

275

weak, and they have this chance to seize power? With the arrogant Pazzi family, we saw how far pride extends." He picked up a bronze medal displayed in a wooden case on his desk and played his fingers over it.

It was the medal Lorenzo had commissioned to commemorate the attack on him and Giuliano in the Cathedral. Small but intricate and swirling with detail, on one side Lorenzo fought off his attackers. On the other, Francesco de' Pazzi raised his knife high over Giuliano, who already lay lifeless on the church floor.

Guid'Antonio pulled back in his chair, straightening his shoulders. He felt surrounded by all things Medici, with no means of escaping his memories.

"Listen," Lorenzo said, "before I left for Naples, there was grumbling in the streets because of the war. While I was there, our detractors whispered I might meet my death at King Ferrante's hands. Yet here I am. I compromised myself by going to Ferrante and suing for peace, since it meant identifying my house so closely with the city's continuing problems. I know that, and don't regret it a whit, since I did it in the name of peace. I certainly didn't expect to have my efforts come back and bite me in the ass."

Amerigo laughed, then fell quiet as

Guid'Antonio said, "You believe the rumblings within our ranks pose a genuine threat to the regime?"

Lorenzo bent toward him, his cheeks unusually thin, almost sunken, in the candlelight. "As dangerous as when ruthless men tried to replace my father and grandfather as the leaders of our city. And more recently, me."

"They failed miserably," Guid'Antonio said. The Albizzi, the Pitti, the Pazzi families.

"Not without tremendous cost. I live with the death of my brother every day."

*So do I,* Guid'Antonio thought. *And you know it very well.*

Lorenzo pressed the medal to his lips before returning it to its case with Giuliano's image face up. "This is no time to drag our feet."

"Do you have a plan?"

"Not quite yet" — Lorenzo looked away — "only a few ideas involving change."

Guid'Antonio's thoughts were worn, wooly threads seeking some design or pattern. "Find Camilla, expose the painting —"

"I'm speaking of our government and our party," Lorenzo snapped. "About our lives and the lives of our families. About our impending ruin. When the time comes to

277

make a move, I'll need you with me." A smile slipped across his full lips. "You're my voice of reason."

By "change," what, exactly, did Lorenzo mean?

Resistance crept up Guid'Antonio's legs and settled in his chest beneath the ties of his sweat-soaked tunic. Magnificent to behold, suddenly the windowless little study felt hot as the flames of hell. He sat thinking while moments marched past, his gaze on the wall in the shadows at Lorenzo's back. There on a shelf sat small sculptures and vases and a blue and white onyx cameo in a frame: *Noah and His Family Emerging from the Ark.* His eyes traveled to the painted chest on the floor. On the wooden chest lay a velvet cloak. The cloak was familiar. Inky black with bands of crimson satin sewn along the sleeves. The same scarlet made the hood an inner lining. Folded back, in the dark light of Lorenzo's *studiolo,* its contents were transformed into a flowing river of blood.

Guid'Antonio felt off balance. How often had he seen Giuliano with that same cloak slung over his shoulders as he strolled the streets of Florence with his young bloods or rode with the hunt, his arrow whistling into the stout heart of a wild boar or a magnificent stag? The last time, as Giuliano lay dead on the Duomo floor. Guid'Antonio swallowed hard. He did not need to see the familiar cape to be reminded of Giuliano's limp body, his skull split in two halves. The image of Giuliano's corpse was seared into Guid'Antonio's blood, guts, and bones.

"I want to show you something."

Guid'Antonio flinched, startled by the sound of Lorenzo's harsh voice breaking into his thoughts.

Lorenzo blew out all the candles save one and beckoned to his guests.

# EIGHTEEN

Lorenzo opened a door panel hidden in the *studiolo*'s back wall and led them along a narrow passage before beckoning them down a twisting stone stairway. When they reached an oaken door with cast-iron fittings, he extinguished the candle and added it to others within an iron container attached to the wall. "The outside exit is here." The iron inner bolt screeched like a wounded bird when Lorenzo pulled it back. Heat and a slab of daylight poured in the door.

On the street, while Lorenzo locked the door behind him with a key, Guid'Antonio glanced around to get his bearings. Red-gowned men on foot hurried past, and a horseman clattered by, almost trampling a miller whose donkey was laden with a precious half sack of flour. Shops with barred doors and shuttered windows outnumbered those doing business.

They were on Via Larga, Florence's broad main street. Guid'Antonio looked toward his right. Midway down the block, a messenger carrying a leather satchel hurried through the main gate into the Medici palazzo. Keeping to the wall, Lorenzo walked in the opposite direction, north toward San Marco.

"Sometimes avoiding the main gate affords a bit of privacy," Lorenzo said, smiling round with an air of easy grace. Men in rich scarlet robes smiled back at him. Peasants from the *contado*, laborers and chicken farmers, looked slowly away.

"Are you armed?" Guid'Antonio said.

"Now? No."

"I am," Amerigo said.

Lorenzo had said avoiding the main gate afforded him some privacy, but there was none on Via Larga today. Tall and athletic, publicly bright and energetic, Lorenzo de' Medici's singular figure never went unnoticed in these streets. Except, perhaps, when he slipped from his *studiolo* and out into Florence under the veil of night. *To meet whom?* Guid'Antonio wondered. Lucrezia Donati, who was married to Ambassador Niccolò Ardinghelli, as Nastagio Vespucci had pointed out on Monday evening? God! Just two nights ago. Unbelievable.

Regarding Lorenzo thoughtfully, Guid'Antonio opened his mouth to suggest they return to the safety of the palace, but Amerigo was in the midst of accepting Lorenzo's offer to borrow a few manuscript pages of Francesco Berlinghieri's work in progress, *The Seven Days of Geography.* When published, the book, an Italian verse translation of Ptolemy's *Geografia,* would come with an introduction by Marsilio Ficino, as well as with updated maps of France, Italy, Spain, and the Holy Land, apparently.

In the light of his companions' unbridled enthusiasm, Guid'Antonio felt the curmudgeon, the one always wary of this, that, and the other thing; so, he bit off a warning that they should turn back while they had the chance and kept his fears to himself.

Halfway down the block, Lorenzo unbolted a gate and strolled into a grassy forecourt scented with rosemary and basil and pots of prickly yellow roses. Amerigo fell back a pace, glancing at Guid'Antonio. Lorenzo had brought them to the town apartment, in the Medici holdings, of his ward, Lorenzino de' Medici. Lorenzino and his younger brother, Giovanni, lived here when they left their villa at Castello and rode into the city. And, yes: Lorenzino and Giovanni were those same two young

Medici cousins whose inheritance Lorenzo de' Medici had looted to help fund the war. In response to Amerigo's silent question, Guid'Antonio could only shrug; he had no idea why Lorenzo would bring them here today.

From the courtyard, they went into the junior Medici's *sala.* High vaulted ceiling, wool and silk tapestries decorated with flowers and foliage, leather chairs, and a credenza laden with enameled glass and gilt goblets, silverware, trays, candlesticks, and plates. Yes, yes, yes. Very impressive. Even for a Medici.

Lorenzo opened an ornately carved door and, unannounced, they invaded Lorenzino de' Medici's bedchamber. Seventeen and weak of chin, Lorenzino was alone, his nose buried in the leaves of a book as he absentmindedly stroked the plump gray cat dozing on his lap. Lorenzino jumped up at once. "Cousin!" Fur spiking, the cat hissed and skittered across the marble floor.

"Stop it, Your Grace," Lorenzo said, shaking his finger playfully at the disgruntled feline. "You're not as fierce as you would have us believe."

The cat sped under the trestle table and rested on her spreading haunches, glaring from beneath the table's white linen cloth.

Lorenzo clasped his young cousin to his breast and kissed him on both cheeks. "We're not inconveniencing you, I hope."

"Of course not," Lorenzino lied, coloring to the roots of his hair. "Amerigo! I'm happy you're back. I missed you. Florence has been quiet with you gone."

"Thank you, I think," Amerigo said, smiling.

Graciously, though a bit shakily, Lorenzino offered wine all around. Sipping the Chianti, more than a little embarrassed by this incursion into Lorenzino de' Medici's private space, Guid'Antonio marked the raw emotions flickering across the younger man's pocked cheeks. Surprise, awe, resentment. Plainly, this pale, young Medici knew about the 54,000 florins his older cousin had borrowed from his and Giovanni's trust fund, and he did not much like it, either.

While Lorenzo talked with his ward, Guid'Antonio cast an eye around the chamber, a spacious room that was close kin with countless others in his world: a bed with summer hangings and a counterpane, a pinewood armario with a backboard and cornice set against one wall. On the cornice, which served as a shelf, Lorenzino had assembled a collection of astrolabes and spherical models of the universe. Guid'Antonio reckoned the massive armario was at least thirty-three feet long. A great tondo of the Virgin and Child in a gilt frame caught his attention: he had heard these round paintings were gaining popularity in prosperous homes.

"Amerigo," Lorenzino was saying, "I sent a note to you this morning to let you know I was here in the city."

"Did you? I'm in Florence but rarely home."

"We've been busy," Guid'Antonio said.

Understanding and a trace of malice flickered in Lorenzino's heavy-lidded brown eyes. The youth looked down at his hands. Soft and plump, like a child's. And like a child, was he hot for revenge against his sticky-fingered kinsman? Lorenzino de' Medici had good reason for wanting to take his magnificent cousin down a peg or two.

Smiling, Lorenzo said, "We won't keep you, Cousin. I didn't believe you would mind the intrusion, as you and Amerigo are favorite friends. And I wanted to show them your latest commission." He gestured toward the younger man's pine daybed and the large rectangular painting fixed above it on the wall. "It's Sandro's. A depiction of spring. Guid'Antonio?"

In the white frame above Lorenzino de'

Medici's daybed was the painting Sandro had mentioned in his shop yesterday. Instantly, Guid'Antonio knew this was one of the most complex paintings he had ever seen. Astonishingly beautiful, the horizontal panel resembled a tapestry. Venus — or was it the Virgin Mary? — graced the center of a grassy meadow blooming with wild strawberries, coltsfoot, and red roses in such vivid array, Guid'Antonio would swear he smelled the earth and the deep scent of the flowers scattered across it. Looking left across the painting, he saw the Three Graces in filmy gowns holding hands and dancing, bodies radiant against the dark glade. Sandro had captured the center maiden glancing over her shoulder. She was tall and golden-haired, with a wistful smile on her pale pink lips: a young woman's face too beautiful to be completely of this world.

As, indeed, it wasn't.

The girl was Simonetta Vespucci, Marco Vespucci's wife and Giuliano de' Medici's lover, dead these last four years. Guid'Antonio's breathing slowed as he followed Simonetta's gaze to the figure of Mercury on the far left side of the painting. Youthful and beautiful, Mercury was naked but for the brief red cloak hiked up over his cocked hip, his feet shod in winged leather boots as he reached up with his caduceus to banish a gathering of gray clouds from the sky: Giuliano de' Medici, perfectly rendered by Sandro Botticelli.

"Jesus, meek and mild," Amerigo said, "Sandro has put Giuliano and Simonetta in the world again."

Amerigo spoke as if this were a wonderful thing, and Guid'Antonio supposed it was if you were not consumed with sorrow and guilt at each passing image of Giuliano de' Medici. This painting of Giuliano was *real,* and it made Guid'Antonio shiver with despair.

Lorenzo ran his hand over his face in a gesture of deep emotion. "Sandro painted it for Lorenzino while the rest of us were off in other directions. I saw it the first time when I came home from Naples. My brother was always otherworldly in his beauty." Tears sprang into Lorenzo's eyes; he neither blinked nor turned away.

Nor did Lorenzino, who chatted casually about how, over a river of wine, Botticelli and Brother Giorgio Antonio Vespucci — along with Marsilio Ficino, Angelo Poliziano, and Lorenzino himself — had discussed the painting to be placed above Lorenzino's new bed. "Their combined feeling was, since I am engaged to marry, why not an allegory of marriage and the kindling of love?"

Lorenzino blushed crimson. "Or of physical desire, as Angelo Poliziano would have it." As if on cue, everyone glanced at the three maidens' transparent gowns and their breasts so engagingly revealed. Beneath the gauzy fabric their breasts were white, their nipples peaked.

Lorenzino cut his brown gaze to his cousin. "This was when our Angelo was still welcome among us and not isolated up north in Mantua."

Lorenzo's gaze on his young ward burned with dark emotion. "No one forced Angelo Poliziano to run off to Mantua. Angelo did so of his own accord, rather than die of his own cowardice for refusing to accompany me to King Ferrante's fearsome court. Unfortunately, Lorenzino, for the rest of us life is not all spring meadows."

Chastened, Lorenzino said, "Of course not, Cousin. Forgive my insensitivity."

Guid'Antonio cast Lorenzo a measuring look. Why had Lorenzo brought him to see this haunting painting? The *Primavera* was glorious, yet for Guid'Antonio it vibrated with sorrow and memories of the dead. Of Giuliano and Simonetta and, by association, of Simonetta's cuckolded husband,

288

Marco Vespucci, and Marco's incarcerated father, Guid'Antonio's kinsman, Piero Vespucci.

Lorenzo de' Medici did not do anything by chance.

They took their leave with all outward signs of cordiality. Lorenzino and his cat, the latter's bushy gray tail unfurled like a banner over her furry back, accompanied them into the courtyard, the youth chatting with Amerigo about his betrothal to Semiramide d'Appiani and their wedding, set for two years hence.

" 'Zino, where's your brother?" Lorenzo asked, one hand on the gate latch.

"At Castello with our grandmother. He chose to stay there rather than ride to town this week." Lorenzino gathered up the cat and nuzzled her head with his cheek. "I wanted to return some books to Brother Giorgio and give him my Greek exercises for corrections. Amerigo, ride back with me tomorrow? We can amuse ourselves with my errors and escape the heat."

Amerigo's face lit with pleasure. "I'll tell you about France."

"No, you won't," Guid'Antonio said.

Lorenzino looked owlish and surprised. Amerigo turned pink.

"Next week, perhaps," Guid'Antonio said. "At present, life holds us here."

"Of course it does," Lorenzino said, glancing pointedly at his guardian.

"But only if that suits you and your grandmother Genevra," Guid'Antonio said.

Lorenzino nodded and addressed the sullen-faced Amerigo: "Ride out when you're free to do as you please." Patting the cat's head, smirking, he turned away.

Lorenzo chewed his lip. "I'm glad you two are friends, Amerigo, no error. He thinks of you as an older brother. Otherwise, he has only Giovanni, who's just thirteen."

" 'Just'?" Amerigo said. "When last I saw Giovanni, he was barely eleven." He cast a brooding look at Guid'Antonio. "Two years ago."

"A lot changes in that much time," Lorenzo said, smiling as they left the garden and stepped back out into the street. "Boys become men."

"But often are not given credit," Amerigo said.

"Credit comes when credit is due," Guid'Antonio said. "You earned a lot of it in France."

In silence the trio walked south along Via Larga to Lorenzo's main gate. "Well, friend," Lorenzo said, "what's next on your list?"

"It's on my mind to seek Camilla's nurse," Guid'Antonio said, his hawk's eyes keen on the steady stream of people traversing the thoroughfare. Some turned to the right at the corner of Via Larga and Via Gori, heading toward San Lorenzo Church and market; others kept straight in the direction of Florence Cathedral. He flicked his eyes away from Brunelleschi's red brick dome, toward the cheese and egg sellers hawking meager wares in the marketplace.

"Palla questioned the old woman. I told you yesterday."

"I'll speak with her, nonetheless."

"Only if you ride to the Rossi farm in Vinci, since that's where she is."

A spasm of irritation shook Guid'Antonio. Why had he assumed Camilla's nurse was here in Florence and easily available? Because she was a member of Castruccio Senso's household. Or so he had thought. "And the slave boy?" he said.

"He's there, too. And now?"

Guid'Antonio had only one answer he cared to divulge. "Along with the nurse and boy, I mean to take a closer look at Ognissanti, or at least at the good brothers of the Humiliati residing there. They can't all be

291

so cold and tight-lipped as they would have us believe. Or so innocent."

Lorenzo laughed his throaty, low laugh. "Inquire too closely there, and you may uncover all manner of mischief having nothing to do with the *Virgin Mary of Santa Maria Impruneta.*" He inclined his head. "Please God, end this soon, Guid'Antonio *mio.* On my soul, I am tired of it and ready to move on to other things."

*So am I,* Guid'Antonio thought, eyeing Lorenzo as he called a merry greeting to the man mopping the arcaded loggia before hurrying up the broad curving stairs to his private quarters. The question pressing on Guid'Antonio's mind now was what Lorenzo de' Medici meant to move on to — and when.

"Sandro's painting for Lorenzino is a mighty piece of work," Amerigo said as he and Guid'Antonio walked through the market past San Lorenzo Church. Our Botticelli's to be congratulated."

"He's probably happy just to have been paid."

"Did you notice the Pallas and centaur above the door to 'Zino's antechamber?"

"How could I not? Sandro, again."

"The figure of Pallas was —"

"Yes, Semiramide d'Appiano, Lorenzino's intended," Guid'Antonio said.

"Do you think —" Amerigo looked perplexed. "I wonder if Lorenzino minds marrying her. Since she's our deceased Simonetta Vespucci's niece. *De-ceased:* what an interesting word! And Giuliano was supposed to marry Semiramide. Before he died, I mean, since Simonetta was already married to our Marco. Mayhap Lorenzino feels he's getting cold soup? Particularly since Lorenzo arranged this marriage, and there's no love lost betwixt them. Lorenzo and Lorenzino, I mean. God! Why does everyone we know have the same name? And then there are the letters Marco and Piero Vespucci have sent Lorenzo's mother." Wide-eyed, Amerigo shook his head in wonder. "This is akin to incest."

It flashed across Guid'Antonio's mind to wonder about baby Giulio's mother, who had borne Giuliano his by-blow, another precious Medici heir. Who was she? And where? Lorenzo had not said. Ah, well. What did it matter, truly?

"Lorenzino understands marriage," Guid'Antonio said. "His alliance with Semiramide helps bind the Piombino family with us against the Pope. No doubt you'll hear exactly how Lorenzino feels about the young lady when you ride off to visit him."

"If I ever do. Who knows what may happen next?" Amerigo hesitated. "Uncle Guid'Antonio?"

"Yes."

"Lorenzo must have noticed you didn't offer an open answer when he mentioned making a change in our government. I don't believe he liked your lack of enthusiasm."

"Nor do I like being manipulated," Guid'Antonio said.

That night, a hot, airless Wednesday in mid-July, as Guid'Antonio thrashed in bed dreaming of lush, sweet lips brushing his, someone painted Lorenzo de' Medici hanging from a gallows on the wall of the Medici Palace, directly across the street from San Lorenzo, the oldest Christian basilica in Florence and, for well over one hundred years, the Medici family church. On the stone bench beneath the crude drawing, the malefactor had deposited a set of horns butchered from a cow and above them had written: SEE HERE THE HORNS OF THE DEVIL LORENZO DE' MEDICI WHO RESIDES WITHIN!

Large and heavy-fisted. In a dark liquid very much resembling blood.

# NINETEEN

*1470*

*Via Saturnia, Florence*

*Magnificent Lorenzo, to whom Heaven has given charge of the city and the State; first citizen of Florence, doubly crowned with bays for the victory in Santa Croce, amid the acclamations of the people, and for poetry, on account of the sweetness of your verses, give ear to me who, drinking at Greek sources, am striving to get Homer into Latin metre. This second book, which I have translated (you know we have the first by Messer Carlo d' Arezzo), timidly crosses your threshold. If you welcome it, I propose to offer you all the* Iliad. *It rests with you, who can, to help the poet. I desire no other muse or other gods but only you; by your help I can do that of which the ancients would not have been ashamed. May it please you therefore at your leisure to give audience to Homer. . . .*

*Your servant,*
*Angelo Poliziano*

*By your help.*

Well situated in Mantua in the summer of 1480, Angelo Poliziano was not isolated, having been given an appointment in the court of Federigo Gonzaga, the Marquis of Mantua. Yet in his heart, where it mattered most, Angelo existed in a cold world, abandoned and alone. Never mind that in the sun-baked garden beneath his villa window, the hot perfume of crimson and butter-colored roses scented the air beneath the high, hot sun, and that in the distant fields tan-faced *contadini* wore their sweat-soaked sleeves rolled up as they toiled. Since hastily packing his bags and riding out from Florence eight months ago, Angelo had roamed homeless through northern Italy, drifting from Bologna to Mantua, Verona, Padua, and Venice, wandering through libraries and visiting other scholars, before finally settling in this city commanded by the Gonzaga lords: soldiers, scholars, patrons of the arts.

On Angelo's writing desk there resided a bowl of golden pears the likes of which the field workers never would see, let alone taste. He consumed the plumpest of the speckled fruits, searching his mind for any means of mending his rift with Lorenzo de' Medici — he might just as well have thrown his conciliatory letters to Lorenzo into a black pit — and returned in thought to last December. He could no longer avoid the realization Lorenzo had indeed expected him to accompany Lorenzo's emergency delegation to Naples, where King Ferrante's cellars hid the skulls of rotting men. Unlike Lorenzo the Magnificent, Angelo was no brave heart. He was no soldier or politician. He was a defenseless poet.

Yes, Angelo's translation of the *Iliad* from Greek into Latin had ushered him across the threshold of the Medici Palace ten years ago, when Angelo was just sixteen. Needy, his cloak threadbare, his shoes hand-me-downs, living with his uncle and a family of rowdy stonemasons on one of the Oltr'Arno's poorest backstreets. Angelo's face burned when he recalled that thin, ungainly lost boy. But he had found Lorenzo, and in him had found his savior. Lorenzo possessed a superb mind and the green freshness of youth, and by mid-January 1470, he was the twenty-one-year-old prince of the city, his father having died just one month earlier. Lorenzo lauded

Angelo's translation, took him into his home, gave him decent clothes and rooms on Via Larga, and provided him with the best tutors in Italy: Latin under Cristoforo Landino, translator of Aristotle and commentator on Dante; Greek under Andronicus Kallistos and Argyropoulos; and Platonic philosophy under Marsilio Ficino, all at *Studio Fiorentino,* Florence's acclaimed university.

Lorenzo had given him a *home,* finding in him a close companion who shared his interests in poetry and scholarship; Lorenzo had given him respect and friendship, even supporting Angelo during the thunderstorm with Clarice Orsini, Lorenzo's *pathetic* little Roman wife, and had allowed him to embark upon the ruling passion of his starved soul — the collection and translation of the manuscripts in the Medici library and the study of ancient coins and inscriptions.

*But Naples, for God's sake?*

Angelo abhorred violence. Just the thought of it made him sweat and fall into a panic. Two years ago, he had stood gasping for breath with Lorenzo and a few other friends in the Cathedral's north sacristy where they had eluded Lorenzo's attackers and bolted the heavy bronze doors even as men, women and children fled the church, convinced

Brunelleschi's dome was about to collapse on their heads. Rioters had filled the streets, armed with bricks, rocks, and spears. "Down with the Pazzi family! Medici, Medici! *Palle, palle!*" they had screamed till their throats were raw and they could scream no more.

At the palace later that day, the sight of Giuliano's body wretchedly fouled with the blood of so many knife wounds, nineteen in all, it had been said, had made him vomit Easter Sunday's blood and bread. Later, with hands trembling, he had written not about woodland groves, fauns, nymphs, and Simonetta Vespucci, but about greed and slaughter. *This* he had done, although it had meant stepping back in time to when he was a boy. *This* he had done, although it meant revisiting himself as an awkward child of nine, watching, horrified, as thugs threw his father to the ground, thrust their pikes into his body, slit his throat, and rode from the hill town of Montepulciano, laughing and congratulating themselves for murdering the man who had sent one of their lousy relatives to jail. Angelo had ripped the scab off that putrid wound and penned his commentary on the Pazzi Conspiracy, *Della Congiura dei Pazzi: this* he had done as a gift to Lorenzo, to Florence, and to all future generations. Did no one appreciate how the effort had wrenched his soul? Wasn't that bravery enough?

*I am not a coward,* he told himself. *Men react to violence in different ways.* His face smarted with heat. He had heard the gossip on every Florentine's lips: Angelo Poliziano backed away when the whole city was in danger and Lorenzo ready to place his life in the hands of the Neapolitan king.

The sound of a squirrel chattering in the garden brought him back to the Mantuan countryside. On these long afternoons, he usually tossed the little animal a bit of food to eat. The squirrel stared up at him now, white paws placed together in supplication, as if even it knew how to pray. "There's your handout," Angelo said gloomily, tossing down the pear's fleshy white core. Anything rather than quit his rooms and thereby risk an encounter with the Gonzaga court painter, Andrea Mantegna, a crusty, short-tempered, querulous old snot of a man. Although, admittedly, talented with a brush.

All Angelo wanted to do was write, teach, and share his ideas with a company of good men in the City of Flowers, where Italy's best and brightest dwelled. Mantua was a court rather than a meeting place of friends. In Florence, there was the Medici library.

His heart sank when he thought of the disarray Lorenzo's priceless manuscripts must have fallen into during his absence these past eight months. He felt his anger flare. Lorenzo simply did not understand that handing precious writings over to every beggar who wanted to borrow them was a serious mistake. Who was keeping those records today? Who was protecting the written records Angelo had painstakingly created and kept a quick eye on every single day, no matter that he had students knocking and poems and letters beckoning him to his *studiolo* tucked in the heart of the Medici Palace?

His sharp brown gaze fell on the latest correspondence from Alessandra Scala. One of Florentine Chancellor Bartolomeo Scala's five daughters, Alessandra was Angelo's dear, devoted student and friend. *You remain much out of favor and it is useless for you to return here. My hope, Angelo, is that you will write, write, and write, for your own illumination and the comfort of your soul.*

*Useless,* Alessandra said. Alessandra, whose blazing intelligence matched her incomparable beauty, was not one to mince words. A sad smile touched Angelo's full, pouting lips. *Write,* Alessandra said, the pupil instructing the master. Wasn't that what he always had done? Poor, he may once have been, but his mind was not impoverished. Nor was it today, no matter how his heart ached when he remembered he would celebrate — no, merely *observe* — his twenty-sixth birthday two days hence in a foreign city situated between Venice and Milan. *Not Florence.* Although to the town of Mantua's credit, Virgil had been born near here, and S. Andrea, a former Benedictine monastery church, did possess the *Preziosissimo Sangue,* a vial of blood from Christ's wounded side.

Along with the letter, Alessandra Scala had sent Angelo a birthday gift, a tiny pebble she had picked up in front of the Medici Palace, a small piece of home. Eyes closed, he pressed the stone to his lips. Alessandra had written of turmoil in the streets and of the *tramontano* blowing toward Lorenzo with such force, it threatened to topple him and his supporters. She had written of a missing girl and of the *Virgin Mary of Santa Maria Impruneta* weeping in Ognissanti Church.

*Bone Deus!* Could it be that with Giuliano de'Medici's death, the golden days of Florence were gone with the wind? No. Angelo refused to believe it. He would not believe it! In the last few months, he had composed epigrams and verses. Now, he had in mind a different sort of composition for Cardinal Francesco Gonzaga, a secular play with musical accompaniment, perhaps even singing voices. Composed in Italian rather than Latin, that the play's spectators might better understand the words. Lorenzo, who from the days of his youth, had encouraged Florence's poets to write in Italian, to bring poetry back down to earth and the common people, would like that.

Nothing like this proposed play, one with singing parts, had been done in recent memory. Why not throw caution to the wind? What did he stand to lose? Ten years ago, his translation of the *Iliad* had taken him inside the Medici Palace's hallowed doors. Perhaps *Orfeo* would take him back. It *must*, for then and only then would the fullness of the fallen angel's dreams rise and walk again.

# TWENTY

"Whoever attacks Lorenzo attacks every last man of us." Lord Prior Pierfilippo Pandolfini cast a grave look around Lorenzo's *sala,* his dark eyes blazing with fury.

" 'Attacks'? There's a strong word," Piero di Nasi said. "Revelers may have put the horns on the bench. Bravos, carousing."

"Then it's a dangerous joke," Lorenzo said, his voice cold and commanding.

In a nervous flurry of robes and papers, Bartolomeo Scala burst into the chamber. "Maddalena's in bed with fever and chills. She's four months along. I fear —" The Chancellor's satchel slipped from his hands; pens spilled over the floor.

"God bless her and keep her well," Lorenzo said.

*He'd like to break the table with his fist,* Guid'Antonio thought. His eyes shifted to the other Medici men seated around the table. A good many of Lorenzo's partisans

304

were in attendance, along with the Priors, transforming the chamber into a sea of red.

"The drawing may have been made by some of the Pazzi family," Piero di Nasi said. "Not all are in jail."

"They are now," Lorenzo said.

Antonio Capponi slid unceremoniously into a chair. "As always, bringing up the rear," Pierfilippo Pandolfini said.

"Have it how you will," Antonio shot back. "Lorenzo, now your palace is sparkling clean again, why are we here?" Very early this morning Lorenzo had sent messages to the men of the Medici faction, telling them about the blood-spattered effigy and requesting their presence here this evening. Not exactly a summons, but still.

A muscle jumped in Lorenzo's jaw. "We're here because I'm the target of men who mean to destroy me."

Piero di Nasi drew back. "We won't know anything firm until Palla imposes a curfew and loosens a few tongues."

"Curfew?" Pierfilippo Pandolfini snorted. "That'll show them."

"Violence against me is violence against you," Lorenzo said.

Tommaso Soderini drew his robe closer around his shoulders. "Other than drawing and quartering every man, woman, and child in the Golden Lion district, what do you suggest we do?"

"Reform the government," Lorenzo said.

Silence hummed in the room, thoughts scattering, tumbling here and there. *Ah,* thought Guid'Antonio. Carefully, he said, "Reform it how? Do you mean you want the Lord Priors, many of whom are now present, to call for a *balìa*?" A *balìa* was a special commission created in times of extreme crisis and war. Dictatorial, it could suspend the Florentine constitution and override the law. It could name Lorenzo de' Medici duke or king and place Florence in the hands of one man for the first time in the city's history.

"I do," Lorenzo said.

"Because of a crude effigy?" Antonio Capponi said. "Sweet Jesus, what have we come to?"

Lorenzo jumped up and knifed forward, as if he meant to grab Antonio by the throat. *"My* effigy, Antonio! *My* house! Next time, *you* go to Naples, and I'll stay home! You watch *your* brother die for the Republic and wake every morning wondering if today's the day a madman will stick a knife in *you.*"

Lorenzo slung himself back into his chair, still watching Antonio Capponi, who slunk down, his pale skin scorched with heat.

There was a minute silence. "*Our* city and government," Lorenzo said, and in his voice there remained an undercurrent of fury. "We're mired in debt. War, weeping paintings. Who can blame people for wanting to tear off our heads? We've become a place of curving streets and dead ends in more ways than one."

Pierfilippo Pandolfini's brown eyes darted around the faces of the other men. "I agree. It's time for reform. For change."

"What shape would that change take? Exactly," Guid'Antonio said.

A smile played on Tommaso Soderini's colorless lips. *Bravo, Guid'Antonio. Dig your own grave.*

"Whatever it takes to establish a stronger government," Lorenzo said.

"But a *balìa*?" Tommaso said. "However would we manage it? People are suspicious of us as it is. They would think we're up to no good." He smirked. "Imagine that."

"What is this? You know how it works. *We* wouldn't manage anything. We have a Republic, remember?" Lorenzo arranged two small bowls of olive oil and a large plate of bread and cheese in front of him in a straight line, setting the single large plate slightly apart. "The first bowl of oil is the nine Lord Priors, the second bowl, our other legislative councils. First, a majority of the nine would have to agree to ask the other councils to consider the appointment of the special commission, the *balìa.*"

He tapped the second bowl of oil. "If, and *only* if, those councils agreed would the commission be appointed." He touched the plate. "In turn, *that* commission, whose members would consist of a great body of men, would determine what reforms should be set in place. *Exactly,* I mean," he said, his brown eyes fixed on Guid'Antonio.

"Even if a majority of the nine agreed to initiate the proposal —" Reaching over, Guid'Antonio slid the first bowl of oil away from the other small bowl and the plate. "What makes you think the other legislative councils would vote for the creation of an emergency committee? They might not agree we have an extreme crisis on our hands."

He moved the second bowl away from the plate. "And as Tommaso says, God help us if the *popolo minuto* get the wrong idea. If they think we mean to seize the government, they'll hang us all, no questions asked."

The *sala* was quiet and tense. Bartolomeo Scala looked up from his notes and put down his pen. Like Guid'Antonio, he was here only as a member of the Medici party's inner circle. And like the rest of the men present, he was willing to let Guid'Antonio butt heads with Lorenzo the Magnificent.

Lorenzo drew his hands back through his hair, holding it away from his face. "I woke to blood on my walls. Who's next? You, Guid'Antonio? Your family? All I am saying is the Lord Priors should consider moving forward. All I hope to do is to strengthen the government, not for me, but for the people."

He sopped a piece of bread in the first bowl of oil and chewed it a while. "Every Prior currently in office would sit on the final commission. Along with a good number of other qualified men. Many of whom are sitting here now."

Of course, yes: it was the law. Lorenzo surveyed the meeting table. "You, Capponi. You, too, Di Nasi." Lorenzo gazed at his uncle. "You, Tommaso Soderini." His eyes locked on Guid'Antonio. "And you, as well as everyone present and many of our closest friends."

"As qualified men," Guid'Antonio said.

Lorenzo's lips quirked in a smile. "Yes."

Tommaso turned the plate, the emergency commission, the *balìa,* in a circle with the tips of his fingers. "No harm in thinking about it, surely."

*No harm,* Guid'Antonio thought, *since we will be the men who benefit most from any changes made in the Republic.*

"The quieter we proceed, the better," Tommaso said. "If we are to consider our necks."

"It's always about our necks, isn't it?" Guid'Antonio said, his words dying into silence in the vast room.

And so, amid the light of many candles, the men parted, gathering their cloaks, many of them with thoughts blurred, not altogether unsuspicious of Lorenzo's true motives. At the door Lorenzo said, "Guid'Antonio, a moment alone, *per favore?*"

Guid'Antonio closed his eyes, seeking a small bit of rest, before opening them again. "Certainly."

"You know all this will come down to numbers and influence. That is, if we get it going in the first place."

"It almost always does. Come down to numbers and influence, I mean. Are you worried? People listen to you," Guid'Antonio said.

Lorenzo laughed. "Not so much anymore, as you just witnessed. Whereas everyone values your good opinion and takes note

310

when you withhold it."

"Still?"

Lorenzo smiled and touched him lightly on the shoulder. "You know they do."

Sharply aware his was the solitary shadow on the wall, Guid'Antonio walked through the loggia arcade in the light of dimly burning torches, his mind bounding over the events of the last four long days, to Ognissanti Church, to the weeping Virgin, and back again to Lorenzo. Lorenzo vulnerable, Lorenzo declaring in the privacy of his *studiolo* his firm belief the Medici party must strengthen itself or face the city's ruin along with the ruin of all their families. Lorenzo "hanged" in effigy, his palace smeared with blood, and now Lorenzo urging the men within the inner circle to consider tampering with the constitution of the Florentine Republic. Guid'Antonio breathed deeply, liking neither the direction of his thoughts nor the shrinking feeling they occasioned in the pit of his belly.

Just beyond the main gate, two guards stood watch, assigned by Palla Palmieri to their new post earlier today. Guid'Antonio passed the armed men, slowing at the figure of Lorenzo's uncle, Tommaso Soderini, seated on the stone bench facing Via Larga, his head resting against the front wall of Lorenzo's palazzo. Nighttime shadows furrowed the length of Tommaso's crimson robe. He said, "What took you so long?"

Guid'Antonio sat beside him. The street was quiet, shop doors and shutters locked, the night air warm but pleasant. At this hour, San Lorenzo market just around the corner was closed down.

"I spoke briefly with Bartolomeo to say Maddalena is in my prayers and to ask if she needs anything," Guid'Antonio said.

"I didn't see him."

"He left by the garden gate."

"And does she? Need anything?"

"Prayers, only. His daughter Alessandra and her four sisters are in close attendance."

Tommaso nodded, smiling. "Five daughters. Remarkable."

"Yes."

"Do you remember when Cosimo de' Medici built this palace?"

"Tommaso, I was only eight or so when Lorenzo's grandfather started construction here."

"It must be your hair, all that silver you're sporting now. Also, it seems as if you've always been around. Like a not altogether unpleasant odor lingering in the air."

"Thank you," Guid'Antonio said. "I think."

"Cosimo commissioned Brunelleschi for a design," Tommaso said. " 'Too grand!' Cosimo believed, so he hired Michelozzo, instead. This, after Brunelleschi already had built the Cathedral's magnificent brick dome. And after Cosimo had hired him to rebuild San Lorenzo. Cosimo knew the danger of flying too high. The old man said so many times. And yet, he devoted much of his life not only to books and learning, but to fine craftsmanship, as well. I was among the first to stroll through the loggia arcade there at our backs. To gasp at Donatello's little *David,* perched on a pedestal in the garden in all his naked glory. In those days, people considered that delicious sculpture pagan."

"They still do," Guid'Antonio said.

Tommaso chuckled. "No one had seen anything like it since the Greeks and Romans. Which was precisely the point. Ironic, isn't it, that Cosimo had it done for this palace as a symbol of Florentine liberty, as David conquered Goliath, so Florence conquered blah, blah, blah."

Guid'Antonio relaxed with his hands in his lap, content to let the old man reminisce. He had heard enough stories about Cosimo de' Medici from his elders to fill a book. Several books. Upon Cosimo's death, the Florentine government had named him the Father of His Country, and him, yes . . . a private citizen.

"Alas, Lorenzo's father, Piero, lacked the physical energy to match Cosimo's fervor when it came to rebuilding Florence," Tommaso said. "But even Piero understood the political importance of maintaining the *status quo*. Tamper with it, and you're risking your neck. Your family. You have a son named Giovanni, Guid'Antonio?"

"I do, yes."

"Is he a good boy? Will he follow in his father's footsteps?"

"I don't know yet," Guid'Antonio said, tucking away the implied compliment.

The old man puffed out a breath of air. "You had best find out." He coughed, a terrible hack, causing the guards to stir and glance in their direction.

Alarmed, Guid'Antonio turned to the old man. "I'm fine," Tommaso said. Coughing had weakened his voice. "We're bound by time and loyalties, my friend. You, our magnificent Lorenzo, and me. We may not always agree with one another —" He managed a laugh. "But we remain within his golden circle. Do you know why?" The little laugh gave way to another series of rasping coughs.

"Why?" Guid'Antonio asked.

Tommaso's pale blue eyes opened wide on him. "Because you and I are the only ones who dare tell him it's raining when he says the sun is shining. We tell him the *truth.* And he loves us for it. That's why he wants your approval in all things, my friend. For validation and to ease his conscience in the days ahead."

Tommaso stood, drawing his cloak close about his shoulders. Bird wings. "I'm almost eighty years old. My nephew has nothing to fear from me. Weeping paintings to turn the populace against him? Hanging him in effigy?" Tommaso's mouth crimped in a smile. "Not me." He raised his brow. "Not anymore."

In silence, with Guid'Antonio acting as escort, they walked through wide dark streets to Ponte Trinita and then alongside the river to the next bridge, Ponte alla Carraia. Across this bridge lay Tommaso's palace in the Green Dragon district of the Santo Spirito quarter. Beyond the river, torches flickered here and there, chasing shadows from the dark piazzas and deserted streets.

Guid'Antonio let Florence's premier

elected official walk unescorted across the bridge spanning the Arno's warm, dark water, but kept an eye on Tommaso's slight figure as he approached the Soderini Palace gate. Satisfied the old man was safe, Guid'Antonio turned from Ognissanti and walked in the direction from which they had just come, setting a course now for Santa Croce and the Del Vigna household.

There, through the iron gates, he had a clear view of Maria's moonlit garden. The house was dark and silent. At this hour, she slept, Maria, his sometimes lover, his wife. Here was a woman who gave her mother brave comfort; surely in good time he, too, would benefit from her devotion. Shaken somehow, and not at all certain why he had made this discomforting, nocturnal visit, Guid'Antonio withdrew and trod back toward his home in Ognissanti.

# TWENTY-ONE

*"Giorno."* Strolling into the kitchen at noon the following day, dressed in traveling clothes, Guid'Antonio squeezed Amerigo's shoulder, kissed Domenica on both cheeks and gave Cesare, whom he had seen in his apartment a short while earlier, a nod of acknowledgment. Olimpia Pasquale looked up from the stone sink, smiling, swishing basil in a basin of water to clean it.

*"Giorno,"* Domenica said. "Praise God for a miracle, you're happy again!" She crossed herself. "Olimpia, for God's precious love, don't crush the leaves."

"What difference does it make?" Olimpia said back. "We're only going to pulverize them."

"My happiness is so rare it bears commenting on?" Guid'Antonio said, smiling. The kitchen smelled deliciously of basil and garlic, pine nuts, and Parmesan cheese.

"This week, yes," Cesare said, stepping

quickly from the sink to the cold hearth in a move calculated to hide the bulky object looming beside the fire irons.

Guid'Antonio narrowed his eyes, watching his willowy — and wily? — manservant.

"All the more remarkable when one considers there's no rest for Medici men," Amerigo said.

"Does the entire town know about the meeting at Lorenzo's house last night? And the vandalism that occasioned it?"

They stared at him wonderingly, as if he had just asked whether they knew there was a river running through town called the Arno. "Word of the attack on Lorenzo and the subsequent meeting swept Florence like wildfire," Cesare said.

Attack. "And?" Guid'Antonio said.

"The *popolo minuto* wonder, 'What next?' as they always do when there's a nocturnal meeting at Palazzo Medici. They're calling Lorenzo's hanging an act committed by Satan to claim Lorenzo as his own. They're saying they wish they had done it themselves, rather than leave it to the Prince of Darkness."

Domenica snapped her damp wiping towel at her son. "Cesare, if there's a prince of darkness in Florence, it's you! I should box your ears for repeating malicious gossip."

"If you do, watch the earring, Mama, it's new from Verrocchio's." Cesare danced away from his mother's wrath, grinning impishly.

"Domenica," Guid'Antonio started, but hesitated as the object behind Cesare shook itself vigorously and rose up from the fireplace. "God's flesh. What is that?"

A touch of uncertainty crossed Cesare's face. And then he stepped aside to reveal a huge, hunch-shouldered, hairy beast: it was the mastiff dead at the hand of Bartolomeo Scala's secretary. Guid'Antonio's mouth dropped open. Miraculously, it appeared that in the past week the animal had gained weight; very little, of course, but in any event, the dog's ribs no longer seemed about to poke holes through his skin. Cesare had hidden him away. He had bathed and brushed the animal, too. For all his scars and beatings, the *cane corso Italiano* looked amazingly well. And what of the cur Alessandro Braccesi had killed at Lorenzo's palace gate? Well. Florence had a multitude of stray, starving dogs.

The grinning animal dared take a shaky step toward him. Guid'Antonio raised a hand: "Stop." Amazingly, the dog obeyed.

Guid'Antonio stifled a smile.

"Tell him to sit," Cesare said.

Guid'Antonio did, and again the animal obeyed. Amazing. Guid'Antonio stared hard at Cesare. "This explains the bits of leftover roast you squirreled away the other evening. Not to mention Elisabetta's missing charity blanket."

Cesare met his eyes straight on. "It certainly does."

"And you were out yesterday morning in the rain."

"Walking him," Amerigo said. "I saw them together."

"And covered for them, too," Guid'Antonio said.

Domenica poured pine nuts into a mortar bowl and ground them with the pestle, her expression grim. "I warned Cesare the lady Elisabetta Vespucci would skin him like a rabbit meant for the pot, should she find out. Worse, she would have him tossed in the Stinche."

Cesare lifted his chin. "I believe she would be overruled." His eyes sought Guid'Antonio.

"No one's being tossed in the Stinche," Guid'Antonio said.

"Except, of course, our kinsman, Piero Vespucci," Amerigo kicked in.

"Amerigo, must you always —" Guid'Antonio stopped and drew a deep breath. "So you think your mother doesn't know about —" He indicated the *cane corso Italiano.* *"This?"*

"Actually, my mother does know," Amerigo said. "Somehow, she, ummm, gained the impression he has your permission to stay. Nor is she happy about it, either."

"His fur makes her sneeze," Cesare said.

The rare smile breezed along Guid'Antonio's lips. "Welcome, you," he said to the dog. "No! Stay away from me. Cesare, you're the one feeding him. Why is he making calf eyes at me?"

"You fed him in Mercato Nuovo," Amerigo said.

"I spit some spoilt cheese on the ground."

"Yes."

Cesare turned up both palms in a gesture of helplessness. "He loves you unconditionally."

*A dog.* "Get him out of here," Guid'Antonio said. "Dogs don't belong in the kitchen with the —" He glanced at the table. "The pesto."

"Amen," Domenica said. "Olimpia! You've spilled the olive oil again! My God, girl!"

"You'd be wise to burn the blanket," Guid'Antonio told Cesare. "No need in providing Elisabetta fuel for her anger."

"I'm grieved my mother is such a bone of contention," Amerigo said. Glancing at the dog, he grinned. "No pun intended."

"Never fear, there wasn't one," Guid'Antonio said.

The dog straggled after Cesare, glancing back over his hefty shoulder at Guid'Antonio, his dog-smile open and adoring. "Amerigo," Guid'Antonio said, "let's get going. Do we have food for our trip?"

Amerigo drew himself up in his boots and brown leather pants. "I wrapped cold roast pork in greased paper and packed my saddlebags hours ago. Before Cesare informed me we weren't leaving for Morba at the crack of dawn today, as planned. Although he didn't say why you changed our time of departure."

"I was with Maria," Guid'Antonio said. Thank God he had gone back to see her this morning, after leaving her gate without venturing inside the house last night.

Olimpia grinned and Domenica glanced up from the mortar bowl. "Ah, *que bella Maria*," she said.

"That explains your smile," Amerigo said. "And this delay."

"How's her mother?" Domenica asked.

Alessandra del Vigna was as dead now as

if she had already drawn her last breath. In fact, she might already have done. "The lady is grave," Guid'Antonio said.

But nothing, not even the memory of Maria's mother in pain upon her daybed, could spoil his joy at having spent a few hours with Maria earlier today. Hours he had stolen when, upon jerking awake at dawn, he had felt the emptiness in his soul and realized how hungry he was to see his family. Ridiculous, unconscionable: he had been in Florence almost five days and spent no time to speak of with them, damn the extenuating circumstances.

Dressing quickly, he had retraced his steps of the previous night and gone to Santa Croce to fetch her and the boy. Strolling together from the Del Vigna courtyard, his little family had struck out across the piazza, stepping lightly into the sun-gilded square, where this morning there was no sign of a ghostly Giuliano de' Medici celebrating his snow-bound tournament. Maria lifted her face to the sun, soaking up its warm, healing rays. She was as much a prisoner in the twilight sadness of her mother's house as Guid'Antonio's kinsman, Piero Vespucci, was in the dark night of the Stinche.

Watching Maria, Guid'Antonio saw a woman in her middle twenties, with thick dark lashes brushing her cheeks and black tendrils of hair escaping the cowl meant to cover her head and neck from the roving eyes of the public. Love thickened his throat, and he was grateful to God he had delayed his journey to Morba until later in the day.

In no hurry, they walked amongst vendors and dodged boys playing ball, Guid'Antonio's spirits so elevated, he hardly noticed the ramshackle appearance of the poor wooden houses and shops encircling Piazza Santa Croce. From two *venditrici,* women peddling their wares outside the guild-endorsed shops, he purchased a packet of sewing needles and a lace cap for Maria. Giovanni's gift was a marionette dangling from a web of strings.

"See, Giovanni." Laughing, Guid'Antonio made the wooden spider's legs clack and dance in the street.

The boy stared, amazed: not at the toy, but at his father. "Mama," Giovanni said. "He does so know how to laugh!"

Heat stung Guid'Antonio's cheeks; his smile faded.

"Giovanni! Of course he does." Embarrassed, Maria placed her hands on Giovanni's shoulders; leaning down, she kissed the boy's cheek. "Why don't you try working the puppet?"

To Guid'Antonio, his wife sounded nervous and exhausted, too tired to tolerate much more conflict and weight. He touched her arm. "It's all right, Maria."

"No. But one day —" She let the sentence drift. *One day, my mother — my constant presence won't be required at my mother's house.*

Giovanni squinted up at Guid'Antonio. "May I play with the spider puppet?"

"Of course. It's yours. Try not to get it tangled."

But Giovanni was already concentrating on the puppet and the relationship of the strings to his childish fingers. His parents took the opportunity to sit together on the stone bench encircling the fountain, where the morning sun poured down on them, and the water in the fountain gurgled and glistened, spurting from the mouth of a reclining stone lion. "Guid'Antonio, such a thing for 'Vanni to say."

"Well. If it's the truth."

"But it isn't." She placed her hand high on his thigh, and he felt a spasm of desire shoot through his groin, here in crowded Piazza Santa Croce with russet buildings thrusting skyward all around them, and Santa Croce Church watching from the piazza's far end.

A band of adolescent boys strolled past. One grabbed his crotch. *"Que bella Signora,* best you should try this long ripe fruit!"

Stone-faced, Guid'Antonio eased his dagger from its sheath. The brazen boys hurried on, but they were not so threatened that they desisted from flashing wicked grins over their shoulders at Maria.

"Bold," she fussed. "Traveling in packs, wearing one another's colors with knives at their hips. Blessed Mother, if ever I hear of Giovanni strutting about like that."

"You won't," he assured her. "Hear of it, I mean."

A little frown creased her brow; she caught his smile, and grinned. "You're teasing me."

"Yes."

With a show of delicacy, Maria removed her hand from his leg. *"Cara,* over here," she called to Giovanni. "Don't wander into the alley."

Dutifully, the boy moved away from the shadowy backstreet, toward his parents. At that same moment, bell towers and churches all over Florence pealed the hour, high and bright, shivering through the air. It was almost noon.

Guid'Antonio said, "Amerigo and I are setting out for Morba today."

326

"Morba? Isn't that where the girl disappeared? That's a lengthy journey."

"We meant to leave at dawn." He made a light shrug. "Instead, I brought you and Giovanni here. Actually, Morba town's not our destination. I mean to go only as far as the place where Camilla Rossi vanished. Anyway, now we'll have to stop in San Gimignano for the night and take the road again early tomorrow morning."

Maria shaded her eyes with her hand, blocking the sun. "Why are you involved with her in the first place?"

Of course — Maria didn't know about his investigation of the missing girl and the weeping painting. She didn't know someone appeared to be using Camilla Rossi da Vinci's disappearance to stir up a world of trouble in Florence. "I'm concerned about what happened to her," he said.

Fine lines appeared around Maria's dark eyes. "But Turks would have left no trace."

He blinked. "You believe Turks took her, Maria?"

"On my soul, yes." She crossed herself. "Everyone knows they did." Tears rimmed her eyes, and her voice had the reedy sound born of certainty and fear.

What could he say to this? He did not mean to mock Maria or demean her beliefs.

What he must do was learn from her expression of dread.

He squeezed her arm gently. The fabric of her full-length summer cloak felt hot beneath his fingers. "I believe we're safe from Mehmed the Conqueror. Presently, at least."

"You do? Good!" She looked at him inquiringly, wanting to believe. Then frowning. "But why do you have to go? Surely, the police have already been."

Yes, they had, in the slender shape of Palla Palmieri. The place Camilla Rossi da Vinci had vanished was an extended ride from Florence. He and Amerigo would have to find beds in San Gimi, and then ride a bit farther west, toward Volterra town. Palla Palmieri had inspected the scene the day after news of Camilla's disappearance had reached Florence and found — nothing.

But Guid'Antonio wanted to see for himself. To smell the atmosphere and touch with his fingers the place where Camilla Rossi da Vinci had ended her journey with Tesoro, with her nurse, and with her slave boy. He wanted to fill his lungs with the same air, feel the worn ruts in the road, and wander in the surrounding forest. To discover if he could feel what had happened that particular Saturday. Perhaps there on the road to Bagno a Morba, home of Lucrezia de' Medici's healing sulfur springs, he would find his own cure. Fool. He smiled to himself.

He said, "I only want to see if I might uncover additional information concerning what might have become of the girl. With Fortune's blessing, I'll be back late tomorrow evening. Meanwhile, do you need anything? More medicine for your mother?"

Maria shook her head, still frowning, regarding Guid'Antonio thoughtfully. "She's calmer now, thanks to Luca Landucci's potions. The wolfsbane helps her most."

If only Luca's talents extended to discovering how the *Virgin Mary of Santa Maria Impruneta* was being made to weep! Late last night, Cesare had brought Guid'Antonio a sealed note from Luca, who had written he had a brilliant idea: what if someone were using a pig's bladder filled with water to squirt the painting's face at opportune moments? Luca, having tried this at home and discovered it worked, hinted he might slip into Ognissanti and —

Christ on the Cross! Guid'Antonio had paled at the thought of the druggist sneaking into Ognissanti and aiming an animal organ at the *Virgin Mary of Santa Maria Impruneta.* What if Luca were caught? Abbot

Ughi would have him drawn and quartered. Luca had suggested chemicals, too. A powder of some kind that became liquid under the proper conditions. In that way, the tears could be controlled. But what powder? What liquid? And what conditions? Luca was working on it.

In his hastily written reply, Guid'Antonio had told the man he should not go to Ognissanti and experiment under any conditions. It was too dangerous. Also, Luca might damage the revered old painting. God's pants, to see Gostanzo win the *palio* next month, this was how far Luca Landucci would go to appease Guid'Antonio Vespucci?

Yes.

"I'm glad your mother is resting," he said before rising from the circular stone bench. "Giovanni, come along."

Now, with his wife and son safely home in Santa Croce, and Amerigo walking with him to the Vespucci stable, Guid'Antonio felt awash in light and hope. How could the gently stirring breeze and the summer sun warming his shoulders through the fabric of his plain brown tunic and linen undershirt be anything other than a benediction?

Shadows fell in bands across the sunlit road

as they traveled south on Flora and Bucephalus. Florence was not far behind them when the road widened and flame-shaped cypress trees gave way to rolling hills carpeted with scarlet poppies, brilliant yellow *genestra,* and sweet-scented wildflowers, ravaged by bees. On and on they rode, saddles pleasantly creaking, past simple churches and stone farmhouses.

Sighting the crumbling castles and fortified villages dotting the countryside, Amerigo shuddered. "Imagine what it was like living back in the gloomy old days. Utter cold. Bleak. No books to read. Not that many people could read then. Or if they once could, they had forgotten how. Can you imagine not holding a book in your hands?"

Guid'Antonio glanced at him. "In the great scheme of things, it wasn't that long ago."

It was the Dark Ages, as people sometimes called it, a time in the dark past when violence ripped the Tuscan countryside apart as if it were soft flesh. A time when safety and power depended upon individual strength, and families sought refuge from axe-wielding enemies in lofty towers and walled strongholds, raining rocks and boiling pitch down on their heads. The skin of

Guid'Antonio's scalp prickled. He saw Bernardo Bandini's axe slice down on Giuliano's head and saw Lorenzo race toward the sacristy with Angelo Poliziano at his back. Francesco Nori, manager of the Florence branch of the Medici Bank, had died at the altar that day. Instead of running, Francesco had stepped in front of Lorenzo and been stabbed in the heart.

Guid'Antonio scrubbed his hand over his face. Not the Dark Ages, but a mere two years ago. These, the rich and the celebrated, living in the fullness of light and the new, blossoming genius of the day, scrambling to keep power and place, not to mention their lives: because, in fact, the fundamental trick remained simply to *stay alive.*

In the violet dusk of evening, they approached San Gimignano, built high upon a hill. "Hear my confession and call me a sinner," Amerigo said. "I'm always amazed by the number of towers in this small city."

"Yes. Seventy or more."

After showing the guard their traveling papers, they passed through the gate and rode down a narrow, rocky street lined with workshops. Another tight lane led them to Piazza del Duomo. They dismounted, and

Amerigo set out in search of the public stable, having secured the horses at a water trough, while Guid'Antonio walked in twilight to the church on the main square, seeking a relatively safe place for them to rest their heads for the night. These tasks accomplished, they sought *La Buca,* the town tavern. Looking around at the care-worn faces in the light of stubby candles set on tables in the hot little bar, they made a filling supper of wild boar ham and tiny sweet peas washed down with pottery cups of Vernaccia, the local white wine.

Guid'Antonio swept a glance around the tight eatery: curious, each and every man supping and drinking at the wooden tables, all of them eager to exchange gossip and information. "Ah. You're traveling to Morba for the soothing waters? Watch your backs. The road is lined with blood-sucking Infidels. You know at midnight, they become werewolves and eat our flesh!"

"Yes, yes, *Signore.* Not long ago, they attacked an innocent. A girl! Of course, that's what they like, slaves for the market. And for themselves."

Guid'Antonio shook his head in sorrow. "We heard about the attack. Where did it happen?"

"You'll find the place marked with a cross,

two reeds twisted together, like those protecting our crops."

Later, after buying the tavern a round and checking on Flora and Bucephalus in the stable, Guid'Antonio and Amerigo extinguished their night candles and fell exhausted onto their pallets in the sanctuary of the pitch-black church. Amerigo whispered, restless: "Uncle Guid'Antonio, I can't sleep."

"You're exhausted, Amerigo. Good night."

Amerigo's voice was animated. "It's not that. How can you close your eyes, surrounded by these hellish frescoes? They're, they're —"

"Taddeo di Bartolo's *Last Judgment*," Guid'Antonio murmured. "The proper word for them is 'breathtaking,' though they do depict the souls of the damned being tortured in hell. In fact, the frescoes are nowhere near, but at the back of the church, on the far walls of the nave. Besides, 'tis midnight black in here. Those gold stars painted on the ceiling above our heads are not shining down on our heads."

Amerigo said, "I saw Ghirlandaio's frescoes in the chapel of Saint Fina when we arrived this afternoon. His depiction of the girl's piety is quite satisfying."

"I'm sure Ghirlandaio would be ecstatic

to hear you say it." Guid'Antonio, too, had seen Domenico Ghirlandaio's fresco cycle in the chapel today and had read the words inscribed on Saint Fina's tomb: *Are you looking for miracles? Observe those that the vivid images on these walls illustrate. 1475.*

*Yes,* Guid'Antonio thought. *I am.*

"Have you seen Ghirlandaio's new fresco in Ognissanti?" Amerigo said.

Guid'Antonio blew out a tired breath. "The *Saint Jerome* near Sandro's *Saint Augustine*? In passing, yes."

"No, no. The one in the refectory. *The Last Supper* on the far end wall."

"No." Guid'Antonio's body felt as if it had been whipped for the last week, and then flung onto a stone bed. Well — after all, he was on the floor.

"Nor have I. Uncle Giorgio commissioned it," Amerigo said.

"Perhaps we should start calling Brother Giorgio 'Brother Moneybags,' " Guid'Antonio said.

"Uncle —"

"Amerigo, has Sandro begun your portrait?"

"Alas, no. As you say, who's had time? Though I'm sure he'll chase me down soon, so he can begin collecting payment. *Buona*

335

*notte,* Uncle. Um, when tomorrow are we leaving?"

"Early, lest we're trampled beneath the monks' feet."

They rode from San Gimignano wrapped in a blanket of drizzle and white clouds so thick, they could barely make out the noses of their horses. "God!" Amerigo exclaimed. "I had hoped to produce a map of this place. How, when we can't see where we're going?" He bit into the apple he had purchased from the peddler setting up his wares near the church at the first pink glimmerings of dawn.

Guid'Antonio pulled his hood up against the early morning damp. "Just think how men must feel when they first set sail on the uncharted ocean, my beloved nephew. Nothing but water and sky as far as the eye can see." He felt, rather than saw, his nephew straighten in the saddle.

"I have thought of it. Daunting, to say the least." Amerigo paused, thinking. "But there is a school which holds —"

Guid'Antonio smiled, letting Amerigo prattle as they rode on, picking their way, trusting the horses, descending at last from the veil of clouds into a lush valley. Hoods lowered, cloaks soggy, they rode westerly across green hills and through glittering, clear steams, slowing their mounts when the trees bordering their passage thickened and became forest. "There," Guid'Antonio said, indicating the reed cross stuck in the grass beside the road.

They dismounted and removed their cloaks. Amerigo fetched a hunk of thick chewy bread from his saddlebag and tore it in half, wordlessly handing Guid'Antonio a portion. They drank from a trickling stream and ate sausages with the bread before wiping their hands on their pants and approaching the cross.

Rough, yes. Two reeds, twisted together.

Arms crossed, with his right finger pressed against his mouth, Guid'Antonio observed his surroundings. The road was narrow here, little more than a sun-dappled clearing.

"Room enough for a thundering horde to waylay a young woman with no sign of struggle?" Amerigo said.

"No. And of course Palla was here almost immediately and says he saw no sign of a disturbance."

"That's good, am I right? Since it's proof Camilla left her husband of her own will, with nary an anti-Christian in sight?"

"With a lover, you mean?"

Amerigo shrugged. "What else?"

"Good as far as it goes, Amerigo. Meaningless when it comes to frightened people who consider the Turks half devils capable of all manner of cruel deeds. Also, a few ordinary thieves could have waylaid her. Plenty of room for that."

Amerigo cocked his head. "If Camilla *did* leave of her own will — and there's a leap for a lady — what about the nurse and boy? It's they who cried 'Turks' in the first place."

Distantly, Guid'Antonio said, "Precisely." And then: "What did you say?"

"It's they who cried —"

"No, about the leaping lady."

Amerigo looked impatient. "What girl of Camilla Rossi da Vinci's standing would dream of quitting her husband? Well." He grinned. "Plenty of them may dream of it, but when did one ever do it?"

Right. Guid'Antonio wondered what in hell he had been thinking when he jumped to the conclusion Camilla Rossi had run off of her own accord with some strapping, hot-blooded youth. For one thing, this assumed she was miserable with her husband, Castruccio Senso. Who could say for certain? For another, divorce was possible in Florence. He had handled one such case, successfully, in the end. But when had a young

338

woman ever actually flown off with her paramour? Actually, several times he could recall. But in each instance, the girl had been hunted by her family and sent to a nunnery to live out the days of her life. Another, in despair over her impossible situation, slit her own throat.

What, then? What other possible scenarios were even remotely possible? Why were the boy and the nurse lying about Turks? He must question them. But the town of Vinci, like Morba, lay a good distance from Florence. He was tired of traveling. He was tired of everything.

They walked the woods on either side of the road and up brambly hills, sniffing the green smell of the ferns and the fecund odor of damp decay. "Nothing," he said.

They made their way back to the horses and stood in the sunlight filtering through the trees, Guid'Antonio sucking in great breaths of air. He got down on his knees and sifted the dirt through his fingers. A tranquil place. A safe, fair place. He pressed his hands to the ground, inhaling the mix of earth and heat, and it seemed to him for one wondrous moment, he felt against his flattened palms the thumping of his heart connected to the earth, to all ages past and all yet to come.

And then he had an odd feeling that something had, indeed, spoiled the quiet of this golden place. Something . . . he rose to his feet, shaking his head to clear it.

Something terrible and violent.

"Where to now?" Amerigo said. "The baths?"

Guid'Antonio swung into Flora's saddle, frowning, slowly shaking his head. "Why would we go all that way when our young lady never reached her destination? We're going home, Amerigo. To Florence."

# TWENTY-TWO

"That's your rain cloak?" Cesare's violet-blue eyes swept Guid'Antonio up and down. Gingerly, he accepted the sopping wet fabric and draped it over the corner rope in the courtyard garden, to dry it in the sun.

Guid'Antonio had yanked his tunic up over his head by the time he reached the stairs from the courtyard to his private apartment. "That cloak has more than earned its cost, first coming from France, then now," he said.

Riding home the previous afternoon, he and Amerigo had run afoul of a raging summer storm, complete with black, bursting rain clouds accompanied by silver shards of lightning and volleys of thunder that saw Flora and Bucephalus slipping in the muddy road and rolling their eyes in terror. When Castellina in the Chianti Valley drew near, they turned toward that little town and sought shelter. This morning, it was on to Florence, past cypress trees and scarlet poppies beaded with raindrops sparkling in the sun like gemstones.

Behind him now, following him up the stairs, Cesare said, "If you hadn't returned soon, I was mounting a search for you. These days who knows what the mob might be about?"

Guid'Antonio growled. He did not want to be met by gloom and doom every time he came back home from — somewhere. "I don't believe Amerigo and I are in any particular danger."

"Humph," Cesare said. "By the way, your nephew Ser Antonio Vespucci is gone."

"Gone? Gone where?" Another question he asked often these days. He turned down the hall and into his chamber.

"San Felice, yesterday. With his wife and children to escape the heat." No need for Cesare to add the rest of it: "And to tend his father, Nastagio Vespucci, in residence at the villa since your entry back into our lives one week ago. Antonio left you this." Cesare bolted the door and pressed a sealed note into Guid'Antonio's hand.

*Guid'Antonio mio:*
*Whilst you were gone, wild rumors of a*

342

balìa *began creeping through town. People are saying Lorenzo means to make himself prince of the city, officially, once and for all. Don't ask me the source of this astonishing speculation. I honestly don't know, for Lorenzo de' Medici is nothing if not closemouthed. There is talk, too, of dissension within the Lord Priors' ranks. Some fear the power a* balìa *could render our Lorenzo. There are murmurs Lorenzo means for the Signoria to change the laws so he can make himself a duke like Ercole d'Este in Ferrara or Montefeltro in Urbino. Some speak of armed rebellion if this happens, others of mounted Medici troops in the streets. Others say Lorenzo is our prince in all but name, anyway, and he is a good man, so what harm if the Signoria makes it official?*

*Pray Mary that if any changes come about they favor us, as the future of our House depends on maintaining our position within the Republic, whatever shape it may take. Destroy this document, since as yet we know not whose side we are on. Stay safe.*

*Antonio di Nastagio Vespucci*
*Saturday, 15 July 1480*

"Burn this," Guid'Antonio said.

343

"Done. There is some good news."

"Thank God."

"You know the lady in Ognissanti wept when Camilla Rossi's horse rode into the city two days ago now. Last night, the Virgin Mary's eyes went dry as a witch's tits."

Cool air smelling of old stone brushed Guid'Antonio's face the moment he opened the door to Ognissanti and entered the church with Amerigo. "I see you continue robbing people of their earnings," Amerigo said, addressing Brother Bellincioni, who was standing by the holy water font with his collection box in his hands. "Even when our Virgin Mary isn't weeping."

"What do you know of earnings? Pah!" the monk spat. "Either of you, in your boots of fine leather and rich clothes."

"Amerigo, don't waste your breath," Guid'Antonio said, pushing past the bitter old man.

Within the sanctuary, he glanced around and took a step back. Was it possible? Oh, joy, good luck at last! "Amerigo!" he said. "Look there!"

Hurrying along the south wall were two brothers of the Benedictine Order of the Humiliati, the smaller fellow a novitiate, the other the tallish young monk who, racing from the cloister in pursuit of his fleet, dark-haired brother last Monday, had burst straight into Guid'Antonio.

It was Brother Paolo Dolci and his little shade, Ferdinando Bongiovi.

"Here's one prayer answered. *Andiamo,* Amerigo. Brother Paolo, hold!"

Brother Paolo Dolci turned slowly around, his face suffused with a look of wonderment: him, singled out in the church by a voice at once demanding and unfamiliar? His pale blue eyes widened as Guid'Antonio and Amerigo Vespucci elbowed through the people in the sanctuary, coming near, and he shrank back. "I meant you no harm, Messer Vespucci. I swear!"

Amerigo bristled. "Harm him? *You?* It would take more than the rude bump you gave us last week."

"Brother Paolo," Guid'Antonio said, "I mean only to have a word with you. Nothing more."

"Oh," Paolo said. "I thought —" Delicate fingers brushed back a missing lock of hair; a ghost lock: so, Brother Paolo was newly tonsured. "May God bless you for your mercy," Paolo said, casting his eyes down.

"I need to talk with you," Guid'Antonio said. "Not here. Somewhere hidden. Somewhere safe."

"I —"

"He'll not go anywhere with you," Ferdinando Bongiovi huffed. "Father Abbot says you're in league with the devil and on the path to hell. He says sinners may spend their last florin in church, but they cannot buy entrance to heaven."

"Well then, Uncle, do you think we should stop trying?" Amerigo said, grinning malevolently.

"Ferdinando," Brother Paolo said, "for God's sake, hold your tongue, or one day it will get us both into such trouble, we'll never see our way back into the light. Ignore him, Messer Vespucci. He's an ignorant boy."

But after all, a loose tongue was Guid'Antonio's aim. And it seemed unlikely he would ever get Paolo alone anywhere. "Ferdinando," he said, quietly addressing the boy, "we came late to the weeping Virgin —"

"Praise Mary, ever Virgin, who brings us overwhelming joy," Ferdinando chanted, crossing himself.

"Ferdinando, hush," Brother Paolo said. "Joy certainly," he added, turning to Guid'Antonio. "Still, it's a sad kind of joy that springs from Mary's sorrow and her disappointment in us."

"Us?" Ferdinando drew himself up to his full height, which was sadly lacking. "Nay. Not in us, but in *Il Magnifico.* Father Abbot says Lorenzo and his lackeys are Satan's footmen."

"How dare you, you little rodent!" Amerigo said.

"Amerigo, you're not helping," Guid'Antonio cut in.

"Ferdinando," Brother Paolo said, "be still or I'll hang you up by the ears."

"If you don't, I will," Amerigo said, his volume increasing. People stared in their direction. A boy nearby began crying.

"Quiet!" Guid'Antonio demanded and seized the moment: "Brother Paolo: have you or any of your brothers ever been here in the church when tears begin coursing down the Virgin's face?"

Brother Paolo pondered this as if Guid'Antonio had just spoken to him in Portuguese. "Begin coursing — ? I don't understand."

Guid'Antonio prayed for forbearance. "You come into the sanctuary, the Virgin's eyes are as dry as witch — as dry they are today, and then she weeps." He gestured encouragingly.

Regret clouded the monk's blue eyes. "Sadly, no. That special blessing belongs to

Brother Bellincioni and our blessed Father Abbot."

"Ah. Well," Guid'Antonio said, "perhaps one day." He pulled his earlobe, as if deep in thought, and flicked his eyes back to Brother Paolo. "Have you seen Lorenzo here when Mary has just begun to weep?"

"Lorenzo?" Amerigo softly wondered.

"Lorenzo?" Brother Paolo said.

"De' Medici," Guid'Antonio said, smiling tightly.

Whereupon Brother Paolo shook his head. "Lorenzo the Magnificent has been here only once to my knowledge, shortly after the tears were first seen by a child in the congregation and he pointed them out to his mother."

Paolo's eyes searched the sanctuary even as his fingers strayed toward the iron latch on the sacristy door. "I pray for Lorenzo each night. I don't think he's the bad man Father Abbot believes him to be."

Ferdinando stepped back, appalled. "You contradict Father Abbot? Father Abbot says the painting is weeping for the devil on Via Larga as much as for the sins of Brother Martin."

*Brother Martin?* Guid'Antonio and Amerigo shared a glance.

"Hush, hush, hush!" Brother Paolo flung

his arm down across Ferdinando's thin chest, then grabbed him and gave him a vigorous shake. "Ferdinando, desist! Should anyone overhear, we'll be in such peril, we'll never see our way clear."

"Trouble in paradise," Amerigo said.

"This Brother Martin is the same fellow you chased down Borg'Ognissanti last week, yes?" Guid'Antonio said.

"No," Paolo said.

"It is, too," Ferdinando said. "And he has been missing ever since."

Paolo groaned, whether from Ferdinando's blathering or from Abbot Roberto Ughi's sudden presence, Guid'Antonio had no way of knowing. In silence, the sacristy door had swung back to reveal the abbot of Ognissanti. A formidably austere man and the head of the Benedictine Order of the Humiliati, Ughi gazed at Guid'Antonio from eyes as cold and pale as a gutted fish.

"Brother Paolo," the abbot said, his voice dangerous and low. "Get you gone. At once, or you'll be late for prayers. Take Ferdinando with you. How, may I ask, is the lad to make a monk with you his whining example?"

"I —" Brother Paolo's eyes sparked with a flash of heat.

Good. No matter that the youth immediately smothered his passion, beneath Paolo's tonsure and robe, a shimmer of fire still burned.

Jaw clenched, Brother Paolo did as he was told.

"For once you come to us in daylight, Messer Vespucci," Abbot Ughi tartly observed.

"Praying, as usual, to catch a glimpse of you," Guid'Antonio said.

The abbot's chilly eyes narrowed. Add to the black marks on Guid'Antonio's soul the sin of disrespect. "Why are you here?" he said, his tongue darting in and out of his mouth.

"This is my family church."

"This is a holy place, and I will not have you stirring up the passions of our young men."

Amerigo snickered, but held his tongue.

"And I will do whatever I deem necessary to gain a more intimate knowledge of the weeping Virgin," Guid'Antonio said.

Ughi's narrowed eyes acknowledged Guid'Antonio's careful wording. "Messer Vespucci," he said, glancing toward the painting and the people at the altar, "the Lord works in mysterious ways. Why can't you accept that?"

"While you reap all the benefit."

"Come now. This is no impoverished church."

"Thanks in no small measure to us," Amerigo pointed out.

"Still," Guid'Antonio said, "this controversy keeps Ognissanti invigorated, does it not? In a city bursting with churches, that fact alone is worth the effort of hosting a miracle."

Ughi gazed upon him with raw dislike. "Controversy? Hosting? If that is how you describe the miracle of the weeping *Virgin Mary of Santa Maria Impruneta,* I advise you to look into your soul, for it is in grave peril."

"No doubt," Guid'Antonio said. "But Father Abbot —" Using the man's title disgusted him, but in this instance, it was necessary if he meant to gain any ground. "On the two occasions the painting has wept. Why is it, do you think? What does Christ's mother want? And if not offerings and importance, what do *you* want?"

Ughi glared. "To see the wicked devil in Rome!"

Guid'Antonio shrugged. "He's already there."

A squeal of distress escaped Ughi's lips. "Do you mean our Holy Father, Pope Sixtus IV?"

"Interpret it how you will."

The fire of outrage crept into the abbot's face. "Hear me well, Messer Guid'Antonio Vespucci: the tears are a sign of God's wrath and glory to come. As the abbot of your family church, I implore you to ask yourself this: Do the Virgin Mary's tears offer you reprieve or reproach? Or do you, like Lorenzo de' Medici, place yourself above God and Church?"

In one swift move, Father Abbot Roberto Ughi turned and marched toward the altar, his commanding figure separating the people in his path like a ship dividing the ocean waters.

"Father Abbot," Guid'Antonio called after him. "You have a monk missing and have not reported it?"

Roberto Ughi stiffened, then turned slowly around. "Don't believe everything young monks tell you. Particularly novitiates."

Watching him vanish into the crowd, Amerigo said, "If he were any other man, he would feel my fingers around his wrinkled throat."

Guid'Antonio took a deep breath, calming the thrum of pure hot anger roaring in his veins. "*Chi va piano va sano e va lontano,* Amerigo."

Slow and steady wins the race.

"No wonder our good Saint Augustine casts his eyes towards heaven," Amerigo said, thumbing toward the left wall as they strode back to the church entrance. "I would, too, if I spent much time in this place. Or in any church, come to that."

"Ummm?" The loquacious novice, Ferdinando Bongiovi, rather than Sandro Botticelli's *Saint Augustine* occupied Guid'Antonio's thoughts. "Amerigo, Abbot Ughi says the painting is weeping for the devil on Via Larga as much as for the sins of Brother Martin. What sin might this Martin fellow have committed so foul, in Ughi's eyes at least, it could make a painting weep?" He still remembered the young, black-haired monk clearly: high emotion and hot tears as Brother Martin fled this place and ran down Borg'Ognissanti.

"Who knows? Steal a pat of butter? For that alone the abbot would condemn the poor fellow to hell." Amerigo cocked his eyebrow. "Or perhaps the youth fled the abbot for other, more personal, reasons."

"For some clandestine mischief in one of the chapels?" Guid'Antonio said as they stepped outside into the heat of Piazza Ognissanti.

"Between him and one of the other brothers?"

"Or with Abbot Ughi himself." Guid'Antonio blinked. On Borg'Ognissanti the sky was spectacularly sunny, the stones radiating heat. Beyond the waist-high parapet, the Arno glistened like a silvery snake slithering between Florence proper and the Oltr'Arno.

"I think —" He slowed his stride, drawing a bead on *il Leone Rosso,* the Red Lion, and the squat little man rushing headlong down the tavern steps toward the open door.

"What?" Amerigo said.

"Unless my eyes and memory deceive me, Castruccio Senso just flew into the Red Lion. Camilla Rossi's husband."

# TWENTY-THREE

The Red Lion was smoky, dimly lit, and thick with the ripe odor of hard-laboring men. Craftsmen and vendors, mostly, spooning from pottery bowls small white beans anointed with fruity olive oil and washing this down with thick red wine. Guid'Antonio and Amerigo stepped over the yellow dog snoozing in the narrow entry. *"Sogni d'oro,* dreams of gold, *Biscotto."* Amerigo rubbed the animal's graying ears in a gesture of affection.

Slowly, Guid'Antonio's eyes adjusted to the pale light of the tavern and inn.

Artisans and shopkeepers in plain belted tunics and mended hose crowded the rough wooden tables and the hinged service counter. Many wore *foggette,* the soft, floppy caps of the *popolo minuto.* Seated on stools or standing at the counter, a few peered at the newcomers with ripe curiosity. A purse maker Guid'Antonio recognized from the Santa Croce quarter narrowed his eyes before lowering his gaze. In a far corner, Camilla Rossi da Vinci's husband, Castruccio Senso, argued heatedly with a young man Guid'Antonio did not recognize.

Heatedly, at least, on Castruccio Senso's part. A rough young fellow by his stained and muddy appearance, taller than Castruccio Senso by a good two heads, the stranger listened with cool attention to the missing girl's husband, curving his lips up in a contemptuous smile.

At the bar, Neri Saginetto, the tavern's owner, threw down his bar cloth, clapped his hands with pleasure, and hurried from behind the counter to greet Guid'Antonio and his nephew. "Two years gone! Mama! Evangelista! The traveling Vespuccis are here!"

Neri snapped his fingers at the girl behind the counter, washing dishes. "Bring them a jug of the Chianti we just purchased, you know the one. Yes!" Neri tossed Evangelista a key. "There, the top cask."

"That can't be little Evangelista?" Amerigo said.

"My daughter. It can be and is."

A quietly pretty girl, Evangelista's black eyes glowed, acknowledging the compliment she heard in Amerigo's voice. "Fourteen now, and not much longer for this place," Neri assured them. "Much too pleasing on the eye. Have a seat. Evangelista will bring the wine."

"And *salame*?" Amerigo said. "I'm starving." They claimed a vacant bench, placing the wall at their backs, offering Guid'Antonio a clear view of Castruccio Senso and his tall companion.

A slim, dark figure slipped past *Biscotto* and on into the tavern. Palla Palmieri. Guid'Antonio pursed his lips. Palla was making good his promise to shadow Castruccio Senso, and he was doing it himself, rather than leaving it to his men.

Palla glanced around the smoky chamber and caught Castruccio in his sight. His sweeping gaze came to rest on Guid'Antonio seated against the wall. Smiling faintly, he moved smoothly back past the sleeping dog and on out the tavern door, his exit accompanied by a general easing of tension amongst Neri's customers.

Beside Guid'Antonio, Amerigo, who had been watching Evangelista place the *salame* along with some cheese and bread on a platter, sighed with unadulterated pleasure, not only in tribute to the food. "Such a difference in a girl in two years. But for all that, where is this elusive Castruccio Senso, now we're here?"

"In yon corner with that dangerous-looking fellow."

Amerigo gave a hushed cry. "God! That fat toad? No wonder his wife disappeared."

Age had yellowed Castruccio Senso's white hair. This he wore cropped around a reddened face beaded with sweat. He had on the simple short gown of a successful merchant, the brown folds belted high over a barrel-shaped belly. Skinny legs and knobby knees sheathed in soled brown hose protruded like twigs from beneath his gown.

Amerigo said, "He seems more agitated and angry than bereaved."

"Decidedly."

"He is wearing a black mourning band, though. Who's that tall tree with him?"

"Good question, Amerigo."

Whoever the man was, he was an unkempt fellow, watching Castruccio Senso with an almost disturbing calm, his muscular arms anchored over his chest, the heel of one boot propped against the wall. A jagged red scar ran from the line of his cheekbone to the edge of his upper lip. Unkempt or no, he stood in controlled silence before Castruccio's shrill outbursts.

Evangelista served the food and returned with two pottery cups and a pitcher of wine.

This was the red wine her father had yesterday purchased from Castruccio Senso, the
wine merchant, she explained, nodding
toward the far corner. " 'Tis a Chianti from
Montepulciano."

Fleetingly, Guid'Antonio thought of Angelo Poliziano. Montepulciano was the
poet's hometown, built so high in the Tuscan hills that when strolling its streets you
walked in the clouds. "Castruccio's one of
your father's suppliers?" Guid'Antonio said.

"Yes, *Signore.*"

"Do you know the fellow with him?"

Aversion flickered in the girl's black eyes.
"Nay. Nor do I wish it." She shivered,
whispering, "He's boarding here. Not for
long, pray."

It was not the crimson weal on his cheek
that caused Evangelista's dislike of the rug-
ged young fellow; Guid'Antonio sensed
that. For all the ragged redness of that mark,
he had a comely face. "His name?"
Guid'Antonio said.

"Salvestro Aboati," Evangelista whispered
and withdrew, casting Aboati a secret look.

Amerigo drizzled olive oil on his *salame*
and bread. "What manner of business could
Castruccio Senso have with him? Aboati's
no customer of wine and oil, surely."

"I shan't discount anything. A wine transaction gone wrong, perhaps?" In truth, Guid'Antonio did not believe it.

Castruccio, breaking off in the midst of his diatribe, glanced across the crowded tavern, spied Guid'Antonio, and from him received a smiling inclination of the head. Castruccio whirled around and uttered a few sharp words to Aboati, who spread his hands in a shrugging gesture of innocence.

Castruccio poked him in the chest. Once, twice.

"There's the fool," Amerigo said.

Salvestro Aboati's fixed smile vanished. He slapped Castruccio's hand as if slapping a fly, the scar on his cheek crimson.

Castruccio flinched. "You dare touch me, you — !"

A stiletto flashed in Salvestro's hand. "Yes?"

Castruccio made a squeaking sound and scurried from the corner, bumping into stools and tables. Keen eyes followed his flight to the tavern door, where he scampered up the stone steps, his foot kicking *Biscotto* hard in the ribs on the way.

The old yellow dog yelped in surprise and pain.

Evangelista, pouring wine at a table, gasped. Her pottery pitcher hit the floor and shattered. Red wine splashed her simple dress. The fellow holding his cup out to her hopped off his stool, swearing and wiping the front of a much-worn tunic not easily kept clean.

*"Bastardo!"* Neri raced after Castruccio. "You, Castruccio Senso!" Purple-faced with outrage, Neri stood in the stone doorway, shaking his fist and shouting after a wine seller now fleeing Ognissanti as fast as his spindly legs would carry him, Guid'Antonio would bet his house.

"I'll have your cock in a stew for kicking my dog, you son of a murdering Turk!" Neri bent down: *"Biscotto,* are you all right?"

The dog, mercifully unharmed, licked his hand.

"I'll coldcock Senso myself the next time I see him," a hard-eyed old man swore, a cobbler or slipper maker by trade, judging from the leather punch in his belt.

With all eyes on him now, Salvestro Aboati strolled to the counter, where he put down two coins and ordered wine all around from Evangelista, a request met with good-natured swearing and cheers. He rested his lean back against the bar, but did not partake of the wine himself. He smothered a yawn and handed Evangelista a coin from his scrip. "For your spoiled gown." The girl stared, her eyes bright and questioning.

"Take it," her father said, his expression grim.

Everyone watched Aboati's departure from the tavern; gently his fingers brushed *Biscotto*'s pale yellow fur as he sauntered up the steps.

"Do you think Castruccio Senso is safe with that cutthroat shifting along behind him?" Amerigo said.

"Palla's with Castruccio, too," Guid'Antonio said.

Together, he and Amerigo approached the counter. Neri was vexed, wringing out a wine-stained cloth vigorously, as if it were Castruccio Senso's neck. "Those two villains." He leaned toward Guid'Antonio, offering him a whiff of the garlic on his breath. "That tall blade. A southern Italian, of course. From Naples, I'd wager my right arm. Though he's tight-lipped enough about his origins and his reason for lingering here in Florence."

"Naples?" The domain of King Ferrante and Prince Alfonso, when Alfonso wasn't riding herd over Tuscany, down Siena way.

"Yes," Neri said. "The fellow's foreign speech and rough manners give him away."

Guid'Antonio wondered why a Neapolitan would have intimate dealings with Castruccio Senso. Surely, Castruccio wasn't selling wine to foreign families; not so far as Naples on Italy's southern tip, past Rome and on down. "Neri, when did Salvestro Aboati first show his face in the Red Lion?"

"A few days ago."

"And took accommodations?"

"Yes. And spreads his coins around as few others do."

"Has he stayed here before?" Guid'Antonio said.

"No, he's a stranger."

"Did Castruccio visit him soon after he checked in?"

"Ahhh." Neri lowered his voice. "The Vespuccis are investigating something involving those two." He motioned towards the back room. "Come."

To his patrons, the tavern owner shouted, "If any one of you so much as glances at my daughter, I'll torture you with red-hot pincers and set fire to your feet before hanging you!"

Like dutiful children, Guid'Antonio and Amerigo followed Neri into the storage room. Wooden casks lined the walls. Whole hams, *prosciutti,* dangled from the rafters alongside fat *salame* seasoned with black pepper and garlic. Neri bolted the door from the inside. "You know everything I know about Salvestro Aboati. As for Castruccio Senso, he's a Medici man, yes?"

Guid'Antonio made a dismissive sound down in his throat. "Only insofar as any other wine merchant who may occasionally broker wine for Lorenzo's family."

Neri leaned over, thumping his chest with his fist. "I'm a true Medici man, like my father and his father before him. I'm proud to say it. For that reason, I tell you this, but don't say where you heard it: There's talk — hushed — that evildoers dispatched Castruccio Senso's wife and have been causing the Virgin Mary to weep, all to blacken Lorenzo's good name. To rid Florence of his supporters, men like you and me. Turks? Pah!"

"You mean evildoers here in the city."

"Yes."

"Are there many who believe as you do?"

Neri hiked his shoulders. "As I say, talk is hushed. No one takes any chances."

Guid'Antonio nodded. If they were smart, they didn't. "Neri, what do you know about Camilla Rossi da Vinci?"

"Mama." Neri kissed his fingertips. "Such a beauty. And married to that rabbit! If such a woman were mine, I never would let her out of my house, much less put her on the road alone."

"She had traveling companions," Amerigo said.

"A slave boy of twelve and a half-blind old woman. A crone in worse shape than my dog, *Biscotto*. And here's *this:* Castruccio, in his cups, brags he toasts Bacchus often because he first glimpsed Camilla Rossi while purchasing wine for resale at the Rossi farm in Vinci."

"And?" Guid'Antonio said.

Neri blinked in wonderment at Guid'Antonio's lack of understanding. "And she brought with her a sizable dowry. If I wanted to know who killed her, I'd have a close look at Castruccio Senso's accounts. The money's now as free and clear to him as he is of her. And if it should happen he owes money to a thug like Aboati and can't repay it —" Neri made a slashing motion across his throat.

"Why," said Amerigo, "would Castruccio Senso owe Salvestro Aboati money? How does he even know him?"

"That," replied Neri, his palms touching as if in prayer, "is for you and your uncle to discover."

"Neri," Guid'Antonio said, and he was thinking perhaps he should have spoken with Neri sooner, "there's been no talk of the lady and a liaison of any sort?"

"A what?"

"An affair of the heart," Amerigo said, twinkling.

"Ah. The husband, a cuckold?" Neri unlocked the door. "Evangelista!"

But no, Evangelista Saginetto had heard nothing of the kind. In fact, all the mothers of Florence offered Camilla Rossi da Vinci as an example of virtue: Camilla, that flawless beauty, with wisps of curly black hair caught up in a pearl and lace cap peeking from her hood as she made her way to church, was an obedient wife and devout Christian. "Messer Vespucci," Evangelista said, "people say before she went missing, she spent every free moment on her knees in church."

"And which church was that?"

"Yours, Messer Vespucci. Ognissanti."

# Twenty-Four

*Who is Brother Martin, and why did Brother Paolo shadow me under the cloak of darkness the first night I set foot back in our walled city? For I suspect strongly it was he. Brother Paolo's anxious manner today in Ognissanti indicated guilt about something concerning me, and although he said only one word to me in the alley — "No!" — after hearing his voice again, I believe I have my man. Why tail me and risk his neck? To whisper some information, surely. If so, has fearsome Abbot Roberto Ughi found him out? If so, there is no way in hell the trembling fellow will approach me again, particularly with Ferdinando tailing him.*

Guid'Antonio ceased writing and inserted his pen in the inkwell on his desk, aware of night creeping steadily across the bed-chamber. Near to hand, he found a lamp and oil; the wick flared and held. A pool of

367

light illuminated his papers, nothing more. He smoothed the curling parchment, squinting. It was a wonder he wasn't blind as Plutus.

*Who's angry and afraid? Camilla's Rossi da Vinci's husband, Castruccio Senso.*

*Why?*

*Who is Salvestro Aboati?*

*Who's lying?*

*Everyone again, again, and again.*

He rubbed his face. *Jesu,* he was weary. A memory flashed in his mind: Palla Palmieri, a shadow this afternoon in the Red Lion, slipping in, and then quietly out again.

The *studiolo* door creaked and swung open. Guid'Antonio leapt up, almost knocking over his chair. His eyes locked on the woman standing on the threshold. She stood before him in a dark brown mantle, hair spilling from her hood, silk ties loosely tied at her throat. He put down the dagger in his hand.

"Am I dreaming?" he asked. "How, when I'm not in bed? Do you mean to say after all this time — ?"

"You will be in a moment, Guid'Antonio. In bed, I mean."

Undoing the ties, she let her cloak drift slowly to the floor.

# TWENTY-FIVE

This was Maria's scent, the soft touch of her flesh, her fingers caressing his face. He stroked her hair, the curve of her breasts, lying with her in a tangled sea of pillows and sweaty sheets. "Is your mother sleeping?"

"Praise God, she is. Was it wicked of me to leave her tonight? And to leave Giovanni, too, although a nurse and Olimpia are with him."

"I'm sure they're fine, Maria." He kissed her hair, her throat, and nuzzled her nipples with his lips.

Breathlessly, she laughed. "What have you been doing besides traveling to Morba? Have you learned anything concerning the girl?" She lowered her voice: "Did you see the Turks?"

He slid his hand between her legs, up high. "Nothing much. No sign of Turks or any others."

She placed her hand on his and gave it a gentle push, quivering with delight. "I can't breathe."

He moved his finger softly, rhythmically, back and forth, teasing her. "I've been checking our accounts." He nibbled her ear. "And attending meetings at Palazzo della Signoria."

She gasped with pleasure. "Mother Mary, you're stealing my breath." In reply, he ran his tongue along her belly and down.

"Slower . . . ," she said.

He was not certain how much longer he could wait. Two years was long enough. She drew a sharp breath, her laugh weak and pleased. "Oh!" she panted and slid her hands over his back, pulling him to her. He held on, his limbs consumed with heat. This fire, this was worth the wait.

He entered her with one hard, blazing thrust and she bucked then moved rhythmically with him, gazing at him through half-closed lids, her head tilted back. The candles on the bedside chest flared, oozing melting wax. Finally exhausted, they fell apart. "I wanted you," he breathed.

"And I, you." She touched his lips with her fingers and smiled, her eyes shrewd with satisfaction. "Has anyone ever mentioned you have a beautiful mouth?"

"Yes." In the light of the sputtering candles, his eyes roamed her body, the rosy patches of color splotching her naked breasts. "You."

She snuggled into the curve of his arm. "You never did tell me about France. I know the women adored you there."

He gazed silently at her, stroking her glossy black hair, surprised she had returned to this topic. The pretty young widow Ameliane Vely had been half in love with him, he was almost sure. He would not let his thoughts linger on Francesca Vernacci. Not when he was in bed with his wife. Since coming home, he had had no excuse — no valid reason — to consult with Francesca in Spedale dei Vespucci.

He felt himself harden. So quickly, too. He pressed himself to his wife, his skin hot with desire. He said, "They adore Lorenzo more."

"Lorenzo? He's never been there."

"Where?"

"France!" She punched him playfully. "They've heard about him, nevertheless. Everyone has. They admire him, too."

Maria kissed the silver tangle of hair on Guid'Antonio's chest. "Have they heard his heart belongs to Lucrezia Donati?"

Lucrezia Donati again. "She is pretty," he

371

said, loosening his arms around Maria.

"I suppose. If you like willowy blondes without any coloring. Apparently, our Sandro covets her for his paintings, now Simonetta's in her tomb."

"There's no need for you to be jealous, Maria." Not anymore.

She gave him a little smile. "I'm not."

"I am."

"You know I would never betray you."

"Nor I, you."

There was silence in the room. Then: "I wish this could last forever." She made a sweeping motion, indicating him, the quiet apartment. "Instead —" Her words, muffled against his chest, were inaudible to him.

He frowned, puzzled. "What's wrong," he said, adding to himself, *now.*

"I'm afraid."

"Of what?"

"Losing you."

He stared at her, uncomprehending. "What in God's name do you mean, Maria?"

"Must you always answer every question with a question?" she flared. "I know you'll leave again. It's just a matter of when Lorenzo demands you go on some mission or other for him."

*Mama Mia.* He said, "I've done my duty

as an ambassador, Maria. Several times, as you have already pointed out. Now it's time for me to tend my house. Antonio can't handle the family business without my help, and Amerigo's help, too, particularly now their father is in San Felice and unable to lend a hand." He brushed her hair from her face and kissed the skin at her temple. "I'll not be leaving Florence anymore." Except, mayhap, for short trips, he reminded himself.

"What about Lorenzo?"

He sat up against the headboard. "What about him?" he said.

"You'll tend *him*. You have obligations to him. Made all the more serious because you're cohorts, and he depends on you."

"As does our government," Guid'Antonio said. "That's my —" He had started to say, "That's my life, Maria." Instead: "That's my lot in this life, Maria. But I don't have to leave Florence to serve her. Not if it means leaving you again for any length of time. And Giovanni."

One corner of his mind had already tripped down the street and across town to the Golden Lion district in the San Giovanni quarter of Florence. It was still very early morning. He meant to go to the Medici Palace today and speak with Lo-

373

renzo and Giuliano's mother, Lucrezia Tornabuoni. But would Lucrezia receive him? Once upon a time, the prospect of visiting Lucrezia would have filled him with immense joy; he liked Lucrezia and relished her company. She was kind and exceedingly intelligent. Over the years, they had become close acquaintances. Now the thought of facing her twisted in his gut like a sharp blade. Because of him Lucrezia Tornabuoni de' Medici had lost Giuliano, her beautiful young son.

"What is it?" Maria said, her face watchful as she sat up beside him in the bed.

"Nothing. Maria, did you ever notice Camilla Rossi at Mass in Ognissanti?"

If Maria considered the question an odd one to ask at this particular moment, she hid it well. "She seemed a sweet girl. But sad."

"Sad? How?"

"Her movements were melancholy, and she looked around frequently, as if she had lost something."

"What, I wonder?"

Maria smiled. "Why is a girl, or woman, ever sad or watchful, Guid'Antonio, if not because of an inconstant lover? But, of course, Camilla was married."

Of course, yes, with no hint of wantonness about her, according to those he had asked about her character — Lorenzo, Evangelista — she was a proper, even timid, girl.

"I have something for you," he said. A necklace of pearls painstakingly chosen from Paris's finest jeweler, a man Ameliane Vely had recommended highly. Beautiful in their simplicity, their color a delicate peach blush, the pearls would glow against Maria's luminous skin.

He retrieved the pearls from the casket locked in the drawer beneath the bed and presented the packet to her, smiling as she gasped with pleasure, plucking the necklace from its black velvet wrapping. "Guid'Antonio, they're beautiful!" She twisted up her hair, and he clasped the pearls around her throat, symbols of purity, according to the Romans, the Greeks, and Ameliane Vely, who had helped Guid'Antonio choose them.

He kissed the tender flesh at the back of Maria's neck, and she laughed, shivering, fingering the costly beads. "They feel cold against my skin."

He drew back.

"Oh, no, they're lovely!" she said. "We need more light to see them properly."

She rose, naked, sweeping aside the damp, tangled sheets with one hand, and replaced the spent tallow candles beside the bed with a single tall one of creamy beeswax. Suspended like precious jewels in the wax were cloves for affection, leaves of jasmine for the sweet perfume of happiness, and lemon verbena, meaning, *You have bewitched me.* The sizable candle burned with flames of pure light, suggesting the unquenchable, the utterly enchanting. Swarms of bees had traveled long distances collecting nectar from clover and other wildflowers to produce not only honey, but also the honeycombs that had yielded this single candle of costly beeswax.

"There's a dear candle," Guid'Antonio said, smiling. "Where did you get it?"

"Lorenzo brought it from Naples."

In the stuffy warmth of the bedchamber, Guid'Antonio felt a sudden chill. "He did."

"Yes, he came home with gifts for his closest friends." Maria unclasped the pearls, rewrapped them, and slid back into the bed, her hair a sea of black flowing over her shoulders. They made love quickly, panting in the slippery heat, Guid'Antonio's blood pulsing as he kissed her feverishly, thinking, *One day I will eat you alive.*

Afterward, with Maria asleep in his arms, he lay awake in a sultry haze, watching the candle's steady flame.

The church bells tolled at dawn. He stood at the bedroom window, listening to a melody of sound as monks across the city and in the surrounding hills and valleys gripped strong ropes woven in Pisa, arms pumping, faces tilted toward the day's first glimmering rays of sun. From the southeast, a particularly sweet, ringing peal echoed down from San Miniato al Monte.

He rested his hands on the stone windowsill and cast his gaze toward the church, considering the decapitated Greek soldier who had taken up his head and flown with it across the Arno to the hill where he wanted his head buried with his body. What happened in that old monastery at night? Did the monks hear Saint Miniato's ghost rustling in the nave as his footstep skimmed the images of lions and lambs inlaid in the marble floor? Did they hear the long-dead soldier descend step-by-step into the crypt, where human corpses lay moldering amongst dust and bones? Did they hear the sighs of young lovers made bold by passion, heightened enough to risk slipping into the unlit chapels under the cover of night, the youngsters' feelings for one another thwarted by arranged marriages, most often between girls of thirteen and fourteen and prosperous, withered guildsmen? Most men in Florence did not marry until their late twenties or even well afterward, hence Amerigo's single status. The city teemed with budding, married maidens and hot young bachelors. The secret corners and shadows of churches made lively meeting places. This Guid'Antonio Vespucci knew with certainty.

More bells rang, cocks crowed loudly. He glanced toward Maria, sleeping in their rumpled bed. Her face appeared peaceful and unguarded. He watched himself walk over and kiss her on the mouth, her perfect lover and trustworthy friend. In addition to Lucrezia Tornabuoni de' Medici, he meant to speak with Luca Landucci today, to see if the druggist was making any progress on how the Virgin's tears might have been manufactured, not once, but twice now, although they had since gone dry, praise God and all the saints. While at the Sign of the Stars, he would buy Maria a bouquet tied with ribbons and scented with dried herbs. Amaranth for unfailing love, lavender for devotion, and oregano — *You add spice to my life.* No lie there.

His brow puckered into a frown. Spice; was that the essential ingredient his nature lacked? Was he too solemn, too intense? Too — dare he think it? — *removed?* Any man, whether cloth dyer, tailor, or lawyer and diplomat, could be hardworking, but cheerful and lively, as well: light and dark in equal measure. Couldn't he? Spice. What might he accomplish then? What, if he insisted, demanded, claimed, *took,* as other men did?

He started to the bed and heard a quiet knock at the door. Barefoot, he walked over and eased up the iron bolt.

Cesare regarded him from the depths of the hall, his face livid in the yellow glare of a solitary torch. Guid'Antonio stepped into the passage, the soles of his feet cool on the stone floor. "Maria's mother?"

"Yes. During the night."

Guid'Antonio crossed himself. "How did you come to know?"

"Olimpia Pasquale came to me disguised as a boy."

"Olimpia? *You?*" Guid'Antonio said.

"Ummm. She makes a good courier." Cesare pursed his lips roundly. "Never fear. The dead lady's nurse is there with Giovanni."

Behind Guid'Antonio, Maria stirred restlessly in the bed. "I'll be down in a moment," he said.

Cesare faded along the corridor. In the

shadows at the top of the stairs, he checked. "The Pope has spies watching constantly to see how Florence treats his interdict. In the coming days, all eyes will be on you."

Not a child christened, not a couple married within the walls of any holy sanctuary, not one corpse buried in blessed ground. In the end, it was Guid'Antonio Vespucci who was in the Pope's glaring light. He had known he would be, all along.

Beneath his fingers, Maria's flesh tingled with warmth, with life. Slowly, she came up from sleep. Within the instant, she knew. Her arm fell hard back upon the bed, as if he had bent over and placed a heavy stone in her hand.

At the washbasin, he dampened a cloth to cool her fiery cheeks. He would have wagered his soul that on this day she would cry fiercely, rant, and throw pottery and silver on the floor in a protest of rage and grief. She did not. Instead, she curled on her side in the bed, as if by making herself small, she might disappear into the sheets.

The mattress sank beneath his weight. "I'm sorry," he said. "I was fond of your mother." They remained like this for what felt to him a very long time, Guid'Antonio aware that elsewhere the wheels of Florence were turning forward with the news of Alessandra del Vigna's passing. Town criers would add her name to their lists of the newly deceased. Speculation concerning Guid'Antonio Vespucci's plans for her funeral would grow by leaps and bounds.

A second soft knock sounded at the door. It was Cesare's mother, Domenica, with bread, pesto butter, wine, and cheese. Silently, with a nod to Guid'Antonio, Domenica came and went from the bedchamber. Shadows receded into far corners and sunshine streamed through the open windows, washing the bedchamber in a blaze of bright white light. Below in Piazza Ognissanti, a horseman clattered past, and a milkman shouted out his wares.

"Guid'Antonio?"

He started. "Yes?" On impulse he bent down and kissed Maria's shoulder.

"Now I am completely alone," she said and fell, exhausted, back to sleep.

Guid'Antonio stared at his wife. Surely, she meant that with her mother's passing, she was bereft of her natural family, her father, brothers, sisters and now, her beloved mother. All, all gone from her forever, while here in the natural world, she had him and Giovanni.

Why, then, did he feel as if he had plunged into an icy lake?

Completely alone. Yes. He knew how she felt.

# TWENTY-SIX

Weeping painting or no, it seemed to Guid'Antonio everything had been leading up to this: Alessandra del Vigna's illness, her death, and his public response to it in the eyes of Sixtus IV and the city. There had been religious rites in Florence these last two years, quietly and humbly held. Tiptoeing disobedience. In the opinion of the town, it was men like Guid'Antonio Vespucci and his cronies who trod the perilous line between heaven and hell, more so than everyone else. Men who deserved to be struck down for mocking not only Rome, but God Himself. God the Almighty, capable of floods and fire, of plagues, and of casting people into the hands of their enemies.

He could arrange a private Mass and burial for Alessandra del Vigna in Santissima Annunziata, Alessandra's family church. This would defy Sixtus IV's dictates, but meekly, without commotion, a semi-nod to the Pope's authority. Or he could honor the lady's death with all the public display his wife's mother deserved: a solemn procession of powerful men through the city with caparisoned horses and Vespucci family banners displayed.

Guid'Antonio Vespucci: Disobedient. Rebellious. Proud. Was he unafraid? No. God aside, there was the possibility of assassination. Why play with a weeping painting and hangings writ in blood, when all it would take to change Florence forever was an arrow through the heart of the man, or men, who walked together through the city's slow, twisting streets from Santa Croce to Santissima Annunziata? Guid'Antonio and his kinsmen, along with Lorenzo de' Medici, Chairman Tommaso Soderini, Chancellor Bartolomeo Scala, the Capponis, and the Pandolfinis: the glorious, longtime leaders of the Florentine Republic.

He glanced at Maria in their bed. In a moment, he would leave her sleeping and tread downstairs into the garden, where he would find Amerigo and Cesare waiting to do his bidding. First he would instruct Cesare to fetch Annunziata's infirmarian to confirm the lady's death and to prepare her body for her entombment in Annunziata's church crypt. Then he would ask Amerigo to tell Lorenzo and the Lord Priors he planned to observe all the public ceremonial funeral display befitting his kinswoman.

In two days' time, before all the people of Florence, he would put heaven to the test. Risking himself, his family and his friends, he would challenge God head-on.

# TWENTY-SEVEN

Guid'Antonio squinted up at his nephews' black-clad figures moving against the sky, shading his eyes against the glare as they struggled to take the litter bearing Alessandra del Vigna's corpse from the hands of the neighborhood religious fraternity and settle it onto the funeral wagon's scarlet-draped platform. A light breeze stirred the lady's gossamer veil and the sleeves of her crimson velvet gown, distributing the perfume of white roses and the lady's stink across Piazza Santa Croce.

The four horses hitched to the wagon stirred restlessly, glossy black coats and decorative metal trappings glinting, expensive and beautiful, for the world to see and envy. Resplendent in rich brown tunic and hose, Cesare waited alone in front of the caparisoned animals, poised to lead the funeral procession on its lengthy journey to the Holy Church of the Annunciation, Santissima Annunziata, when Guid'Antonio gave the signal.

Shoemakers and laborers who worked for the dyers and finishers on Corso dei Tintori lurked in the doorways of shops and houses, men, women, and children taking stock of the lithe shield bearer, the proud horses, the scarlet-draped catafalque and the white robes worn by the men of the confraternity, all in direct contrast to Guid'Antonio and his nephews' smothering black cloaks. These were voluminous, hooded affairs, each sewn from fourteen arm-lengths of cloth, or more, and worth enough money to put soup in the workers' bellies for a year.

Amerigo's hands slipped. "Holy Mary. Antonio, there she goes!"

Antonio made a grab for the litter and caught it, swearing beneath his breath. He had returned from San Felice yesterday, having left his wife and children there with Brother Giorgio Vespucci, "For their safety," Antonio had said.

Fresh sweat streamed beneath Guid'Antonio's arms. "Steady, there."

"Would you could say as much to our audience," Amerigo said. "They're taking our measure, clog makers and whores alike, or I'm not Amerigo Vespucci. Where are our famous friends now? Has everyone but the confraternity abandoned us today?"

"Yes," his brother said.

No gifts of wine and food.

No Lord Priors. No Chancellor Scala. No Lorenzo standing beside Guid'Antonio Vespucci. In the air, he smelled the whiff of betrayal and fear. A mangy white cat shot past his feet, toward the horses. Cesare jumped away from the wagon, a dancer in brown leather slippers, and Antonio swore again as the horses pranced and snorted. "Thank God yon skittish feline wasn't black."

"Careful!" Guid'Antonio called to Cesare, his voice sharper than he intended it to be. He didn't like the frisson of fear he felt when he thought of Cesare walking alone in front of the procession to Santissima Annunziata in the Miniver district of the San Giovanni quarter of the city. A walk of one half hour at least. He wished this were done with and they were back in Santa Croce. Well, if wishes were horses, all men would ride, wouldn't they?

He scanned the stone balconies surrounding the piazza. The balconies and tile rooftops appeared all clear. "Amerigo, Antonio, come down now."

Antonio jumped to the ground, and Amerigo landed lightly on his feet beside him, his cape swirling like a black cloud. "We do have one friend." He thumbed toward the fawn-colored canine parked on his haunches near the Del Vigna gate.

The mastiff's mellow brown eyes flicked back and forth between Amerigo and Guid'Antonio and settled on the taller of the two, his gaze one of pure adoration. Bathed and brushed, the dog's short thick coat had a glossy sheen. And good God was he getting big. One day the mastiff would reach the size of two lesser dogs combined. Or three!

"Amerigo, don't think for a minute that animal's going with us."

But Amerigo, staring at a point past Guid'Antonio's shoulder, whispered, "Look here."

Guid'Antonio twisted around. Antonio Capponi ambled across the piazza toward them, his scarlet cloak clasped with a sparkling, jeweled gold pin. "Surprised?" he said, clapping Guid'Antonio on the arm.

"Relieved," Guid'Antonio said.

Capponi grinned. "I would have been here sooner, but I found a barber and had a shave." He blew a stray lock of pale blond hair off his cheek. "If God's sending me to hell today, I may as well be presentable when I greet Satan at the mouth of his cave."

Capponi's cocky smile faded. "I know what you're thinking. 'Capponi, least of all, you.' But I'd rather be struck dead at the hand of God or murdered by the mob than act the spineless coward." He half turned and gestured back across the square. "Sometimes, people will surprise you in varied and wondrous ways."

In a wave of crimson cloth, Pierfilippo Pandolfini, Bartolomeo Scala, and Piero di Nasi advanced toward them, robes whipping about their heels. Tommaso Soderini was not with them. Fine. Another absence rent Guid'Antonio's soul like the tip of a stiletto.

Capponi raised his brow: "No Lorenzo?"

"No." Aware of the restless, shifting eyes watching them all around, Guid'Antonio walked into the piazza to greet his supporters.

A short time later, he raised Maria's damp palm to his lips, while the other men whispered and stirred in crimson cloaks whose necklines were drenched with sweat. Standing in the garden loggia with her, he felt light-headed, his heart pounding a deep, slow rhythm. In a few moments, he would embark upon an action that in the end could see him and his nephews slaughtered and their heads displayed on pikes around the city. Here was a truth new to Guid'Antonio Vespucci: he did not relish this role as the leader of other men.

He lifted Maria's filmy black veil, memorizing the firm curve of her chin. Violet rings shadowed the tender skin beneath her eyes. Had he said everything he wanted her to hear?

"Should anything happen to me today, hurry with Giovanni to San Felice. Brother Giorgio will keep you safe there. All our accounts have been temporarily transferred to Urbino. Duke Montefeltro's a trustworthy man; through his banker, he'll see you and Giovanni have everything you need."

"I heard the duke fights for our Holy Father in Rome," Maria said, staring up at him with eyes blurry and red-rimmed.

"For Rome one day, for Florence the next," he said. "But I know Montefeltro, and I believe he's a man of his word, no matter who hires his services as *condottiero* from one war to the next."

From his cloak, he withdrew an iron key. "This fits the lockbox beneath our bed. The Vespucci family papers and my journal are there."

"And so?"

"The papers are for Brother Giorgio to pass down as he sees fit. Save the journal for Giovanni. Someday, these events may prove of interest to him. Or even, mayhap, to others." A light smile: "Who knows what some people might find interesting reading?"

A troubled look creased her brow. "Don't make light, Guid'Antonio. I'm afraid."

He wanted to say, "So am I, Maria." Instead: "We must be brave."

"Easy for you to tell me."

*No, it isn't. Give me some credit, Maria.* "I do love you," he said.

She took his hands in hers and kissed them. "You had better go."

He summoned a smile, nodding. "Yes. Given the friars of Annunziata's reticence in this affair, I mustn't keep them waiting."

"You mustn't keep Lorenzo waiting, either."

He whirled around. A lone man had appeared in the piazza, his figure bathed in slanting bands of light. Graceful, sturdy, tall and dressed in the brown shade of mourning reserved for the closest family friends, striding toward them in his swirling cape, Lorenzo de' Medici resembled some dark angel come to rescue them from all the wickedness of hell.

Whispers sighed around the square like a light wind. "Lorenzo the Magnificent."

"God keep you, my love." Lowering her veil, Maria slipped into the house in a crackle of expensive black silk.

Lorenzo embraced Guid'Antonio, his lips a disarming smile. "I see you warrant a soft touch. My wife is among those who believe I've put us on the road to perdition and may as well pack my bags and go there straightaway myself. But then, she's Roman, born and bred, so I don't pay her opinions much heed. Good morning," he said all around before adding in a soft aside to Guid'Antonio, "so few supporters today?"

"So it seems."

"I'm only sorry I'm late."

Was he?

Lorenzo moistened his lips. "Let's get this over with. No offence to the deceased." He crossed himself.

"Cesare," Guid'Antonio called. *Andiamo, per favore.*" A pair of eyes bored into him. "Oh, come on," he said.

The mastiff scrambled up. Gliding over, jowls dripping, the huge brown dog posted himself beside Guid'Antonio's right hip and grinned.

■ ■ ■ ■

The funeral wagon lurched and the huge wheels creaked and rolled.

Cesare marched into the piazza. The feeling reverberating among the men now was one of extreme caution. Surely, the townspeople were in the mood to expect terrible things from the Creator.

Behind Guid'Antonio, Lorenzo's stride sounded sure and smooth, his boots an easy pace in front of Bartolomeo Scala and the three Lord Priors who were spread out behind the *de facto* ruler of Florence like a scarlet fan.

"Bull's-eye," Amerigo whispered when they reached Piazza Santa Croce's midpoint. "Here we are dead center. Remind me again why we're doing this?" He gestured toward the shadowed artery they would enter after passing behind the Stinche on their left.

"Because fear doesn't change anything, it only robs us of what we have," Guid'Antonio said.

Behind them, Lorenzo said, "Well put, friend. We have the right to walk freely in our town."

"Along with the right to die in it," Amerigo said.

"That, too," Lorenzo said.

They followed the rattling wagon into the alley, where children peeped at them from stone doorways. The sound of a muttered prayer wafted from a workshop. Just when Guid'Antonio became convinced they had made a wrong turn and were trapped in a dead end, Cesare led them out into full light again. Draped over a balcony, a coarse canvas sheet snapped in a gust of wind. A window shutter slammed. Amerigo jumped. Alarm widened Antonio Vespucci's eyes. The mastiff growled.

Guid'Antonio touched the dog's head. "Easy everyone. We're not alone."

Amerigo muttered, "God holds us in His hands."

"I mean Palla's here," Guid'Antonio said. A short while earlier, he had glimpsed Palla Palmieri light-footing it from corner to corner, maintaining a brief lead ahead of them. From the rooftops Palla's men peered down, bows cocked, arrows at the ready.

"Protection," Lorenzo said.

"Let us hope," Guid'Antonio said.

They entered an alley so narrow the wagon skinned the walls. Guid'Antonio's breath came fast. He was not sure of Palla. He was not wholly sure of anyone. He kept

395

walking, one heavy boot step after the other.

An eternity passed. With a profound sense of relief, he emerged with the others into the fresher air of a sunny space where a young woman slouched in a doorway with sleeves pushed up, revealing red, work-roughened forearms. Her eyes raked the mourners and stopped at Lorenzo. She bent, whispering, to the naked toddler clutching her leg. The boy drew back, his brown eyes focused on Lorenzo in awe and fear.

*"Giorno,"* Lorenzo said, smiling at the child, who ducked his head and looked quickly back up, frowning. And then an answering smile crept around his lips. *"Giorno,"* he said, and winced, feeling his mother's pinch.

Slowly, the men twisted right and walked straight northeast with the massive bulk of the Cathedral and Brunelleschi's red brick dome looming up behind them. Guid'Antonio kept his eyes dead ahead. Here the ground was so rough, he thought Alessandra del Vigna might bounce off the cart. Beside him, the mastiff kept a steady pace.

At the close of the passage, Cesare paused, content for the moment to remain in the safety of the shadows.

Straight across Piazza della Annunziata

sat Santissima Annunziata, its facade stark and unyielding in the light of the sun's white glare. Both lawn and church appeared deserted. There was no sign of Palla or his guards now. Guid'Antonio felt Amerigo's apprehensive glance. With the sound of his heartbeat thrumming in his ears, he waited for Cesare to raise his shield and lead them into the open for the last leg of their journey. The horses snuffled and neighed, and Cesare squared his shoulders. Beside Guid'Antonio, the mastiff waited. Reaching down, he brushed his hand over the dog's furry big head for the second time that day.

# TWENTY-EIGHT

The wagon advanced into the light.

Guid'Antonio's eyes traveled toward his right side, where the *Ospedale degli Innocenti,* the Hospital of the Innocents, lay in bands of shadow. The hospital, designed by Brunelleschi as Europe's first orphanage, showed no signs of life. A glance to the opposite side of the piazza revealed a clutter of houses and shops shoved one up against the other. From open windows and doors, murderous eyes stared back at the funeral party as it began its slow progress across the grassy square.

"We're being watched again," Antonio Vespucci said.

Amerigo gave a hollow laugh. "Does this surprise you?"

The inhabitants of this district were not gifted master tailors whose perfumed hands worked with damasks and brocaded velvet cloth, small silvered ornaments, and silken gold thread which bore Florence great fame, but poor wool carders, combers, sorters and the like, men and women whose place in the city's cloth industry was firmly fixed on the bottom rung.

Guid'Antonio concentrated on the death wagon and the path its wheels pressed in the grass. Within the walls of the orphanage, a baby cried, shrilly, relentlessly. Antonio Vespucci said, "That child sounds as if its heart has suffered a terrible wound and is about to break."

"I suppose it has and is," Guid'Antonio said as they passed the basin where people deposited babies without fear of being seen. One too many mouths to feed? Not enough medicine to go around? A female rather than a coveted male heir? Better the Ospedale and life as an orphan than suffocation at its father's hands.

At the doors of Annunziata, Cesare halted, holding the Vespucci shield stiffly erect. Long moments passed, while sweat dripped down Guid'Antonio's neck and back. "Where are the friars?" Amerigo said. "We look like fools standing here."

"Surely the Servants of Mary won't betray us now," Antonio Capponi said, his voice tight with fear.

"Do they," Lorenzo said, "and I'll remind

them my father commissioned Michelozzo to restore this place. And to design the marble tabernacle for their own painting of a miraculous Virgin."

Ignoring the others, Guid'Antonio stepped alongside the wagon for a clear view of the church front. It was then Annunziata's doors swung open and two of the black-robed Servants of Mary stepped out onto the lawn. From beneath his wrinkled brow, Brother Bardi, one of two infirmarians who had tended Mona Alessandra's corpse, glared at him. "God has watched you with a careful eye today."

"Praise Him," Guid'Antonio said.

Brother Bardi gestured toward his companion, a thin, pale fellow who blew out his cadaverous cheeks and in a high, reedy voice began the funeral Mass. "With God's grace and mercy, Mona Alessandra del Vigna has departed this blasphemous world."

" 'Blasphemous,' " Amerigo said, bristling with indignation. "He means us."

"Bow your head," Guid'Antonio said.

"Why do you think they wear long cassocks?" Lorenzo whispered behind them. "So they can kick you before you see their leg move."

"Wish to God he would get this over with," Pierfilippo Pandolfini hissed. "We're ready targets out here in the piazza."

"As always, Pierfilippo, thank you for stating the obvious," Antonio Capponi said.

". . . Amen." The friars spun and vanished inside the church in a flurry of black robes.

Amerigo nodded toward the horses and wagon. "A gold florin says when we return the animals are gone."

Guid'Antonio looked around. "You." He gestured toward the funeral cart: "Go, sit. Stay." Regarding him happily, the mastiff crossed the grass on huge paws and planted himself beside the funeral cart.

"Well," Guid'Antonio said. "Good dog."

Resuming his measured pace, Cesare led them thorough the church portal and into the *Chiostrino dei Voti,* where bodies dangled from the rafters, tied to the beams with brown ropes. "God's wounds! They surprise me every time," Amerigo said, staring up at the wood and wax effigies of men who had commissioned their likenesses from craftsmen like Andrea del Verrocchio, and then had them strung up in the cloister as a sign of their piety.

"And me," Guid'Antonio said.

Heavy, dark-colored cloths draped the sanctuary windows. Slowly, Guid'Antonio's eyes adjusted to the somber atmosphere

401

circling them all around. Within the darkness of Annunziata, all seemed well. Still, the church seemed eerily quiet for a space enclosing twenty anxious men.

They followed Cesare past vacant chapels, toward the black hooded figures present on the high altar. "The place seems safe enough," Lorenzo said.

"We're blind as ship mice in here," Antonio Capponi hissed. "Yet not one of us thought of it."

"I did," Palla Palmieri said, his slight form stepping from the gloom.

"Christ!" Pierfilippo Pandolfini said, his voice uncertain.

"Mary!" Bartolomeo Scala said, clutching his chest.

Guid'Antonio's fingers touched the dagger hidden in his cloak.

A smile appeared on Lorenzo's lips. "Now we are completely safe, my friends."

Palla gestured lightly toward his sergeants, dark-clad shades interspersed at intervals along the chapel walls, their forms part and parcel with the bulky dark. "Let us hope," he said, and melted back into the folds of the church.

"Did you invite him here?" Guid'Antonio said.

Lorenzo shook his head. "Just doing his

job, I think."

At the altar, the Servants of Mary gazed on the mourners with indifferent expressions. At a sign from one of them, a trio of friars set the Vespucci family's beeswax offering alight. The flames sputtered and flared, and the men on the wall at Guid'Antonio's side jumped to the floor. "Christ!" he shouted, jerking back.

Antonio Capponi chuckled darkly. "No, it's only Andrea del Castagno."

With wildly pounding heart Guid'Antonio watched the men of the religious confraternity set the litter bearing Alessandra del Vigna's corpse on the church floor. He had forgotten the expressive frescoes "Andrea without mistakes" had painted on Santissima Annunziata's sanctuary walls. *Saint Julian, Saint Jerome.* He glanced around, heat climbing up his throat and into his face. None of the other men had been affected so by the wall painting.

He knelt at the altar and at the far end of the rail saw Giuliano de' Medici on his knees, praying. A wave of nausea threatened to overwhelm him.

Beside him, Lorenzo whispered, "I didn't think to tell you. That wood and wax image of my brother was crafted while you were gone."

Guid'Antonio rose with the others, shaking. "And it's his exact likeness, too."

The figure's wooden framework had been covered with waxed cloth arranged in lifelike folds, the head and hands copied from life and painted in oil. A swath of lustrous human hair the color of Giuliano de' Medici's rich black locks brushed the figure's painted cheeks. The face was Giuliano's impossibly beautiful countenance.

*Please, don't look over at me,* Guid'Antonio thought, and it occurred to him he was mad. On the morning he and Amerigo first returned to Florence, hadn't he seen Giuliano sink to his knees in the mud, blood gushing from his broken head? Later that same day, hadn't the *Virgin Mary of Santa Maria Impruneta* whispered his name? Now, he saw century-old saints leaping from Annunziata's walls and imagined the wax figure kneeling at the altar was Giuliano de' Medici in the flesh.

If only that were so. If only Giuliano could finish his communication with God, stand, and join Alessandra del Vigna's mourners as they stepped back into the piazza's molten glow. But for all the perfect likeness, the clothing and human hair, even Andrea del Verrocchio could not work that particular miracle.

In sandals fashioned from the finest calf leather, the friars accompanied them toward the *Chiostrino dei Morti,* the Cloister of the Dead, where Maria's mother would be laid to rest. "There I am, too," Lorenzo said, shifting his gaze back toward the tall wax figure standing near that of his brother kneeling at the altar rail, but deeper in the shadows, dressed in the long red gown of the Florentine citizen. "In case you hadn't noticed."

"Oh, I had. Verrocchio again?"

"With his help, yes."

"Two Lorenzos, one in wax and one in the flesh," Guid'Antonio said, still rattled and uneasy.

"Actually, there are several more," Lorenzo told him, grinning. "Another one here in Florence in the church of the nuns of Chiarito in front of the miraculous crucifix, and one in Santa Maria degli Angeli in Assisi before the precious Madonna." A spark of self-mockery animated Lorenzo's voice.

In the Cloister of the Dead, the marble slab with access to the underground vault had been pushed aside in readiness for their coming. Rough-hewn steps plunged down into the crypt. Foul odors wafted up. Guid'Antonio covered his mouth with his hand. It struck him then how kind — not to mention *brave* — the twelve men of the religious confraternity were to accompany them here today. One fellow backed awkwardly down the steep short steps, holding a sputtering torch aloft, awkward in his bulky white robe, but managing it nonetheless. Two others, having secured Alessandra's corpse to the litter with straps, manhandled the unwieldy business down into the dark, and then helped their brother place the lady on her stone bed.

Grunts and soft oaths floated up the steps. In a whisper, Guid'Antonio called Cesare's name. The time had come for them to depart, while the confraternity remained to heft the marble slab back into place.

Back outside again, where white light seared the piazza, Guid'Antonio peered toward the funeral wagon. The four horses whickered and lifted their heads, and the mastiff fetched up a lopsided grin, jowls dripping. On the ground beside him, someone had placed a pottery bowl chipped around the rim and filled it with water for him to drink.

Amerigo, glancing around Maria's crowded *sala,* said, "When have people felt so happy to have survived a funeral procession?"

"Never in my memory." A feeling of

profound ecstasy fluttered in Guid'Antonio's throat. In the courtyard, Cesare had collected sweat-stained cloaks from the men. Now, standing with Amerigo, looking around the modest chamber, Guid'Antonio saw Alessandra Scala approach her father, Bartolomeo, her face illuminated with joy. Alessandra's mother, Maddalena Scala, still lay abed, waiting for the birth of the Scala family's next baby girl.

In a swirling haze, Guid'Antonio saw Lorenzo's two sisters, Nannina Rucellai and Bianca de' Pazzi, but not Lorenzo's wife, the disapproving Clarice Orsini from Rome, who surely believed that if God had not struck them down today, it was because He had not got around to it yet. He saw tables draped with white linen cloths. On the tables were small alabaster vases tied with yellow silk ribbons and filled with poppies the dark red color of blood. He saw Maria speak with Antonio Capponi on her way to the kitchen, and heard Elisabetta Vespucci caw, "Domenica! Quick, the roasts! Olimpia! Not that one, you brainless twit!"

Maria had rushed to him the instant he entered the house and wrapped her arms, sheathed in black silk, around him. "Bless Mary, you're safe, Guid'Antonio."

And he had answered softly: "I'm here,

and I'm whole."

Amerigo touched his arm now. "You're not listening."

"Not completely, no."

"I was asking what we will name our dog."

"Our dog? No. Give an animal a name and it owns you."

Amerigo straightened his shoulders. "He stood by us today. Along with everyone else."

*Not everyone,* Guid'Antonio thought. Many in the Medici inner circle had not shown their faces, among them Tommaso Soderini. His gaze went to the trestle tables, where Olimpia was tending the poppies. Cesare flashed by and her hand shot out. Scarlet petals and water bled across the linen tablecloth. Guid'Antonio blinked.

"Olimpia!" Amerigo's mother shrilled, poking her head out from the kitchen. "Get in here!"

"Alexander the Great named a city in India after his dog," Amerigo said stubbornly.

Across the room, Cesare whisked up the flowers, uttered reassurances to Olimpia, and retrieved fresh cloths from God only knew where. "Alexander the Great conquered the world. I doubt either you or I ever will," Guid'Antonio said. What had he just witnessed? Olimpia and Cesare? Really?

"Never say 'never,' Uncle Guid'Antonio. And by the way —" Amerigo narrowed his eyes spitefully. "Didn't you mean to speak with Lucrezia Tornabuoni regarding Camilla Rossi da Vinci? Lucrezia is here today." Lucrezia Tornabuoni de' Medici: Lorenzo and Giuliano's mother.

Guid'Antonio's body flashed hot with dread. Lucrezia's figure was so petite, he had missed her in the milling crowd. She and another woman were standing by the credenza, staring directly at him.

"Smell that food?" Amerigo said, inhaling deeply. "Roast chicken stuffed with artichoke hearts. Alessandra Scala and her flock of sisters brought it. Everyone brought something, food, wine. I can hardly wait."

"Then don't," Guid'Antonio said, glancing away from Lucrezia de' Medici, feeling panicked, a sensation that was to him quite new.

Cesare floated back into the *sala* trailed by a phalanx of trim young men carrying steaming food on silver trays aloft in their hands. On his tunic just above his breast, Cesare wore a scarlet poppy tied with a ribbon of narrow yellow silk.

Guid'Antonio smiled slightly before bracing himself and turning back toward the credenza, and then all around, surveying the crowd. Lucrezia de' Medici had vanished, leaving no sign she had ever been in the house.

All right then: next stop, the Medici Palace.

A servant escorted Guid'Antonio up the stone staircase and down the hall to the Medici Chapel. Was it his imagination, or did a shadow pass over Lucrezia's face when he appeared at the chapel door? If so, she banished it at once. "Guid'Antonio, welcome to our house," she said in the melodious voice he recalled from memory. "Join me here."

He lowered himself into the pew facing the altar, feeling light-headed now he was here, wrapped in the glory of Benozzo Gozzoli's luminous *Adoration of the Magi* encircling the chapel walls. *"Grazie, Mona Lucrezia."*

She surprised him by reaching over and placing her slim fingers lightly on his arm, just as she might have done before. "It's good to have you home, Guid'Antonio *mio.*"

*My Guid'Antonio.* He tucked that away. "Thank you, my lady." Anything more would have been much too complicated.

"A friend and I had given our word we

410

would deliver food to some of the particularly needy this afternoon. We couldn't disappoint them. Has the banquet ended?"

"Not yet. People are still visiting with Maria. Your Lorenzo included."

Lucrezia gave him a curious look from hooded brown eyes, and silence filled the chapel. Her white cowl framed a strong nose, pleasing lips, and an even chin. Although petite, she radiated strength. He thought silver must streak her dark hair, now she was in her mid-fifties. "Are you still writing poetry?" he said.

"Am I still breathing? Yes."

Blockhead! Why had he thought she might quit writing? Like Lorenzo, Lucrezia Tornabuoni de' Medici was a widely known poet of considerable talent. A writer of religious poems, only, very unlike her son.

"Although," she said, "I'm busy these days with so many other things. Grandchildren. The household. Letters from everywhere. Prioresses needing assistance, priests, even the queen of Bosnia. Mostly, they ask what I can do for them." She smiled. "Like they do Lorenzo."

"Bosnia?" he said.

She nodded. "The queen asked me to find bankers who will pay her in cash and not cloth in these troubled times." A small smile

411

crept across Lucrezia's thin lips. "Everyone thinks I have some sway over my son."

Guid'Antonio relaxed a little. "Everyone knows you do."

This she acknowledged with a modest tilt of her head. After her husband Piero's death just a little over ten years ago, despite her quiet nature, Lucrezia Tornabuoni de' Medici had stood as a visible presence alongside her two sons and her daughters, Bianca and Nannina, as well as her husband's illegitimate daughter, Maria, as matriarch of the Medici family. It was no secret young Lorenzo had leaned on his mother for support and advice. He still did. People sought her help with him for pardons, charity, and letters of recommendation. This, along with her own accomplishments as writer, businesswoman, and patron of the arts had made her arguably the most powerful woman in Florence. Observing her now, Guid'Antonio tried not to think of his kinsman, Piero Vespucci, and the pleading letters Piero had written Lucrezia and Lorenzo from the Stinche.

She touched the plain gold cross on a chain at her neck. "Unfortunately, here at the close of an already difficult day, I have crushing news for him. Tommaso sent a note from the Signoria a short while ago."

"Our chairman?" Guid'Antonio sat back in the pew. "What did Tommaso say?"

"That Sinibaldo Ordelaffi, the poor, unfortunate boy, died yesterday. Now Girolamo Riario will brutalize Forlì exactly as he did our Giuliano."

Guid'Antonio sucked in his breath. Of course Riario would. With the Pope's blessing, Girolamo Riario would add Forlì to the list of towns in his possession and stay on the hunt for more, all the while staring at Florence with an army of plundering mercenary soldiers at his command.

The Pope's monstrous nephew was in the chapel now as surely as if he stood before them in the flesh, soiling everything beautiful and good. Assassin. Instigator. What could they do about him? Beyond staying on the alert and watching their backs in Tuscany?

"Lucrezia," Guid'Antonio said, "that day in the Cathedral —" He stopped and started again. "I must confess —"

She touched his arm again. "No, Guid'Antonio, pray. I've heard enough confessions for one lifetime. I know the Lord gives and the Lord takes away. I know He took my son from the world and gave it Giulio, my precious little grandson. I know you're a good man. I'm sorry to disappoint you but

413

no, you are not God, not even approaching perfect. Who besides Our Heavenly Father is? I don't know one. Being good must be enough."

She said: "Lorenzo mentioned you met Giulio the other day."

Guid'Antonio nodded affirmation. A second chance. A healing feeling was unfolding in him now. "He's the image of his father." Rosy cheeks, hair black as jet, eyes brown and liquid.

"Bianca has taken him in hand," Lucrezia said.

"I can see how she would." Did Bianca ever see her exiled husband, Guglielmo de' Pazzi? Did she want to? She had been such a devoted sister to Giuliano.

"How's your little boy? Giovanni?" Lucrezia said.

Guid'Antonio shifted in the pew. "Something of a stranger."

"That's honest enough." She cocked her head, smiling. "He'll come around. So will you. Are you still going to Poggio with Lorenzo and the boys tomorrow morning?"

Poggio a Caiano. He had almost forgotten the trip Lorenzo had proposed to him early last week. "Maria's for it," he said. "She has to set her mother's house in order and believes the outing would be a tonic for

Giovanni and me."

"We all need a rest," Lucrezia said. "Lorenzo, too." She inhaled deeply. "Piero and I had such great expectations for our daughters and sons. The girls made good marriages. Well, when it comes to Bianca and Guglielmo de' Pazzi, hindsight is everything. For the boys, nothing was impossible. Lorenzo and Giuliano grew up believing there were no limits to what they might achieve. Do you think he's careful enough, Guid'Antonio? Of his person, I mean?"

He thought of Lorenzo walking the streets today on the way to Santissima Annunziata, a target like the rest of them. "No," he said.

"You'll do your best to help him?"

"I always have." Unlike with Giuliano, whom he had failed.

She nodded her gratitude. "But Guid'Antonio, a friendly conversation isn't what you came here for today."

"No. Lucrezia, are reservations necessary to attend your baths at Morba?"

A surprised smile tipped the corners of her lips. "That's sudden. Only if you wish to stay there," she said, her manner lightly teasing. "The place has been amazingly popular since I remodeled it. Everyone wants a long soak in the hot springs." She massaged her arthritic hands. "The hotel for paying visitors is almost always full. But why do you ask? Would you like to take Maria there?"

He felt embarrassed. The farthest thing from his mind had been a vacation with his wife. Another woman occupied his thoughts these days. Two, actually: The *Virgin Mary of Santa Maria Impruneta* and Camilla Rossi da Vinci. Three, if you would have the whole truth. "Sometime, perhaps," he said. "Right now I need to know if Camilla Rossi had reservations there the day she disappeared. She's the girl —"

"I know who she is. Aha." In Lucrezia's eyes, the light of understanding dawned. "That's where she was supposed to be going. If the hotel wasn't expecting her, that could mean she was never meant to arrive. Excuse me while I fetch the reservation book."

Lucrezia was gone a good long while and returned flustered. Abruptly, she sat down in the pew. "It's lost! Angelo always kept it in the library. With him gone, everything's a shambles. His assistant knows nothing of the book's whereabouts and has been too frightened to tell me. My God. There is no way of knowing whether or not Camilla's husband ever intended for Camilla to reach her destination."

Angelo Poliziano again. "Other than to ask him," Guid'Antonio said, adding, "Castruccio Senso, I mean." Questioning Camilla's husband was something he intended to do the instant he returned from the brief outing to Poggio with Lorenzo and the boys. As Lucrezia had said, no reservations made in Camilla's name might mean Castruccio Senso knew his wife would never reach her destination. It was as simple as that. This was circumstantial evidence and would never hold up in court to convict Castruccio of the crime of murder; but in a case with precious few clues, it would have provided a decent start.

He wondered if Castruccio, assuming he was guilty, had realized his mistake and had somehow stolen the reservation book in order to protect himself. The Medici library doors were open to everyone, a policy Guid'Antonio knew Angelo Poliziano vehemently disapproved. The entire book, missing. Countless reservations lost, creating all manner of mayhem for Lucrezia de' Medici and the proprietor of the Bagno a Morba Hotel.

Before descending the stairs, he looked back down the hall, watching Lucrezia de' Medici's slight figure pass into her bed-

417

chamber, thinking he would not want to be the lady's assistant librarian just now.

Alone in her chamber, Lucrezia sat with eyes closed, repeating in her mind a passage from the poem Angelo Poliziano had begun in celebration of Giuliano's winter joust five years ago. Five years. That was all. How could that be true? Tears wet her cheeks, and she felt a jab of pain in her womb so sharp, she bent over, breathless. The *Stanzas on the Joust of Giuliano de' Medici* was meant to be a long poem, but it had never been completed, given Angelo's pen never touched it again after 26 April 1478.

*In the lovely time of his green age, the first flower yet blossoming on his cheeks, fair Giuliano, as yet inexperienced in the bittersweet cares that Love provides, lived content in peace and liberty, sometimes bridling a noble steed, the glory of the Sicilian herds, he would race, contending with the winds.*

# TWENTY-NINE

"I could work these country fields all day and never look like him." Amerigo gulped water and flicked a glance at Lorenzo breaking rocks in the ground beyond the farmhouse in Poggio a Caiano. Lorenzo was naked from the waist up, the muscles rippling along his powerful arms and back, glistening with sweat.

Grumpily, Amerigo added, "And yet he's my senior."

"By five years only," Guid'Antonio reminded him.

"I'd go help, but my head's pounding like he's hitting it with his mallet."

Guid'Antonio accepted the water ladle and drank deeply. It was midday and hot, birds chirping in the trees. "That's not too surprising, given you imbibed a vat of Medici wine last night. Anyway, I believe he's enjoying this time by himself."

The warmth of the sun was a balm, soothing Guid'Antonio, calming him. But only to a point. Now they were in Poggio a Caiano, Wednesday's harrowing roundtrip trek to Santissima Annunziata seemed far away. Still: that long walk and Sinibaldo Ordelaffi's demise rumbled and muttered in the back of his mind. When Girolamo Riario mustered his forces and took Forli, as he surely would, the people of Florence would look into the mirror of war and see the Pope's nephew gazing back at them.

They had ridden into Poggio late yesterday, traveling by cart and horseback northwest toward the small town of Pistoia and beyond. A long and oft tedious but blissfully safe journey, praise Jesus, Mary's son, its only downside had come when Guid'Antonio let the two Medici boys' bickering crawl under his skin and set up house, like ringworms or ticks. Bossy and impudent, at age eight Lorenzo's eldest son, Piero di Lorenzo de' Medici, reveled in lording it over the younger boys, the two Giovannis, trotting ahead of them on his pony, Bella, calling back, "Little babies, can't keep up!" his voice mocking as the children bumped along the country roads in a wagon loaded with small traveling chests pulled by a donkey whose mane was twined with pink and white ribbons. Lorenzo's dimple-cheeked, fleshy son, Giovanni de' Medici, stuck his tongue out at his older brother, while Guid'Antonio's Giovanni Vespucci giggled and clamped his treasured seashell to his ear.

At dusk, at the crest of a hill, Lorenzo had pulled up in the saddle and hushed his squabbling boys. His wide, sweeping gesture had encompassed the far off mountains, the swampy curve of the River Ombrone and, closer in, the mill and a ragtag assembly of wood and stone buildings clustered near a brushy lake surrounded by rough fields. "Guid'Antonio, Amerigo, I warned you. The place is rustic." Lorenzo's eyes sparkled as he spoke, and he grinned.

"Is it quiet?" Guid'Antonio said.

"Except for the rooster."

"That's all I ask," Guid'Antonio said.

Lorenzo grasped the donkey's nose halter and negotiated the cart carrying the boys down the gently sloping hill to the farm, while Piero de' Medici rode ahead, his thin behind bouncing in the pony's leather saddle. "Careful!" Lorenzo called after him. "You'll break your head, and we're a long way from *nostro medico*." For reply, Piero slapped Bella's flank and shot down the hill.

Guid'Antonio and Amerigo kept Flora and Bucephalus reined in, their eyes trained

421

on Lorenzo and the three children. "We're alone out here," Amerigo said. "In the midst of nowhere with Lorenzo de' Medici and his first two heirs."

"With mine, too," Guid'Antonio said. He did not need Amerigo to remind him they made attractive targets here in the *campagna*.

A pebble skipped behind them in the road. Flora and Bucephalus danced; Guid'Antonio and Amerigo jerked around in the saddle, alarmed. It was only a goat, separated from the herd.

Later, while there was still light in the western sky, they found sleeping places in the plain stone farmhouse and set torches, tinder, and night-lights near to hand. That done, they gathered around the trestle table shaded by cherry trees near the kitchen door. The early evening air was fine. A lamb, skewered on an iron spit, sizzled, juices steaming and hissing in the stone pit banked with chunks of wood. "We played at guessing what meat you'd cook for us," Lorenzo told his farm manager, Falcone Bellaci.

"It came from your neighbors," Falcone said. "A plump gift to welcome *Il Magnifico* home to Poggio. A little olive oil, some herbs." Falcone kissed his fingertips.

"Piero!" Lorenzo said. "Catching fireflies

is one thing; pulling their wings off is quite another. Stop it." The boy ignored him. Lorenzo snatched the pottery jar from his son's fist and shook the remaining insects free, prompting Piero to glare at the ground, simmering with heat.

Guid'Antonio glanced at the two Giovannis. The pair were taking turns holding the seashell to their ears to listen to the sound of waves roaring along some distant shore. *Which one?* he idly wondered.

In the pit, the fire was dying to a red glow, the wood ashy around the edges. It was then, as they settled down to eat, that Falcone became stupid and talkative. "Have the Turks attacked Rhodes yet? Did our Christian Knights put up a good fight, or did the Turkish Infidels slaughter them like dogs? And the girl, murdered. Despoiled. Maybe in that order." Falcone's eyes shone in the heat radiating from the wood fire. "Maybe —"

"Falcone!" Lorenzo cut his farm manager off with a sharp gesture of his hand. "Not around the boys. There's no news from Rhodes beyond the fact the Turks are reconnoitering the island. Regarding the lady, whatever happened, it wasn't at the hands of Infidels."

"What does 'reconnoitering' mean?" Giovanni de' Medici said.

"They're merely looking around." Lorenzo sucked meat from his fingers. "Boys, do you want more wine? Yes?" He poured the children's wine from a separate pitcher, watered down to a rosy hue, and changed the subject from Mehmed the Conqueror's campaigns to his own plans for the dairy farm.

"We had cows brought from Lombardy. One hundred of them." He regarded Guid'Antonio's son. "Giovanni, did Piero tell you about our pet calf, *Belfiore*?"

"*Sì, Il Magnifico.*" Giovanni placed his wooden spoon on the table. "He said we're going to eat her."

Lorenzo gasped. "Eat her? No!"

Solemnly, Giovanni nodded. "Piero said the Ombrone has snakes, and if we try to swim in it, they'll kill us dead."

Lorenzo gave his smirking older son a razor glance. "Piero has a bold imagination. One day, I fear it will be his undoing. Falcone found one harmless green snake by the river and took care of it. And we are *not* going to eat *Belfiore.*"

In an aside to Guid'Antonio, Amerigo said, "Not tonight, anyway."

"Father, why don't we kill the bad men back?" Giovanni de' Medici said.

"Giovanni. Exactly which bad men do you mean?"

"The Turks. Everyone says they're going to kill the crusaders, then skin us alive and feed our eyes to the lions in the piazza." Giovanni de' Medici's mouth, shiny with meat grease, turned, trembling, down at the corners.

*Little pitchers,* Guid'Antonio thought. His own son's dark golden eyes shone with confusion and fear. Extending his hand, he patted the child's knee. "Giovanni, they're just pretending."

"The Turks are far off in another land, Giovanni," Lorenzo said, addressing his son. "As soon as we're back home, I'll show you a map."

"I want to kill the Pazzis," Piero said. "For murdering Uncle Giuliano."

In the sudden silence, Giovanni de' Medici said, "What about Uncle Guglielmo de' Pazzi? Will we kill him? Won't that make Aunt Bianca sad?" Tears formed in his eyes and threatened to spill down his cheeks. "Cousin Giulio might cry, too."

For the uncle whose brother killed his father? Guid'Antonio doubted it. His eyes traveled to Lorenzo, who said by way of protest, "What kind of vacation is this? Uncle Guglielmo is safe outside the city

425

gates. Piero, all the men who killed your uncle Giuliano have been punished. Anyway, we don't kill people on a whim. We leave that to the Pope."

"Are all Popes evil?" Giovanni de' Medici said.

"Only those like Sixtus IV."

"Piero says it's illegal for us to pray."

"Your brother's wrong," Lorenzo said, exasperated now. "It's almost never wrong to pray. Although it depends on what you're praying for. The Pope is using that kind of language to batter us down."

In the distance a dog or wolf howled, and Guid'Antonio thought of the loyal, if lumpy, *cane corso Italiano* back home in Florence. Where did the animal spend his nights? At the garden gate, alert and remembering, with one ear cocked toward the Vespucci Palace?

"I think it's time we called it a night," Lorenzo said. "Past time, in fact. Falcone, see the fire's extinguished, will you?"

After lighting torches to illuminate the night, Guid'Antonio and Lorenzo escorted the boys to their *camera* and put them to bed, and to Guid'Antonio, how odd it felt. Afterwards, deep into the night the three men leaned forward with their elbows resting on the rough kitchen table, playing cards and consuming musky red wine while the boys tossed and turned in a largely empty room flooded with moonlight and phantom Turks who flew in through the open windows wielding bloody bayonets.

Now, Lorenzo strode languorously toward Guid'Antonio and Amerigo across the sun-baked field, swiping the sweat from his eyes with his forearm. He removed a towel from the trestle table and dried his muscled torso. "So, friends, how are you this morning?"

*"Bene,"* Guid'Antonio said. He had not slept a moment last night. Thinking, reconsidering, and turning inside out all the events of the last twelve days. Leaning first one way, then the other. Indecisive? No. Yes. Weighing all the options, not just for himself, but for his family for generations to come as well. This morning, after seeing to the horses (both Flora and Bucephalus, since Amerigo was a layabout), he had begun reading Simplicius' commentary to Aristotle's *Physics,* but couldn't concentrate for the nattering in the farthest reaches of his mind. In the last few days, the Lord Priors had not moved one foot closer to proposing a *balìa* to the other councils. They had been far too busy bickering about it amongst themselves. What would become

of those government changes Lorenzo wanted? Something? Nothing?

"I expected Sangallo to arrive by now," Lorenzo said, and cast a glance toward the road as if hoping his master architect, Giuliano da Sangallo, would ride toward them through the hazy morning light. "We agreed on Friday morning."

"It's almost noon," Guid'Antonio said. "Perhaps he started late."

"I could ride out for him." Amerigo let the suggestion hang.

"Don't worry yet. Thanks." Lorenzo poured well water over his face and chest. "Where're the children?"

"Taking turns riding in the donkey cart," Guid'Antonio said.

"All three of them?"

"No, Piero's catching butterflies with a net."

Lorenzo sighed, shaking his head. "Let's hope he enjoys the sport of it and releases them soon."

After a light meal of cheese and bread, they accompanied the boys to the stables, where Lorenzo instructed everyone to wait outside till he came back out. Moments later, he returned leading a horse whose chestnut coat shone in the light of the afternoon sun.

"There's a magnificent animal," Amerigo said. "What, about sixteen hands?"

"On the mark," Lorenzo said. "Not too close, boys, she's restless." The mare shifted her hooves, tail switching, as if to prove the point.

"Eeeeee!" The two Giovanni's jumped back, squealing. Piero shied away, intimidated by the size and presence of the horse.

"She's a secret," Lorenzo said.

"What kind of secret?" Piero said.

"She's our horse in the *palio* next year."

*Next year?* Guid'Antonio pursed his lips.

"A mare?" Amerigo snickered.

Lorenzo smiled. "I'll put her up against two of your studs anytime."

"What's her name?" Giovanni Vespucci said.

*"La Lucciola."* Firefly.

"Why?"

"Because when she races, she's quick as a lightning bug."

"Piero says you never lose the *palio.* Do you?" Giovanni Vespucci said.

"What do you mean 'next year'?" Guid'Antonio said.

"I mean *La Lucciola*'s not going to Florence till then, and I'm running a different horse in the *palio* finals next month. Giovanni, in answer to your question, no, I

429

don't."

The three men were in a grassy meadow later that afternoon, armed with bows and arrows, when a rider crested the hill and galloped down the sloping hill toward them. He rode with his body bent forward and one hand clamped on his feathered cap to prevent it from blowing off his head.

Amerigo shaded his eyes. "Who in Hades? Not your architect, surely."

Lorenzo dropped his bow and wiped sweat from his eyes. "Sangallo? No. A courier from Florence, I think."

The fellow slid from the saddle. *"Il Magnifico! Buon giorno."* He bowed. "I've two messages. First —" He caught his breath. "Maestro Giuliano da Sangallo sends word he's ill and won't be here this weekend. He regrets the inconvenience and will speak with you in town."

Lorenzo grunted his disappointment. "What else?"

"Is Messer Guid'Antonio Vespucci here?"

Guid'Antonio started. "I am."

The courier handed him a sealed note. Impressed in the red wax seal were the initials LTM. *Lucrezia Tornabuoni de' Medici.*

Lorenzo raised his brow as Guid'Antonio broke the seal and scanned the words

430

penned in Lucrezia's small, firm script. *Grazie Madonna.* Slowly, Guid'Antonio smiled.

"Good news?" Lorenzo said.

"Yes. What was lost has been found." Guid'Antonio told them about the missing reservation book, not truly missing after all, but misplaced. Before revealing more, he glanced at Lorenzo, who sent the exhausted courier to the kitchen, where Falcone, having returned there with the boys after a visit with *Belfiore,* would put out bread and wine for the fellow's repast.

"I asked your mother if Camilla Rossi da Vinci had a reservation at Bagno a Morba the week she disappeared. And, no, she did not. The lady's name does not appear anywhere in the reservation book."

Amerigo scratched his head. "Mona Lucrezia sent word all the way out here to tell you that?"

"It is of the utmost importance," Guid'Antonio said. And explained how the lack of a reservation implied Castruccio Senso knew his wife would never reach the baths.

"*Mon Dieu!* That old toad had her killed?"

"Perhaps," Guid'Antonio said. "But he can come up with all kinds of stories."

By common consent, they moved to the shaded table. "Castruccio didn't think to make false arrangements?" Lorenzo said,

431

eyes glowing. "There's stupidity personified. It could go far in proving he knew his wife never would arrive at Morba."

"You said yourself, Castruccio Senso's not a bright man," Guid'Antonio said. "He can, and no doubt will, say he forgot to make arrangements before sending her on her way. Given his reputation as a fool, the court may believe him. And, yes, I do mean to have Palla arrest him straightaway."

"But why harm his wife? And use Turks as the culprits? There's a colorful touch," Lorenzo said. "There remain the nurse and boy, as well. Surely, they didn't go along with Castruccio's villainy."

"Stranger things have happened," Guid'Antonio said. "As for why, Amerigo has suggested a new dowry as motive."

"Or there could be another woman involved," Lorenzo said. "Think, though: that doesn't require killing your wife."

Guid'Antonio thought, *Love? Please. Lust?* And what, if anything, did any of this have to do with the painting of the *Virgin Mary of Santa Maria Impruneta* in Ognissanti?

"Now what?" Amerigo said.

"I want to question that little man as soon as possible," Guid'Antonio said. "In the morning, we'll ride straight to Florence."

This meant returning home Saturday rather than Sunday, as they had originally planned to do. But something told him he must get to Castruccio Senso immediately.

"In the meanwhile," Lorenzo said, "I'll dispatch the courier with a note to Palla. He'll know what to do. Apply pressure with the rope, and Castruccio Senso will squeal like a pig."

Guid'Antonio pictured the corpulent little wine merchant stripped to the waist and hoisted toward the ceiling by his wrists. Till Castruccio confessed to something, Palla's men would give the cord a hard jerk, a *strappado.*

"I want to interrogate him myself," he said.

"Both you and Palla, then. We'll all leave at first light tomorrow. A departure by you and Amerigo alone would leave the three boys and me traveling the road solo. I agree you must question Castruccio at once."

That evening, after looking in on Giovanni and bidding Amerigo good night, Guid'Antonio stepped out into the side yard off the kitchen and found Lorenzo sitting alone at the trestle table beneath a glittering canopy of stars, gazing toward the distant hills. Guid'Antonio sank onto the wooden bench beside him, feeling curiously calm.

Lorenzo said, "I'd like to go six months to some place where Italian affairs were never mentioned. Even here in the country it's hard to forget about Girolamo Riario and the Pope. And so many other things."

Crickets chirped and fireflies lit the grounds, their starry pulse fading across the meadows. On the table a solitary candle burned with a pale yellow flame. Not scented beeswax, but plain cheap tallow.

Lorenzo went on, "Do you honestly believe Castruccio Senso had Camilla killed? Whoever heard of such a thing? Not often, anyway."

"I believe it's far more complicated than that," Guid'Antonio said. "I hope our young courier doesn't run afoul of thieves tonight."

"Given the florin I promised the lad to hurry, not even *La Lucciola* could catch up with him. Why wouldn't Camilla be suspicious when Castruccio Senso told her he was sending her to Morba? In my experience, Castruccio isn't a generous man."

Guid'Antonio tucked away Lorenzo's "experience" of a man who, only recently, he had professed not to know beyond a casual acquaintance. "What choice would she have but to go?"

"True."

In the farmhouse there was muffled laughter: the two Giovannis. "They get along," Lorenzo said, nudging Guid'Antonio, smiling. "Like you and me."

"They do," Guid'Antonio said. *And I will do anything to protect them.*

"In Florence, I'd like them to visit often. I think yours is good for mine." Lorenzo mock-grimaced. "Maybe your Giovanni will rub off on my Piero."

"My Giovanni? Good? How?"

Lorenzo laughed down in his throat. "Are you that surprised? He's quick. And generous to a fault. He gave, well, loaned, Piero his seashell tonight, so Piero could listen to it before falling asleep."

"It's Giovanni's prized possession," Guid'Antonio said. "Such a little thing." Not the painted wood puzzle he had brought Giovanni from Paris and not the marionette he had bought the boy in Piazza Santa Croce.

"I'm glad he likes the shell," Lorenzo said. "I brought it back from Naples."

Guid'Antonio sat rooted to the spot. Seashells and beeswax candles beset with cloves, with jasmine and lemon verbena. "You are generous to a fault, *Il Magnifico.*"

Lorenzo's mouth quirked in a smile. "I enjoy sharing."

435

"As do I. Depending what it is."

In the gathering darkness, Guid'Antonio saw Lorenzo's smile widen. "Guid'Antonio, I brought back a trunk full of gifts, something for the families of my most trusted friends. Quite a small trunk, I might add."

Guid'Antonio let it go at that. He was a Medici man. More than that, he was an Italian, as married to the soil and stones of Tuscany as he was to his wife and family. He said, "I'll speak with Capponi and Di Nasi and the others when we're back in Florence. See if I can persuade them to vote for making a call to the other councils for your *balìa.*"

Lorenzo sat up straight, staring at him. "Mary and all the saints. I thought —"

"I may have some influence, since I've been one of them," Guid'Antonio said.

"And will be again. But that's not what I meant. Why change your mind now?"

"I want Florence in the best hands. Yours. And mine."

"We will make all the decisions, Guid'Antonio," Lorenzo said earnestly.

"I know."

"You know, too, I have no desire to be a lord. Everything I want is here: this farm, a peaceful night, time with my family and friends."

"In the end, that's all any of us want," Guid'Antonio said.

Now the words were spoken, there was no turning back, this he knew with absolute certainty. His destiny was tied to the Medici; it had been from the time of his birth and his baptism a few days later in the Baptistery in Piazza San Giovanni a few feet from the Cathedral doors in the Golden Lion district of Florence. The Baptistery that Florentines could not, or should not, now darken with their newborn babes because of the Pope's feud with Lorenzo.

Whatever the circumstances, Florence, Lorenzo, and Guid'Antonio, the Medicis and the Vespuccis, were one and the same. Wasn't that what he had worked for his entire life? To defend one was to defend the other. He had fallen down once; he would not do so again.

They sat in silence for what seemed to Guid'Antonio a long time, watching the fireflies, listening to the frogs croak in the yard. "It's late," Lorenzo said at last, yawning. "Dawn will break early in the morning."

"I'll stay a moment longer."

Lorenzo turned to go.

"One more thing," Guid'Antonio said.

Lorenzo swung back. For an instant in the

pale light of the solitary candle, he appeared exhausted, his eyes glazed with fatigue. "Yes?"

"If not *La Lucciola,* which horse will you run in the *palio* next month?" In late August, when Luca Landucci's brother, Gostanzo, would race astride his dragon through Florence's crowded streets, from the starting point in the meadow near Ognissanti Church to the finish line at San Piero Maggiore.

"Since when did you take an interest in horse racing?" Lorenzo said, tilting his head slightly.

"Since I was born a Florentine."

*"Il Gentile,"* Lorenzo said, grinning. "He's stabled at San Pietro in Grado, at our house west of Pisa. Under wraps till the day before the race. That *Draghetto* of Gostanzo's —" He kissed his fingertips. "There's a formidable horse. I don't mean to lose to him."

"I'm sure you don't."

Lorenzo's gaze swept the countryside, the fields, the River Ombrone. "One day I'll have fish ponds, mulberry trees and gardens as far as the eye can see. For now, I like the fact the place is rough and free, like my own nature."

"You are neither."

"Nor are you, my friend."

Guid'Antonio remained alone at the table for a long while, thinking and watching heat lightning play across the sky. Somewhere, a twig snapped. A stag or a doe, perhaps. A hare or a fox. Off in the woods, something screamed and died a slow death. He recognized the sound.

A hare, after all.

The following morning, Saturday, it was Lorenzo's son, Piero, who spotted the horseman first. Their small party had set off from Poggio shortly after dawn and had already traveled several hours. Now they could see the Palazzo della Signoria watchtower soaring toward the sky high above Florence's walls, Giotto's bell tower, and the Cathedral's softly rounded red brick dome. "We'll drop the boys off and go straight to the Bargello. That's where Palla will hold Castruccio till we get there," Lorenzo was saying when Piero pointed to the rider pounding toward them from the Prato Gate.

"Another courier?" Lorenzo said, his tone dubious.

"No." Amerigo straightened in the saddle. "What the devil? It's Cesare!"

Guid'Antonio started to question this but in the next instant recognized the lithe figure of his manservant who had, they learned in the next moment, set out for Poggio to tell them that when Palla Palmieri's captain went to Castruccio Senso's house to take him in for questioning earlier this morning, he had found the wine merchant sprawled facedown on the floor of his house with his head bashed in.

# THIRTY

Camilla Rossi da Vinci's husband lay on his stomach in the *sala* of his house off Piazza Santa Maria del Carmine in the Santo Spirito quarter, his brains spilling onto the carpet in a lake of gore and blood. Guid'Antonio forced his thoughts from another, similar, setting and quickly surveyed his surroundings. Leaves of writing parchment ripped from Castruccio Senso's account ledgers littered the floor. A *forziere,* a strongbox bound with iron straps and fitted with locks, had been pitched against the tiered sideboard, then battered open, and the box emptied of its contents. Pottery lay everywhere in shards.

Near Castruccio's corpse lay a pewter candlestick polished to resemble silver, the upper portion smeared with blood. Castruccio's right hand was outstretched, his fingers twisted in the strings of the rush hanging that had fallen from the portal separating the *sala* and the kitchen.

In his mind's eye, Guid'Antonio saw the dead man scramble toward the back room, grasp the curtain, lowered at the time, and stumble under his pursuer's attack. He saw the candlestick slice Castruccio's head.

Palla Palmieri, on his knees beside the body, rocked back on his heels, glancing up. "This is no robbery gone wrong. There was a battle here and demon anger to boot. You're here quickly."

"Yes, once I heard the news."

From the Prato Gate, Lorenzo and Cesare had escorted the three boys home, while Guid'Antonio and Amerigo nudged their horses into a trot across Ponte alla Carraia to the Santo Spirito quarter on Florence's left bank, Guid'Antonio cursing himself for a fool. The trip to Poggio had cost him dearly in more ways than one.

"That fat little man did put up a fight," Amerigo said. "I've never seen so much blood other than at hog killing season."

"Aptly put, Amerigo," Palla said dryly.

Guid'Antonio's gaze flicked to the black boy huddled by the towering sideboard, as distant from the corpse as he could get. Gently, Guid'Antonio approached. "Who's this?" he said, although, of course, he knew. This was Camilla Rossi's slave, about twelve years old, tall for his age, his whip-thin body struggling to catch up with his skinny legs and arms. He had been told the boy was not here, but in Vinci town, along with Camilla Rossi da Vinci's nurse, whoever the woman might be.

The boy's cheeks and brow were bunched up in terror, and his dark skin had a chalky pallor. Amerigo removed a handful of sugared almonds from his scrip and offered them to the child. "What's your name?"

The boy refused the sweets. "Luigi." He shrank back into the corner, clenching his fist behind his back. "Don't hurt me, please!" he said, and burst into tears.

Amerigo cast a silent plea to Guid'Antonio, who shrugged and nodded for him to proceed. "All right, then, Luigi," Amerigo said. "I'll place the almonds in your scrip, and you can have them whenever you wish." He bent down and slipped the sweets into the child's purse.

"*Signore,* don't kill me!" the boy said, weeping. "I've done nothing wrong. I swear!"

Guid'Antonio's heart dropped. "We're not going to hurt you. We're here to help you, child." *And to question you,* he thought. Luigi, the little slave, had witnessed not one crime now, but two: Camilla Rossi's disappearance and the death of her husband, Castruccio Senso. How coincidental was that? And how lucky could Guid'Antonio get? He almost danced. "Would you like to go out into the sunshine? Yes?" He gave Palla a sideways look.

Luigi's eyes flicked from one to the other of them. Guid'Antonio pictured himself, Amerigo, and Palla through the boy's eyes: a trio of men gazing down at him, one taller than the other two, his black hair threaded with silver, all three dressed in plain brown clothes and boots, while the wiry, sharp-eyed police chief wore a wide leather belt with his dagger in full view. *"Sì, Signore,"* Luigi said meekly.

"We passed some sort of test," Amerigo commented quietly as they left the murder scene.

"Now let's see if he does." Every nerve in Guid'Antonio's body was aware of the boy's hand clenched behind his back.

In the courtyard, a cardinal landed on the limb of a lemon tree and flew off again, searching for his mate. "Palla," Guid'Antonio said beneath the sound of water gurgling in the fountain. "What happened?"

"Just this: when your courier arrived from Poggio this morning, I sent a man straight here to arrest Castruccio. Instead, the fel-

444

low returned shaken, saying he had found Castruccio Senso murdered. I came at once." Palla's eyes creased in the hint of a smile. "Guid'Antonio, are you questioning me?"

"Take it how you will."

While Amerigo stood near the garden gate, blocking the house from the view of gawkers in the piazza, Palla settled with the boy, Luigi, on the stone bench encircling the fountain. Guid'Antonio, finding a stool with a rush seat, assumed a relaxed pose facing them.

"Luigi," Palla said, "I spoke with you a couple of weeks ago in Vinci. It concerned your mistress, Camilla Rossi. You remember, yes?"

Fresh tears rolled down Luigi's cheeks. "You're the police."

"Guilty as charged. Luigi." The boy would not look at him. "How came you here? I thought you were in Vinci."

"Ser Jacopo brought me here when he came to Florence," Luigi said so softly, Guid'Antonio could just make out the words. "He — he had to go to a wine merchant in Orsanmichele, but he came here first."

Guid'Antonio glanced at Amerigo. That was last week, when they encountered the fiery Jacopo Rossi da Vinci in the crowded marketplace amongst peddlers and money changers. The same Jacopo who had eluded Amerigo when Amerigo gave chase.

"And so last night when your master, Ser Castruccio Senso, was killed, you were here," Palla said. The boy nodded and seemed about to burst into tears again. "Did you see what happened?" Palla said.

Luigi clutched his toes in the tips of his sandals. "No!"

Palla made a dismissive sound. "Luigi, the house is small. You must have seen something. Where were you?"

"On my pallet in the fireplace."

Across from Luigi, Guid'Antonio leaned back. "In the fireplace?"

"You heard him," Palla said.

"You were in the hearth? In the main room of the house?" Guid'Antonio said.

*"Sì, Signore."*

"You didn't rise when you heard the ruckus?" Guid'Antonio said, still not sure he understood the boy's meaning.

"No." Luigi kept his head down.

"Well, of course not, Uncle," Amerigo inserted from his post at the gate. "He was scared."

A steady stream of tears had wet the collar of Luigi's tunic, a tunic appropriately

446

short and skimpy, befitting the boy's role as a slave. All Castruccio Senso's pride of ownership was on display: Luigi's shirt was not uncolored cloth, but sewn from a cotton-linen blend dyed a warm white hue to emphasize his dark skin. His hose were relatively inexpensive brown jersey, but fit him well, and so were probably new to accommodate his constant growth.

Guid'Antonio removed his handkerchief from his scrip. "Wipe your eyes." Luigi accepted the handkerchief with his free hand and did as he was told. "The intruder didn't notice you in the fireplace?" Guid'Antonio said.

Luigi went very still. "Either he did, or he didn't," Guid'Antonio said, staring at him.

A small snuffling sound escaped Luigi's lips. "Master Senso had filled the opening with the chimney board. Every night he did the same. In the mornings, he let me out."

Amerigo gasped. "He boarded you up?" Slaves were a commonplace in Florence, as was true throughout Italy. Tartars from the Black Sea, Russians, Greeks, Turks, Moors, and Albanians: all were fair game for purchase, so long as they weren't Christian. Although slaves were meant to work hard, usually as family servants, they generally were not mistreated. "The bastard," Amerigo said.

"And since you were behind the board you couldn't see anything," Palla said. "But what did you *hear,* Luigi?"

"They — they yelled at Master Senso."

*"They?"* Guid'Antonio pounced. "There were two of them or more?"

"Yes! Ten or twenty, at least!" Luigi sobbed as if his heart might break.

The boy had survived a terrifying experience, yes, but this? From what Guid'Antonio had seen inside the house, to say a dozen men or more were there last night was preposterous. But why lie about it? It was then he realized they knew nothing of Luigi's character. Luigi could be a liar. He could be a thief. Guid'Antonio caught Palla's eye: *Go easy, or we will learn precious little from him.*

"Luigi, Luigi, you're all right now." Palla placed his arm around the boy, his black eyes fast on Guid'Antonio over the top of Luigi's head.

"Luigi," Guid'Antonio said, "we need to know as much as possible about last night so we can catch the men who did this and chain them in the Stinche."

"You'd like to help us do that, wouldn't you?" Palla said.

Luigi's glance slipped away from them,

toward the middle distance. "Yes," he said in an emphatic, clear voice.

"Last night was terrible," Guid'Antonio said, careful to keep his knees from bumping the boy. "I'm glad you were in the fireplace, nice and safe from those bad men. Sometimes it's best to keep quiet, isn't it?"

"Yes. That's what Margherita said."

"And Margherita is?" Guid'Antonio asked.

"My lady's nurse."

"Ah. Where is Margherita now?" Guid'Antonio said, hoping against hope Camilla's nurse was here in Florence.

"Vinci," Luigi said.

Guid'Antonio glanced at Palla, who chose then to stand and arch his back, easing the soreness in his muscles. "Luigi, do you know what things Castruccio Senso kept in his strongbox?" Palla said.

Luigi eyed Guid'Antonio but answered Palla softly. "Ser Senso hid some florins there. And my lady's jewelry. He didn't know I saw him do it," he said, smirking.

Jewelry. The jewelry Camilla did not take on her trip, was not allowed to take in all probability. And now stolen by Castruccio Senso's killers. "Luigi, did Castruccio keep a private journal?" Guid'Antonio said, tilting his head, hoping.

449

"They stole it," Luigi said.

"How do you know that?"

"It was in the strongbox. It's gone now."

Guid'Antonio gritted his teeth. Where was Lady Fortune when he needed her? Castruccio Senso's journal might have gone a long way in revealing the fate of Castruccio's lost wife. But Lady Fortune helped those who helped themselves. And Luigi had become very quiet again.

"Here come the *beccamorti*." Amerigo thumbed toward the sound of creaking wagon wheels. The grave diggers would wash, shave, and anoint Castruccio's body and also report his name, parish, and quarter to the doctors' and spicers' guild. Unless his family spoke up for him, he would be buried with little or no pomp, given the umbrella of excommunication the Pope held over the city. *Give me that rascal, Lorenzo de' Medici.*

"Luigi, I'd like to see the item you're holding in your hand," Guid'Antonio said.

The boy hunched his shoulders. "What item?" Palla said.

Guid'Antonio held out his palm. "It's important, Luigi. If you found something in the *sala* this morning, it could help your lady."

There's a cheap shot, Palla's expression

said. Well done.

"You have no choice, Luigi," Guid'Antonio said.

The boy wilted, and Guid'Antonio took a small swatch of white cotton fabric from his shaking hand. "It's her *guardacuore,*" Luigi said.

"Her nightgown?" Amerigo said, incredulous.

"A piece of it, yes."

"Wherever did you get this? It has blood on it." Palla's friendliness had evaporated. Now, he was alert as a cat and ready to pounce.

Luigi glanced from the courtyard to the door leading back into the household. "I found it on the floor when your sergeant fetched me from the fireplace and then ran to fetch you," he said, looking away from Palmieri. "I borrowed it. Please don't chop off my hand!" He cried again, aching tears from a bottomless well.

"Luigi. Swear on the Bible, no one is going to do anything bad to you." Guid'Antonio handed Palla the small white cotton scrap. On it were embroidered the initials CR. And, yes, the cloth was damp with blood; Castruccio Senso's, Guid'Antonio guessed, though there could be no way of knowing with certainty. It could be the

451

blood of a cat. Or a dog.

"Those are my lady's initials," Luigi said, appearing about to faint. "Camilla Rossi da Vinci." Anything to say her name.

"Well, well," Palla said. "Show me exactly where you found it. Then —" Taking Luigi by the hand, glancing at Guid'Antonio, he escorted the boy into the house.

"Then *what*?" Amerigo's stare at Luigi's retreating back said it all: What about that boy, now he has neither master, nor home, nor anywhere to live? To the foundling hospital in Piazza Annunziata to grow up as an orphaned slave boy? Luigi was far too valuable for that. Someone would take him, perhaps in trade. He was twelve, fatten him up, and he might live and toil for a long time, a strong, healthy slave.

"Senso's relatives?" Guid'Antonio said.

Palla, having returned to the garden with his charge, used his handkerchief to wipe dried tears from the boy's face with water from the fountain. "Castruccio Senso has no family," Palla said. "I found that much out when *I* was actively investigating Camilla's —" He glanced down at Luigi. "Departure," Palla said.

"Where did Luigi find the fabric?" Guid'Antonio said.

Palla grinned. "Beside the body, of

452

course."

Amerigo said, "He'll be in grave danger should Castruccio Senso's killers realize Luigi was listening from the safety of the fireplace during the night. He might recognize their voices if ever he hears them again. They'll figure that out."

Luigi looked surprised, and his sobs filled the garden, louder and louder.

A starving dog and now a mistreated boy. Guid'Antonio frowned unhappily. "Amerigo, take him home and tell Domenica to get some food in his stomach. Give him a clean pallet. Tell everyone to keep quiet about him. We don't want anyone to know his whereabouts. Certainly not Castruccio Senso's killers."

Palla arched his brow. "Not that you asked, but I agree. For now."

The gate closed on Amerigo and Luigi with a soft click. After a moment, from Piazza Santa Maria del Carmine there came the fading sound of Amerigo talking to his charge. Palla plucked a twig of rosemary from a nearby bush and sniffed it thoughtfully. "Our little slave knows something."

"Yes." From inside the Senso household there came the sounds of the *beccamorti* cursing as they heaved Senso's corpse onto the litter.

"Now what?" Palla said.

*Later, I'm going to have Luigi tell me exactly what happened on the road to Morba,* Guid'Antonio thought. He said, "I think we should go to church."

"Excellent idea," Palla said.

After giving instructions for his sergeants to stand watch over the crime scene, with a graceful wave of his arm, Palla swung open Castruccio Senso's gate.

They stood together in Santa Maria del Carmine Church, gazing up at *The Expulsion of Adam and Eve from Paradise* painted fifty or so years earlier in Cappella Brancacci, Eve with her head thrown back in a howl, her face wracked with anguish. Overcome by shame and grief, she covered her naked breasts and nether region with her hands. Gone forever were the days of flat renderings of angels and saints.

"I know how she feels," Guid'Antonio said, and immediately regretted expressing his feelings to anyone, flippantly or no.

Palla's laugh echoed softly in the chapel. "Masaccio would be proud," he said, and let it go at that, chewing the rosemary twig reflectively. "Luigi claims he heard voices besides Castruccio Senso's. Could be he knows them. Could be he was in league with them."

"All ten or twenty?" Guid'Antonio said skeptically. "He also claims Turks kidnapped his lady."

"That's my point."

Guid'Antonio waved his hand. "Much as I dislike eliminating any possibility, I don't think Luigi's one of them, however many there were. Were they some of Castruccio Senso's disgruntled clients? If so, in the past Luigi would have been around them enough to distinguish one voice from the other. But why not finger them? Because he's afraid they'll get to him?" he said, half to himself.

"My money's on Salvestro Aboati," Palla said.

"The Neapolitan you tailed after the argument at the Red Lion. Maybe." They moved to the right toward *The Tribute Money* frescoed on the church wall.

"I left Salvestro Aboati when his path turned opposite Castruccio's," Palla said. "I'll have my men search the taverns and inns for him again. By the way, they scoured the countryside for evidence of where Camilla's horse might have been held captive these last weeks and found nothing."

"That would have been too good to be true," Guid'Antonio said. "Why bother looking for the Neapolitan? If he was involved in Castruccio's death, he's long gone by now. Along with whoever might have assisted him."

"I'll leave no stone unturned," Palla said.

"What of the account sheets torn from the ledger?" Guid'Antonio said. "Find Salvestro Aboati's name there and —"

"I'll sift through the papers," Palla said, "though surely if any of them incriminated Aboati or anyone else, they've been destroyed. There's the motive, perhaps."

Somewhere in the chapel, a door opened. Skirts swished across the nave; in a far corner, a door closed. Quietly, Palla said, "Killing a man's one thing. The scene in Senso's house is quite another."

True. There had been more than avarice in Castruccio Senso's household last night. There had been malice and extreme cruelty, the likes of which Guid'Antonio had witnessed only once before. For an instant, he saw Giuliano's knees buckle as he sank to the Cathedral floor, saw Francesco de' Pazzi stab him relentlessly, ten, twenty times, and more. . . .

"What do you think about the fabric?" Palla said.

"Countless possibilities," Guid'Antonio said, swallowing hard.

Palla turned his shrewd dark eyes him. "But what do you *think* about it, since thinking is our *modus operandi?*"

Palla would press him. So while good Saint Peter poured water over the head of a muscular, barely clothed young man in Tommaso Masaccio's *Saint Peter Baptizing the Converts,* and a viper tempted the naked and unashamed couple in the Garden of Eden in Masolino's gentle *Temptation of Adam and Eve,* Guid'Antonio removed the monogrammed fabric from his scrip. "The cloth is smoothly cut and in a rectangular form. Done with scissors, not ripped. Deliberate, then. The fabric is good quality, albeit not fine. Still, any decent clothing is precious to its owner. Not many people would cut up a woman's shift." He slid the small piece of cloth back into his purse.

Palla smiled. "I will want that back. Cut by Castruccio Senso himself, mayhap? Why?"

"Or someone else and why, again?"

"If he had her killed, why keep the fabric? There's a macabre souvenir."

"But remember the blood on it is fresh," Guid'Antonio said. "This bit of nightgown has been recently soiled, while the girl's been missing almost three weeks now."

By silent agreement they turned and

strode down the single nave enclosed by a barrel vault. Despite the rough stone face Santa Maria del Carmine showed the world, its interior was rich with frescoes lit by candles and natural light provided by ten large arched windows. Turning to Palla, Guid'Antonio said, "What did the elusive nurse Margherita state when you questioned her in Vinci?"

"Nothing. 'Cept she, Camilla, and the boy were beset by Turks, and you know the rest."

"No, I do not," Guid'Antonio said. Luigi: He would go softly when questioning the boy or risk losing him completely. Patience, patience. But look what patience and procrastination had cost him already. It sickened him.

"By the by," Palla said. "She's doing well."

"Who is?" Guid'Antonio said.

"The doctor of the house."

Guid'Antonio felt hot color rise in his cheeks. "Ah," he said.

"You haven't spoken with her about this case." It was a statement, not a question.

"No need," Guid'Antonio said.

Palla made a light, laughing sound down in his throat. "Need comes in many guises, my friend."

"How well I know," Guid'Antonio said.

Casually, Palla said, "She is that rarest of

458

Florentine women. Beautiful, unmarried, and dependent on no man."

Still not married, then. Guid'Antonio sought and failed to find the slightest comfort in that.

They stepped into the piazza, shading their eyes with their hands. "What are you going to do next?" Palla said.

"Keep thinking." Turks. How in God's name had Margherita and Luigi come up with that outrageous tale? And Margherita had told the boy to keep quiet.

Why?

"Castruccio Senso, murdered? So much for that louse as our culprit regarding Camilla Rossi da Vinci," Lorenzo said, storming up and down the *sala* in his house.

"Not necessarily. I believe Castruccio was involved in whatever happened on the road that day." From Santa Maria del Carmine, Guid'Antonio had ridden Flora across Ponte Trinita to the north bank and straight to the Medici Palace.

"So? With Castruccio's death, we've lost the chance to question him about the reservations, about everything." Lorenzo whipped around, glowering, his eyes black points of light. "Tell me now Mary isn't weeping for that miserable little wine merchant!"

"No. The streets are quiet." The painting hadn't wept since Camilla's horse, Tesoro, had galloped into town, thank God in all His radiant glory. "No one has taken advantage of this latest turn. Yet," Guid'Antonio said.

"Senso was robbed as well as having his head bashed in?"

"Maybe only as an extra dividend," Guid'Antonio said. "Or to throw us off the killer's actual motive."

"What actual motive? A *vendetta*?" Lorenzo said, twirling one finger in the air.

A family seeking revenge on Castruccio's house for some slight, whether real or imagined? Camilla's husband was a man well disliked, and the murder seemed a personal one. Still, it had been an ugly kill. "If a *vendetta,* we'd know by now. His killers would make sure of it."

"Killers?"

"Two, at least."

"Why can't we catch these morons who keep committing crimes beneath our noses? Missing girls, paintings weeping when they have a will," Lorenzo said, scowling.

"Castruccio was only *just* murdered," Guid'Antonio reminded him. "And Palla's fast on it." He couldn't resist adding, "Morons, they may be but, so far, they're getting away with it."

"What will you do now?"

*Make a list of the people asking me that same question,* Guid'Antonio thought darkly to himself. "I'll go home to the wife I haven't seen since Thursday. I'll study our accounts. I'll visit Verrocchio's workshop." Another item on his list he had yet failed to do.

"Verrocchio's?" On Lorenzo's lips, the word was an explosion. "Is this truly the time to be thinking about commissioning a sculpture or painting?"

Did he have a life of his own? Apparently, not. "I aim to question his apprentice, Leonardo da Vinci."

Lorenzo whirled around, facing him again. "Leonardo? Why, for God's sake?"

"One never knows where one might find a connection," Guid'Antonio said and refused to elaborate.

"Leonardo's no longer with Verrocchio," Lorenzo said, frowning. "He opened his own shop while you were gone off to France." He resumed pacing, his dark eyes darting here and there. "You know people will accuse me of having a hand in this, if not of actually wielding the candlestick, of

461

causing Castruccio Senso's death in some secret way. Never mind I had no reason to destroy the little man. Just the opposite. A murder in our town. It sickens me."

But it was not Castruccio Senso's violent death for which the populace blamed Lorenzo de' Medici. Rather, it was the alarming news from southern Italy delivered to City Hall by a courier on horseback later in the day. After reconnoitering Rhodes, Mehmed the Conqueror's Turkish army had encamped on the island. For more than a week now, enemy soldiers had been firing messages into the fort held by the Christian Knights of Saint John. "They say the Turkish admiral has seventy thousand soldiers backed by an armada of one hundred ships, and the Knights a force of only six hundred men," the courier said, wiping tears from his eyes with his fist.

"They say the assault is imminent. Against them, our good Knights haven't *any* chance."

# THIRTY-ONE

*"Seventy thousand against six hundred."
Imagine cheeks going pale as Tommaso Soderini repeats the news in Palazzo della Signoria: the Turks say the Knights of Rhodes
are on the verge of such bitter fighting as they
have never witnessed nor imagined in their
wildest dreams. The Turks say that at the end
of the day, they will fly their black flag high
atop the fort tower, sack the city, and slaughter
or enslave its Christian men, women, and
children.*

*Imagine Lorenzo's powerful body bent over
a parchment map unfurled and its corners
weighed down with pebbles on the meeting
table. "Here's Italy's southern tip with King
Ferrante on the Bay of Naples. Moving south-
southeast across the Mediterranean, here's
the island of Rhodes, her battlements blown
open by Admiral Mesih Pasha's artillery."*

*No one present in the hall needs this geog-
raphy lesson; we all know exactly where*

Rhodes is located. We know its defeat will give Mehmed II naval command of the Mediterranean along Italy's eastern shore. We know Mehmed wants to create a new world Islamic Empire.

Lorenzo's presence in City Hall as the unofficial ruler of the Florentine Republic is remarkable and yet undisputed. All eyes follow his ringed finger up the map. "After devouring Rhodes, the Turks will take Naples, then march north to Rome."

"My God," Pierfilippo Pandolfini gasps, and Bartolomeo Scala rubs his temples hard. Just the thought of Turks on Italian soil gives our Lord Chancellor a roaring headache.

Lorenzo's finger taps the parchment. "Overland travel from Rome north to Tuscany takes less than two weeks. By ship and horseback, it is at most four days."

Piero di Nasi laughs shrilly. "Boats off the coast of Naples? Then Rome and Tuscany besieged? What happened to 'There are no Turks in Italy'?"

A scarlet line streaks Lorenzo's neck. "The defeat of Rhodes will wash them up on our shores."

"And we're to prevent this how?" Chairman Tommaso Soderini's faded blue eyes are unnaturally round, his voice sour.

"By presenting a united front against them.

464

Florence, Rome, Naples, Venice, and Milan."

"Oh, please." Antonio Capponi rallies once more. "You are a dreamer, man."

Lorenzo regards him with an intensity that makes Antonio squirm in his seat. "Where are we without dreams, Antonio?"

The Italian peninsula's five major powers constantly bicker and war amongst themselves. Pope Sixtus IV and King Ferrante against Florence, the Sforza in Milan against their own kinsmen, the Lion of the Adriatic against everyone else, including the small but mighty independent states like Urbino and Ferrara led by dukes and despots of every stripe. The notion of a united Italy surfaces from time to time, a puff of smoke riding the air only to evaporate when it loses strength. Yet somehow Lorenzo still believes in it, just as his grandfather, Cosimo de' Medici, did when Cosimo negotiated the Peace of Lodi in 1454 after the fall of Constantinople to Turkish forces.

Moments drag by in silence. Finally, I say, "Will we propose a general league to Milan and all the others?" We. I include myself in the question, though I am not currently one of the nine Lord Priors.

"No," Lorenzo says. "We'll let them stew awhile. They will have received this same news and be thinking hard upon it."

*Imagine Piero di Nasi making a last feeble protest. "Maybe the Knights of Rhodes will beat the Infidels back. On their side the Knights have God and the Virgin Mary."*

*"Di Nasi!" Antonio Capponi shouts. "It's David and Goliath all over again! This time, with an army of thousands at his command, the giant will win!"*

*In the end, we say a prayer for the good Knights and the island of Rhodes and abandon them both. After all, what can we do for them now? For all we know, the Knights are already dead, along with the island's other inhabitants. It is our own future, our own dreams, our own safety we protect. And so, we speak of closer issues, how to placate our town, a festival, perhaps? And of the Pope, Girolamo Riario, and Prince Alfonso of Naples, a trinity of devils already plaguing our city.*

*Think of Lorenzo saying in an undertone to me as I shrug into my roomy, crimson cloak, "Whether City Hall likes it or not, I will unite our homeland."*

*22 July In the Year of Our Lord 1480*
*Guid'Antonio Vespucci, Florentine*

# THIRTY-TWO

"You miss your lady, don't you?"

Luigi gave Guid'Antonio a measuring look and pressed his lips shut.

They were in the Vespucci courtyard, seated on the stone bench encircling the fountain. Coming in from the meeting at the Signoria, he had found Luigi in the kitchen with Giovanni and Maria and been glad to see his son showing the other boy his seashell from the Neapolitan shore. As for sending Luigi home with Amerigo, Guid'Antonio could kick himself. Now the entire town knew Luigi had been in Castruccio Senso's house when Castruccio was bludgeoned to death with the candlestick. Thus, Luigi was a witness, and Guid'Antonio fretted for his safety. Still, where else could the boy have gone? To the Bargello? At least there at the city jail, he would have been under Palla's watchful eye. He would have been scared to death there. And silent as a clam.

Guid'Antonio had told Amerigo to post guards here at home, and this had been done. His feeling of urgency regarding questioning the boy had not abated. If Palla *did* find Salvestro Aboati, would Luigi say whether or not it was Aboati's voice he had heard last night? No matter what Luigi said, could they believe him?

In the garden now, the dog was their sole company, soaking up the sun and the touch of Luigi's hand on his shoulder. Calming the boy. Good. The gate latch squeaked. "Been to Mass?" Guid'Antonio said, glancing up.

"It happens, Uncle. *Mattina.*" Yawning deeply, Amerigo joined the little garden party.

Guid'Antonio gestured to Luigi, smiling. "We're having a chat."

"One-sided, hey?"

"Not for long."

"I mean to go to the stable and rescue Tesoro from that sorry stable keep," Amerigo said. "Since there's no one else to claim her. And I had better go soon. That ass will sell her and worry later about the fact the mare is evidence."

And now an Andalusian horse.

Luigi licked his lips, breathing rapidly.

Amerigo's mention of Tesoro had struck a chord. Hmmm. Guid'Antonio touched the boy's shoulder. "Luigi. In a moment you can find Giovanni in the nursery, or go see Domenica and Cesare. You saw Amerigo latch the gate. You're safe."

Luigi kept his silence.

"When you were in the fireplace, what happened first? Did the men come in and wait for your master? Or did he admit them?"

Luigi scrunched his toes in the tips of his sandals. "I think . . . he let them in."

"You couldn't tell?"

"I'm not sure, *Signore.*"

"He knew them?" Guid'Antonio pressed.

Luigi closed his eyes and bent his head. "I don't know, *Signore.*"

"I'm not sure" and "I don't know," would not suffice for this. "Did they have a conversation? Or did the yelling start immediately?"

"They talked, of course, *Signore,* but I — I couldn't distinguish what they said. Then one of them screamed at my master, and he shouted, 'No! No!' and ran. After that it was quiet except when one of them smashed the strongbox."

"One more thing, then you can scoot to the nursery," Guid'Antonio said. "The piece of fabric you had in your hand . . . did your lady's nurse pack the gown it came from on the day the three of you left on your trip?"

Luigi hesitated. "I think so, *Signore.* Yes."

Hedging, again. "And was the gown whole? Of a piece, I mean?"

Luigi looked offended. "Whole, *Signore*! My lady would not wear torn clothing."

Guid'Antonio closed his eyes, smiling. So. Camilla had the gown in her possession of a whole, and yet later a piece of it was in Castruccio Senso's hands. "Did your master have the piece of fabric before last night?" he said.

The boy looked confused: how should he answer this? "I don't know," he said, falling back into evasion.

"Maybe he doesn't," Amerigo cut in.

"Luigi, did you actually see Turks accost your lady the day you accompanied her on the road?" Guid'Antonio said.

"No! No, *Signore.* I didn't," Luigi said, beginning to tremble again.

"Then how do you know that's who they were?"

"I mean — yes."

Luigi's eyes fluttered with such violence, Guid'Antonio feared the boy might faint, or have a seizure. "*Grazie,* Luigi, you may go now," he said quietly. "Go."

Luigi couldn't have vanished from the garden and up the apartment stairs faster if he had sprouted wings and flown.

"Uncle Guid'Antonio," Amerigo said, "he's just a boy."

Guid'Antonio held up his hand. "Time is of the essence. Palla will be much harder on him. And we don't know what mischief is afoot or how Camilla fares in all this."

"Well, what do we know?"

"Something wicked happened on the road to Morba. And I believe Luigi holds the key to unlocking that terrible secret. Something niggles at me."

"Only 'something'?" Amerigo said as they ascended the palace stairs. "I'm completely in the clouds. Come along, Dog."

So the cur bore an appellation now, insignificant as the name was. "No," Guid'Antonio said. "Animals belong in the yard. Especially one as big as he is." And plush. The dog's fur was growing thicker by the hour. In a month or so — Guid'Antonio didn't want to think about it. His mind was already an explosion of facts and semi-facts and curious wanderings.

He said: "Whoever killed Castruccio Senso must know about the boy, whether he, or they, had anything to do with Camilla's disappearance or were disgruntled business patrons, or whatever. Why didn't they tear the house upside down, looking for Luigi to prevent him from bearing witness?"

"They didn't know he was there," Amerigo said. "They thought he was still in Vinci, like we did. That reminds me, Luigi told me Castruccio Senso was selling him. That's why Jacopo Rossi brought Luigi to town last Tuesday. Good God. You don't suppose Luigi killed Castruccio to prevent that happening? As cruel as Castruccio was, at least he was a known entity."

"Luigi's no killer, Amerigo."

"Let us hope. Speaking of killers, is there any news of Forli and Count Girolamo Riario?"

"No. The boy, Sinibaldo Ordelaffi, has only been dead four days."

Amerigo laughed dryly. "Silence is dangerous. How long do you think Riario needs? What is it, Uncle? You look pale."

Guid'Antonio shook his head. Only the uneasy feeling he was back in the grassy lawn at Poggio a Caiano watching Lorenzo fix his arrow and shoot it straight into the eye of the target.

# THIRTY-THREE

"You could set Sandro Botticelli's workshop down in here a dozen times." Amerigo glanced back over his shoulder into the byway. "No, no, Dog, stay here. In the alley, *Signore.*"

Guid'Antonio scrunched up his face, as if that would help him hear Amerigo over the noise in Andrea del Verrocchio's enormous *bottega:* nails banged into picture frames and hammered into furniture under construction, a heated argument between apprentices over whose cartoon drawing of an angel would best suit the master. "Sorry?" he shouted over the din.

Amerigo raised his voice. "Andrea's busy as always, no matter what mischief and misery happens in our town."

"Yes." Guid'Antonio's roving glance found stout Andrea del Verrocchio standing in the midst of Verrocchio and Company with a tall young fellow studying drawings laid out on a trestle table. Ah: Leonardo da Vinci. One of Leonardo's apprentices had told Guid'Antonio where his master could be found this morning.

"Come along, Amerigo." Guid'Antonio picked a path around goods packed in wooden crates set for delivery throughout Italy, dodging the boy dashing toward them with an armload of brass candlesticks.

"Look who's ventured to our part of town." Andrea del Verrocchio's plump cheeks lifted in a cherubic smile. "Welcome, Messer Guid'Antonio, Amerigo. Welcome."

All the typical questions followed. They had been back from Paris for how long now? Two weeks? And been met by the devil's own news: kidnappings, weeping paintings, murderers loose in town, terrible, terrible. "And now, the Turks at Rhodes," Andrea said, crossing himself. "You'd think it was the end of the world."

Above the babble and buzz of activity of the workshop, Guid'Antonio answered by rote: two weeks, yes. God help the last of the Christian crusaders. And, yes, the girl was gone and her husband killed. "But Palla is on it," he said. "And the painting is quiet."

"I see you brought a friend," Leonardo da Vinci said, indicating Dog, who sat with one paw just over the threshold, smiling at them with drool on his jowls.

"Not really," Guid'Antonio said.

"Who wanted those two out of the way, do you think," Andrea said, his forehead a dimpled frown. "The wife, and now, him. Someone must have had a grudge against him. Else that fellow sold truly terrible wine."

Guid'Antonio smiled. Poor wine as a motive for murder? Well, in Italy, perhaps. He said, "No murderers, only a robbery gone wrong."

"But Uncle," Amerigo said.

"Do you have something to add?" Guid'Antonio said, whipping around.

"No. Not now."

"Because a murderer running loose would cap all our troubles," Guid'Antonio said.

"It certainly would."

Guid'Antonio glanced at Leonardo and told Andrea del Verrocchio he and Amerigo just happened to be in Sant'Ambrogio parish and thought they would stop by to say hello.

Andrea's eyes showed he did not believe this for a moment. Just happen to be in Sant'Ambrogio? Come round on a whim? It was not in Guid'Antonio di Giovanni di Vespucci's nature to just happen by anywhere. Moreover, Andrea's *bottega,* the

475

largest and most productive in the city, sat no short distance from Ognissanti, east of the Cathedral toward Porta alla Croce in the Keys district of the San Giovanni quarter. "I am honored," he said.

Smiling, Guid'Antonio regarded Andrea's former apprentice, Leonardo da Vinci. Leonardo was slender with light auburn, almost blond, hair worn well past his shoulders. His loose white linen shirt lay open at the throat, revealing a mass of golden chest hair. "I hear you have your own shop now," Guid'Antonio said. Small talk with this talented craftsman who shared his hometown with Camilla Rossi and her father, Jacopo Rossi da Vinci.

"I do," Leonardo said, nodding. "But —"

"But!" Andrea gestured wildly around the shop and back toward a room where plaster casts of hands, feet, and knees lined the shelves, models for his apprentices to work by. "I have boys to teach, a silver relief to finish for the baptistery altar, the monument of Forteguerri for Pistoia to complete, and the *Doubting Thomas* for Orsanmichele to wrangle into place. I did finish a bust of our Lorenzo. Terracotta. Good as it turned out."

"I wouldn't expect otherwise," Guid'Antonio said.

"By comparison, in my own shop I've precious little work," Leonardo said, and grimaced. "Of the sort that pays."

Andrea pushed back his cap, revealing a receding hairline, and swiped perspiration from his forehead. "He's a great help to me. Keeps me calm when I see everything crashing down."

"I do what I can," Leonardo said, smiling.

"So you don't have much work of your own," Amerigo said.

"Not since the portrait I painted of Genevra de' Benci. A Madonna or two, and some drawings, also an alterpiece here and there. Nor do many of our craftsmen, given the present economy, except Andrea, which is only just, since he taught most of us."

"No, no," Amerigo protested, "I know for a fact our Botticelli is doing extremely well. Moreover, he's set to paint me."

"Good for Sandro," Leonardo replied neutrally.

"Leonardo whiles away the hours dreaming up ideas for Florence's future defense: canals, weapons, all manner of outrageous machines," Andrea said.

"Not outrageous. Only time-consuming," Leonardo said. "Given the war and now the Turks breathing down our necks, someone needs to think about homeland security.

477

Messer Guid'Antonio, do you know how it goes with the Pope's new chapel in the Vatican?"

"I've no idea," Guid'Antonio said, not wanting to go into it and thinking of Sandro, who had asked him the same question at Botticelli and Company.

"Oh," Leonardo said. "That would be a good commission."

"If you don't mind working for the devil in Saint Peter's," Amerigo said.

Glancing away from him, Leonardo said, "Along with all the rest, Verrocchio will no doubt win the right to do the latest sculpture planned by the Venetians." He indicated the drawings on the table.

"What is it?" Guid'Antonio said. Time enough in a moment to get down to the true nature of his business with Leonardo da Vinci.

"An equestrian monument of Bartolomeo Colleoni. Big!" Andrea said. "Means traveling north. How I long for the days when Sandro and Leonardo were in this shop together, frescoes, portraits, wedding chests. Easy work."

"The air wasn't always so quiet when Botticelli and I were apprentices here," Leonardo said, smiling again, "and any man like our Andrea who can mount a sphere and cross atop the Cathedral dome as easily as he paints tournament banners can do anything."

"Having Leonardo around sounds a good arrangement for you both," Amerigo said. "His help is a boon to you, Andrea, and it keeps him off the streets."

Hot color crept into the flesh of Leonardo's delicate countenance, and his smile faded. He adjusted the front of his tunic, pulling the hem tighter beneath the wide leather belt encircling his hips, and tucked a stray lock of hair behind his ear. Andrea looked appalled. The silence was deafening.

"Don't mind him," Guid'Antonio said, wanting to throttle his nephew. "Amerigo's memory is sharp when it comes to his grandfather." Amerigo's comment had been a neat double slur, referring both to the public charge of sodomy an unidentified accuser had made against Leonardo a few years back, and to the long ago afternoon when Leonardo chased Amerigo the Elder through town, whispering to himself and drawing hastily in his sketchbook to capture the frightened old man's ancient likeness on paper.

Leonardo relaxed a bit. "I knew my fascination with his grandfather displeased your nephew, Messer Guid'Antonio. That's why

I gave one of those rough sketches to him. Though I thought he might tear it up in retaliation." He offered Amerigo a conciliatory smile. "Better than a knife in the heart, I suppose."

"No," Amerigo said, his anger diffused, though his cheeks still appeared warm. "The drawing was much too good to destroy. I still have it."

Andrea looked around from one to the other of them, tapping his fingers on the table, clearly wondering what in hell the Vespuccis were actually doing in his shop.

"Leonardo, you're from Vinci," Guid'Antonio said.

"Born there, yes. But I've lived in Florence almost twenty-eight years, since I came here as a boy."

"What do you know of Jacopo Rossi da Vinci?"

"Jacopo? Oh. The father of the girl —"

"Who is still missing, yes," Guid'Antonio said, leaning forward, motioning with his hands.

"Never met the man," Leonardo said. "Nor the girl, either."

Guid'Antonio grunted his disappointment, aware Andrea and Leonardo were staring at him. He didn't care. "Are you sure?"

"Yes. But my uncle Francesco da Vinci might know Jacopo," Leonardo said. "Francesco's still on the farm where I spent my early years. If it's information about Jacopo Rossi you want, I'll send Francesco a message asking what he can find out about him."

"No. Or, anyway, not yet." Guid'Antonio must go to Vinci himself. Soon.

Then what? Leonardo's eyes asked, and Andrea cleared his throat loudly. He had work to do. So did Leonardo.

"Leonardo, how would you go about making a painting weep?" Guid'Antonio said.

Andrea stepped back. "The Virgin Mary in Ognissanti? Surely, the hand of God has been in that."

Leonardo's mouth quirked. "I could find a thousand ways."

"I'll settle for one." Guid'Antonio turned back to Andrea. "The hand of God, you say? You believe the tears, intermittent as they are, are an indictment of Lorenzo?"

"Of course not. No," Andrea del Verrocchio, a craftsman commissioned by the Medici for decades, said.

"Apply a dry compound of a dead animal's blood to the eyes, then squirt the painting with liquid," Leonardo said. "Or —"

481

"Wouldn't that make tears of blood?" Guid'Antonio said.

"Absolutely," Leonardo said.

"God's knees, don't think it," Amerigo said.

"But if it's translucent tears you want?" Leonardo raised his brow questioningly.

"I don't want them, but I have them," Guid'Antonio said. True, the Virgin Mary hadn't wept in well over a week, but who knew when the tears might begin again, and him no closer to exposing the perpetrator today than on the Monday he first heard about them?

Smiling, Leonardo said, "I understand."

"He'll be inside Ognissanti this very night studying the painting from every angle known to man," Amerigo said, leading the way back toward the Unicorn district through shadowed stone passages and skinny side streets.

"Let us hope," Guid'Antonio said.

"Did you notice the emblem 'broidered around the neck of his tunic?"

"I did." Leonardo's emblem was a plow in an oval setting with the motto *Impedimento non mi piega. No obstacle will stop me.* Guid'Antonio prayed not. He heard Dog

482

panting behind him. "Go on," he said. "Get back."

"The tunic was made of fine cotton, too," Amerigo said. "But then, his family's wealthy and cares not he's a bastard. God, it's hot today."

The hairs prickled on the back of Guid'Antonio's neck, a warning to take care. Why? He glanced over his shoulder before starting with Amerigo across a sunny piazza. Despite the heat, alms seekers loitered near the shops, stretching their hands out to passersby. People with wooden buckets crowded toward the public well, sweating, fanning themselves, and awaiting their turn at the spout.

There was something menacing here. Something hit Guid'Antonio in the back, hard. In the next instant a warm breath brushed his cheek, and a familiar voice whispered urgently in his ear, "Brother Martino, and him still gone!"

"Uncle!" Amerigo whipped around, brandishing his knife. A woman screamed. People scattered. Empty buckets struck the ground and rattled across the square.

Dog had already launched his massive body toward the dark-draped figure hurrying toward a nearby alley. "You! Dog!" Guid'Antonio shouted. "No!"

The animal jerked around, looking askance at him, confused. "Good dog! Stay! It's only Brother Paolo," Guid'Antonio told Amerigo, excited, his heart beating rapidly. "He meant no harm. He had something to tell me." Amazing. In the blink of an eye, they were alone in the square. So much for people coming to their rescue. He glanced at the *cane corso Italiano.* The dog's attempt to protect him was pure instinct on its part, nothing more.

"Never. How do you know? That it was Paolo, I mean." Amerigo sheathed his weapon, breathing hard. "That fellow was uncommonly tall, but his cowl did hide his face."

"His voice," Guid'Antonio said.

Perplexed, Amerigo said, "Paolo didn't care if you understood it was him? Why risk having me knife him rather than just coming out with — what was it, by the way?"

"He said, 'Brother Martino, and him still gone!' With an exclamation point." Guid'Antonio raised his eyebrows, thinking about this as they started walking, quickly now.

"But we knew Martin was gone," Amerigo said. "Didn't we? He's the lout who plowed into us in Ognissanti and kept running the first day we were back in town."

"Indeed. But we didn't know he hadn't come back, did we? And Brother Paolo risked everything to tell me that. Why, Nephew?"

"The mind reels," Amerigo said.

They threaded south toward the Arno through the Ox and the Black Lion districts, stepping every so often into a piazzetta where sunlight illuminated the buildings, transforming their ochre facades into russet and gold stone. Thoughtfully, as they passed into a bleak passageway, Amerigo said, "In church last week the novice Ferdinando Bongiovi swore —"

"The *Virgin Mary of Santa Maria Impruneta* is weeping for Martin's sins, yes, yes. But now the question is where Martino may be found. And why he ran from church in the first place."

"I think we're sidetracked," Amerigo said.

"Then don't think," Guid'Antonio said.

"If I were you, I'd be asking why chatty Brother Paolo didn't tell you Brother Martin's whereabouts rather than continuing this game of hit and run."

"Because clearly Brother Paolo doesn't know and is hoping I'll find out."

Outside Ognissanti Church, street urchins played and dogs scavenged for vegetables and fruit oozing with flies. Guid'Antonio opened the church door, glancing sideways down the street, watching Amerigo unlatch the Vespucci courtyard gate and disappear into the garden. Meanwhile, Dog lay curled into a huge ball at the church entrance with his nose resting on his massive paws, prepared to snooze and wait for Guid'Antonio to come back out.

What persistence. Stepping inside the church, Guid'Antonio breathed deeply and glanced around. The sanctuary was quiet, with only three or four people praying at the main altar. Behind him, the door opened, admitting a crack of light. The two women who entered craned their necks for a better view of Sandro's *Saint Augustine* before continuing past Guid'Antonio to the church front. A figure swathed in black crept toward him through the shadowed nave. It was Brother Battista Bellincioni, the doughy almoner of the church, and him ever on the prowl.

Guid'Antonio narrowed his eyes. Was Bellincioni the culprit who had manufactured the tears? If so, why had he stopped? On orders from Abbot Ughi, who feared they might get caught, now Guid'Antonio Vespucci was on the case? He smiled to himself, acknowledging his own sense of self-

486

importance.

"Messer Vespucci," Brother Bellincioni said, sneering. "You again."

"And you. You look undressed without the collection box in your hands."

"You look undressed without your costly red cloak," Bellincioni said.

"I would speak with Brother Martin."

A shuttered look closed the monk's face. "There is no Brother Martin here."

"Not anymore, you mean."

Bellincioni blinked. "I mean there is no such person here."

"The novice Ferdinando Bongiovi, then." Guid'Antonio's little talker.

Bellincioni snapped his fingers, his expression gloating. "Gone!"

A sliver of fear slid up Guid'Antonio's throat. "Gone where?" Surely they wouldn't hurt the boy.

"I wouldn't know," Bellincioni said.

Quite possibly, this was true. Probably the worst thing that had happened to young Ferdinando was that he had been sent to another church somewhere outside the town walls, squirreled away to keep him from blabbing about Brother Martino and his whereabouts. All three young brothers of the Humiliati Order, Paolo, Martino, and Ferdinando, held the key to some secret

Ognissanti did not want revealed. Guid'Antonio was certain of it now.

He hardly dared say it: "And Brother Paolo Dolci?" Could Paolo have reached here so soon after bumping into him? Yes. He would have run, run, run, timid and scared as a mouse.

"Unavailable," Bellincioni said.

"He had better not come to any harm. Nor any of them."

"We protect our own," Bellincioni said.

"From what?"

"Themselves," Bellincioni hissed.

"Abbot Ughi, then."

"Gone. To Rome." A smile snaked across Bellincioni's lips. "To meet with the Pope."

Sixtus IV. This was interesting. Guid'Antonio's eyes sought and found the Virgin Mary on the distant altar. The two women who had come into the church with him were kneeling before Mary's painted image. Ognissanti and the Pope in collusion over the tears did not seem such a stretch anymore. But it was not too much to say that the *Virgin Mary of Santa Maria Impruneta* was Florence's most revered icon. Would Abbot Ughi dare tamper with the painting? He thought of the Pope's support of Giuliano's murder and of the abbot's frosty stare. The tears meant money in the coffers and Lorenzo's reputation soiled. Two for one, and both men benefited, abbot and Pope.

He said: "Abbot Roberto Ughi can't stay in Rome forever, although it might be best for Florence if he did. Mind this, Bellincioni, playing with the Pope can be dangerous."

*"Playing?"* Bellincioni quailed. Recovering, his countenance sour and outraged, he turned without further words and scurried deep into the sanctuary.

Guid'Antonio glanced at the wall on his right side. In the gloom, the *Saint Augustine* — the old man's gold-and-white robe — jumped out at him. "Old fellow," he said, noting the beseeching expression on the saint's face and how his eyes were turned toward heaven, seeking answers, "I know just how you feel."

Near the sacristy, a shadow, watching Guid'Antonio, vanished.

Guid'Antonio's skin prickled. What would they have done with little Ferdinando? Would they have sent him home or, indeed, to another church? If Brother Paolo were still here, tucked away somewhere, did he fear some personal harm? Paolo had risked his neck by contacting Guid'Antonio out in the open just now, no matter how briefly. And where was Brother Martino? He and

Camilla Rossi da Vinci disappeared. Camilla gone *before* the young, dark-haired monk, and then Camilla's horse, Tesoro, sent into the city.

One thing he did know: he must find Martino, if only because Brother Paolo Dolci desperately wanted him to do it and believed that he could.

# THIRTY-FOUR

A beam of light shone over Guid'Antonio's shoulder.

Startled, he glanced around. A dark shape hovered within the church door, its shadowed form surrounded by a halo of golden light. He strode forward, toward whatever good or evil stood waiting for him.

"Uncle Guid'Antonio?"

"Amerigo." Guid'Antonio closed his eyes a moment. It was his angel nephew, backlit by the sun pouring down on Piazza Ognissanti with Dog drooling at his heels.

"Luigi's fine now," Amerigo said. "I'm happy you sent me to check on him. He was crying in his bed. What have you learned here?"

"Abbot Ughi is in Rome."

"Rome! And now?"

"Let's —" Guid'Antonio glanced back at Sandro's fresco of Saint Augustine, frowning, his eyes traveling up the length of the painting. "Amerigo," he said, advancing toward the church wall, "open the front door far as it will go. Yes, look there, just beneath our coat of arms."

"Where? Oh, some lines scribbled in the saint's geometry book. In the shadows, I hadn't seen them before."

"I had. But in shadow, as you say." Guid'Antonio squinted. And read the lines aloud.

*"Is Brother Martino anywhere about?"*
*"Brother Martino just slipped out!"*
*"Slipped out where?"*

Where, indeed? Guid'Antonio hardly dared breathe, lest he wake to find himself not in Ognissanti, but home, swimming up from a dream featuring clues painted at the top of frescos, and how ridiculously improbable was that?

Hoping against hope, heart pounding rapidly, he read the fourth and final line:

*"Through the Prato Gate for a breath of fresh air!"*

Martin had been running in that direction, yes. "Amerigo," Guid'Antonio said softly, "Alessandro Botticelli could hold the key to Brother Martin's whereabouts. Please God, we'll find our neighbor in his house."

Those golden eyes.

"You've discovered the writing," Sandro said, fixing Guid'Antonio with a wide yellow stare. "It was lightly meant, with no harm done to the commission."

"Clever, too," Guid'Antonio said.

"I knew if anyone ever saw those lines, it would be you." Sandro cocked an eyebrow. "It was only after including them I realized my little jest might seem inappropriate." He smiled.

Amerigo said: "Or even sacrilegious."

"Even that," Sandro said.

"Is that why you were nervous when we came to your shop the other day?" Amerigo said.

Sandro conceded the point with a nod of the head. "Amerigo, you are a sharp knife, as always."

"What did you see the last day you were employed in Ognissanti?" Guid'Antonio said.

Sandro glanced at his apprentices, three boys gilding, drawing, tracing. "I was almost finished with your wall when this monk, a certain Brother Martino as it turned out, came flying from the sacristy, feverish and yelling."

"Yelling?" Guid'Antonio said.

"That he had defiled Ognissanti. He didn't want to live."

493

"Defiled Ognissanti?" Amerigo straightened. "How?"

"What else happened?" Guid'Antonio said.

"He fell before the Virgin, sobbing, claiming he had brought God down on our heads. By 'our,' I took it he meant Florence. He said he was Satan's brother."

"That is a bit much," Amerigo said.

Sandro's puckered brow indicated he disagreed. "Brother Martin believed everything he said. The word *murder* flew from his lips."

*"Murder?"* Guid'Antonio and Amerigo said.

"Who was murdered?" Guid'Antonio said.

Grim-faced, Sandro shook his head. "That he did not say."

"Why didn't you tell Palla about this? Or me?"

"You didn't ask. How should I know it was important? Anyhow, the boy was overwrought, no more, no less. Murder? No."

Guid'Antonio massaged his temples, thinking. "The other monks chased him — Paolo Dolci and little Ferdinando."

"They did."

"What did they say? Besides the exchange you jotted down for all posterity to read?"

"You mean till someone paints over the

494

fresco or cuts a door in the wall?" Sandro laughed sourly. "They called loudly to him, or rather, Brother Paolo did: the tall, pretty one with the silver hair. Tonsured, sadly. Paolo seemed to think Martino had committed some particularly vile sin. His concern appeared to be that if Brother Martino ran off, the abbot would have his head."

Amerigo snorted. "Most like he already did."

"So," Guid'Antonio said. "Martin thought, or thinks, he committed some grievous wrong. Paolo does as well, but you don't?"

"I don't want to think it," Sandro said.

"The question remains, run where?" Guid'Antonio said. "Pisa? Lucca? Straight into the sea? I saw Martino run toward the Prato Gate, but that particular gate leads everywhere."

A light dawned in Sandro's eyes. "That's what you want to know? Where Brother Martino went that day?"

"Yes."

Sandro glanced at his apprentices' bent heads and the candles burning around the shop, adding a whisper of light to the dim illumination offered by the open windows. "Seems smaller to me every year. Messer Guid'Antonio," he ventured softly.

"Yes."

"I want to go to Rome."

"Yes, yes, to paint the chapel for the Pope."

"You remember."

"I remember everything. Including the new building in the Vatican. And its naked walls." *And you — and Leonardo da Vinci — nattering about how it is the end of the world if you don't go there immediately and leave your painterly marks upon them.*

"Those who go will need a strong recommendation from Lorenzo. You could whisper my name in his ear."

"I could," Guid'Antonio said.

"You'll tell no one else what I'm about to say? For I have no wish to bring trouble to Brother Martino or any of ours in Ognissanti."

"Of course I won't."

"Peretola," Sandro said.

"Peretola?" Guid'Antonio stiffened. "That's the Vespucci family seat."

"I know. And Peretola was the last word I heard on Brother Martin's lips."

"Yes, I know Martino Leone," Niccolò Vespucci said.

Guid'Antonio and Amerigo were in Niccolò's tavern in Peretola a short distance from Florence, having hastily saddled Flora and Bucephalus and ridden hard through the Prato Gate. "I know the boy's family, at least. The Leones keep a farm nearby. Their son, this Martino Leone, came home, oh, a good two weeks ago now. Left the church, probably in disgrace, but his family took him back willingly. Not every son makes a monk."

Two weeks. Guid'Antonio smiled to himself. Two weeks ago was when Martino bumped into him in the street.

"Thank God for that," Amerigo said. "I would not want to enter the church myself, though I believe Uncle Giorgio hoped I might." He fanned himself, his face dripping sweat, then gulped the Chianti his uncle Niccolò Vespucci had poured for him and his kinsman, Guid'Antonio. Seated at one of the tavern's many tables, with a plate of cheese and fruit alongside a plate of *zucchini fritti,* eggplant fried in olive oil then sprinkled with parsley, spread before them, Guid'Antonio wiped his hands on his pants and casually said, "Do you think Martino's still there? At the Leone farm, I mean?" Please, God, please.

"Where else would he go?" Niccolò poured more wine from the carafe.

"Did — does he have a young woman with

497

him?" Amerigo said.

"A young woman?" Niccolò fluttered his hand. "What family would allow such indecency as that?"

"None, surely," Amerigo said.

They asked for directions to the Leone farm; Niccolò Vespucci told them the way; and then as quickly as they had come, Guid'Antonio and Amerigo were off and gone yet again.

In the fields, the apple and pear trees dripped with maturing fruit. Bees buzzed beneath the sun, buried themselves in wild flowers, and returned to their hives with pollen. Crickets sang ceaselessly. A wooden cart rattled along the road, its load a basket of ripe cherries. The old man pushing the cart waved as Guid'Antonio and Amerigo rode by. "Can things be looking up?" Amerigo said, waving back. "All seems well here."

"We can hope." In a few weeks, the sun would scorch the green meadows stretching out on either side of them, bleaching the grass into the thin yellow shade of straw.

They found Martino Leone gathering root vegetables in the narrow terraces surrounding the Leone farmhouse. A young girl walking down the road with a string of dead pigeons in her hand had directed them here. Roasted, the birds' meat would fill several bellies. Crushed, their bones would yield a hearty soup stock.

Martino started when he saw the two riders approaching. He glanced toward the stone house. The windows were open and empty. The mutt lounging in the door didn't lift its head. Everything in Martino's manner shouted, "Run!"

"No," Guid'Antonio said, sliding from the saddle. "We want only to talk. You've nothing to fear." For now.

Martino hesitated and approached them heavily, as if his feet were weighed down with stones. He held out his hands, crossed at the wrists, waiting to have them bound. "Take me to the Stinche. Or to Abbot Ughi. Whoever sent you, I'm your prisoner now."

Guid'Antonio gave Martino an appraising look: glossy black hair, a remarkably beautiful face, a face that might have been drawn by Botticelli himself. He said, "For what crime, pray tell?"

"Murder. Cowardice."

Guid'Antonio took in the trembling, slender hands, newly calloused and raw. When had they ever toiled? Not in Ognissanti, certainly. Not at hard labor, at any rate. He said, "No one sent me. I'm neither the church nor the police."

"You are both," Martino said. "I know who you are. I defiled Ognissanti. Your place of worship."

"Defiled it how? Why did you leave there?"

"Because they killed her. Camilla," Martino said, her name soft on his lips.

Guid'Antonio's heart picked up a pace. "They?" he said.

"The Turkish Infidels. Because of me! And caused the Virgin Mary painting to weep, all, all because of me." Hot tears streaked Martino's dusty cheeks.

"Holy hell," Amerigo said, "you take a lot on yourself."

"I repeat, Martin Leone: how? And why?" Guid'Antonio said.

"Because of our sins. Me, a monk, and her, a married lady. We couldn't help ourselves. We were in love. I love her still."

Amerigo gave Guid'Antonio a look from beneath half-lowered lids: *I knew it.*

"And this in Ognissanti?" Guid'Antonio said.

Martino swiped at the tears on his cheeks. "Yes, in one chapel after another when she came to say her prayers."

"And had them answered," Amerigo said.

"Where is everyone?" Guid'Antonio said, glancing around. Deserted road, empty

500

meadows and fields.

"The market fair a short way down from here. Vegetables, fruit."

"And you didn't go?"

"I told you I'm a coward. I neither want to see anyone nor to be seen."

"Nor to be caught. You're out of luck today," Amerigo said.

Guid'Antonio indicated the stone steps leading into the house. "Let's sit down."

This they did, the old dog shuffling to the narrow shade of a plane tree. "You left Ognissanti a few days after word came the Turks had kidnapped Camilla and the painting began to weep."

Martino covered his face with his hands, sobbing. "Yes. Why did God punish her instead of me? I've asked it over and over, but have no answer. But this —" He thumped his chest. "The pain in my heart is my eternal punishment. Camilla's sweet and good. But I — I had lust in my heart. God is punishing me. He's leveling his righteous fury on all Tuscany because of me."

His gaze slid to Guid'Antonio. "The interdict still stands?"

"Yes."

"Oh, Mary!"

"You believe Camilla's dead?" Guid'Anto-

501

nio said.

"Naturally. Her nurse came back to Florence and said —"

"We know what her nurse said. Have you any news at all from town?"

"Why should I? I don't care what happens there anymore."

Guid'Antonio narrowed his eyes, watching him closely. "You might care about this: Castruccio Senso is dead."

Martino whipped around on the step. "Camilla's husband? Dead? Good. How?"

"Murdered," Guid'Antonio said.

"Murdered?" Martino gasped, licking his lips, blinking rapidly. "Don't look at me for this. I despised Castruccio Senso, but I never would kill him. But had I done that early on, we could have —"

His voice sharp, Guid'Antonio said, "You could have done nothing." Beyond the hot passions released in the murky shadows of the church, Martino Leone and Camilla Rossi da Vinci had had no choices open to them. As Martino had said, they were a monk and a married lady. Where would they go? How would they live once they arrived there?

"How did Castruccio die?" Martino said, his words a dry whisper in his mouth.

"A burglary. In his house," Guid'Antonio

said vaguely.

"Then may he burn in the hottest corner of hell. Surely, I'll see him there." Martino shook his head in wonder. "If it had happened differently, him killed and her not going to the baths, then we —"

They left Martin Leone like that, on the stone step alone, building an airy castle of maybes and what-ifs, Guid'Antonio content to let him do so if it eased the fellow's tortured soul. He thought about the baths, the nonexistent reservation, Castruccio Senso's murder, and the ill-starred lovers, and in his heart he still resisted the notion God decided everything.

They rode home in the early evening through an atmosphere perfumed with the ripe, hot scent of fig trees and fennel, and on through the Prato Gate. In the Vespucci garden, Maria ran to him, her smile markedly brighter than he had seen it in the five days since her mother's burial. "Oh!" She stepped back, pretending to shudder. "You're all sweaty."

"Enjoy," he said, smiling back at her.

"Guid'Antonio!"

"I thought you liked me this way."

"I do, but people can hear you. Where have you been all day?"

*"Buena sera,"* Amerigo said to Maria, grinning, and went on into the kitchen for a late supper.

To Verrocchio and Company. To Ognissanti Church. To Sandro's *bottega* just around the corner. "To Peretola," Guid'Antonio said. *Turks,* he thought. *A missing girl. A weeping painting. A husband murdered.*

"Did you learn anything?"

"Some." She looked young and pretty in the twilight, even in her mourning gown and veils, black, and even more black silk enveloping her all around. How did she breathe?

She glanced toward the fountain where Luigi, Giovanni, and Olimpia were playing cards. Nearby sat Cesare on a stool brushing Dog's coat with a silver brush. *I have lost control of our house,* Guid'Antonio thought. Obviously, Dog had been the victim of another bath. Olimpia, her eyes adoring, watched Cesare work the bristles through the cur's lustrous fawn coat.

Here was a pretty scene. Why did it make him uneasy? Dog, having spotted him, grinned and struggled to rise from his haunches. "He doesn't want you," Cesare reminded the animal, pressing its rear end down. "Stay."

"The boys do get along," Maria was saying. "Can we keep him? Luigi, I mean."

"He's not a pet, Maria," Guid'Antonio said, drawing his eyes back to her.

"I know that," she said with considerable heat. "I mean to care for Luigi, as we do all our family."

The Vespuccis didn't own any slaves, though most wealthy families in Florence counted several in their households. Lorenzo de' Medici's grandfather, Cosimo, had a son by a slave girl; his name was Carlo de' Medici. Again, there was Lorenzo's half sister born of Lorenzo's father, Piero, under the same circumstances. "I don't know, Maria," Guid'Antonio said. "Castruccio Senso seems not to have heirs, but if someone does eventually come forward, they'll claim the boy. Luigi is valuable on the market. We'll have to wait and see." Buy the boy? *Luigi.* Not his true name, of course. "If we should take him in, we'll free him when he comes of age."

"Good." She kissed him there in front of everyone. Long. Hard.

His blood stirred. "Let's go upstairs."

A smile curved Maria's lips. "Olimpia, watch the boys."

Dog, released from his grooming, followed Guid'Antonio with yearning eyes as they crossed the garden, while Cesare caught Giovanni up and swung him around, causing the boy to giggle, and Luigi stood back, his face filled with longing.

What might a man do if he believes his wife is cuckolding him?

Guid'Antonio trailed his fingers down Maria's belly, his eyes on her face, drinking her in. Beat her? Beat him? Send her on vacation to remove her from the other man? Murder her, having already collected the balance of her dowry? And all this, or some part of it, swirling around Lorenzo and the weeping *Virgin Mary of Santa Maria Impruneta* in All Saints Church. Guid'Antonio shook his head to clear it, damning himself for the direction of his thoughts here in his bed.

"You're thinking about him and all his troubles," Maria whispered, her lips soft against the hairs on his chest.

"I just want to forget him for now," he said.

"I will if you will," she said and drew him down to her, her mouth hungry, seeking his.

# THIRTY-FIVE

"No wonder Leonardo's so good. Who couldn't draw if he was born with this view?" Amerigo said.

"Me." Guid'Antonio lifted a spoonful of *ribollita* to his lips.

The view from the village inn Leonardo da Vinci's family owned in the hilltop town of Vinci was a panorama of dark green cypresses, ancient olive trees, flowering almonds, and sparkling, darting streams. Guid'Antonio wondered if in the last few hours Leonardo had had any luck with making paintings weep. So far, Luca Landucci had sent Guid'Antonio only two notes, the second one as vague as the first: Luca's attempts continued apace. Guid'Antonio sighed, sipping wine. At least Luca and Leonardo were trying. He had an image of them slipping into Ognissanti under the cover of night and bumping into one another — no matter that he had cautioned Luca about going there — one tall, slender, and fair, the other olive-skinned and stocky, the picture of the successful, honest druggist whom no one would ever suspect of prowling the streets with a pig's bladder secreted beneath his cloak.

"What are you hoping to find at Jacopo Rossi's farm?" Amerigo said. "Don't forget Palla was there and came away with nothing."

"I'm not Palla," Guid'Antonio said, sopping up the bits of beans and carrot in his bowl. Palla hadn't found a clue in Castruccio Senso's account books, either. Yet another dead end. Well. Jacopo Rossi's homestead was not far from the center of this small town. Pray the man was there.

He said, "I just want any little hint." His voice trailed off. Along with Jacopo Rossi da Vinci, he wanted to speak with Margherita Whoever-She-Was, the old nurse who had accompanied Camilla and Luigi on their ill-fated ride toward the baths at Morba one month ago, now. Despite Martino's protestations to the contrary, had Martino and Camilla concocted a plan to flee to some faraway town and convinced Margherita and Luigi to go along with it, conjuring up Turks, a kidnapping, and so on?

No. In that case, Martino would have

known what had actually happened on the road. He would be with Camilla, for God's sake. Instead, he had remained in Florence the whole while, wrapped in a cloak of misery, till escaping to the Leone family homestead.

"I just recalled something odd Francesco da Vinci mentioned while we were talking recently," Amerigo said. "I saw him in the marketplace."

"Leonardo's uncle? In Florence? Odd? How?"

"He mentioned Camilla's ghost to me."

Guid'Antonio, who had pushed back from the table, intending to retrieve a few coins from his scrip for the tavern keeper hovering near the service counter, sat back down, hard. "What are you saying?"

"He spoke of Camilla's, ah, ghost wandering around Vinci." Amerigo gestured toward the town beyond the tavern door. "So outrageous, I didn't think —" He pulled a face. "You know how superstitious these villagers are."

"Villagers? Villagers, my ass," Guid'Antonio said brusquely. "Superstitious? Have you forgotten all the talk of miracles in Florence, and why we're here?" He called the taverner over to them. This was Giovan, a friendly, red-faced fellow cast from the hearty and talkative tavern owner's mold. "My nephew tells me Vinci has a ghost." Guid'Antonio's own manner had undergone a rapid change, become effusive, gossipy.

"We do. We did." Giovan poured more Chianti into their jug and placed both hands on the table, towering over them. "I saw the specter myself. None other than Camilla Rossi, wandering through the town at midnight, wailing as if her heart might break."

Guid'Antonio inhaled a sharp breath. "Ah. You're certain it was she?"

"Never a doubt. Pretty a girl as a man ever did see, but now her black hair gone all wild, and her under gown —" Giovan had the grace to redden beneath his already rosy coloring. "Her under gown clinging — well . . . but her dead and all, you see. Never did you witness such —"

"Would that I had," Amerigo said.

"Giovan, had you seen this apparition before? Have you since?" Guid'Antonio said.

"No, 'twas only that once. Right after she was violated and murdered." Giovan crossed himself. "God rest her soul and bring her peace and send the Ottomans to hell."

"Did anyone else see her?" Guid'Antonio pressed.

Giovan shook his head. "The hour was late, and I was closing up the place. I yelled, and in a flash, she evaporated." He snapped his fingers and shivered, though the tavern was hot and close.

"So, Amerigo," Guid'Antonio said, when they were riding out from Vinci, "what make you of that?"

Amerigo turned slightly in the saddle. "I'm not sure, Uncle."

Guid'Antonio laughed dismissively. "You're a help."

Amerigo flared. "What I mean is this: obviously either Camilla is or was here in Vinci in the flesh after her disappearance, or the taverner has been imagining things."

Guid'Antonio nudged Flora into a canter. "The question is, which is which. Far be it for me to discount visions."

A cockerel crowed and strutted near the front door of the Rossi homestead, decrying the arrival of the two riders on horseback. Jacopo Rossi da Vinci's stone house was commodious, with two levels, and shutters propped open to allow air within. The farm sat on the edge of a deep woodland. West of the house, a vineyard stretched far as the eye could see. All in all, exactly what Guid'Antonio would expect for a prosperous winegrower. One who could provide his daughter a pretty dowry, he reminded himself, dismounting.

"By what authority will we say we've come?"

"Authority?" Guid'Antonio laughed. "Ah, darling nephew."

Near the south side of the house, there was a stable. Amerigo made short work of leading Flora and Bucephalus to the trough to drink before dropping their reins to the ground. "Uncle," he said, turning.

"Yes. I see."

Jacopo Rossi had come outside, sour-faced, his visage dark, smoldering with raw fury. His eyes narrowed on Guid'Antonio, who flinched inwardly, feeling a jolt much like the one he had experienced when he and this same Jacopo locked eyes in Orsanmichele.

"What do you want, Messer Vespucci?" Jacopo said, the surname a snarl on his lips.

"To inquire about your daughter." *Never mind how it is you know my name.*

"Here's your answer: she's dead."

Guid'Antonio's eyebrows rose. "That's coldly said."

"The truth is cold. You're a Medici man. You know about death better than most."

"Listen —" Amerigo said.

512

"And after all, Jacopo," Guid'Antonio cut in, "Camilla disappeared four weeks ago. Plenty enough time to mourn her, no matter who stole her life."

Jacopo's eyes flickered, but he held his tongue.

"Fetch the girl's nurse. I want to speak with her," Guid'Antonio said.

"Gone," Jacopo said, snapping his fingers.

"There's a surprise. Where?"

"To tend her sick son."

"Amazing, how everyone concerned with this business disappears."

"What's that to do with me?"

Looking past Jacopo, Guid'Antonio saw a girl of about four years peek around the doorjamb. "There's the matter of the dowry," he said. "Apparently, Castruccio Senso had no relatives. If none come forward, it could revert to you. You do know he's dead?"

"No!" Jacopo gasped, stepping back. "And you think what? That I murdered and robbed him?" A smile widened Jacopo's mouth.

"No one mentioned murder and robbery."

Purple color crept into Jacopo's face. His quick words could hang him.

Guid'Antonio said, "Did you know someone sent your daughter's horse into the city two weeks ago with its saddle bloodied?"

Jacopo recovered quickly. "Odd, isn't it, the Turks would do that? And I do mean to have Tesoro back. The horse is valuable."

"You'll have to find it first," Amerigo said.

"Keep Tesoro from me, and I'll —"

"You'll what?" Amerigo said, advancing a step.

And Guid'Antonio said, "You'll do nothing, Jacopo. Tell me what you know about the weeping painting. The *Virgin Mary of Santa Maria Impruneta.*"

"What I know is that when Mary comes to Florence, she has every reason to weep," Jacopo said. Jacopo's challenge to Guid'Antonio was strong: *You can't figure this out and you know it.*

*Watch me.*

"Is this another daughter?" Guid'Antonio said, glancing past the man.

Jacopo jerked around. "Isotta! Get back inside. I told you."

Isotta Rossi da Vinci flinched, standing just a foot behind her father, clutching a doll to her chest. "Isotta," Guid'Antonio said, "there's a pretty name." He smiled down at the child. And started, glancing quickly at Amerigo, who looked back at him questioningly.

Calming himself, Guid'Antonio knelt

down. "What a pretty doll, Isotta. Will you show it to me, please?"

"Isotta Rossi!" Jacopo roared. "Do as I say!"

Guid'Antonio looked up at him. "What is it to you?"

Jacopo clenched his teeth. If he had any notion of challenging Guid'Antonio, he saw Amerigo's fingers tracing the hilt of his dagger and abandoned it.

Isotta, all dimples and curly black hair and dressed in a light summer shift, glanced at her father, walked forward, and handed the doll to Guid'Antonio. His heart lurched in his chest. The doll's dress was sewn from the same fabric Luigi had found in Castruccio Senso's *sala* the morning after Castruccio was murdered. Clearly, the tiny dress had been made from the same material.

"Isotta," Guid'Antonio said, "what a lucky girl you are to have such a pretty doll. And such a pretty dress. Has she worn it long?"

Isotta shook her head, the pride of ownership overcoming her shyness. "It's new. My —"

"Isotta!" Jacopo bellowed. "Go now, or —"

"Or what?" Amerigo said, stepping close to him.

"Never mind, Amerigo." Guid'Antonio

regarded the child, who was trembling in the shadow of her father. "Thank you, Isotta. Now you'd better go inside as you're told."

"I know."

Jacopo, casting his interrogator a final black glare, took the child's hand, stalked inside the house, and slammed the door.

"Well," Amerigo said.

"Well, indeed, Amerigo."

" 'You think what? That I murdered and robbed him?' " Amerigo said, softly mimicking Jacopo's words to Guid'Antonio. "Not for one moment did he think Castruccio Senso might have, oh, died in his sleep."

They started toward the horses. "And the fabric used to make a new doll's dress," Guid'Antonio said. "Clearly, Camilla was here after the alleged abduction."

"But why? And where is she now? Dead? Though I do hate to say it."

"That's the crux."

"But we can't just leave."

"Jacopo would be a tough nut to crack if we took him in now, even for Palla's men. Anyway, I have another idea." Guid'Antonio nodded toward the open kitchen window, where moments earlier he had seen a wrinkled face watching them from the shadows.

516

Margherita, Camilla Rossi's nurse, he felt it in his bones. "You know, Amerigo," he said, raising his voice as he swung into Flora's saddle, "we could with a little help bring Camilla's disappearance to a conclusion, given Castruccio Senso's murder."

A cry emanated from inside the kitchen. A woman's cry. Yes, Margherita's cry, Guid'Antonio knew this with certainty.

"True," Amerigo said. "And tonight we'll sleep at the inn in Vinci?"

"True again, Nephew."

Chickens scattered from Bucephalus and Flora's path. Once again, the cockerel crowed, fussed, and scratched in the dirt. "Now what?" Amerigo said as he and Guid'Antonio turned onto the bumpy path back toward the village.

"We take a room and wait."

And wait and wait and wait.

Margherita did not venture into Vinci town that evening, and although Guid'Antonio was disappointed, he was not surprised. How could she, a domestic servant, escape Jacopo Rossi's piercing eyes? And so late July melted into the first day of August, and a lid of summer heat pressed down on Florence, turning the alleyways into ovens and the walls of shops and houses into burning umber and tan surfaces. In Ognissanti, the Virgin's eyes remained dry as sand. Still Camilla's nurse did not make contact.

Guid'Antonio had lost at gambling before. He would give Margherita a few days more, and then ask Palla to bring Jacopo Rossi into Florence for questioning. He worried about Camilla. Was she still alive? Pray God, it was so.

"You actually hoped the old nurse would come to you?" Lorenzo said. They were in the Medici kitchen, where *Il Magnifico* stood bent over the sink, rinsing soap from his lengthy brown hair.

"Or send me a note," Guid'Antonio said.

Lorenzo grabbed a towel. "Why not just bring Jacopo Rossi in now? Today? Why go through the old woman?"

"I wondered if in doing that we would get the whole story."

"Aren't you afraid for the girl? And the nurse? Isn't time of the essence?"

"Yes."

Tossing aside the towel, Lorenzo sat at the kitchen table, anchoring his hair behind his ears. "Jacopo Rossi da Vinci. What could he possibly have to do with the weeping Virgin? And with me? Strange." He tapped his fingers on the table's wooden surface. "I hear Maddalena Scala's worse. Bleeding now, along with the fever and chills."

Guid'Antonio felt a wave of regret for the Scala family, for Chancellor Bartolomeo Scala and his daughters, but particularly for Maddalena and her unborn baby. "May Christ help her." He crossed himself.

"We had twins who died," Lorenzo said. "Clarice and I."

Guid'Antonio nodded, thinking of Taddea and their baby, both gone these ten years and more.

Amerigo said, "You did?"

"When we first married," Lorenzo said. "After our little Lucrezia was born. Boys. Stillborn. Praise God, all our other children are thriving. Though Giovanni lives to eat. I do need to get him outside, playing ball. Wouldn't that be something, though? Me with twin boys as my heirs."

"The mind staggers," Guid'Antonio said.

From Palazzo Medici, Guid'Antonio and Amerigo walked in separate directions, Amerigo down Via Larga to visit young Lorenzino de' Medici, who was in town, having ridden in from Careggi, and Guid'Antonio to Borg'Ognissanti, Maria, and Giovanni. That night, after climbing quietly from bed, he slipped back into his pants and shirt and was about to put pen to paper when Cesare tiptoed in.

"Cesare, sometimes you do startle me," Guid'Antonio said, glancing at Maria sleeping soundly in their bed, oblivious to Cesare's presence in the chamber.

"And you me," Cesare said, looking pointedly down at Guid'Antonio's hand, idly scratching the top of Dog's head.

"Christ," Guid'Antonio said, but made no move to banish the dog grinning up at him. When in Hades had the creature slipped in the door? The dog and now Cesare. "What is it?" he said.

"Not what — *who,*" Cesare said, sparkling with excitement.

"Who, then," Guid'Antonio said.

"Leonardo."

"Da Vinci?"

"The same. My God, he's tall."

Within the instant Guid'Antonio was on his feet. Maria stirred in the bed. "Where is he? What does he want?" Guid'Antonio said softly.

"He has news for you," Cesare said. And explained how Leonardo had come to the Vespucci Palace in the middle of the night bearing a message, not about the mechanics behind the weeping Virgin — here, Cesare didn't even bother to lift an eyebrow — but concerning Camilla Rossi da Vinci, whose nurse, Margherita, was at that moment waiting for Guid'Antonio before the altar in Ognissanti Church.

Shadows appeared and disappeared in the dark spaces of the sanctuary, robes rustled and slipped over the stone floor. A woman dressed in black knelt before the *Virgin Mary of Santa Maria Impruneta.* Leonardo was close by, kneeling, his reddish-blond hair shimmering like gold in the light of the votive candles. With them at the rail there was another man: Leonardo's uncle, Francesco da Vinci. Guid'Antonio glanced at Cesare. "How did Margherita get here?"

"Francesco brought her from his farm. Margherita sought him there."

They walked forward through the church, past the Vespucci family chapel, past Domenico Ghirlandaio's *Saint Jerome* and Sandro Botticelli's *Saint Augustine,* the only sounds Guid'Antonio and Cesare's breathing and the soft fall of their footsteps. Francesco and Leonardo looked around and nodded, acknowledging their presence.

Guid'Antonio made a quiet prayer and lifted his eyes to the altar, where the Virgin Mary had begun weeping again, translucent tears wetting her pale, painted cheeks.

■ ■ ■ ■

In the church garden a short while later, they situated the nurse on a bench and sat with her in silence, waiting for her to speak. *Is there truly a woman in there?* Guid'Antonio wondered, drinking in Margherita's black cloak and the hood falling forward over her head and face.

At last, she spoke. She had, after all, sought him for this purpose; once she began, the story spilled out, with little prompting from him.

"It started the day we — I, my lady, and the boy — started for the baths. Those the wealthy do frequent at Morba. A hot, sunny day it was, my lady wrapped in a *mantello* over her gown, sweltering, but she laughed in her lilting way. She was filled with happiness to be free of her husband for even a short while. We hadn't been gone long from Florence when she removed the cloak and made it into a bundle and fixed it behind her on Tesoro's back. How she loved that horse. I told her they were a pretty pair, both with hair so shiny, those black curls. At San Gimignano we spent the night in the church and started back on the road the next day. And then —" Margherita faltered.

"Is she — ?" Francesco da Vinci said.

"Go easy, *Nonna,*" Guid'Antonio said, shooting a quelling glance at the other man. "We're your friends."

Margherita gulped in air. With great care, Leonardo covered her hands with his. Cesare, standing behind them, touched Leonardo's shoulder.

"A rider descended on us, screaming. A demon from hell, yelling gibberish, waving fantastic scarves and bangles, screaming he was a Turk. He grabbed my lady and attempted to wrench her from her horse. Tesoro shrieked, shying away. My lady grappled with her attacker and tore the scarf from his face."

All four men leaned in closer to catch Margherita's next words.

"Horrible!" she said. "A terrible scar slashed along his cheek."

Guid'Antonio drank this in, his thoughts retreating to Salvestro Aboati arguing with Castruccio Senso in the Red Lion. Yes, yes, the Neapolitan with the jagged red weal on his face.

"My lady screamed. The fiend screamed back, saying he would kill her for revealing his face. I wept. He looked at us with eyes both pained and evil. He threatened us, saying our lives were worth less than a rabbit's.

He would cut us up and fry us in oil should we ever describe him to anyone. Who would I describe him to? Poor little Luigi. The boy quaked with fear, his color washed out beneath his skin. Our abductor herded us —" Margherita wept again.

Guid'Antonio wanted to shake her. "Herded you where?"

"I couldn't credit it. Neither could my lady. This madman, instead of butchering us or taking us for slaves, arrived with us at our home place. Messer Vespucci, you say her husband, Castruccio Senso, is dead. Given that, Camilla could be free. Instead, her father has locked her away. But little Luigi, where is he?" she snuffled, looking around.

"He's safe," Guid'Antonio said. "Jacopo locked her where?"

Sobs of relief wracked the woman's body. "Please," Guid'Antonio said, hastening to quiet her as much as was possible. Surely, ears were listening, Brother Bellincioni and who else? But he wanted her to talk. Parts of the puzzle were sliding into place, but not all of them. *Slowly, slowly,* he cautioned himself. "Margherita, it was Jacopo who had Camilla kidnapped? Her own father?"

She sniffed. "Who else?"

Who else, indeed? "But why?" he said.

*Where, where?* his mind ranted. Surely, Camilla was safe, for now, at least.

"For her terrible sin."

"And that would be?"

"Daring to love, Messer Vespucci."

"Cesare," Guid'Antonio said, glancing around, but Cesare had already posted his supple figure at the garden gate and was standing beside Amerigo, who had slipped in a few moments earlier, both now listening for any little sound. It would not do for anyone on Borg'Ognissanti to overhear this conversation.

"Love," Guid'Antonio said, thinking, *Brother Martino. Yes.*

Margherita lowered her voice. "She met a young man here, and he was smitten with her at once, as what man wouldn't be? But he — he —"

"He was a monk."

"Yes. Kind and gentle, my lady said. And her hungry for such. Ser Senso used to beat her." Margherita said this with such hatred, Guid'Antonio flinched.

"And Jacopo knew about this," he said. "About the monk and Castruccio's beatings."

"Yes on both counts. Jacopo saw her bruises once when he visited us here in Florence. Ser Jacopo and Castruccio Senso had a terrible fight over it. Ser Castruccio Senso told Jacopo he suspected my lady of cuckolding him. At first, Jacopo didn't believe it. His pious daughter? No! But then, he did. He may have had her watched. Shortly thereafter is when he sent us off to Morba. Ser Castruccio Senso, I mean. And now Ser Jacopo means to bundle her off to some cloistered nuns who will lock her in darkness forever. They'll silence her tongue, chop off her hair."

Margherita's voice broke. "That's why I had to come to you, to save my sweet Camilla, whilst I still can."

A relieved sigh escaped Amerigo's lips. "She is safe, then."

"Margherita," Guid'Antonio said. "What happened to Camilla's horse once Salvestro Aboati delivered you to Jacopo?"

"The mare was home at first, then vanished. Like my lady."

"You do know where Camilla is being held?"

"Yes. Locked in a stone tower in the woods near her father's house. She escaped him early on and wandered, dazed out of her wits, she was so frightened, into Vinci town. Jacopo couldn't have that. People might see her and talk. He caught her and took her back home. But she's well enough,

*Signore.* Jacopo put her in my care, and I've done my best for my sweet girl. As much as I could with her heart broken."

Leonardo's hand went to his breast. "When is Jacopo sending her to the nunnery?" he said. "Where is it?"

"Tomorrow afternoon," Margherita answered softly. "All I know is, it's far, far away. I had to seek you now. Before I left, I filched the tower key."

# THIRTY-SIX

In a scatter of dust and stones, they reined in before Jacopo Rossi da Vinci's farmhouse. "Go, Amerigo!"

Quickly, Amerigo turned Bucephalus toward the woods to release Camilla from the woodland tower, while Guid'Antonio paced the foreyard and Palla and his men subdued the girl's father. Not that Jacopo Rossi da Vinci wanted subduing.

Before Palla reached the farmhouse door, Jacopo strode outside, his face a mask of impotent fury, yet acknowledging when he was beaten. With an air of expertise that was handmaiden to years of experience, Palla tied the other man's hands behind his back for the ride to Florence, where he would be interrogated at police headquarters.

"What will you do with my daughters?" Jacopo asked as they set off from the farm accompanied by armed guards.

"Better ask what we'll do with you," Palla said. "Keep silent or I'll cut out your tongue."

Guid'Antonio turned in the saddle, glancing over his shoulder. With Camilla's arms around his waist, Amerigo had ridden from the woods to the house, there to fetch the girl, Isotta, and hasten them to Peretola, where they would remain at Niccolò Vespucci's inn till matters concerning them were resolved. And, yes, Camilla Rossi was a vision of loveliness, with cascading black hair and startlingly pale blue eyes that would make many a fellow forget his vows, be he monk or married man. Camilla's eyes met Guid'Antonio's probing gaze, and they shared a slight smile of acknowledgment before he turned Flora toward home.

In bed with Guid'Antonio a few nights later, Maria said, "What happened with our secret lovers? I've never been so curious."

Guid'Antonio smiled. "Yes, you have." Two days had passed since Amerigo had freed Camilla Rossi from the tower. Satisfying days if hot, dusty, and long. He fingered Maria's hair, his palm caressing her belly, but then contented himself for the moment with kissing her mouth and settling alongside her with his arm over her waist. "You know today Amerigo, Lorenzo and I rode to Peretola. Camilla and Isotta have been staying there with Amerigo's uncle, Niccolò Vespucci, and his family."

"Yes. And our two lovebirds behaved how?"

"As you might expect. Amazing. Martino's lost all sense of guilt and wants only to wed Camilla the instant they arrive in France."

"And she?"

"Agrees, judging from the smile on her pert lips. No nunnery for that one."

"*Amore,*" Maria said, pleased. "They're going where?"

"Plessis-les-Tours." Lorenzo had assured the young couple he would make arrangements for them, Margherita, and Isotta with King Louis XI. ("How can they make a life together in Florence?" Lorenzo had asked Guid'Antonio. "Impossible. Besides, *they're in love.*") Love, love, love. In the end, it all came down to that. Before departing Peretola, Guid'Antonio had given Camilla a missive for Ameliane Vely, to catch Ameliane up on events. Inquiring in a playful way how she was faring without him there.

"Was Camilla very happy?" Maria asked, craving the details.

"Lit from within. Hair shining, aglow like

some black sun, the beauty of her flowing locks matched only by those of her lover and her horse, Tesoro."

Maria punched him playfully. "You're mocking me."

"Not at all. Amerigo almost swooned."

"Cesare would have." Maria laughed, snuggling closer. "It's nice, having you lighthearted for a change. I love you for helping that unfortunate girl. But I don't understand why our monks were so determined to stop Martino from leaving their order. You said the one called Paolo was beside himself to find Martino and fetch him back again."

"They were afraid word of Martino's behavior would blacken their name," Guid'Antonio said. "Stop the flow of contributions by fathers now fearful their daughters might be ruined at the groping hands of hot-blooded young monks."

"Guid'Antonio," Maria said chidingly.

"Or that one of their own might be accused of murdering her," he said. "Since she was having an affair with a brother monk. Maria, I wasn't helping Camilla so much I was helping Lorenzo." *And myself,* he thought. *Good Medici man that I am. Myself and my family.*

She held his eyes with hers. "Say what you

531

will. I know better."

No, she did not. He nuzzled her ear and heard her breath change and quicken.

Tonight, all Florence was happy. In the last two days it seemed the entire town had learned Camilla Rossi da Vinci had not only been found: she had been found alive, well, and in love. Now that she was a widow — but who needed details? Vague, titillating musings of a clandestine affair were enough. They were young, they were beautiful, and Florence was safe from the Infidels.

Because there was more on that front, too. The good news had arrived this afternoon. Impossibly, one week ago the six hundred brave Christian Knights of Saint John had beaten back 70,000 or more Turks at Rhodes and planted the flag of faith over the fortress town. Upon hearing the news, the population of Florence had poured forth through the streets, cheering and beating their breasts to the riotous tune of clanging church bells. Not a man to take to the streets on any occasion, Guid'Antonio had smiled till his mouth ached, his chest filled with gladness and no small amount of surprise at the Knights' victory, till he heard how the Infidels had panicked and run like the Prince of Darkness himself when a vision of Mary and Saint John the Baptist led by a cross of gold and accompanied by a dazzling band of Christian warriors had appeared in the sky above the Turks' heads.

How could the Christian Knights of Saint John lose in the face of a miracle such as that?

He made love to Maria slowly, one renegade part of him still with Palla and Lorenzo during Jacopo Rossi's confession at the Bargello earlier in the day. Jacopo had been neither scared nor cagey, till the last. Still, there had been no need for the *strappado*.

*"Why is he here?"* Jacopo said, glaring at Lorenzo.

*"I'll ask the questions."* Palla circled Jacopo like a cat, dark eyes shining, ready to pounce.

*"And I'll answer them,"* Jacopo said. *"I know when I'm caught."*

*"Did you kill Castruccio Senso?"* Palla asked.

*"Yes."*

*"Why?"*

*"I hated him."*

*"Why?"*

*"He paid a Neapolitan thug to kidnap my daughter and sell her into slavery."*

*Guid'Antonio and Lorenzo glanced at one another. Salvestro Aboati, of course.*

*Palla said, "Why did he do that? Castruccio Senso, I mean?"*

"Because she was screwing a horny monk."

"But this hired man, and we know his name, this Salvestro Aboati, brought her to you instead of putting her on some foreign ship."

"Why ask me? You know everything."

"Why did Salvestro Aboati do that?" Palla said.

"Salvestro didn't act on Castruccio Senso's scheme. He sold the information to me. We changed Castruccio's plan. Salvestro would take Camilla, but deliver her to me rather than to the slave market. Then we would blackmail Castruccio Senso by threatening to expose his wickedness. To sweeten the pot, we determined to let the horse loose in Florence with its saddle bloodied, so Castruccio would believe Salvestro had murdered my daughter."

"You did hate him. Why so completely?"

"He beat her."

"Reason enough. So, you went forward with your plan."

"Right again, Palmieri."

"What happened next?"

"After taking Camilla, Salvestro and I went to Castruccio's house to blackmail him. Things went sour, and I brained him."

"You went there planning to kill him," Palla said.

Jacopo grinned. "Yes."

"Why did you drop the fabric there? Evidence that might get you hanged."

"It was an accident."

Guid'Antonio and Lorenzo laughed. Accident? Too crazy to believe.

"It's true!" Jacopo said, offended. "I took it with me to cause Castruccio grief. When I picked up the candlestick, I dropped the bit of cloth without realizing it."

"And the cloth had blood on it?" Guid'Antonio said.

"Yes. Camilla's, I wanted him to think."

"Whose was it?"

"That of a cat I gutted in the street."

"Weren't you concerned Luigi would witness your attack on his owner?"

"Castruccio told me he was selling the boy. I thought he had done so. Anyway, Luigi wasn't around. I looked."

Guid'Antonio and Lorenzo shared another glance. Now they knew why Luigi hadn't revealed Jacopo's terrible secret to the authorities: the child was scared for the lady he loved above all else and wanted only to protect her. Tell anyone Jacopo had murdered Castruccio Senso, and Jacopo might kill Camilla for pure meanness.

"Then what?" Palla said.

"We ran."

"What about the money you took?"

"I didn't want Castruccio Senso's money. I

535

*threw it in the Arno."*

*"Where's Salvestro Aboati now?"*

*"Gone."*

*"Gone where?"*

*Jacopo grinned malevolently. "He tried to blackmail me, much as we had planned to blackmail Castruccio. I couldn't allow it."*

*"And?"*

*"I made him a counteroffer."*

Maria's breathing softened and slowed as she drifted into slumber. Hardly knowing what he was doing, Guid'Antonio eased from bed, dressed, and went out into the street. At this midnight hour, Borg'Ognissanti was deserted and quiet. He walked in the direction opposite Ognissanti, toward Florence Cathedral. At intervals along his route, torches shed pools of yellow light on the walls of the buildings. He caught sight of no one else, although he knew guards stood watch every few blocks or so after curfew.

He advanced up the Cathedral steps with a quick pace, exactly as he had done a little over two years ago, on 26 April 1478. He opened the door. Vast the sanctuary, deserted and still. Was there ever another darkness like this, so tranquil and complete as here in the Duomo? He walked to the spot where he had stood that Easter Sunday morning and peered through space toward Giuliano positioned apart from the congregation cloaked in the black velvet *mantello* with the hood lined in scarlet satin.

Odd. Francesco de' Pazzi and Bernardo Bandini were with him.

Guid'Antonio hesitated, cried out and in the next instant found himself struggling to squeeze through knots of screaming, frightened people. He felt a sudden snap of release, gained ground, and knelt beside Giuliano, weeping. Had they looked into one another's eyes then, surprised and smiling? *Yes.* And then Giuliano died, with Guid'Antonio holding Giuliano close to his chest as he took his last breath and his soul winged its way to heaven. Guid'Antonio had that last, precious moment with him. A moment of love and sorrow no one else had experienced, nor did anyone else know about.

He glanced around now, his heart skipping in his chest. What had he hoped to find in this empty, dark place? Some sign, some whisper of his lost friend? Some feeling of forgiveness and release?

He fell to his knees and placed his palm upon the marble floor, so hard and cool to the touch. "Giuliano, I'm sorry," he said.

"You are sorely missed. A lot has happened this summer. These last two years."

Beneath his fingers, the pavement became as supple and warm as living flesh, and something soft brushed the top of his head. He looked up. Giuliano stood over him. "Guid'Antonio," he said in a whisper so faint, Guid'Antonio didn't know if the words came from Giuliano's lips or from the depths of his own soul. "Florence is my beating heart. Both then and now. It always will be, my stalwart friend."

Hardly daring to breathe, Guid'Antonio watched Giuliano move toward the front of the church and vanish through the door. Guid'Antonio followed, his fingers turning the handle, his solid footsteps leading him outside into Piazza San Giovanni. Directly across from the Cathedral he saw the baptistery, intact and real. He turned back toward the Cathedral, looking up, his gaze seeking the wooden platform encircling Brunelleschi's red brick dome. One winter morning Guid'Antonio and Giuliano had stood up there a few feet from the iron safety rail. So very close to the edge. *Too close for comfort,* Guid'Antonio had thought even then. In their private meeting place overlooking the city, away from listening ears, Giuliano had spoken of Lorenzo, his beloved brother, and about what the future held in store for all of them. "I fear that by grasping for too much, we will lose everything," Giuliano had confided that snowy morning in 1476.

Perhaps. Perhaps. So be it.

Alone in the piazza now, Guid'Antonio drew a deep breath. What he had learned this night was that Giuliano de' Medici still walked the byways of Florence. Well, he had already known that, hadn't he? Giuliano still laughed back in time with his companions and with Lorenzo, still rode out into Piazza Santa Croce, flying his painted standard for the world to see, still handed violets to his Queen of Beauty, Simonetta Vespucci. He still lived in the face of his son, Giulio, and in the blood of all their descendants. Like Giuliano de' Medici, Lorenzo and Guid'Antonio were everywhere in Florence, the amazing, beautiful city they were creating with their minds, hearts, and hands.

They always would be.

And they were all forgiven.

# EPILOGUE

*Six months later, January 1481*

Shimmering snow blanketed the valley and dressed the rolling countryside in immaculate white robes. High above Florence, a solitary man on horseback sat straight in the saddle with the church of San Miniato al Monte at his back, his cloaked figure a crimson speck against the frozen landscape. A chill breeze ruffled his black hair streaked with silver and brushed his finely chiseled cheeks, not unpleasantly, but with an edge suggestive of the icy blasts the month of February would let fly like sharp spears across the Arno valley. Alone on the hillside, he closed his eyes and watched the days of full-blown winter hurry past.

Within the walls of Florence, icicles descended like daggers and shattered into glistening shards on winding cobblestones. Chestnuts roasted over hot coals, while youngsters, rosy-cheeked and laughing, skated across the frozen Arno. Cesare lifted extra blankets from wooden trunks, and cold air made Maria and Giovanni's breathing visible as they hastened along Borg'Ognissanti to church, bundled in fur-lined cloaks, past Spedale dei Vespucci, where Francesca Vernacci toiled in her mantle of plain white cloth.

He opened his eyes, blinking against the dazzling glare of bright sunshine on ice. Who knew when he might see his family again, now he was going to Rome as the newly appointed Administrator and Attorney General of the Florentine Republic?

*Sì, Roma.*

Guid'Antonio Vespucci, not Lorenzo, despite the Pope's living itch to see Lorenzo there at his feet.

This time, Guid'Antonio was traveling alone.

It happened like this:

In the latter days of August, the heat, always suffocating in summer, had brought its fist down hard on the city. Flies had buzzed and settled in piles of dung, whose stench cooked in the sweltering atmosphere. At night the bed Guid'Antonio and Maria shared had made a constant tangle of clammy sheets soaked with the sticky perfume of their lovemaking. In the Unicorn

541

district, tempers flared. Cats yowled, and stray dogs barked at the moon. He and Maria, lying awake deep into the night, whispered drowsily about the odd twists and turns late summer had taken.

With Camilla Rossi da Vinci and Martino Leone's departure to France, the weeping Virgin's tears had ceased once again. (Had the tears been for Camilla's lost innocence? Or for his own, Guid'Antonio wondered.) Soon thereafter, the dry-eyed — and for the time being nonjudgmental — painting had been borne to its church home in Impruneta, where it would rest on the altar until the next drought or festival required its presence in the nearby city.

Ognissanti had become blessedly quiet after Brother Martin's exodus, although one evening Abbot Roberto Ughi broke a tooth on the gold coin he bit while eating fish stew. This had occurred just after a young boy caught Salvestro Aboati's bloated corpse in the fishing net he cast into the waters of the Arno River.

In Via Larga, Lorenzo penned a letter to Angelo Poliziano, inviting Angelo to return to Florence, now as Professor of Latin and Greek Eloquence at *Studio Fiorentino*. Notoriously, Angelo opened his homecoming lecture with the declaration, "They say the female mouse is madly lustful."

Some came home to Florence, while others left. Soon, at Lorenzo's request, Sandro Botticelli and Domenico Ghirlandaio would travel to Rome to fresco the walls of the Sistine Chapel, along with several other painters. But not Leonardo da Vinci, because who knew if he would finish the job?

Against all odds, Luca Landucci's brother, Gostanzo Landucci, won the grand *palio* riding *Draghetto* against Lorenzo de' Medici's entry, *Il Gentile.* Not surprisingly, Brother Paolo Dolci remained at Ognissanti, whether out of piety or to protect little Ferdinando — who after a short absence had returned to the church — from the unsavory abbot, Guid'Antonio was unsure.

Long, lazy days and nights these, hot and fat with small worries and moments of intense satisfaction. Then everything had changed. The church bells had scarcely stopped ringing for the victorious Knights of Rhodes before news reached Florence that 14,000 Turks had landed at Otranto in southern Italy and slammed the small coastal town to its knees. Infidels chopped the archbishop and governor in halves, slaughtered 12,000 men, women, and children, and enslaved the remaining inhabitants.

*Muslim armies on Italian soil.* Surely now, exactly as Lorenzo had predicted, the Ottomans would advance across the ankle of the Italian peninsula, ravage Naples, and march north to Rome, where they would plant the Holy Standard of Islam in the heart of the Vatican. Fueled by fear and outrage, Sixtus IV had called for all Italy to unite in the face of the common enemy and had then melted down his collection of finely wrought silver to help finance the coming battle. For his part, Prince Alfonso of Naples had abandoned Siena and scurried home to defend his future kingdom in southern Italy. Did it surprise Guid'Antonio when both Rome and Naples turned to Lorenzo for help? No. No.

In Lorenzo's name, the Florentine government had agreed to support their former enemies if Sixtus IV lifted the ban of excommunication against the city and if King Ferrante restored all the lands Florence had lost to Naples in the aftermath of the Pazzi Conspiracy. Under the circumstances, what could Pope and king do but agree?

No surprise that in Florence the populace did a quick turnaround. How could they have been so mistaken? The Infidels weren't in Tuscany, but down south — a sure sign God was angry not with their Lorenzo de'

Medici, but with King Ferrante and Pope Sixtus IV! Once again, Lorenzo was their shining hero, a man who knew how to recognize Fortune when he saw her and pin her to the ground. Once again — for the first time in thirty years — Italy was united, exactly as Lorenzo had vowed to Guid'Antonio it would be.

Wisely, Lorenzo had not addressed the suggestion whispered in Palazzo della Signoria that events couldn't have turned out better for him if he had orchestrated the Turkish invasion of Italy himself.

A brownish-purple cardinal lit on the icy finger of a nearby tree. The male, following his mate, landed in a feathery display of scarlet. Snow plopped on the ground. Guid'Antonio patted Flora's shoulder with gloved fingers. In November, he had been one of twelve Florentine ambassadors who had traveled to Rome to kneel at the Pope's feet in Saint Peter's to receive absolution on behalf of the people of Florence for sins they might possibly have committed against the Pope's person and office in the last two years.

Twelve distinguished Florentines in place of one Lorenzo de' Medici.

By that time, though, Guid'Antonio had

already served on the committee of 240 handpicked citizens granted full powers to decide the reforms necessary for the good government of the city. Within a week of its creation, the committee had suspended the constitution and paved the way for sweeping changes in the Florentine government.

A wry smile lifted the corner of Guid'Antonio's mouth. There had been dissenters who had muttered phrases like "princely ambitions" and "a dangerous departure" when they understood reforming and strengthening the government meant strengthening the position of the Medici circle with Lorenzo at its core. But what would they prefer? Some other family lording it over the city? Some loose cannon? *Someone like the Pazzi family?* In truth, the creation of the *balia* had passed the legislative councils by only one vote. Guid'Antonio took some comfort in that. The Florentine Republic remained a government of men who refused to let Tuscany be entirely ruled by any one man or family. Gowned in robes of flowing crimson cloth, they would argue, accuse, give sway, refuse, and cast their ballots before God and the people.

He took comfort in a good many things. In September, the hermit who seemed set to assassinate Lorenzo at Poggio a Caiano had failed, praise God in His infinite mercy. Guilty or not, the man had died after being questioned: the soles of his feet skinned, then burnt when his torturers in the Bargello held them in the fire till the fat dripped off. Guid'Antonio's kinsman, Piero Vespucci, was fortunate not to have suffered a similar fate. Instead, at Lorenzo's behest, Piero had been released from the Stinche, and a black mark thus removed from the Vespucci family name. This had come shortly after Guid'Antonio pledged to back Lorenzo's call for a *balìa*.

And then in late October in Via di Pinti, Bartolomeo Scala, his wife, and their five daughters had celebrated the safe arrival of Maddalena Scala's sixth child, a boy.

They named him Giuliano.

Guid'Antonio stroked Flora's neck gently, grateful for the familiar presence of the solid animal, and inhaled a cold, calming breath. Seriously ill now, Nastagio Vespucci had given Amerigo his power of attorney; one day soon Amerigo would handle all Nastagio's legal obligations. At Guid'Antonio's request, since Amerigo would not be going to Rome this time around, Lorenzo had taken Amerigo into his service. Good. No matter where Guid'Antonio went or how long he was gone, he would have eyes and ears fixed on Via Larga.

He snugged his scarlet cape close around his body, thankful for the cloak's thick ermine lining. Flora whinnied and stamped, glancing around with a restless eye. Once Guid'Antonio turned toward the road, the blood would heat in his veins and his fingers would thaw. "Hush, Flora. Just another moment."

Behind him he heard a scraping and *shhhussing* sound and twisted in the saddle. One of San Miniato's white-robed monks was making an icy path to the church well, carrying an axe, his formless figure ghostly against the frozen atmosphere. Pocking the snow with huge prints, a darker, fawn-colored shape bounded past the old religious and on around the church in pursuit of what? A squirrel or a rabbit? Guid'Antonio settled back around in the saddle.

Where had all this left him, a man on a mission for his own salvation? He gazed across the valley, where the cypress trees were skeletons furred with snow and a veil of white lay over the city. At Florence's heart, the Cathedral presided over all, its marble interior gathering the cold to its breast, while close by in Ognissanti, Sandro Botticelli's *Saint Augustine* raised his hoary countenance toward God, struggling to understand lightness and dark, compromise and truth. Guid'Antonio understood now he could not have saved Giuliano, even if he could have sprouted wings and flown across the sanctuary that cold April morning. What must be must be. This was life. This was history. In the end, he was a man whose head ruled his heart. So be it.

He touched the diplomatic pouch beneath his cloak and looked around, seeking his sole companion on his new journey. He made a half whistle and broke into a smile when the mighty *cane corso Italiano* barreled back around the monastery, slobbering, grinning, frisking in the snow, then shaking his giant body vigorously, the silver studs on his wide leather collar shining. What a dog!

"Come, Peritas. Unlike Alexander the Great, I doubt I'll conquer any cities and name them for you, but I can take you to Rome." He turned Flora toward the icy road. And then with Peritas at his side and cold air blowing back his hair and the folds of his crimson cape, Attorney General Guid'Antonio Vespucci began the long road south to Rome.

*"Too much knowing causes misery."*
From *A Wood of Love II,*
by Lorenzo de' Medici

# GUID'ANTONIO

Guid'Antonio Vespucci (1436–1501) was the oldest son of Antonia Ugolini and Giovanni Vespucci. By the time of Guid'Antonio's birth, the Vespuccis ranked among Florence's leading families, with holdings in rental properties, vineyards, olive groves, silk shops, and wool. Like the sons of all wealthy Florentines, Guid'Antonio would have been educated in Latin, arithmetic, and logic. As a young man, in Bologna and Ferrara, he studied civil law, rhetoric and poetry, the latter two deemed essential for the Renaissance practice of diplomacy. For his profession, he chose Doctor of Law.

As Guid'Antonio once said, he believed in the maintenance of legal order and the utilization of the abilities of the cities' most able citizens. Thus, from the first days of his career, like his father before him, he supported the Medici family in its private administration of the democratic Florentine government. In his early thirties (when Lorenzo's father, Piero de' Medici, was the *de facto,* or unofficial, ruler of Florence), Guid'Antonio served as one of the Florentine Republic's nine Lord Priors (the state's highest-ranking council). From 1469 (the year of Piero de' Medici's death) onward, Guid'Antonio's close bond with Lorenzo saw them through Lorenzo's troubled ascendancy as the prince of the city until Lorenzo's untimely death in 1492 at the age of forty-three. During those years, Guid'Antonio and Lorenzo survived the Pazzi Conspiracy (1478) and the ensuing war, with Guid'Antonio traveling to Rome and France and back to Rome again as Florence's/ Lorenzo's diplomatic agent.

When Guid'Antonio was about thirty-four, he married his second wife, Maria del Vigna, and, as in *The Sign of the Weeping Virgin,* they had a son, Giovanni. Of all his nephews, Guid'Antonio seems to have been particularly close with Amerigo Vespucci, who did, indeed, accompany Guid'Antonio to France as his secretary in October 1478, eventually spending almost two years with him at the court of King Louis XI. Back home in Florence, Amerigo went to work for Lorenzo, then for Lorenzo's cousin and former ward, Lorenzino de' Medici, finally sailing west and into the pages of history, while his uncle Guid'Antonio played his part as one of the most influential and powerful personages of his time until his death on Christmas Eve in 1501.

Together, they lived in an age when Italians already spoke of the "rinascimento," an era in which a new spirit of rebirth in life, art, and literature prevailed. Nowhere was this more evident than in Florence, a city of about 50,000 souls at this time in history. Within the town's walls, Guid'Antonio and Amerigo rubbed elbows with their neighbors, Sandro Botticelli, Leonardo da Vinci, Paolo Toscanelli, and so many other Renaissance luminaries while at their heart there stood the controversial, charming, and brilliantly talented poet and statesman, Lorenzo de' Medici . . . justly called "The Magnificent."

# AUTHOR'S NOTE

Many of the characters in *The Sign of the Weeping Virgin* are real people, and the story draws on major events in their lives. On 26 April 1478, in a plot driven by Pope Sixtus IV and his nephew, Girolamo Riario, Francesco de' Pazzi and Bernardo Bandini murdered Giuliano de' Medici in an attempt to rid Florence of its two unofficial heads of state. Given Lorenzo de' Medici's escape that bloody Sunday, the plot failed, and the course was set for war between Florence and Rome. Giuliano did leave behind a son named Giulio, the future Pope Clement VII. Lorenzo's son Giovanni became Pope Leo X.

Botticelli did finish his *Saint Augustine* in Ognissanti Church in the summer of 1480, just as Guid'Antonio and Amerigo returned home from Paris. Giorgio Vespucci commissioned the fresco; restorers discovered the dialogue Botticelli wrote at the top of the painting in recent times. Today in the church visitors may see the fresco, as well as Botticelli's tomb marked with the Filipepi family coat of arms in the floor of the Cappella San Pietro d'Alcantara in the south transcept. Botticelli's workshop and home was located on the side street near the Vespucci Palace and Spedale dei Vespucci, the Vespucci family hospital. The palace is no longer intact, but the hospital where Francesca Vernacci would have practiced medicine is still on Borg'Ognissanti near the church. Botticelli's *Primavera,* as well as other paintings by him, lives in Botticelli Hall in the Uffizi Gallery in Florence.

The painting called the *Virgin Mary of Santa Maria Impruneta* resides in the Cathedral of S. M. All'Impruneta, in the small town of Impruneta, near Florence, and has done for centuries. In his diary (*A Florentine Diary from 1450 to 1516*), druggist Luca Landucci describes the painting and the miracles it performed for the good of the people. Luca notes proudly how his brother, Gostanzo, won the *palio* riding his horse called *"il Draghetto"* (the Little Dragon) on several occasions.

Readers familiar with Florence will notice how in some instances I have used present-day names for buildings and streets, while in others they retain their fifteenth-century names. Today the Medici Palace is Palazzo Medici Riccardi; Benozzo Gozzoli's *Procession of the Magi* in the Medici Chapel is available for viewing by the public. Palla Palmieri's police headquarters and jail is today called the Bargello, and I have used that designation. Now a national museum, the Bargello houses Florentine Renaissance sculpture, with rooms dedicated to the works of Michelangelo, Andrea del Verrochio, and many other artists.

For an introduction to the Medici family, interested readers might begin with Christopher Hibbert's *The Rise and Fall of the House of Medici.* For my research on the Vespucci family, I drew heavily on *Amerigo and the New World* by Germán Arciniegas, and then on materials gleaned from Italian Renaissance scholars, whose work has been invaluable to me.

As for the shadowy villain of the piece, Lorenzo de' Medici had Girolamo Riario watched from the time of Giuliano's murder in 1478. In April 1488, almost ten years to the day, Girolamo was himself assassinated while at home in Forli. His widow, Caterina Sforza, married the younger of Lorenzo's two wards, Giovanni de' Medici, brother to Lorenzino, who figures in our story. Caterina then went on to do battle with Cesare Borgia. This is the Italian Renaissance, whose tapestry of relationships is so colorful and tightly woven it seems almost to defy belief. *Almost.*

# THE SIGN OF THE WEEPING VIRGIN
## READER'S GUIDE

**Questions for Discussion:**

Guid'Antonio and his nephew, Amerigo, have returned home to Florence after a two-year diplomatic mission to France. What are Guid'Antonio's expectations upon their arrival in the city? What happens to deflate them?

Guid'Antonio was one of the most powerful men in the Florentine Republic, both as a lawyer and as a politician. At the same time, Lorenzo de' Medici, poet and patron of the arts and known as Lorenzo the Magnificent, was the acknowledged "prince of the city," ruling the government behind the scenes. How might life have been different for Guid'Antonio if he were not a Medici man? Do you think he had a choice in backing the Medici family, and how strongly do you think he actually agreed with their guiding principles?

561

Guid'Antonio and Lorenzo make much of their friendship. Do you consider them friends? What do you make of their rapport?

When Guid'Antonio visits Lorenzo at the Medici Palace for the first time since coming home from France, Lorenzo reveals to him his dead brother Giuliano's illegitimate young son. How does Guid'Antonio respond to the child? Do you think Lorenzo is manipulating Guid'Antonio? If so, how and why?

Lorenzo de' Medici is considered by some the light of the Italian Renaissance, by others a hard-boiled politico who kept his family's death grip on Florence. One of his near contemporaries said, "If Florence had to have a dictator, she couldn't have had a better one." What do you think of him?

A young boy has witnessed the painting of the *Virgin Mary of Santa Maria Impruneta* weeping in Guid'Antonio's family church. Why have Mary's tears caused such fear in the city? Do you think Guid'Antonio is justified in investigating them? Do you think this means he is a nonbeliever?

Guid'Antonio observes that Florence is

"married" to miracles. What leads him to think this?

Although Giuliano de' Medici died two years ago, Guid'Antonio sees him now on several occasions. Why do you think this is, and how do you feel about it? What other possible interpretation is there for Guid'Antonio's visions? What do you think about his final exchange with Giuliano in the Cathedral?

Guid'Antonio and his wife, Maria, have a stormy relationship. He says he loves her. Do you believe him? Does she? Why did he marry her in the first place?

Several times Guid'Antonio thinks about Maestra Francesca Vernacci, the doctor at the hospital Guid'Antonio and his family built and own. What do you think about the reason Francesca gives Guid'Antonio for not marrying him? Were you surprised at the passion his feelings for her arouse in him? What does this reveal about him?

Discuss the role of women in the society of Renaissance Florence. For example, women did not generally attend funerals.

Florence at this time has a small-town air.

Within these gated, stone walls, everyone knows everyone, or, at least, knows who they are, from Guid'Antonio and Amerigo Vespucci to Leonardo da Vinci, Sandro Botticelli, and Lorenzo the Magnificent to the people in the street. Do you believe that this time and place are rightly considered the heart of the Italian Renaissance? How is Florence different from Rome and Naples?

Regarding his decision to assume the role of leadership in the city when he was only twenty, Lorenzo de' Medici later wrote in his journal that he agreed to do so reluctantly, since it fared ill in Florence with anyone who was rich but who did not have any share in government. Why do you think Lorenzo believed this?

What is the role in the story of the *popolo minuto,* the "little" people in the street, who toil from sunup to sundown to eke out a living? How does the stray, starving dog, Peritas, represent the populace? Discuss the irony of Peritas's presence in Guid'Antonio's life at the close of the story.

Lorenzo wrote, "Too much knowing is misery." What do you think he meant? Do you agree with him?

# ABOUT THE AUTHOR

**Alana White**'s passion for Renaissance Italy has taken her to Florence for research on the Vespucci and Medici families on numerous occasions. There along cobbled streets unchanged over the centuries, she traces their footsteps, listening to their imagined voices: Guid'Antonio Vespucci, Sandro Botticelli, Michelangelo, Lorenzo de' Medici. Alana's first short story featuring real-life fifteenth-century lawyer Guid'Antonio Vespucci and his favorite nephew, Amerigo, was a Macavity Award finalist. She is a member of the Authors Guild, Sisters in Crime, the Women's National Book Association, and the Historical Novel Society. Alana loves hearing from readers, and you can contact her at www.alanawhite.com. There, you will find Guid'Antonio's likeness as Domenico Ghirlandaio depicted him in the Sistine

Chapel, along with other images and tales
of 1400s Italy.